THE EVENTS IN THIS BOOK ARE REAL.

NAMES AND PLACES HAVE BEEN CHANGED
TO PROTECT THE LORIEN SIX,
WHO REMAIN IN HIDING.

TAKE THIS AS YOUR FIRST WARNING.

OTHER CIVILIZATIONS DO EXIST.

SOME OF THEM SEEK TO DESTROY YOU.

I AM
NUMBER FOUR

BOOK ONE OF THE LORIEN ⬚ LEGACIES

PITTACUS
LORE

HARPER

An Imprint of HarperCollinsPublishers

Library of Congress Cataloging-in-Publication Data
Lore, Pittacus.
    I am number four / by Pittacus Lore. — 1st ed.
        p.   cm. — (Lorien Legacies ; bk. 1)
    Summary: In rural Ohio, friendships and a beautiful girl
prove distracting to a fifteen-year-old who has hidden on
Earth for ten years waiting to develop the Legacies, or powers, he will need to rejoin the other five surviving Garde
members and fight the Mogadorians who destroyed their
planet, Lorien.
    ISBN 978-0-06-210555-4
    [1. Extraterrestrial beings—Fiction.   2. High schools—
Fiction.   3. Schools—Fiction.   4. Friendship—Fiction.
5. Love—Fiction.   6. Moving, Household—Fiction.
7. Ohio—Fiction.]   I. Title.   II. Title: I am number 4.
PZ7.L87855Iae   2010   2010009395
[Fic]—dc22   CIP
                                                    AC

Typography by Ray Shappell
14 15   OPM/OPM   10 9 8 7 6 5 4
❖
Mass market international edition, 2011

THE DOOR STARTS SHAKING. IT'S A flimsy thing made of bamboo shoots held together with tattered lengths of twine. The shake is subtle and stops almost immediately. They lift their heads to listen, a fourteen-year-old boy and a fifty-year-old man, who everyone thinks is his father but who was born near a different jungle on a different planet hundreds of lightyears away. They are lying shirtless on opposite sides of the hut, a mosquito net over each cot. They hear a distant crash, like the sound of an animal breaking the branch of a tree, but in this case, it sounds like the entire tree has been broken.

"What was that?" the boy asks.

"Shh," the man replies.

They hear the chirp of insects, nothing more. The man brings his legs over the side of the cot when the shake starts again. A longer, firmer shake, and another crash, this time closer. The man gets to his feet and walks slowly to the door. Silence. The man takes a deep breath as he inches his hand to the latch. The boy sits up.

"No," the man whispers, and in that instant the blade of a sword, long and gleaming, made of a shining white metal that is not found on Earth, comes through the door and sinks deeply into the man's chest. It protrudes six inches out through his back, and is quickly pulled free. The man grunts. The boy gasps. The man takes a single breath, and utters one word: "Run." He falls lifeless to the floor.

The boy leaps from the cot, bursts through the rear wall. He doesn't bother with the door or a window; he literally runs through the wall, which breaks apart as if it's paper, though it's made of strong, hard African mahogany. He tears into the Congo night, leaps over trees, sprints at a speed somewhere around sixty miles per hour. His sight and hearing are beyond human. He dodges trees, rips through snarled vines, leaps small streams with a single step. Heavy footsteps are close behind him, getting closer every second. His pursuers also have gifts. And they have something with them. Something he has only heard hints of, something he never believed he would see on Earth.

The crashing nears. The boy hears a low,

intense roar. He knows whatever is behind him is picking up speed. He sees a break in the jungle up ahead. When he reaches it, he sees a huge ravine, three hundred feet across and three hundred feet down, with a river at the bottom. The river's bank is covered with huge boulders. Boulders that would break him apart if he fell on them. His only chance is to get across the ravine. He'll have a short running start, and one chance. One chance to save his own life. Even for him, or for any of the others on Earth like him, it's a near impossible leap. Going back, or going down, or trying to fight them means certain death. He has one shot.

There's a deafening roar behind him. They're twenty, thirty feet away. He takes five steps back and runs—and just before the ledge, he takes off and starts flying across the ravine. He's in the air three or four seconds. He screams, his arms outstretched in front of him, waiting for either safety or the end. He hits the ground and tumbles forward, stopping at the base of a mammoth tree. He smiles. He can't believe he made it, that he's going to survive. Not wanting them to see him, and knowing he needs to get farther away from them, he stands. He'll have to keep running.

He turns towards the jungle. As he does, a huge hand wraps itself around his throat. He is lifted off the ground. He struggles, kicks, tries to pull away, but knows it's futile, that it's over. He should have expected that they'd be on both sides, that once they found him, there would be no escape. The Mogadorian lifts him so that he can see the boy's chest, see the amulet that is hanging around his neck, the amulet that only he and his kind can wear. He tears it off and puts it somewhere inside the long black cloak he is wearing, and when his hand emerges it is holding the gleaming white metal sword. The boy looks into the Mogadorian's deep, wide, emotionless black eyes, and he speaks.

"The Legacies live. They will find each other, and when they're ready, they're going to destroy you."

The Mogadarian laughs, a nasty, mocking laugh. It raises the sword, the only weapon in the universe that can break the charm that until today protected the boy, and still protects the others. The blade ignites in a silver flame as it points to the sky, as if it's coming alive, sensing its mission and grimacing in anticipation. And as it falls, an arc of light speeding through the blackness of the jungle, the boy still believes that some part of him will survive, and some part of him will make it home. He closes his eyes just before the sword strikes. And then it is over.

CHAPTER
ONE

IN THE BEGINNING THERE WERE NINE of us. We left when we were young, almost too young to remember.

Almost.

I am told the ground shook, that the skies were full of light and explosions. We were in that two-week period of the year when both moons hang on opposite sides of the horizon. It was a time of celebration, and the explosions were at first mistaken for fireworks. They were not. It was warm, a soft wind blew in from off the water. I am always told the weather: it was warm. There was a soft wind. I've never understood why that matters.

What I remember most vividly is the way my grandmother looked that day. She was frantic, and sad. There were tears in her eyes. My grandfather stood just over her shoulder. I remember the way his glasses gathered the light from the sky. There were hugs. There were words said by each of them. I don't remember what they were. Nothing haunts me more.

It took a year to get here. I was five when we arrived. We were to assimilate ourselves into the culture before returning to Lorien when it could again sustain life. The nine of us had to scatter, and go our own ways. For how long, nobody knew. We still don't. None of them know where I am, and I don't know where they are, or what they look like now. That is how we protect ourselves because of the charm that was placed upon us when we left, a charm guaranteeing that we can only be killed in the order of our numbers, so long as we stay apart. If we come together, then the charm is broken.

When one of us is found and killed, a circular scar wraps around the right ankle of those still alive. And residing on our left ankle, formed when the Loric charm was first cast, is a small scar identical to the amulet each of us wears. The circular scars are another part of the charm. A warning system so that we know where we stand with each other, and so that we know when they'll be coming for us next. The first scar came when I was nine years old. It woke me from my sleep, burning itself into my flesh. We were living in Arizona, in a small border town near Mexico.

I woke screaming in the middle of the night, in agony, terrified as the scar seared itself into my flesh. It was the first sign that the Mogadorians had finally found us on Earth, and the first sign that we were in danger. Until the scar showed up, I had almost convinced myself that my memories were wrong, that what Henri told me was wrong. I wanted to be a normal kid living a normal life, but I knew then, beyond any doubt or discussion, that I wasn't. We moved to Minnesota the next day.

The second scar came when I was twelve. I was in school, in Colorado, participating in a spelling bee. As soon as the pain started I knew what was happening, what had happened to Number Two. The pain was excruciating, but bearable this time. I would have stayed on the stage, but the heat lit my sock on fire. The teacher who was conducting the bee sprayed me with a fire extinguisher and rushed me to the hospital. The doctor in the ER found the first scar and called the police. When Henri showed, they threatened to arrest him for child abuse. But because he hadn't been anywhere near me when the second scar came, they had to let him go. We got in the car and drove away, this time to Maine. We left everything we had except for the Loric Chest that Henri brought along on every move. All twenty-one of them to date.

The third scar appeared an hour ago. I was sitting on a pontoon boat. The boat belonged to the parents of the most popular kid at my school, and unbeknownst to them, he was having a party on it. I had never been invited to any of the parties at my school before. I had always, because I knew we might leave at any minute, kept to myself. But it had been quiet for two years. Henri hadn't seen anything in the news that might lead the Mogadorians to one of us, or might alert us to them. So I made a couple friends. And one of them introduced me to the kid who was having the party. Everyone met at a dock. There were three coolers, some music, girls I had admired from afar but never spoken to, even though I wanted to. We pulled out from the dock and went half a mile into the Gulf of Mexico. I was sitting on the edge of the pontoon with my feet in the water, talking to a cute, dark-haired, blue-eyed girl named Tara, when I felt it coming. The water around my leg started boiling, and my lower leg started glowing where the scar was imbedding itself. The third of the Lorien symbols, the third warning. Tara started screaming and people started crowding around me. I knew there was no way to explain it. And I knew we would have to leave immediately.

The stakes were higher now. They had found Number Three, wherever he or she was, and Number Three was dead. So I calmed Tara down and kissed her on the cheek and told her it was nice to meet her and that I hoped she had a long beautiful life. I dove off the side of the boat and started swimming, underwater the entire time, except for one breath about halfway there, as fast as I could until I reached the shore. I ran along the side of the highway, just inside of the tree line, moving at speeds as fast as any of the cars. When I got home, Henri was at the bank of scanners and monitors that he used to research news around the world, and police activity in our area. He knew without me saying a word, though he did lift my soaking pants to see the scars.

In the beginning we were a group of nine.

Three are gone, dead.

There are six of us left.

They are hunting us, and they won't stop until they've killed us all.

I am Number Four.

I know that I am next.

CHAPTER TWO

I STAND IN THE MIDDLE OF THE DRIVE and stare up at the house. It is light pink, almost like cake frosting, sitting ten feet above the ground on wooden stilts. A palm tree sways in the front. In the back of the house a pier extends twenty yards into the Gulf of Mexico. If the house were a mile to the south, the pier would be in the Atlantic Ocean.

Henri walks out of the house carrying the last of the boxes, some of which were never unpacked from our last move. He locks the door, then leaves the keys in the mail slot beside it. It is two o'clock in the morning. He is wearing khaki shorts and a black polo. He is very tan, with an unshaven face that seems downcast. He is also sad to be leaving. He tosses the final boxes into the back of the truck with the rest of our things.

"That's it," he says.

I nod. We stand and stare up at the house and listen to the wind come through the palm fronds. I am holding a bag of celery in my hand.

"I'll miss this place," I say. "Even more than the others."

"Me too."

"Time for the burn?"

"Yes. You want to do it, or you want me to?"

"I'll do it."

Henri pulls out his wallet and drops it on the ground. I pull out mine and do the same. He walks to our truck and comes back with passports, birth certificates, social security cards, checkbooks, credit cards and bank cards, and drops them on the ground. All of the documents and materials related to our identities here, all of them forged and manufactured. I grab from the truck a small gas can we keep for emergencies. I pour the gas over the small pile. My current name is Daniel Jones. My story is that I grew up in California and moved here because of my dad's job as a computer programmer. Daniel Jones is about to disappear. I light a match and drop it, and the pile ignites. Another one of my lives, gone. As we always do, Henri and I stand and watch the fire. *Bye, Daniel,* I think, *it was nice knowing you.* When the fire burns down, Henri looks over at me.

"We gotta go."

"I know."

"These islands were never safe. They're too hard to leave quickly, too hard to escape from. It was foolish of us to come here."

I nod. He is right, and I know it. But I'm still reluctant to leave. We came here because I wanted to, and for the first time, Henri let me choose where we were going. We've been here nine months, and it's the longest we have stayed in any one place since leaving Lorien. I'll miss the sun and the warmth. I'll miss the gecko that watched from the wall each morning as I ate breakfast. Though there are literally millions of geckos in south Florida, I swear this one follows me to school and seems to be everywhere I am. I'll miss the thunderstorms that seem to come from out of nowhere, the way everything is still and quiet in the early-morning hours before the terns arrive. I'll miss the dolphins that sometimes feed when the sun sets. I'll even miss the smell of sulfur from the rotting seaweed at the base of the shore, the way that it fills the house and penetrates our dreams while we sleep.

"Get rid of the celery and I'll wait in the truck," Henri says. "Then it's time."

I enter a thicket of trees off to the right of the truck. There are three Key deer already waiting. I dump the bag of celery out at their feet and crouch down and pet each of them in turn. They allow me to, having long gotten over their skittishness. One of them raises his head and looks at me. Dark, blank eyes staring back. It almost feels as though he passes something to me. A shudder runs up my spine. He drops his head and continues eating.

"Good luck, little friends," I say, and walk to the truck and climb into the passenger seat.

We watch the house grow smaller in the side mirrors until Henri pulls onto the main road and the house disappears. It's a Saturday. I wonder what's happening at the party without me. What they're saying about the way that I left and what they'll say on Monday when I'm not at school. I wish I could have said good-bye. I'll never see anyone I knew here ever again. I'll never speak to any of them. And they'll never know what I am or why I left. After a few months, or maybe a few weeks, none of them will probably ever think of me again.

Before we get on the highway, Henri pulls over to gas up the truck. As he works the pump, I start looking through an atlas he keeps on the middle of the seat. We've had the atlas since we arrived on this planet. It has lines drawn to and from every place we've ever lived. At this point, there are lines crisscrossing all of the United States. We know we should get rid of it, but it's really the only piece of our life together that we have. Normal people have photos and videos and journals; we have the atlas. Picking it up and looking through it, I can see Henri has drawn a new line from Florida to Ohio. When I think of Ohio, I think of cows and corn and nice people. I know the license plate says THE HEART OF IT ALL. What "All" is, I don't know, but I guess I'll find out.

Henri gets back into the truck. He has bought a couple of sodas and a bag of chips. He pulls away and starts heading toward U.S. 1, which will take us north. He reaches for the atlas.

"Do you think there are people in Ohio?" I joke.

He chuckles. "I would imagine there are a few. And we might even get lucky and find cars and TV there, too."

I nod. Maybe it won't be as bad as I think.

"What do you think of the name 'John Smith'?" I ask.

"Is that what you've settled on?"

"I think so," I say. I've never been a John before, or a Smith.

"It doesn't get any more common than that. I would say it's a pleasure to meet you, Mr. Smith."

I smile. "Yeah, I think I like 'John Smith.'"

"I'll create your forms when we stop."

A mile later we are off the island and cruising across the bridge. The waters pass below us.

They are calm and the moonlight is shimmering on the small waves, creating dapples of white in the crests. On the right is the ocean, on the left is the gulf; it is, in essence, the same water, but with two different names. I have the urge to cry, but I don't. It's not that I'm necessarily sad to leave Florida, but I'm tired of running. I'm tired of dreaming up a new name every six months. Tired of new houses, new schools. I wonder if it'll ever be possible for us to stop.

CHAPTER THREE

WE PULL OFF FOR FOOD AND GAS AND new phones. We go to a truck stop, where we eat meat loaf and macaroni and cheese, which is one of the few things Henri acknowledges as being superior to anything we had on Lorien. As we eat, he creates new documents on his laptop, using our new names. He'll print them when we arrive, and as far as anyone will know, we'll be who we say we are.

"You're sure about John Smith?" he says.

"Yeah."

"You were born in Tuscaloosa, Alabama."

I laugh. "How did you come up with that?"

He smiles and motions towards two women sitting a few booths away. Both of them are extremely hot. One of them is wearing a T-shirt that reads **WE DO IT BETTER IN TUSCALOOSA**.

"And that's where we're going next," he says.

"As weird as it may sound, I hope we stay in Ohio for a long time."

"Really. You like the idea of Ohio?"

"I like the idea of making some friends, of going to the same school for more than a few months, of maybe actually having a life. I started to do it in Florida. It was sort of great, and for the first time since we've been on Earth, I felt almost normal. I want to find somewhere and stay somewhere."

Henri looks thoughtful. "Have you looked at your scars today?"

"No, why?"

"Because this isn't about you. This is about the survival of our race, which was almost entirely obliterated, and about keeping you alive. Every time one of us dies—every time one of *you*, the Garde, dies—our chances diminish. You're Number Four; you're next in line. You have an entire race of vicious murderers hunting you. We're leaving at the first sign of trouble, and I'm not going to debate it with you."

Henri drives the entire time. Between breaks and the creation of the new documents, it takes about thirty hours. I spend most of the time napping or playing video games. Because of my reflexes, I can master most of the games quickly. The longest it has taken me to beat any of them is about a day. I like the alien war and space games the best. I pretend I'm back on Lorien, fighting Mogadorians, cutting them down, turning them to ash. Henri thinks it's weird and tries to discourage me from doing it. He says we need to live in the real world, where war and death are a reality, not pretend. As I finish my latest game, I look up. I'm tired of sitting in the truck. The clock on the dash reads 7:58. I yawn, wipe my eyes.

"How much farther?"

"We're almost there," Henri says.

It is dark out, but there is a pale glow to the west. We pass by farms with horses and cattle, then barren fields, and beyond those, it's trees as far as the eye can see. This is exactly what Henri wanted, a quiet place to go unnoticed. Once a week he scours the internet for six, seven, eight hours at a time to update a list of available homes around the country that fit his criteria: isolated, rural, immediate availability. He told me it took four tries—one call to South Dakota, one to New Mexico, one to Arkansas—until he had the rental where we're going to live now.

A few minutes later we see scattered lights that announce the town. We pass a sign that reads:

WELCOME TO PARADISE, OHIO
POPULATION 5,243

"Wow," I say. "This place is even smaller than where we stayed in Montana."

Henri is smiling. "Who do you think it's paradise for?"

"Cows, maybe? Scarecrows?"

We pass by an old gas station, a car wash, a cemetery. Then the houses begin, clapboard houses spaced thirty or so feet apart. Halloween decorations hang in the windows of most of them. A sidewalk cuts through small yards leading to the front doors. A traffic circle sits in the center of town, and in the middle of it is a statue of a man on horseback holding a sword. Henri stops. We both look at it and laugh, though we're laughing because we hope no one else with swords ever shows up here. He continues around the circle and once we're through it, the dashboard GPS system tells us to make a turn. We begin heading west, out of town.

We drive for four miles before turning left onto a gravel road, then pass open cut fields that are probably full of corn in the summer, then through a dense forest for about a mile. And then we find it, tucked away in overgrown vegetation, a rusted silver mailbox with black lettering painted on the side of it that reads 17 OLD MILL RD.

"The closest house is two miles away," he says, turning in. Weeds grow throughout the gravel drive, which is littered with potholes filled with tawny water. He comes to a stop and turns the truck off.

"Whose car is that?" I ask, nodding to the black SUV Henri has just parked behind.

"I'm assuming the real-estate agent's."

The house stands silhouetted by trees. In the dark there is an eerie look to it, like whoever last lived in it was scared away, or was driven away, or ran away. I get out of the truck. The engine ticks and I can feel the heat coming off of it. I grab my bag from the bed and stand there holding it.

"What do you think?" Henri asks.

The house is one story. Wooden clapboard. Most of the white paint has been chipped away. One of the front windows is broken. The roof is covered with black shingles that look warped and brittle. Three wooden stairs lead to a small porch covered with rickety chairs. The yard itself is long and shaggy. It's been a very long time since the grass was last mowed.

"It looks like Paradise," I say.

We walk up together. As we do, a well-dressed blond woman around Henri's age comes out of the doorway. She's wearing a business suit and is holding a clipboard and folder; a BlackBerry is clipped to the waist of her skirt. She smiles.

"Mr. Smith?"

"Yes," says Henri.

"I'm Annie Hart, the agent from Paradise Realty. We spoke on the phone. I tried calling you earlier but your phone seemed to be turned off."

"Yes, of course. The battery unfortunately died on the way here."

"Ah, I just hate when that happens," she says, and walks towards us and shakes Henri's hand. She asks me my name and I tell her, though I am tempted, as I always am, to just say "Four." As Henri signs the lease she asks me how old I am and tells me she has a daughter at the local high school about my age. She's very warm, friendly, and clearly loves to chat. Henri hands the lease back and the three of us walk into the house.

Inside most of the furniture is covered with white sheets. Those that aren't covered are coated with a thick layer of dust and dead insects. The screens in the windows look brittle to the touch, and the walls are covered with cheap plywood paneling. There are two bedrooms, a modest-sized kitchen with lime green linoleum, one bathroom. The living room is large and rectangular, situated at the front of the house. There's a fireplace in the far corner. I walk through and toss my bag on the bed of the smaller room. There is a huge faded poster of a football player wearing a bright orange uniform. He's in the middle of throwing a pass, and it looks like he's about to get crushed by a massive man in a black and gold uniform. It says BERNIE KOSAR, QUAR-TERBACK, CLEVELAND BROWNS.

"Come say good-bye to Mrs. Hart," Henri yells from the living room.

Mrs. Hart is standing at the door with Henri. She tells me I should look for her daughter at school, that maybe we could be friends. I smile and say yes, that would be nice. After she leaves we immediately start unpacking the truck. Depending on how quickly we leave a place, we either travel very lightly—meaning the clothes on our back, Henri's laptop and the intricately carved Loric Chest that goes everywhere with us—or we bring a few things—usually Henri's extra computers and equipment, which he uses to set up a security perimeter and search the web for news and events that might be related to us. This time we have the Chest, the two high-powered computers, four TV monitors, and four cameras. We also have some clothes, though not many of the clothes we wore in Florida are appropriate for life in Ohio. Henri carries the Chest to his room, and we lug all of the equipment into the basement, where he'll set it up so no visitors will see it. Once everything is inside, he starts placing the cameras and turning on the monitors.

"We won't have the internet here until the morning. But if you want to go to school tomorrow, I can print all of your new documents for you."

"If I stay will I have to help you clean this place and finish the setup?"

"Yes."

"I'll go to school," I say.

"Then you better get a good night's sleep."

CHAPTER
FOUR

ANOTHER NEW IDENTITY, ANOTHER NEW
school. I've lost track of how many there have
been over the years. Fifteen? Twenty? Always a
small town, a small school, always the same rou-
tine. New students draw attention. Sometimes I
question our strategy of sticking to the small
towns because it's hard, almost impossible, to go
unnoticed. But I know Henri's rationale: it is
impossible for *them* to go unnoticed as well.

The school is three miles away from our
house. Henri drives me in the morning. It's
smaller than most of the others I've attended and
is unimpressive looking, one story, long and low-
slung. A mural of a pirate with a knife between
his teeth covers the outside wall beside the front
door.

"So you're a Pirate now?" Henri says beside me.

"It looks like it," I reply.

"You know the drill," he says.

"This ain't my first rodeo."

"Don't show your intelligence. It'll make them resent you."

"Wouldn't dream of it."

"Don't stand out or draw too much attention."

"Just a fly on the wall."

"And don't hurt anybody. You're far stronger than they are."

"I know."

"Most importantly, always be ready. Ready to leave at a moment's notice. What's in your backpack?"

"Five days' worth of dried fruit and nuts. Spare socks and thermal underwear. Rain jacket. A handheld GPS. A knife disguised as a pen."

"On you at all times." He takes a deep breath. "And keep an eye out for signs. Your Legacies are going to appear any day now. Hide them at all costs and call me immediately."

"I know, Henri."

"Any day, John," he reiterates. "If your fingers start to disappear, or if you start to float, or shake violently, if you lose muscular control or begin to hear voices even when nobody is talking. Anything at all, you call."

I pat my bag. "Got my phone right here."

"I'll be waiting here after school. Good luck in there, kiddo," he says.

I smile at him. He is fifty years old, which means he was forty when we arrived. Being his age made for a harder transition. He still speaks with a strong Loric accent that is often mistaken for French. It was a good alibi in the beginning, so he named himself Henri, and he has stuck with it ever since, just changing his last name to match mine.

"Off I go to rule the school," I say.

"Be good."

I walk towards the building. As is the case with most high schools, there are crowds of kids hanging around outside. They're divided into their cliques, the jocks and the cheerleaders, the band kids carrying instruments, the brains in their glasses with their textbooks and BlackBerries, the stoners off to one side, oblivious to everyone else. One kid, gangly with thick glasses, stands alone. He's wearing a black NASA T-shirt and jeans, and can't weigh more than a hundred pounds. He has a handheld telescope and is scanning the sky, which is mostly obscured by clouds. I notice a girl taking pictures, moving easily from one group to the next. She's shockingly beautiful with straight blond hair past her shoulders, ivory skin, high cheekbones, and soft blue eyes. Everyone seems to know her and says hello to her, and no one objects to her taking their picture.

She sees me, smiles and waves. I wonder why

and turn to see if someone is behind me. There are, two kids discussing math homework, but no one else. I turn back around. The girl walks towards me, smiling. I've never seen a girl so good-looking, much less spoken to one, and I've definitely never had one wave and smile as if we're friends. I'm immediately nervous, and start blushing. But I'm also suspicious, as I've been trained to be. As she nears me, she lifts the camera and starts snapping pictures. I raise my hands to block my face. She lowers the camera and smiles.

"Don't be shy."

"I'm not. Just trying to protect your lens. My face might break it."

She laughs. "With that scowl it might. Try smiling."

I smile, slightly. I'm so nervous I feel like I'm going to explode. I can feel my neck burning, my hands getting warm.

"That's not a real smile," she says, teasingly. "A smile involves showing your teeth."

I smile broadly and she takes pictures. I usually don't allow anyone to take my picture. If it ended up on the internet, or in a newspaper, it would make finding me much easier. The two times it happened, Henri was furious, got hold of the pictures, and destroyed them. If he knew I was doing this now, I'd be in huge trouble. I can't help it, though—this girl is so pretty and so charming. As she's taking my picture, a dog comes running up to me. It's a beagle with tan floppy ears, white legs and chest, a slender black body. He's thin and dirty as if he's been living on his own. He rubs against my leg, whines, tries to get my attention. The girl thinks it's cute and has me kneel down so she can take a picture of me with the dog. As soon as she starts snapping shots, he backs away. Whenever she tries again, he moves farther away. She finally gives up and shoots a few more of me. The dog sits about thirty feet away watching us.

"Do you know that dog?" she asks.

"Never seen him before."

"He sure likes you. You're John, right?"

She holds out her hand.

"Yeah," I say. "How'd you know?"

"I'm Sarah Hart. My mother is your real-estate agent. She told me you'd probably be starting school today, and I should look out for you. You're the only new kid to show up today."

I laugh. "Yeah, I met your mom. She was nice."

"You gonna shake my hand?"

She's still holding her hand out. I smile and take it, and it is literally one of the best feelings I've ever had.

"Wow," she says.

"What?"

"Your hand feels hot. Really hot, like you have a fever or something."

"I don't think so."

She lets go.

"Maybe you're just warm-blooded."

"Yeah, maybe."

A bell rings in the distance and Sarah tells me that it's the warning bell. We have five minutes to get to class. We say good-bye and I watch her walk away. A moment later, something hits the back of my elbow. I turn and a group of football players, all wearing letterman jackets, sweep by me. One of them is glaring at me and I realize that he hit me with his backpack as he walked past. I doubt it was an accident and I start to follow them. I know I'm not going to do anything, even though I could. I just don't like bullies. As I do, the kid in the NASA shirt walks next to me.

"I know you're new, so I'll fill you in," he says.

"On what?" I ask.

"That's Mark James. He's a big deal around here. His dad is the town sheriff and he's the star of the football team. He used to date Sarah, when she was a cheerleader, but she quit cheerleading and dumped him. He hasn't gotten over it. I wouldn't get involved if I were you."

"Thanks."

The kid hurries away. I make my way to the

principal's office so I can register for classes and get started. I turn and look back to see if the dog is still around. He is, sitting in the same spot, watching me.

The principal's name is Mr. Harris. He's fat and mostly bald, except for a few long hairs at the back and sides of his head. His belly reaches over his belt. His eyes are small and beady, set too close together. He grins at me from across the desk, and his smile seems to swallow his eyes.

"So you're a sophomore from Santa Fe?" he asks.

I nod, say yes even though we've never been to Santa Fe, or New Mexico, for that matter. A simple lie to keep from being traced.

"That explains the tan. What brings you to Ohio?"

"My dad's job."

Henri isn't my father, but I always say he is to allay suspicion. In truth he is my Keeper, or what would be better understood on Earth as my guardian. On Lorien there were two types of citizens, those who develop Legacies, or powers, which can be extremely varied, anything from invisibility to the ability to read minds, from being able to fly to using natural forces like fire, wind or lightning. Those with the Legacies are called the Garde, and those without are called

Cêpan, or Keepers. I am a member of the Garde. Henri is a Cêpan. Every Garde is assigned a Cêpan at an early age. Cêpans help us understand our planet's history and develop our powers. The Cêpan and the Garde—one group to run the planet, the other group to defend it.

Mr. Harris nods. "And what does he do?"

"He's a writer. He wanted to live in a small, quiet town to finish what he's working on," I say, which is our standard cover story.

Mr. Harris nods and squints his eyes. "You look like a strong young man. Are you planning on playing sports here?"

"I wish I could. I have asthma, sir," I say, my usual excuse to avoid any situation that might betray my strength and speed.

"I'm sorry to hear that. We're always looking for able athletes for the football team," he says, and casts his eyes to the shelf on the wall, on top of which a football trophy sits engraved with last year's date. "We won the Pioneer Conference," he says, and beams with pride.

He reaches over and pulls two sheets of paper from a file cabinet beside his desk and hands them to me. The first is my student schedule with a few open slots. The second is a list of the available electives. I choose classes and fill them in, then hand everything back. He gives me a sort of orientation, talking for what seems like hours, going over every page of the student manual with painstaking detail. One bell rings, then another. When he finally finishes he asks if I have any questions. I say no.

"Excellent. There is a half hour left of second period, and you've chosen astronomy with Mrs. Burton. She's a great teacher, one of our very best. She won an award from the state once, signed by the governor himself."

"That's great," I say.

After Mr. Harris struggles to free himself from his chair, we leave his office and walk down the hall. His shoes click upon the newly waxed floor. The air smells of fresh paint and cleaner. Lockers line the walls. Many are covered with banners supporting the football team. There can't be more than twenty classrooms in the whole building. I count them as we pass.

"Here we are," Mr. Harris says. He extends his hand. I shake it. "We're happy to have you. I like to think of us as a close-knit family. I'm glad to welcome you to it."

"Thank you," I say.

Mr. Harris opens the door and sticks his head in the classroom. Only then do I realize that I'm a little nervous, that a somewhat dizzy feeling is creeping in. My right leg is shaking; there are butterflies in the pit of my stomach. I don't understand why. Surely it's not the prospect of

walking into my first class. I've done it far too many times to still feel the effect of nerves. I take a deep breath and try to shake them away.

"Mrs. Burton, sorry to interrupt. Your new student is here."

"Oh, great! Send him in," she says in a high-pitched voice of enthusiasm.

Mr. Harris holds open the door and I walk through. The classroom is perfectly square, filled with twenty-five people, give or take, sitting at rectangular desks about the size of kitchen tables, three students to each. All eyes are on me. I look back at them before looking at Mrs. Burton. She is somewhere around sixty, wearing a pink wool sweater and red plastic glasses attached to a chain around her neck. She smiles widely, her hair graying and curly. My palms are sweaty and my face feels flushed. I hope it isn't red. Mr. Harris closes the door.

"And what is your name?" she asks.

In my unsettled mood I almost say "Daniel Jones" but catch myself. I take a deep breath and say, "John Smith."

"Great! And where are you from?"

"Fl—," I begin, but then catch myself again before the word fully forms. "Santa Fe."

"Class, let's give him a warm welcome."

Everybody claps. Mrs. Burton motions for me to sit in the open seat in the middle of the room

between two other students. I am relieved she doesn't ask any more questions. She turns around to go to her desk and I begin walking down the aisle, straight towards Mark James, who is sitting at a table with Sarah Hart. As I pass, he sticks his foot out and trips me. I lose my balance but stay upright. Snickers filter throughout the room. Mrs. Burton whips around.

"What happened?" she asks.

I don't answer her, and instead glare at Mark. Every school has one, a tough guy, a bully, whatever you want to call him, but never has one materialized this quickly. His hair is black, full of hair gel, carefully styled so it goes in all directions. He has meticulously trimmed sideburns, stubble on his face. Bushy eyebrows over a set of dark eyes. From his letterman jacket I see that he is a senior, and his name is written in gold cursive stitching above the year. Our eyes stay locked, and the class emits a taunting groan.

I look to my seat three desks away, then I look back at Mark. I could literally break him in half if I wanted to. I could throw him into the next county. If he tried to run away, and got into a car, I could outrun his car and put it in the top of a tree. But aside from that being an extreme overreaction, Henri's words echo in my mind: "Don't stand out or draw too much attention." I know that I should follow his advice and ignore what

has just happened, as I always have in the past. That is what we're good at, blending into the environment and living within its shadows. But I feel slightly off, uneasy, and before I have a chance to think twice, the question is already asked.

"Did you want something?"

Mark looks away and glances around the rest of the room, scoots his weight up the chair, then looks back at me.

"What are you talking about?" he asks.

"You stuck your foot out when I passed. And you bumped into me outside. I thought you might have wanted something."

"What's going on?" Mrs. Burton asks behind me. I look over my shoulder at her.

"Nothing," I say. I turn back to Mark. "Well?"

His hands tighten around the desk but he remains silent. Our eyes stay locked until he sighs and looks away.

"That's what I thought," I say down at him, and continue walking. The other students aren't sure how to respond and most of them are still staring when I take my seat between a redheaded girl with freckles and an overweight guy who looks at me with his mouth agape.

Mrs. Burton stands at the head of the class. She seems a little flustered, but then shrugs it off and describes why there are rings around Saturn, and how they're made mostly of ice particles and dust. After a while I tune her out and look at the other students. A whole new group of people that I'll yet again try to keep at a distance. It's always a fine line, having just enough interaction with them to remain mysterious without becoming strange and thus sticking out. I've already done a horrible job of that today.

I take a deep breath and slowly exhale. I still have butterflies in my stomach, still the nagging shake in my leg. My hands feel warmer. Mark James sits three tables in front of me. He turns once and looks at me, then whispers something into Sarah's ear. She turns around. She seems cool, but the fact that she used to date him and is sitting with him makes me wonder. She gives me a warm smile. I want to smile back but I'm frozen. Mark again tries to whisper to her but she shakes her head and pushes him away. My hearing is much better than human hearing if I focus it, but I'm so flustered by her smile that I don't. I wish I could have heard what was said.

I open and close my hands. My palms are sweaty and beginning to burn. Another deep breath. My vision is blurring. Five minutes pass, then ten. Mrs. Burton is still talking but I don't hear what she is saying. I squeeze my fists shut, then reopen them. When I do my breath catches in my throat. A slight glow is coming from my right palm. I look down at it, dumbfounded, amazed. After a few seconds the glow begins to brighten.

I close my fists. My initial fear is that something else has happened to one of the others. But what could happen? We can't be killed out of order. That is the way the charm works. But does that mean that some other harm can't befall them? Has somebody's right hand been cut off? I have no way of knowing. But if something had happened, I would have felt it in the scars on my ankles. And only then does it dawn on me. My first Legacy must be forming.

I pull my phone out of my bag, and send Henri a text that says CMEE, though I meant to type COME. I'm too dizzy to send anything else. I close my fists and place them in my lap. They're burning and shaking. I open my hands. My left palm is bright red, my right is still glowing. I glance at the clock on the wall and see that class is almost over. If I can get out of here I can find an empty room and call Henri and ask him what's going on. I start counting the seconds: sixty, fifty-nine, fifty-eight. It feels like something is going to explode in my hands. I focus on the counting. Forty, thirty-nine. They're tingling now, as though little needles are being stuck into my palms. Twenty-eight, twenty-seven. I open my eyes and stare ahead, focusing on Sarah with the hope that looking at her will distract me. Fifteen, fourteen. Seeing her makes it worse. The needles feel like nails now. Nails that have been put in a furnace and heated until they're glowing. Eight, seven.

The bell rings and in an instant I'm up and out of the room, rushing past the other students. I'm feeling dizzy, unsteady on my feet. I continue down the hall and have no idea where to go. I can feel someone following me. I pull my schedule from my back pocket and check my locker number. As luck would have it, my locker is just to my right. I stop at it and lean my head against the metal door. I shake my head, realizing that in my rush to get out of the classroom I left behind my bag with my phone inside of it. And then someone pushes me.

"What's up, tough guy?"

I stumble a few steps, look back. Mark is standing there, smiling at me.

"Something wrong?" he asks.

"No," I reply.

My head is spinning. I feel like I'm going to pass out. And my hands are on fire. Whatever is happening couldn't be happening at a worse time. He pushes me again.

"Not so tough without any teachers around, are you?"

I'm too unbalanced to stay standing, and I

trip over my own feet and fall to the ground. Sarah steps in front of Mark.

"Leave him alone," she says.

"This has nothing to do with you," he says.

"Right. You see a new kid talking to me and you try immediately to start a fight with him. *This* is just one example of why we aren't together anymore."

I start to stand up. Sarah reaches down to help me, and as soon as she touches me, the pain in my hands flares up and it feels like lightning strikes through my head. I turn around and start rushing away, in the opposite direction from the astronomy class. I know that everyone will think I'm a coward for running, but I feel like I'm about to pass out. I'll thank Sarah, and deal with Mark, later. Right now I just need to find a room with a lock on the door.

I get to the end of the hall, which intersects with the school's main entrance. I think back to Mr. Harris's orientation, which included where the various rooms were located in the school. If I remember correctly, the auditorium, band rooms, and art rooms are at the end of this hall. I run towards them as fast as I can in my current state. Behind me I can hear Mark yelling to me, and Sarah yelling at him. I open the first door I find, and shut it behind me. Thankfully there is a lock, which I click into place.

I'm in a dark room. Strips of negatives hang on drying lines. I collapse onto the floor. My head spins and my hands are burning. Since first seeing the light, I have kept my hands clenched into fists. I look down at them now and see my right hand is still glowing, pulsating. I start to panic.

I sit on the floor, sweat stinging my eyes. Both hands are in terrible pain. I knew to expect my Legacies, but I had no idea it would include this. I open my hands and my right palm is shining brightly, the light beginning to concentrate. My left is dimly flickering, the burning sensation almost unbearable. I wish Henri was here. I hope he's on his way.

I close my eyes and fold my arms across my body. I rock back and forth on the floor, everything inside of me in pain. I don't know how much time is passing. One minute? Ten minutes? The bell rings, signaling the start of the next period. I can hear people talking outside the door. The door shakes a couple times, but it's locked and nobody will be able to get in. I just keep rocking, eyes closed tightly. More knocks begin to fall on the door. Muffled voices that I can't understand. I open my eyes and can see that the glow from my hands has lit up the entire room. I squeeze my hands into fists to try and stop the light but it streams out between my fingers. Then the door really starts shaking. What will they think of the light in my hands? There is no hiding it. How will I explain it?

"John? Open the door—it's me," a voice says.

Relief floods through me. Henri's voice, the only voice in the whole world that I want to hear.

CHAPTER FIVE

I CRAWL TO THE DOOR AND UNLOCK IT. It swings open. Henri is covered in dirt, wearing gardening clothes as though he had been working outside on the house. I'm so happy to see him that I have the urge to jump up and wrap my arms around him, and I try to, but I'm too dizzy and I fall back onto the floor.

"Is everything okay in there?" asks Mr. Harris, who is standing behind Henri.

"Everything is fine. Just give us a minute, please," Henri says back.

"Do I need to call an ambulance?"

"No!"

The door shuts. Henri looks down at my hands. The light in the right one is shining brightly, though the left dimly flickers as though trying to gain confidence in itself. Henri smiles widely, his face shining like a beacon.

"Ahh, thank Lorien," he sighs, then pulls a pair of leather gardening gloves from his back pocket. "What dumb luck that I've been working in the yard. Put these on."

I do and they completely hide the light. Mr. Harris opens the door and sticks his head through. "Mr. Smith? Is everything okay?"

"Yes, everything is fine. Just give us thirty seconds," Henri says, then looks back to me. "Your principal meddles."

I take a deep breath and exhale. "I understand what is happening, but why this?"

"Your first Legacy."

"I know that, why the lights?"

"We'll talk about it in the truck. Can you walk?"

"I think so."

He helps me up. I am unsteady, still shaking. I grab hold of his forearm for support.

"I have to get my bag before we leave," I say.

"Where is it?"

"I left it in the classroom."

"What number?"

"Seventeen."

"Let's get you to the truck and I'll go get it."

I drape my right arm over his shoulders. He supports my weight by putting his left arm around my waist. Even though the second bell has rung I can still hear people in the hall.

"You need to walk as straight and as normal as you can."

I take a deep breath. I try to gather any bit of strength I might have on reserve to tackle the long walk out of the school.

"Let's do this," I say.

I wipe the sweat from my forehead and follow Henri out of the darkroom. Mr. Harris is still in the hallway.

"Just a bad case of asthma," Henri tells him, and walks past.

A crowd of twenty or so people are still in the hallway, and most of them are wearing cameras around their necks, waiting to get into the darkroom for photography class. Thankfully Sarah isn't among them. I walk as steadily as I can, one foot in front of the other. The school's exit is a hundred feet away. That is a lot of steps. People are whispering.

"What a freak."

"Does he even go to school here?"

"I hope so, he's cute."

"What do you think he was doing in the darkroom to make his face so red?" I hear, and everyone laughs. Just like we can focus our hearing, we can close it off, which helps when you're trying to concentrate amidst noise and confusion. So I shut out the noise and follow closely behind Henri. Each step feels like ten, but finally we reach the door. Henri holds it open for me and I try to walk on my own to his truck, which is parked up front. For the last twenty steps I drape my arm around his shoulders again. He opens the truck door and I scoot in.

"You said seventeen?"

"Yes."

"You should have kept it with you. It's the little mistakes that lead to big mistakes. We can't make any."

"I know. I'm sorry."

He shuts the door and walks back into the building. I hunch over in the seat and try to slow my breathing. I can still feel the sweat on my forehead. I sit up and flip down the sun visor so I can look into the mirror. My face is redder than I thought, my eyes a little watery. But through the pain and exhaustion, I smile. *Finally*, I think. After years of waiting, after years of my only defense against the Mogadorians being intellect and stealth, my first Legacy has arrived. Henri comes out of the school carrying my bag. He walks around the truck, opens the door, tosses my bag on the seat.

"Thank you," I say.

"No problem."

When we're out of the lot I remove the gloves and take a closer look at my hands. The light in my right hand is beginning to concentrate itself into a beam like a flashlight, only brighter. The burning is beginning to lessen. My left hand still flickers dimly.

"You should keep those on until we're home," Henri says.

I put the gloves back on and look over at him. He is smiling proudly.

"Been a shit long wait," he says.

"Huh?" I ask.

He looks over. "A shit long wait," he says again. "For your Legacies."

I laugh. Of all the things Henri has learned to master while on Earth, profanity is not one of them.

"A *damn* long wait," I correct him.

"Yeah, that's what I said."

He turns down our road.

"So, what next? Does this mean I'll be able to shoot lasers from my hands or what?"

He grins. "It's nice to think so, but no."

"Well, what am I going to do with light? When I'm getting chased am I going to turn and flash it in their eyes? Like that's supposed to make them cower from me or something?"

"Patience," he says. "You aren't supposed to understand it yet. Let's just get home."

And then I remember something that nearly makes me jump out of my seat.

"Does this mean we'll finally open the Chest?"

He nods and smiles. "Very soon."

"Hell, yes!" I say. The intricately carved wooden Chest has haunted me my entire life. It's a brittle-looking box with the Loric symbol on its side that Henri has remained completely secretive about. He's never told me what's in it, and it's impossible to open, and I know, because I've tried more times than I can count, never with any luck. It's held shut with a padlock with no discernible slot for a key.

When we get home I can tell that Henri has been working. The three chairs from the front porch have been cleared away and all the windows are open. Inside, the sheets over the furniture have been removed, some of the surfaces wiped clean. I set my bag atop the table in the living room and open it. A wave of frustration passes over me.

"The son of a bitch," I say.

"What?"

"My phone is missing."

"Where is it?"

"I had a slight disagreement this morning with a kid named Mark James. He probably took it."

"John, you were in school for an hour and a half. How in the hell did you have a disagreement already? You know better."

"It's high school. I'm the new kid. It's easy."

Henri removes his phone from his pocket and dials my number. Then he snaps his phone shut.

"It's turned off," he says.

"Of course it is."

He stares at me. "What happened?" he asks in that voice I recognize, the voice he uses when pondering another move.

"Nothing. Just a stupid argument. I probably dropped it on the floor when I put it into my bag," I say, even though I know I didn't. "I wasn't in the best frame of mind. It's probably waiting for me in lost and found."

He looks around the house and sighs. "Did anyone see your hands?"

I look at him. His eyes are red, even more bloodshot than they were when he dropped me off. His hair is tousled and he has a slumped look as though he may collapse in exhaustion at any moment. He last slept in Florida, two days ago. I'm not sure how he is even still standing.

"Nobody did."

"You were in school for an hour and a half. Your first Legacy developed, you were nearly in a fight, and you left your bag in a classroom. That's not exactly blending in."

"It was nothing. Certainly not a big enough deal to move to Idaho, or Kansas, or wherever the hell our next place is going to be."

Henri narrows his eyes, pondering what he just witnessed and trying to decide whether it's enough to justify leaving.

"Now is not the time to be careless," he says.

"There are arguments in every single school every single day. I promise you, they aren't going to track us because some bully messed with the new kid."

"The new kid's hands don't light up in every school."

I sigh. "Henri, you look like you're about to die. Take a nap. We can decide after you've had some sleep."

"We have a lot to talk about."

"I've never seen you this tired before. Sleep a few hours. We'll talk after."

He nods. "A nap would probably do me some good."

Henri goes into his bedroom and closes the door. I walk outside, pace around the yard for a bit. The sun is behind the trees with a cool wind blowing. The gloves are still on my hands. I take them off and tuck them into my back pocket. My hands are the same as before. Truth be told, only half of me is thrilled that my first Legacy has finally arrived after so many years of impatiently waiting. The other half of me is crushed. Our constant moving has worn me down, and now it'll be impossible to blend in or to stay in one place for any period of time. It'll be impossible to make friends or feel like I fit in. I'm sick of the fake names and the lies. I'm sick of always looking over my shoulder to see if I'm being followed.

I reach down and feel the three scars on my right ankle. Three circles that represent the three dead. We are bound to each other by more than mere race. As I feel the scars I try to imagine who they were, whether they were boys or girls, where they were living, how old they were when they died. I try to remember the other kids on the ship with me and give each of them numbers. I think about what it would be like to meet them, hang out with them. What it might have been like if we were still on Lorien. What it might be like if the fate of our entire race wasn't dependent on the survival of so few of us. What it might be like if we weren't all facing death at the hands of our enemies.

It's terrifying to know that I'm next. But we've stayed ahead of them by moving, running. Even though I'm sick of the running I know it's the only reason we're still alive. If we stop, they will find us. And now that I'm next in line, they have undoubtedly stepped up the search. Surely they must know we are growing stronger, coming into our Legacies.

And then there is the other ankle and the scar to be found there, formed when the Loric charm was cast in those precious moments before leaving Lorien. It's the brand that binds us all together.

CHAPTER SIX

I WALK INSIDE AND LIE ON THE BARE mattress in my room. The morning has worn me out and I let my eyes close. When I reopen them the sun is lifted over the tops of the trees. I walk out of the room. Henri is at the kitchen table with his laptop open and I know he's been scanning the news, as he always does, searching for information or stories that might tell us where the others are.

"Did you sleep?" I ask.

"Not much. We have internet now and I haven't checked the news since Florida. It was gnawing at me."

"Anything to report?" I ask.

He shrugs. "A fourteen-year-old in Africa fell from a fourth-story window and walked away without a scratch. There is a fifteen-year-old in Bangladesh claiming to be the Messiah."

I laugh. "I know the fifteen-year-old isn't us. Any chance of the other?"

"Nah. Surviving a four-story drop is no great feat, and besides, if it was one of us they wouldn't have been that careless in the first place," he says, and winks.

I smile and sit across from him. He closes his computer and places his hands on the table. His watch reads 11:36. We've been in Ohio for slightly over half a day and already this much has happened. I hold my palms up. They've dimmed since the last time I looked.

"Do you know what you have?" he asks.

"Lights in my hands."

He chuckles. "It's called Lumen. You'll be able to control the light in time."

"I sure hope so, because our cover is blown if they don't turn off soon. I still don't see what the point is, though."

"There's more to Lumen than mere lights. I promise you."

"What's the rest?"

He walks into his bedroom and returns with a lighter in his hand.

"Do you remember much of your grandparents?" he asks. Our grandparents are the ones who raise us. We see little of our parents until we reach the age of twenty-five, when we have children of our own. The life expectancy for the

Loric is around two hundred years, much longer than that of humans, and when children are born, between the parents' ages of twenty-five and thirty-five, the elders are the ones who raise them while the parents continue honing their Legacies.

"A little. Why?"

"Because your grandfather had the same gift."

"I don't remember his hands ever glowing," I say.

Henri shrugs. "He might never have had reason to use it."

"Wonderful," I say. "Sounds like a great gift to have, one I'll never use."

He shakes his head. "Give me your hand."

I give him the right one and he flicks the lighter on, then moves it to touch the tip of my finger with the flame. I jerk my hand away.

"What are you doing?"

"Trust me," he says.

I give my hand back to him. He takes hold of it and flicks the lighter on again. He looks into my eyes. Then he smiles. I look down and see that he is holding the flame over the tip of my middle finger. I don't feel a thing. Instinct causes me to jerk my hand free anyway. I rub my finger. It feels no different than it did before.

"Did you feel that?" he asks.

"No."

"Give it back," he says. "And tell me when you do feel something."

He starts at my fingertip again, then moves the flame very slowly up the back of my hand. There is a slight tickle where the flame touches the skin, nothing more. Only when the fire reaches my wrist do I begin to sense the burn. I pull my arm free.

"Ouch."

"Lumen," he says. "You're going to become resistant to fire and heat. Your hands come naturally, but we'll have to train the rest of your body."

A smile spreads across my face. "Resistant to fire and heat," I say. "So I'll never be burned again?"

"Eventually, yes."

"That's awesome!"

"Not such a bad Legacy after all, huh?"

"Not bad at all," I agree. "Now what about these lights? Are they ever going to turn off?"

"They will. Probably after a good night's sleep, when your mind forgets they're on," he says. "But you'll have to be careful not to get worked up for a while. An emotional imbalance will cause them to come right back on again, if you get overly nervous, or angry, or sad."

"For how long?"

"Until you learn to control them." He closes

his eyes and rubs his face with his hands. "Anyway, I'm going to try to sleep again. We'll talk about your training in a few hours."

After he leaves I stay at the kitchen table, opening and closing my hands, taking deep breaths and trying to calm everything inside of me so the lights will dim. Of course it doesn't work.

Everything in the house is still a mess aside from the few things Henri did while I was at school. I can tell that he is leaning towards leaving, but not to the point that he couldn't be persuaded to stay. Maybe if he wakes and finds the house clean and in order it'll tip him in the right direction.

I start with my room. I dust, wash the windows, sweep the floor. When everything is clean I throw sheets, pillows, and blankets on the bed, then hang and fold my clothes. The dresser is old and rickety, but I fill it and then place the few books I own on top of it. And just like that, a clean room, everything I own put away and in order.

I move to the kitchen, putting away dishes and wiping down the counters. It gives me something to do and takes my mind off of my hands, even though while cleaning I think about Mark James. For the first time in my life I stood up to somebody. I've always wanted to but never did because I wanted to heed Henri's advice to keep a low profile. I've always tried to delay another move for as long as I could. But today was different. There was something very satisfying about being pushed by somebody and responding by pushing back. And then there's the issue of my phone, which was stolen. Sure, we could easily get a new one, but where is the justice in that?

CHAPTER SEVEN

I WAKE BEFORE THE ALARM. THE house is cool and silent. I lift my hands from under the covers. They are normal, no lights, no glow. I lumber out of bed and into the living room. Henri is at the kitchen table reading the local paper and drinking coffee.

"Good morning," he says. "How do you feel?"

"Like a million bucks," I say.

I pour myself a bowl of cereal and sit across from him.

"What are you going to do today?" I ask.

"Errands mostly. We're getting low on money. I'm thinking of putting in a transfer at the bank."

Lorien is (or was, depending on how you look at it) a planet rich with natural resources. Some of those resources were precious gems and metals. When we left, each Cêpan was given a sack full of diamonds, emeralds and rubies to sell when we arrived on Earth. Henri did, and then deposited the money into an overseas bank account. I don't know how much there is and I never ask. But I know it's enough to last us ten lifetimes, if not more. Henri makes withdrawals from it once a year, give or take.

"I don't know, though," he continues. "I don't want to stray too far in case something else happens today."

Not wanting to make a big deal of yesterday, I wave the notion away. "I'll be fine. Go get paid."

I look out the window. Dawn is breaking, casting a pale light over everything. The truck is covered with dew. It's been a while since we've been through a winter. I don't even own a jacket and have outgrown most of my sweaters.

"It looks cold out," I say. "Maybe we can go clothes shopping soon."

He nods. "I was thinking about that last night, which is why I need to go to the bank."

"Then go," I say. "Nothing is going to happen today."

I finish the bowl of cereal, drop the dirty dish into the sink, and jump into the shower. Ten minutes later I'm dressed in a pair of jeans and a black thermal shirt, the sleeves pulled to my elbows. I look in the mirror, and down at my hands. I feel calm. I need to stay that way.

On the way to school Henri hands me a pair of gloves.

"Make sure you keep these with you at all times. You never know."

I tuck them into my back pocket.

"I shouldn't need them. I feel pretty good."

At the school, buses are lined up in front. Henri pulls up to the side of the building.

"I don't like you not having a phone," he says. "Any number of things could go wrong."

"Don't worry. I'll have it back soon."

He sighs and shakes his head. "Don't do anything stupid. I'll be right here at the end of the day."

"I won't," I say, and get out of the truck. He pulls away.

Inside, the halls are bustling with activity, students loitering at lockers, talking, laughing. A few look at me and whisper. I don't know whether it's because of the confrontation or because of the darkroom. It's likely that they are whispering about both. It is a small school, and in small schools there is little that isn't readily known by everyone else.

When I reach the main entrance, I turn right and find my locker. It's empty. I have fifteen minutes before sophomore composition begins. I walk by the classroom just to make sure I know where it is and then head to the office. The secretary smiles when I enter.

"Hi," I say. "I lost my phone yesterday and I was wondering if anyone turned it in to lost and found?"

She shakes her head. "No, I'm afraid no phone's been turned in."

"Thank you," I say.

Out in the hallway I don't see Mark anywhere. I pick a direction and begin walking. People still stare and whisper, but that doesn't bother me. I see him fifty feet ahead of me. All at once the thrill of adrenaline kicks in. I look down at my hands. They're normal. I'm worried about them turning on, and that worry might just be the thing that does it.

Mark's leaning against a locker with his arms crossed, in the middle of a group, five guys and two girls, all of them talking and laughing. Sarah is sitting on a windowsill about fifteen feet away. She looks radiant again today with her blond hair pulled into a ponytail, wearing a skirt and a gray sweater. She's reading a book, but looks up as I walk towards them.

I stop just outside of the group, stare at Mark, and wait. He notices me after about five seconds.

"What do you want?" he asks.

"You know what I want."

Our eyes stay locked. The crowd around us

swells to ten people, then twenty. Sarah stands and walks to the edge of the crowd. Mark is wearing his letterman jacket, and his black hair is carefully styled to look like he rolled straight out of bed and into his clothes.

He pushes away from the locker and walks towards me. When he is inches away he stops. Our chests nearly touch and the spicy scent of his cologne fills my nostrils. He is probably six one, a couple inches taller than I am. We have the same build. Little does he know that what is inside of me is not what is inside of him. I am quicker than he is and far stronger. The thought brings a confident grin to my face.

"You think you can stay in school a little longer today? Or are you going to run off again like a little bitch?"

Snickers spread through the crowd.

"I guess we'll see, won't we?"

"Yeah, I guess we will," he says, and moves even closer.

"I want my phone back," I say.

"I don't have your phone."

I shake my head at him. "There are two people who saw you take it," I lie.

By the way his brows crinkle I know I have guessed correctly.

"Yeah, and what if it was me? What are you going to do?"

There are probably thirty people around us now. I have no doubt that the entire school will know what has happened within ten minutes of the start of first period.

"You've been warned," I say. "You have till the end of the day."

I turn and leave.

"Or what?" he yells behind me. I don't acknowledge it. Let him dwell on the answer. My fists have been clenched and I realize I had mistaken adrenaline for nerves. Why was I so nervous? The unpredictability? The fact that this is the first time I've confronted somebody? The possibility of my hands glowing? Probably all three.

I go to the bathroom, enter an empty stall, and latch the door behind me. I open my hands. A slight glow in the right one. I close my eyes and sigh, focus on breathing slowly. A minute later the glow is still there. I shake my head. I didn't think the Legacy would be that sensitive. I stay in the stall. A thin layer of sweat covers my forehead; both of my hands are warm, but thankfully the left is still normal. People filter in and out of the bathroom and I stay in the stall, waiting. The light stays on. Finally the first-period bell rings and the bathroom is empty.

I shake my head in disgust and accept the inevitable. I don't have my phone and Henri is on his way to the bank. I'm alone with my own stupidity and I have no one to blame but myself. I pull the gloves from my back pocket and slip them on. Leather gardening gloves. I couldn't look more foolish if I were wearing clown shoes with yellow pants. So much for blending in. I realize I have to stop with Mark. He wins. He can keep my phone; Henri and I will get a new one tonight.

I leave the bathroom and walk the empty hallway to my classroom. Everybody stares at me when I enter, then at the gloves. There is no point trying to hide them. I look like a fool. I am an alien, I have extraordinary powers, with more to come, and I can do things that no human would dream of, but I still look like a fool.

I sit in the center of the room. Nobody says anything to me and I'm too flustered to hear what the teacher says. When the bell rings I gather my things, drop them into my bag, and pull the straps over my shoulder. I'm still wearing the gloves. When I exit the room I lift the cuff of the right one and peek at my palm. It's still glowing.

I walk the hall at a steady pace. Slow breathing. I try to clear my mind but it isn't working. When I enter the classroom Mark is sitting in the same spot as the day before, Sarah beside him. He sneers at me. Trying to act cool, he doesn't notice the gloves.

"What's up, runner? I heard the cross-country team is looking for new members."

"Don't be such a dick," Sarah says to him. I look at her as I pass, into her blue eyes that make me feel shy and self-conscious, that make my cheeks warm. The seat I sat in the day before is occupied, so I head to the very back. The class fills and the kid from yesterday, the one who warned me about Mark, sits next to me. He's wearing another black T-shirt with a NASA logo in the center, army pants, and a pair of Nike tennis shoes. He has disheveled, sandy blond hair, and his hazel eyes are magnified by his glasses. He pulls out a notepad filled with diagrams of constellations and planets. He looks at me and doesn't try to hide the fact that he is staring.

"How goes it?" I ask.

He shrugs. "Why are you wearing gloves?"

I open my mouth to answer, but Mrs. Burton starts the class. During most of it the guy beside me draws pictures that seem to be his interpretation of what Martians look like. Small bodies; big heads, hands, and eyes. The same stereotypical representations that are usually shown in movies. At the bottom of every drawing he writes his name in small letters: SAM GOODE. He notices me watching, and I look away.

As Mrs. Burton lectures on Saturn's sixty-one

moons, I look at the back of Mark's head. He's hunched over his desk, writing. Then he sits up and passes a note to Sarah. She flicks it back at him without reading it. It makes me smile. Mrs. Burton turns off the lights and starts a video. The rotating planets being projected on the screen at the front of the class make me think of Lorien. It is one of the eighteen life-sustaining planets in the universe. Earth is another. Mogadore, unfortunately, is another.

Lorien. I close my eyes and allow myself to remember. An old planet, a hundred times older than Earth. Every problem that Earth now has—pollution, overpopulation, global warming, food shortages—Lorien also had. At one point, twenty-five thousand years ago, the planet began to die. This was long before the ability to travel through the universe, and the people of Lorien had to do something in order to survive. Slowly but surely they made a commitment to ensure that the planet would forever remain self-sustaining by changing their way of life, doing away with everything harmful—guns and bombs, poisonous chemicals, pollutants—and over time the damage began to reverse itself. With the benefit of evolution, over thousands of years, certain citizens—the Garde—developed powers in order to protect the planet, and to help it. It was as though Lorien rewarded my ancestors for their foresight, for their respect.

Mrs. Burton flicks the lights on. I open my eyes and look at the clock. Class is almost over. I feel calm again, and had completely forgotten about my hands. I take a deep breath and flip open the cuff of the right glove. The light is off! I smile and remove both gloves. Back to normal. I have six periods left in the day. I have to remain at peace through all of them.

The first half of the day passes without incident. I remain calm, and likewise have no further encounters with Mark. At lunch I fill my tray with the basics, then find an empty table at the back of the room. When I'm halfway through a slice of pizza, Sam Goode, the kid from astronomy class, sits across from me.

"Are you really fighting Mark after school?" he asks.

I shake my head. "No."

"That's what people are saying."

"They're wrong."

He shrugs, keeps eating. A minute later he asks, "Where'd your gloves go?"

"I took them off. My hands aren't cold anymore."

He opens his mouth to respond but a giant meatball that I'm sure is aimed for me comes out of nowhere and hits him in the back of the head.

His hair and shoulders are covered with bits of meat and spaghetti sauce. Some of it has splattered onto me. While I start cleaning myself off a second meatball flies through the air and hits me square on the cheek. *Ooh*s filter throughout the cafeteria.

I stand and wipe the side of my face with a napkin, anger coursing through me. In that instant I don't care about my hands. They can shine as brightly as the sun, and Henri and I can leave this afternoon if that's what it comes to. But there isn't a chance in hell I'm letting this slide. It was over after this morning . . . but not now.

"Don't," Sam says. "If you fight then they'll never leave you alone."

I start walking. A hush falls over the cafeteria. A hundred sets of eyes focus on me. My face twists into a scowl. Seven people are sitting at Mark James's table, all guys. All seven of them stand as I approach.

"You got a problem?" one of them asks me. He is big, built like an offensive lineman. Patches of reddish hair grow on his cheeks and chin as though he's trying to grow a beard. It makes his face look dirty. Like the rest of them he's wearing a letterman jacket. He crosses his arms and stands in my way.

"This doesn't concern you," I say.

"You'll have to go through me to get to him."

"I will if you don't get out of my way."

"I don't think you can," he says.

I bring my knee straight up into his crotch. His breath catches in his throat, and he doubles over. The whole lunchroom gasps.

"I warned you," I say, and I step over him and walk straight for Mark. Just as I reach him I'm grabbed from behind. I turn with my hands clenched into fists, ready to swing, but at the last second I realize it's the lunchroom attendant.

"That'll be enough, boys."

"Look what he just did to Kevin, Mr. Johnson," Mark says. Kevin is still on the ground holding himself. His face is beet red. "Send him to the principal!"

"Shut up, James. All four of you are going. Don't think I didn't see you throw those meatballs," he says, and looks at Kevin still on the floor. "Get up."

Sam appears from nowhere. He has tried to wipe the mess from his hair and shoulders. The big pieces are gone, but the sauce has only smeared. I'm not sure why he's here. I look down at my hands, ready to flee at the first hint of light, but to my surprise they're off. Was it because of the urgency of the situation, allowing me to approach without preemptive nerves? I don't know.

Kevin stands and looks at me. He is shaky, still having trouble breathing. He grips the shoulder of the guy beside him for support.

"You'll get yours," he says.

"I doubt it," I say. I'm still scowling, still covered in food. To hell with wiping it away.

The four of us walk to the principal's office. Mr. Harris is sitting behind his desk eating a microwavable lunch, a napkin tucked into the neck of his shirt.

"Sorry to interrupt. We just had a slight disruption during lunch. I'm sure these boys will be happy to explain," the lunchroom attendant says.

Mr. Harris sighs, pulls the napkin from his shirt, and throws it in the trash. He pushes his lunch to the side of his desk with the back of his hand.

"Thank you, Mr. Johnson."

Mr. Johnson leaves, closing the office door behind him, and the four of us sit.

"So who wants to start?" the principal asks, irritation in his voice.

I stay silent. The muscles in Mr. Harris's jaw are flexed. I look down at my hands. Still off. I place them palms down on my jeans just in case. After ten seconds of silence, Mark starts. "Somebody hit him with a meatball. He thinks it was me, so he kneed Kevin in the balls."

"Watch your language," Mr. Harris says, and then turns to Kevin. "You okay?"

Kevin, whose face is still red, nods.

"So who threw the meatball?" Mr. Harris asks me.

I say nothing, still seething, irritated at the whole scene. I take a deep breath to try to calm myself.

"I don't know," I say. My anger has reached new levels. I don't want to have to deal with Mark through Mr. Harris, and would rather take care of the situation myself, away from the principal's office.

Sam looks at me in surprise. Mr. Harris throws his hands up in frustration. "Well then, why in the hell are you boys here?"

"That's a good question," says Mark. "We were simply eating our lunch."

Sam speaks. "Mark threw it. I saw him and so did Mr. Johnson."

I look over at Sam. I know he didn't see it because his back was turned the first time, and the second time he was busy cleaning himself off. But I'm impressed at him saying so, for his taking my side knowing it will put him in danger with Mark and his friends. Mark scowls at him.

"Come on, Mr. Harris," Mark pleads. "I have the interview with the *Gazette* tomorrow, and the game on Friday. I don't have time to worry about crap like this. I'm being accused of something I didn't do. It's hard to stay focused with this shit going on."

"Watch your mouth!" Mr. Harris yells.

"It's true."

"I believe you," the principal says, and sighs very heavily. He looks at Kevin, who's still struggling to catch his breath. "Do you need to go to the nurse?"

"I'll be fine," Kevin says.

Mr. Harris nods. "You two forget about the lunchroom incident, and Mark, get your mind straight. We've been trying to get this article for a while now. They might even put us on the front page. Imagine that, the front page of the *Gazette*," he says, and smiles.

"Thank you," Mark says. "I'm excited about it."

"Good. Now, you two can leave."

They go, and Mr. Harris gives a hard look at Sam. Sam holds his gaze.

"Tell me, Sam. And I want the truth. Did you see Mark throw the meatball?"

Sam's eyes narrow. He doesn't look away.

"Yes."

The principal shakes his head. "I don't believe you, Sam. And because of that, here is what we are going to do." He looks at me. "So a meatball was thrown—"

"Two," Sam interjects.

"What?!" Mr. Harris asks, again glowering at Sam.

"There were two meatballs thrown, not one."

Mr. Harris slams his fist on the desk. "Who cares how many there were! John, you assaulted Kevin. An eye for an eye. We'll let it go at that. Do you understand me?"

His face is red and I know it's pointless to argue.

"Yep," I say.

"I don't want to see you two in here again," he says. "You're both dismissed."

We leave his office.

"Why didn't you tell him about your phone?" Sam asks.

"Because he doesn't care. He just wanted to go back to his lunch," I say. "And be careful," I tell him. "You'll be on Mark's radar now."

I have home economics after lunch—not because I necessarily care about cooking, but because it was either that or choir. And while I have many strengths and powers that are considered exceptional on Earth, singing is not one of them. So I walk into home ec and take a seat. It is a small room, and just before the bell rings Sarah walks in and sits beside me.

"Hi," she says.

"Hi."

Blood rushes to my face and my shoulders stiffen. I grab a pencil and begin to twirl it in my right hand while my left bends back the corners of my notepad. My heart is pounding. Please don't let my hands be glowing. I peek at my palm and breathe a sigh of relief that it's still normal. *Stay calm,* I think. *She's just a girl.*

Sarah is looking at me. Everything inside of me feels as though it is turning to mush. She may be the most beautiful girl I have ever seen.

"I'm sorry Mark is being a jerk to you," she says.

I shrug. "It's not your fault."

"You guys aren't really going to fight, are you?"

"I don't want to," I say.

She nods. "He can be a real dick. He always tries to show he's boss."

"It's a sign of insecurity," I say.

"He's not insecure. Just a dick."

Sure he is. But I don't want to argue with Sarah. Besides, she speaks with such certainty that I almost doubt myself.

She looks at the spots of spaghetti sauce that have dried on my shirt, then reaches over and pulls a hardened piece from my hair.

"Thanks," I say.

She sighs. "I'm sorry that happened." She looks me in the eye. "We're not together, you know?"

"No?"

She shakes her head. I'm intrigued that she felt the need to make that clear to me. After ten minutes of instruction on how to make pancakes—none of which I actually hear—the teacher, Mrs. Benshoff, pairs Sarah and me together. We enter a door at the back of the room that leads to the kitchen, which is about three times the size of the actual classroom. It contains ten different kitchen units, complete with refrigerators, cabinets, sinks, ovens. Sarah walks into one, grabs an apron from a drawer, and puts it on.

"Will you tie this for me?" she asks.

I pull too much on the bow and have to tie it again. I can feel the contours of her lower back beneath my fingers. When hers is tied I put mine on and start to tie it myself.

"Here, silly," she says, and then takes the straps and does it for me.

"Thanks."

I try cracking the first egg but do it too hard, and none of the egg actually makes it into the bowl. Sarah laughs. She places a new egg in my hand and takes my hand in hers and shows me how to crack it on the rim of the bowl. She leaves her hand on mine for a second longer than is necessary. She looks at me and smiles.

"Like that."

She mixes the batter and strands of hair fall

into her face while she works. I desperately want to reach over and tuck the loose strands behind her ear, but I don't. Mrs. Benshoff comes into our kitchen to check our progress. So far so good, which is all thanks to Sarah, since I have no idea what I'm doing.

"How do you like Ohio so far?" Sarah asks.

"It's okay. I could have used a better first day of school."

She smiles. "What happened, anyway? I was worried about you."

"Would you believe it if I told you I was an alien?"

"Shut up," she says playfully. "What really happened?"

I laugh. "I have really bad asthma. For some reason I had an attack yesterday," I say, and feel regret at having to lie. I don't want her to see weakness within me, especially weakness that is untrue.

"Well, I'm glad you feel better."

We make four pancakes. Sarah stacks all of them onto one plate. She dumps an absurd amount of maple syrup over them and hands me a fork. I look at the other students. Most are eating off of two plates. I reach over and cut a bite.

"Not bad," I say while chewing.

I'm not hungry in the least, but I help her eat all of them. We alternate bites until the plate is empty. I have a stomachache when we finish. After, she cleans the dishes and I dry them. When the bell rings, we walk out of the room together.

"You know, you're not so bad for a sophomore," she says, and nudges me. "I don't care what they say."

"Thanks, and you're not so bad yourself for a—whatever you are."

"I'm a junior."

We walk in silence for a few steps.

"You're not really going to fight Mark at the end of the day, are you?

"I need my phone back. Besides, look at me," I say, and motion to my shirt.

She shrugs. I stop at my locker. She takes note of the number.

"Well, you shouldn't," she says.

"I don't want to."

She rolls her eyes. "Boys and their fights. Anyway, I'll see you tomorrow."

"Have a good rest of the day," I say.

After my ninth-period class, American history, I take slow steps to my locker. I think of just leaving the school quietly, without looking for Mark. But then I realize I will forever be labeled a coward.

I get to my locker and empty my bag of the

books I don't need. Then I just stand there and feel the nervousness that begins to course through me. My hands are still normal. I think of throwing the gloves on as a precaution, but I don't. I take a deep breath and close the locker door.

"Hi," I hear, the voice startling me. It's Sarah. She glances behind her, and looks back at me. "I have something for you."

"It's not more pancakes, is it? I still feel like I'm about to burst."

She laughs nervously.

"It's not pancakes. But if I give it to you, you have to promise me you won't fight."

"Okay," I say.

She looks behind her again and quickly reaches into the front pocket of her bag. She pulls out my phone and gives it to me.

"How did you get this?"

She shrugs.

"Does Mark know?"

"Nope. So are you still going to be a tough guy?" she asks.

"I guess not."

"Good."

"Thank you," I say. I can't believe she went to such lengths to help me—she barely knows me. But I'm not complaining.

"You're welcome," she says, then turns and rushes down the hall. I watch her the whole way, unable to stop smiling. When I head out, Mark James and eight of his friends meet me in the lobby.

"Well, well, well," Mark says. "Actually made it through the day, huh?"

"Sure did. And look what I found," I say, holding my phone up for him to see. His jaw drops. I pass by him, head down the hall and walk out of the building.

CHAPTER
EIGHT

HENRI IS PARKED EXACTLY WHERE HE
said he would be. I jump in the truck, still smiling.

"Good day?" he asks.

"Not bad. Got my phone back."

"No fighting?"

"Nothing major."

He looks at me suspiciously. "Do I even want
to know what that means?"

"Probably not."

"Did your hands come on at all?"

"No," I lie. "How was your day?"

He follows the driveway around the school. "It
was good. I drove an hour and a half to Columbus
after dropping you off."

"Why Columbus?"

"Big banks there. I didn't want to draw suspicion by requesting a transfer for an amount of

money larger than what is collectively contained within the entire town."

I nod. "Smart thinking."

He pulls onto the road.

"So are you going to tell me her name?"

"Huh?" I ask.

"There has to be a reason for that ridiculous smile of yours. The most obvious reason is a girl."

"How'd you know?"

"John, my friend, back on Lorien this ol' Cêpan was quite the ladies' man."

"Get out of here," I say. "There is no such thing as a ladies' man on Lorien."

He nods approvingly. "You've been paying attention."

The Loric are a monogamous people. When we fall in love, it's for life. Marriage comes around the age of twenty-five, give or take, and has nothing to do with law. It's based more on promise and commitment than anything else. Henri was married for twenty years before he left with me. Ten years have passed but I know he still misses his wife every single day.

"So who is she?" he asks.

"Her name is Sarah Hart. She's the daughter of the real-estate agent you got the house from. She's in two of my classes. She's a junior."

He nods. "Pretty?"

"Absolutely. And smart."

"Yeah," he draws out slowly. "I've been expecting this for a long time now. Just keep in mind that we might have to leave at a moment's notice."

"I know," I say, and the rest of the trip home is made in silence.

When I get home, the Loric Chest is sitting on the kitchen table. It's the size of a microwave oven, almost perfectly square, a foot and a half by a foot and a half. Excitement shoots through me. I walk up to it and grab the lock in my hand.

"I think I'm more excited about learning how this is unlocked than about what's actually in it," I say.

"Really? Well, I can show you how it's unlocked and then we can just relock it and forget about what's inside."

I smile at him. "Let's not be rash. Come on. What's inside?"

"It's your Inheritance."

"What do you mean, my Inheritance?"

"It's what's given to each Garde at birth to be used by his or her Keeper when the Garde is coming into his or her Legacy."

I nod with exhilaration. "So what's in it?"

"Your Inheritance."

His coy response frustrates me. I pick up the lock and try to force it open as I've always tried doing. Of course it doesn't budge.

"You can't open it without me, and I can't open it without you," Henri says.

"Well, how do we open it? There isn't a keyhole."

"By will."

"Oh, come on, Henri. Quit being secretive."

He takes the lock from me. "The lock only opens when we're together, and only after your first Legacy appears."

He walks to the front door and sticks his head out, then he closes and locks it. He walks back. "Press your palm against the side of the lock," he says, and I do.

"It's warm," I say.

"Good. That means you're ready."

"Now what?"

He presses his palm against the other side of the lock and interlocks his fingers with mine. A second passes. The lock snaps open.

"Amazing!" I say.

"It's protected by a Loric charm, just like you are. It can't be broken. You could run over it with a steamroller and it wouldn't even be dented. Only the two of us can open it together. Unless I die; then you can open it yourself."

"Well," I say, "I hope that doesn't happen."

I try to lift the top of the box, but Henri reaches over and stops me.

"Not yet," he says. "There are things in here you aren't ready to see. Go sit on the couch."

"Henri, come on."

"Just trust me," he says.

I shake my head and sit down. He opens the box and removes a rock that is probably six inches long, two inches thick. He relocks the box, then brings the rock over to me. It is perfectly smooth and oblong, clear on the outside but cloudy in the center.

"What is it?" I ask.

"A Loric crystal."

"What's it for?"

"Hold it," he says, handing it to me. The second my hands come into contact with it both lights snap on in my palms. They are even brighter than the day before. The rock begins to warm. I hold it up to look more closely at it. The cloudy mass in the center is swirling, turning in on itself like a wave. I can also feel the pendant around my neck heating up. I'm thrilled by all this new development. My whole life has been spent impatiently waiting for my powers to arrive. Sure, there were times when I hoped they never would, mainly so we could finally settle somewhere and live a normal life; but for now—holding a crystal that contains what looks like a ball of smoke in its center, and knowing my hands are resistant to heat and fire, and that more Legacies are on the way that will then be followed by my major power (the power that will allow me to fight)—well, it's all pretty cool and exciting. I can't wipe the smile from my face.

"What is happening to it?"

"It's tied to your Legacy. Your touch activates it. If you weren't developing Lumen, then the crystal itself would light up the way your hands are. Instead it's the other way around."

I stare at the crystal, watching the smoke circle and glow.

"Shall we start?" Henri asks.

I nod my head rapidly. "Hell, yes."

The day has turned cold. The house is silent aside from the occasional gust of wind rattling the windows. I lie on my back on top of the wooden coffee table. My hands dangle over the sides. At some point Henri will build a fire beneath them both. My breathing is slow and steady, as Henri has instructed.

"You have to keep your eyes closed," he says. "Just listen to the wind. There might be a slight burning in your arms when I drag the crystal up them. Ignore it as best as you can."

I listen to the wind blow through the trees outside. I can somehow feel them sway and bend.

Henri begins with my right hand. He presses

the crystal against the back of it, then pushes it up my wrist and onto my forearm. There is a burn as he has predicted, but not enough of one to make me pull my arm free.

"Let your mind drift, John. Go where you need to go."

I don't know what he's talking about, but I try to clear my mind and breathe slowly. All at once I feel myself drift away. From somewhere I can feel the sun's warmth upon my face, and a wind far warmer than what is blowing beyond our walls. When I open my eyes I'm no longer in Ohio.

I'm above a vast expanse of treetops, nothing but jungle as far as I can see. Blue sky, the sun beating down, a sun almost double the size of Earth's. A warm, soft wind blows through my hair. Down below, rivers forge deep ravines that cut through the greenery. I am floating above one of them. Animals of all shapes and sizes—some long and slender, some with short arms and stout bodies, some with hair and some with dark-colored skin that looks rough to the touch—are drinking from the cool waters at the river's bank. There is a bend in the horizon line far off in the distance, and I know that I am on Lorien. It's a planet ten times smaller than Earth, and it's possible to see the curve of its surface when looking from far enough away.

Somehow I'm able to fly. I rush up and twist in the air, then torpedo down and speed along the river's surface. The animals lift their heads and watch with curiosity, but not with fear. Lorien in its prime, covered with growth, inhabited by animals. In a way, it looks like what I imagine Earth looked like millions of years ago, when the land ruled the lives of its creatures, before humans arrived and started ruling the land. Lorien in its prime; I know that it no longer looks like this today. I must be living a memory. Surely it isn't my own?

And then the day skips ahead to darkness. Off in the distance a great display of fireworks begins, rising high in the sky and exploding into shapes of animals and trees with the dark sky and the moons and a million stars serving as a brilliant backdrop.

"I can feel their desperation," I hear from somewhere. I turn and look around me. There is nobody there. "They know where one of the others is, but the charm still holds. They can't touch her until they've killed you first. But they continue to track her."

I fly up high, then dip low, seeking the source of the voice. Where is it coming from?

"Now is when we have to be most cautious. Now is when we have to stay ahead of them."

I push forward towards the fireworks. The

voice unnerves me. Perhaps the loud booms will drown it out.

"They had hoped to kill us all well before your Legacies developed. But we've kept hidden. We have to stay calm. The first three panicked. The first three are dead. We have to stay smart and cautious. When we panic is when mistakes are made. They know it will only get harder for them the more developed the rest of you are, and when you are all fully developed, the war will be waged. We will hit back and seek our revenge, and they know it."

I see the bombs fall from miles above Lorien's surface. Explosions shake the ground and the air, screams carry on the wind, bursts of fire sweep across the land and the trees. The forest burns. There must be a thousand different aircraft, all dropping from high in the sky to land on Lorien. Mogadorian soldiers pour out, carrying guns and grenades that hold powers far greater than what is used in warfare here. They are taller than we are, and still look similar except in the face. They have no pupils and their irises are a deep magenta color, some of them black. Dark, heavy circles rim their eyes and there's a pallor to their skin— an almost discolored, bruised quality to it. Their teeth glint between lips that never seem to close, teeth that look filed, coming to an unnatural point.

The beasts of Mogadore come off the planes close behind, the same cold look in their eyes. Some of them are as big as houses, razor teeth showing, roaring so loud that it hurts my ears.

"We got careless, John. That is how we were defeated so easily," he says. I know now that the voice I'm hearing is Henri's. But he is nowhere to be seen, and I can't take my eyes off the killing and the destruction below me to look for him. People are running everywhere, fighting back. As many Mogadorians as Loric are being killed. But the Loric are losing the battle against the beasts, which are killing our people by the dozens: breathing fire, gnashing teeth, viciously swinging arms and tails. Time is speeding along, going much faster than normal. How much has passed? An hour? Two?

The Garde lead the fight, their Legacies on full display. Some are flying, some able to run so fast that they become a blur, and some disappear entirely. Lasers shoot from hands, bodies become engulfed in flames, storm clouds are brewed coupled with harsh winds above those able to control the weather. But they are still losing. They are outnumbered five hundred to one. Their powers are not enough.

"Our guard had dropped. The Mogadorians had planned well, picking that exact moment when they knew we were at our most vulnerable, when the planet's Elders were gone. Pittacus Lore, the greatest of them, their leader, had assembled them before the attack. Nobody knows what happened to them, or where they went, or if they are even still alive. Perhaps the Mogadorians took them out first, and once the Elders were out of the way, that is when they attacked. All we really know is that there was a column of shimmering white light that shot into the sky as far as anyone could see on the day the Elders assembled. It lasted the entire day, then vanished. We, as a people, should have recognized it as a sign that something was amiss, but we didn't. We have no one to blame but ourselves for what happened. We were lucky to get anyone off the planet, much less nine young Garde who might someday continue the fight, and keep our race alive."

Off in the distance a ship shoots high and fast into the air, a blue stream following behind it. I watch it from my vantage point in the sky until it disappears. There is something familiar about it. And then it dawns on me: I am in that ship, and Henri is, too. It's the ship carrying us to Earth. The Loric must have known they were beaten. Why else would they send us away?

Useless slaughter. That is how it all looks to me. I land on the ground and walk though a ball of fire. Rage sweeps through me. Men and women are dying, Garde and Cêpan, along with defenseless children. How can this be tolerated? How can the hearts of the Mogadorians be so hardened as to do all this? And why was I spared?

I lunge at a nearby soldier but go straight through him and fall down. Everything I am witnessing has already happened. I'm a spectator of our own demise and there's nothing I can do.

I turn around and face a beast that must be forty feet tall, broad shouldered, with red eyes and horns twenty feet in length. Drool falls from its long, sharp teeth. It lets out a roar, and then lunges.

It passes through me but takes out dozens of Loric around me. Just like that, every one of them gone. And the beast keeps going, taking out more Loric.

Through the scene of destruction I hear a scratching noise, something separate from the carnage on Lorien. I am drifting away, or drifting back. Two hands press down upon my shoulders. My eyes snap open and I'm back in our home in Ohio. My arms are dangling over the coffee table. Inches below them are two cauldrons of fire, and both of my hands and wrists are completely submerged in the flames. I don't feel the effects at all. Henri stands over me. The scratching I heard a minute ago is coming from the front porch.

"What is that?" I whisper, sitting up.

"I don't know," he says.

We are both silent, straining to listen. Three more scratches at the door. Henri looks down at me.

"There's somebody out there," he says.

I look at the clock on the wall. Nearly an hour has passed. I'm sweating, out of breath, unsettled by the scenes of slaughter I just witnessed. For the first time in my life I truly understand what happened on Lorien. Before tonight the events were just part of another story, not all that different from the many I have read in books. But now I have seen the blood, the tears, the dead. I have seen the destruction. It's a part of who I am.

Outside, darkness has set in. Three more scratches at the door, a low groan. We both jump. I immediately think of the low groans I heard coming from the beasts.

Henri rushes into the kitchen and grabs a knife from the drawer beside the sink. "Get behind the couch."

"What, why?"

"Because I said so."

"You think that little knife is going to take down a Mogadorian?"

"If I hit them straight in the heart it will. Now get down."

I scramble off the coffee table and crouch

behind the sofa. The two cauldrons of fire are still going, faint visions of Lorien still moving through my mind. An impatient growl comes from the other side of the front door. There is no mistaking that somebody, or something, is out there. My heart races.

"Keep down," Henri says.

I lift my head so that I can peer over the back of the couch. All that blood, I think. Surely they knew they were outmatched. But they fought to the end anyway, dying to save each other, dying to save Lorien. Henri grips the knife tightly. He slowly reaches for the brass knob. Anger sweeps through me. I hope it *is* one of them. Let a Mogadorian come through that door. He'll meet his match.

There's no way I'm staying behind this couch. I reach over and grab one of the cauldrons, thrust my hand into it and pull out a burning piece of wood with a pointed end. It's cool to the touch, but the fire burns on, sweeping over and around my hand. I hold the piece of wood like a dagger. *Let them come,* I think. *There will be no more running.* Henri looks over at me, takes a deep breath and rips the front door open.

CHAPTER NINE

EVERY MUSCLE IN MY BODY IS flexed, everything tense. Henri jumps through the doorway and I am ready to follow. I can feel the *thud-thud-thud* in my chest. My fingers are white knuckled around the piece of wood still burning. A gust of wind bursts through the door and the fire dances in my hand and crawls up my wrist. No one is there. All at once Henri's body relaxes and he chuckles, looking down at his feet. There, looking up at Henri through the tops of his eyes, is the same beagle I saw yesterday at school. The dog wags his tail and paws at the ground. Henri reaches down and pets him; then the dog pushes past and trots into the house with his tongue dangling.

"What's he doing here?" I ask.

"You know this dog?"

"I saw him at school. He was following me

around yesterday after you dropped me off."

I put the piece of wood back and wipe my hand on my jeans, leaving a trail of black ash down the front. The dog sits at my feet and looks up expectantly, his tail thumping against the hardwood floor. I sit on the couch and watch both fires burn. Now that the excitement of the situation is over, my mind goes back to what I just saw in my vision. I can still hear the screams in my ears, still see the way the blood shimmered in the grass in the moonlight, still see the bodies and fallen trees, the red glow in the eyes of the beasts of Mogadore and the terror in the eyes of the Loric.

I look at Henri. "I saw what happened. At least the beginning of it."

He nods. "I thought you might."

"I could hear your voice. Were you talking to me?"

"Yes."

"I don't understand," I say. "It was a massacre. There was too much hatred for them to only be interested in our resources. There was more to it than that."

Henri sighs and sits on the coffee table across from me. The dog jumps into my lap. I pet him. He's filthy, his coat stiff and oily under my hand. There is a tag in the shape of a football attached to the front of his collar. It's an old tag, most of the brown paint worn away. I take it in my hand, the number 19 on one side, the name BERNIE KOSAR on the other.

"Bernie Kosar," I say. The dog wags his tail. "I guess that's his name, same as that dude in the poster on my wall. Popular guy around here, I guess." I run my hand down his back. "He doesn't seem like he has a home," I say. "And he's hungry." Somehow I can tell.

Henri nods. He looks down at Bernie Kosar. The dog stretches out, rests his chin on his paws, and closes his eyes. I flip open the lighter and hold the flame over my fingers, then my palm, then run it up the underside of my arm. Only when the flame is an inch or two away from my elbow do I feel the burn. Whatever Henri has done has worked, and my resistance has spread. I wonder how long it will take until all of me becomes resistant.

"So what happened?" I ask.

Henri takes a deep breath. "I've had those visions, too. So real it's like you're there."

"I never realized how bad it all was. I mean, I know you had told me, but I didn't truly understand it until I saw it with my own eyes."

"The Mogadorians are different than we are, secretive and manipulative, untrusting of almost everything. They have certain powers, but they're not powers like ours. They are gregarious and thrive in crowded cities. The more densely populated, the better. That is why you and I stay out of cities now, even when living in one might make it easier to blend in. It would make it a hell of a lot easier for them to blend in as well.

"About a hundred years ago Mogadore began to die, much like Lorien did twenty-five thousand years before that. They didn't respond the way we did, though—didn't understand it the way the human population is beginning to now. They ignored it. They killed their oceans and flooded their rivers and lakes with waste and sewage to keep adding to their cities. The vegetation started to die, which caused the herbivores to die, and then the carnivores weren't far behind. They knew they had to do something drastic."

Henri closes his eyes, remains silent for a full minute.

"Do you know the closest life-sustaining planet to Mogadore?" he finally asks.

"Yes, it's Lorien. Or was, I guess."

Henri nods. "Yes, it *is* Lorien. And I'm sure you know now that it was our resources they were after."

I nod. Bernie Kosar lifts his head and lets out a deep yawn. Henri heats a cooked chicken breast in the microwave, cuts it into strips, then carries the plate back to the couch and sets it in front of the dog. He eats with ferocity, as though he hasn't eaten in days.

"There are a large number of Mogadorians on Earth," Henri continues. "I don't know how many are here, but I can feel them when I sleep. Sometimes I can see them in my dreams. I can never tell where they are, or what they are saying. But I see them. And I don't think the six of you are the only reason there are so many of them here."

"What do you mean? Why else would they be here?"

Henri looks me in the eye. "Do you know what the second-closest life-sustaining planet is to Mogadore?"

I nod. "It's Earth, isn't it?"

"Mogadore is double the size of Lorien, but Earth is five times the size of Mogadore. In terms of defense Earth is better prepared for an offensive because of its size. The Mogadorians will need to understand this planet better before they can attack. I can't necessarily tell you how we were defeated so easily because there's much of it I still don't understand. But I can say for sure that part of it was a combination of their knowledge of our planet and our people, and the fact that we had no defense other than our intelligence and the Garde's

Legacies. Say what you will about the Mogadorians, but they are brilliant strategists when it comes to war."

We sit through another silence, the wind still roaring outside.

"I don't think they're interested in taking Earth's resources," Henri says.

I sigh and look up at him. "Why not?"

"Mogadore is still dying. Even though they've patched the more pressing matters, the planet's death is inevitable, and they know it. I think they're planning to kill the humans. I think they want to make Earth their permanent home."

I bathe Bernie Kosar after dinner, using shampoo and conditioner. I brush him with an old comb left in one of the drawers from the last tenant. He looks and smells much better, but his collar still stinks. I throw it away. Before going to bed I hold open the front door for him, but he isn't interested in going back outside. Instead he lies down on the floor and rests his chin on his front paws. I can feel his desire to stay in the house with us. I wonder if he can feel my desire for the same.

"I think we have a new pet," Henri says.

I smile. As soon as I saw him earlier I was hoping Henri would let me keep him.

"Looks like it," I say.

A half hour later I crawl into bed and Bernie Kosar jumps up with me and curls into a ball at my feet. He is snoring within minutes. I lie on my back for a while, staring into the darkness, a million different thoughts swimming in my head. Images from the war: the greedy, hungry look of the Mogadorians; the angry, hard look of the beasts; the death and the blood. I think of the beauty of Lorien. Will it again sustain life, or will Henri and I go on waiting here on Earth forever?

I try to push the thoughts and images from my mind, but they don't stay gone for very long. I get up and pace for a while. Bernie Kosar lifts his head and watches me, but then drops it and falls back to sleep. I sigh, grab my phone from the nightstand and go through it to make sure Mark James didn't mess with anything. Henri's number is still there, but it is no longer the only entry. Another number, listed under the name of "Sarah Hart" has been added. After the last bell rang, and before coming to my locker, Sarah added her number to my phone.

I close the phone, set it on the nightstand, and smile. Two minutes pass and I check my phone again to make sure I wasn't seeing things. I wasn't. I snap it shut and set it down, only to lift it again five minutes later just to look at her number again. I don't know how long it takes to fall asleep, but I eventually do. When I wake in the morning my phone is still in my hand, resting against my chest.

CHAPTER TEN

BERNIE KOSAR IS SCRATCHING AT my bedroom door when I wake. I let him outside. He patrols the yard, rushing along with his nose to the ground. Once he's covered all four corners he bolts across the yard and disappears into the woods. I close the door and jump into the shower. I walk out ten minutes later and he's back inside, sitting on the couch. His tail wags when he sees me.

"You let him in?" I ask Henri, who is at the kitchen table with his laptop open and four newspapers stacked in front of him.

"Yes."

After a quick breakfast, we head out. Bernie Kosar rushes ahead of us, then stops and sits looking up at the passenger door of the truck.

"That's kind of weird, don't you think?" I say.

Henri shrugs. "Apparently he's no stranger to car rides. Let him in."

I open the door and he jumps in. He sits in the middle seat with his tongue dangling. When we pull out of the driveway he moves into my lap and paws at the window. I roll it down and he sticks half his body out, mouth still open, the wind flapping his ears. Three miles later Henri pulls in to the school. I open the door and Bernie Kosar jumps out ahead of me. I lift him back into the truck but he jumps right back out. I lift him back in again and have to block him from jumping out while I close the truck door. He stands on his hind legs with his front paws on the ledge of the door, the window still down. I pat him on the head.

"Have your gloves?" Henri asks.

"Yep."

"Phone?"

"Yep."

"How do you feel?"

"I feel good," I say.

"Okay. Call me if you have any sort of trouble."

He pulls away and Bernie Kosar watches from the back window until the truck disappears around the turn.

I feel a similar nervousness as I did the day before, but for different reasons. Part of me wants to see Sarah right away, though part of me hopes that I don't see her at all. I'm not sure what I'll say to her. What if I can't think of anything at all and stand there looking foolish? What if she's with Mark when I see her? Should I acknowledge her and risk another confrontation, or just walk by and pretend that I don't see either of them? At the very least I'll see them both in second period. There's no getting around that.

I head to my locker. My bag is filled with books I was supposed to read the night before but never opened. Too many thoughts and images running through my head. They haven't gone away and it's hard to imagine they ever will. It was all so different from what I expected. Death isn't like what they show you in the movies. The sounds, the looks, the smells. So different.

At my locker I notice immediately that something's off. The metal handle is covered with dirt, or what looks like dirt. I'm not sure if I should open it, but then I take a deep breath and force the handle up.

The locker is half filled with manure and as I swing the door open, much of it comes pouring out onto the floor, covering my shoes. The smell is horrendous. I slam the door shut. Sam Goode was standing behind it and his sudden appearance from out of nowhere startles me. He is looking forlorn, wearing a white NASA T-shirt only slightly different from the one he wore yesterday.

"Hi, Sam," I say.

He looks down at the pile of manure on the floor, then back at me.

"You, too?" I ask.

He nods.

"I'm going to the principal's office. Do you want to come?"

He shakes his head, then turns and walks away without saying a word. I walk to Mr. Harris's office, knock on his door, then enter without waiting for his reply. He is sitting behind his desk, wearing a tie that is tiled with the school mascot, no less than twenty tiny pirate heads scattered across the front of it. He smiles proudly at me.

"It's a big day, John," he says. I don't know what he is talking about. "The reporters from the *Gazette* should be here within the hour. Front page!"

Then I remember, Mark James's big interview with the local paper.

"You must be very proud," I say.

"I'm proud of each and every one of Paradise's students." The smile doesn't leave his face. He leans back in his chair, locks his fingers together, and rests his hands on his stomach. "What can I do for you?"

"I just wanted to let you know that my locker was filled with manure this morning."

"What do you mean 'filled'?"

"I mean the whole thing was full of manure."

"With manure?" he asks confusedly.

"Yes."

He laughs. I'm taken aback by his total lack of regard, and anger surges through me. My face is warm.

"I wanted to let you know so it could be cleaned. Sam Goode's locker is filled with it, too."

He sighs and shakes his head. "I'll send Mr. Hobbs, the janitor, down immediately and we'll make a full investigation."

"We both know who did it, Mr. Harris."

He flashes a patronizing grin at me. "I'll handle the investigation, Mr. Smith."

There's no point in saying anything further, so I walk out of his office and head to the bathroom to run cold water over my hands and face. I have to calm down. I don't want to have to wear the gloves again today. Maybe I should do nothing at all, just let it slide. Will that end it? And besides, what other choice is there? I'm outmatched and my only ally is a hundred-pound sophomore with a penchant for the extraterrestrial. Maybe that isn't the whole truth—maybe I have another ally in Sarah Hart.

I look down. My hands are fine, no glow. I walk out of the bathroom. The janitor is already sweeping the manure from my locker, lifting out books and placing them in the trash. I walk past him and into the classroom and wait for class to start. Rules of grammar are discussed, the main topic being the difference between a gerund and a verb, and why a gerund is not a verb. I pay closer attention than I did the day before, but as the end of the period nears I start to get nervous about the next class. But not because I might see Mark . . . because I might see Sarah. Will she smile at me again today? I think it'll be best to arrive before she does so I can find my seat and watch her walk in. That way I can see if she says hello to me first.

When the bell rings, I dash out of class and rush down the hall. I'm the first one to enter astronomy. The classroom fills and Sam sits beside me again. Just before the bell rings Sarah and Mark enter together. She's dressed in a white button-up shirt and black pants. She smiles at me before sitting down. I smile back. Mark doesn't look my way at all. I can still smell the manure on my shoes, or maybe the odor is coming from Sam's.

He pulls a pamphlet from his bag with the title *They Walk Among Us* on the cover. It looks as though it was printed in somebody's basement. Sam flips to an article in the center and starts reading intently.

I look at Sarah four desks in front of me, at her hair pulled back in a ponytail. I can see the nape of her slender neck. She crosses her legs and sits straight in her chair. I wish I were sitting beside her, that I could reach over and take her hand in mine. I wish it were eighth period already. I wonder if I'll be her partner in home ec again.

Mrs. Burton begins lecturing. She's still on the topic of Saturn. Sam takes out a sheet of paper and begins scribbling wildly, pausing at times to consult an article in the magazine he has opened beside him. I look over his shoulder and read the title: "Entire Montana Town Abducted by Aliens."

Before last night I would have never pondered such a theory. But Henri believes the Mogadorians are plotting to take over Earth, and I must admit, even though the theory in Sam's publication is ludicrous, at its most basic level there might be something there. I know for a fact that the Loric have visited Earth many times over the life of this planet. We watched Earth develop, watched it through the times of growth and abundance when everything moved, and through the times of ice and snow when nothing did. We helped the humans, taught them to make fire, gave them the tools to develop speech and language, which is why our language is so similar to the languages of Earth. And even though we never abducted humans, that doesn't mean it's never been done. I look at Sam. I've never met somebody with a fascination in aliens to the point of reading and taking notes on conspiracy theories.

Just then the door opens and Mr. Harris sticks his smiling face in.

"Sorry to interrupt, Mrs. Burton. I'm going to have to snag Mark from you. The *Gazette* reporters are here to interview him for the paper," he says loudly enough so everyone in the class can hear.

Mark stands, grabs his bag and casually strolls out of the room. From the doorway I see Mr. Harris pat him on the back. Then I look back at Sarah, wishing I could sit in the empty seat beside her.

Fourth period is physical education. Sam is in my class. After changing we sit beside each other on the gymnasium floor. He is wearing tennis shoes, shorts, a T-shirt two or three sizes too large. He looks like a stork, all knees and elbows, somewhat lanky even though he's short.

The gym teacher, Mr. Wallace, stands firmly in front of us, his feet shoulder width apart, his hands clenched into fists on his hips.

"All right, guys, listen up. This is probably the last chance we'll get to work outdoors, so make it count. One-mile run, as hard as you can. Your times will be noted and saved for when we run the mile again in the spring. So run hard!"

The outside track is made of synthetic rubber. It circles around the football field, and beyond it are some woods that I imagine might lead to our house, but I'm not sure. The wind is cool and goose bumps traverse the length of Sam's arms. He tries to rub them away.

"Have you run this before?" I ask.

Sam nods. "We ran it the second week of class."

"What was your time?"

"Nine minutes and fifty-four seconds."

I look at him. "I thought skinny kids are supposed to be fast."

"Shut up," he says.

I run side by side with Sam towards the back of the crowd. Four laps. That is how many times I must circle the track to have run a mile. Halfway around I begin to pull away from Sam. I wonder how fast I could run a mile if I really tried. Two minutes, maybe one, maybe less?

The exercise feels great, and without paying much attention, I pass the lead runner. Then I slow and feign exhaustion. When I do I see a brown and white blur come dashing out of the bushes by the entrance of the grandstand and head straight towards me. *My mind is playing tricks on me*, I think. I look away and keep running. I pass the teacher. He is holding a stop-watch. He yells words of encouragement but he is looking behind me, away from the track. I follow his eyes. They are fixated on the brown and white blur. It is still coming straight for me and all at once the images from the day before come rushing back. The Mogadorian beasts. There were small ones too, with teeth that glinted in the light like razor blades, fast crea-tures intent on killing. I start sprinting.

I run halfway around the track in a dead sprint before I turn back around. There is noth-ing behind me. I have outrun it. Twenty seconds have passed. Then I turn back around and the thing is right in front of me. It must have cut across the field. I stop dead in my tracks and my perspective corrects itself. It's Bernie Kosar! He's sitting in the middle of the track with his tongue dangling, tail wagging.

"Bernie Kosar!" I yell. "You scared the hell out of me!"

I resume running at a slow pace and Bernie Kosar runs alongside me. I hope nobody noticed how fast I ran. Then I stop and bend over as though I have cramps and can't catch my breath. I walk for a bit. Then I jog a little. Before I finish the second lap two people have passed me.

"Smith! What happened? You were dusting everyone!" Mr. Wallace yells when I run by him.

I breathe heavily, for show. "I—have—asthma," I say.

He shakes his head in disapproval. "And here I thought I had this year's Ohio state track champion in my class."

I shrug and keep going, stopping every so often to walk. Bernie Kosar stays with me, sometimes walking, sometimes trotting. When I start the last lap Sam catches up to me and we run together. His face is bright red.

"So what were you reading in astronomy today?" I ask. "An entire Montana town abducted by aliens?"

He grins at me. "Yeah, that's the theory," he says somewhat shyly, as though embarrassed.

"Why would an entire town be abducted?"

Sam shrugs, doesn't answer.

"No, really?" I ask.

"Do you really want to know?"

"Of course."

"Well, the theory is that the government has been allowing alien abductions in exchange for technology."

"Really? What kind of technology?" I ask.

"Like chips for supercomputers and formulas for more bombs and green technologies. Stuff like that."

"Green technology for live specimens? Weird. Why do aliens want to abduct humans?"

"So they can study us."

"But why? I mean, what reason could they possibly have?"

"So that when Armageddon comes they'll know our weaknesses and be able to easily defeat us by exposing them."

I'm kind of taken aback by his answer, but only because of the scenes still playing in my head from the night before, remembering the weapons I saw the Mogadorians use, and the massive beasts.

"Wouldn't it be easy for them if they already have bombs and technologies far superior to our own?"

"Well, some people seem to think that they're hoping we'll kill ourselves first."

I look at Sam. He is smiling at me, trying to decide whether I'm taking the conversation seriously.

"Why would they want us to kill ourselves first? What is their incentive?"

"Because they're jealous."

"Jealous of us? Why, because of our rugged good looks?"

Sam laughs. "Something like that."

I nod. We run in silence for a minute and I can tell Sam is having a tough time, breathing heavily. "How did you get interested in all this?"

He shrugs. "It's just a hobby," he says, though

I get the distinct feeling that he's keeping something from me.

We finish the mile at eight minutes fifty-nine seconds, better than the last time Sam ran it. Bernie Kosar follows the class back to the school. The others pet him, and when we walk in he tries to come in with us. I don't know how he knew where I was. Could he have memorized the way to the school this morning on the ride in? The thought seems ridiculous.

He stays at the door. I walk to the locker room with Sam and the second he catches his breath he rattles off a ton of other conspiracy theories, one right after another, most of which are laughable. I like him, and find him amusing, but sometimes I wish he would stop talking.

When home ec begins Sarah isn't in class. Mrs. Benshoff gives instruction for the first ten minutes and then we head to the kitchen. I enter the station alone, resigned to the fact that I'll be cooking alone today, and as soon as that thought occurs to me, Sarah walks in.

"Did I miss anything good?" she asks.

"About ten minutes of quality time with me," I say with a smile.

She laughs. "I heard about your locker this morning. I'm sorry."

"You put the manure there?" I ask.

She laughs again. "No, of course not. But I know they're picking on you because of me."

"They're just lucky I didn't use my superpowers and throw them into the next county."

She playfully grabs my biceps. "Right, these huge muscles. Your superpowers. Boy, they are lucky."

Our project for the day is to make blueberry cupcakes. As we start mixing the batter, Sarah begins telling me about her history with Mark. They dated for two years, but the longer they were together, the more she drifted from her parents and her friends. She was Mark's girlfriend, nothing else. She knew she had started to change, to adopt some of his attitudes towards people: being mean and judgmental, thinking she was better than them. She also started drinking and her grades slipped. At the end of the last school year, her parents sent her to live with her aunt in Colorado for the summer. When she got there, she started taking long hikes in the mountains, taking pictures of the scenery with her aunt's camera. She fell in love with photography and had the best summer ever, realizing there was far more to life than being a cheerleader and dating the quarterback of the football team. When she got home she broke up with Mark and quit cheerleading, and made a vow that she was going to be good, and kind, to everyone. Mark hasn't gotten over it. She says he still considers her his girl-friend, and believes she's going to come back to him. She says the only thing she misses about him are his dogs, which she hung out with when-ever she was at his house. I then tell her about Bernie Kosar, and how he showed up at our door-step unexpectedly after that first morning at the school.

We work as we talk. At one point I reach into the oven without the oven mitts and pull out the cupcake pan. She sees me do it and asks if I'm okay, and I pretend to be hurt, shake my hand as if it's burned, though I don't actually feel a thing. We go to the sink and Sarah runs lukewarm water to help with the burn that isn't there. When she sees my hand, I just shrug. As we're frosting the cupcakes, she asks about my phone, and tells me she noticed there was only one number in it. I tell her it's Henri's number, that I lost my old phone with all of my contacts. She asks if I left a girlfriend behind when we moved. I say no, and she smiles, which just about ruins me. Before class ends, she tells me about the upcoming Halloween festival in town, and says she hopes to see me there, that maybe we can hang out. I say yeah, that would be great, and pretend to be cool, even though I'm flying inside.

CHAPTER ELEVEN

IMAGES COME TO ME, AT RANDOM times, usually when I least expect them. Sometimes they are small and fleeting—my grandmother holding a glass of water and opening her mouth to say something—but I never know the words because the image vanishes as quickly as it came. Sometimes they are longer, more lifelike: my grandfather pushing me on a swing. I can feel the strength in his arms as he pushes me up, the butterflies in the pit of my stomach as I race down. My laughter carries on the wind. Then the image is gone. Sometimes I explicitly remember the images from my past, remember being a part of them. But sometimes they are as new to me as though they never happened before.

In the living room, with Henri running the Loric crystal up each of my arms, my hands suspended over flames, I see the following: I am young—three, maybe four—running through our front yard of newly clipped grass. Beside me is an animal with a body like a dog, but with a coat like a tiger. His head is round, his body barrel chested atop short legs. Unlike any animal I have ever seen. He crouches, poised to leap at me. I can't stop laughing. Then he jumps and I try to catch him but I'm too small and both of us fall to the grass. We wrestle. He is stronger than I am. Then he jumps in the air, and instead of falling back to the ground as I expect, he turns himself into a bird and flies up and around me, hovering just beyond my reach. He circles, then comes down, shoots between my legs, lands twenty feet away. He changes into an animal that looks like a monkey without a tail. He crouches low to lunge at me.

Just then a man comes up the walk. He is young, dressed in a silver and blue rubber suit that is tight on his body, the kind of suit I've seen divers wear. He speaks to me in a language that I don't understand. He says the name "Hadley" and nods to the animal. Hadley runs over to him, his shape changing from a monkey to something larger, something bearlike with a lion's mane. Their heads are level, and the man scratches Hadley beneath the chin. Then my grandfather comes out of the house. He looks young, but I know that he must be at least fifty.

He shakes hands with the man. They speak

but I don't understand what they are saying. Then the man looks at me, smiles, lifts his hand out, and all of a sudden I'm off the ground and flying through the air. Hadley follows, as a bird again. I'm in full control of my body, but the man controls where I go, moving his hand to the left or to the right. Hadley and I play in midair, him tickling me with his beak, me trying to get a grip on him. And then my eyes snap open and the image is gone.

"Your grandfather could make himself invisible at will," I hear Henri say, and I close my eyes again. The crystal continues up my arm, spreading the fire repellent to the rest of my body. "One of the rarest Legacies there is, developing only in one percent of our people, and he was one of them. He could make himself and whatever he was touching completely disappear.

"There was one time he wanted to play a joke on me, before I knew what his Legacies were. You were three years old and I had just started working with your family. I came to your house for the first time the day before, and as I came up the hill for my second day the house wasn't there. There was a driveway, and a car, and the tree, but no house. I thought I was losing my mind. I continued past it. Then when I knew I had gone too far I turned back and there, some distance away, was the house that I swore wasn't there before. So I started walking back, but when I came close enough the house again vanished. I just stood there looking at the spot where I knew it must be, but seeing only the trees beyond it. So I walked on. Only on my third time by did your grandfather make the house reappear for good. He couldn't stop laughing. We laughed about that day for the next year and a half, all the way till the very end."

When I open my eyes I am back on the battle-field. More explosions, fire, death.

"Your grandfather was a good man," Henri says. "He loved to make people laugh, loved to tell jokes. I don't think there was ever a time that I left your house without having a stomachache from laughing so hard."

The sky has turned red. A tree rips through the air, thrown by the man in silver and blue, the one I saw at the house. It takes out two of the Mogadorians and I want to cheer in victory. But what use is there in celebrating? No matter how many Mogadorians I see killed, the outcome of that day will not change. The Loric will still be defeated, every last one of them killed. I will still be sent to Earth.

"I never once saw the man get angry. When everyone else lost their temper, when stress encompassed them, your grandfather stayed calm. It was usually then that he would bring out his best jokes, and just like that everyone would be laughing again."

The small beasts target the children. They are defenseless, holding sparklers in their hands from the celebration. That is how we are losing—only a few of the Loric are fighting the beasts, and the rest are trying to save the children.

"Your grandmother was different. She was quiet and reserved, very intelligent. Your elders complemented each other that way, your grandfather the carefree one, your grandmother working behind the scenes so that everything went off as planned."

High in the sky I can still see the trail of blue smoke from the airship carrying us to Earth, carrying us Nine and our Keepers. Its presence unnerves the Mogadorians.

"And then there was Julianne, my wife."

Far off in the distance there is an explosion, this one like the kind that comes from the liftoff of Earth's rockets. Another ship rises in the air, a trail of fire behind it. Slowly at first, then building speed. I'm confused. Our ships didn't use fire for liftoff; they didn't use oil or gasoline. They emitted a small blue trail of smoke that came from the crystals used to power them, never fire like this one. The second ship is slow and clumsy compared to the first, but it makes it, rising through the air, gaining speed. Henri never mentioned a second ship. Who is on it? Where is it going? The Mogadorians shout and point at it. Again, it causes them anxiety, and for a brief moment the Loric surge.

"She had the greenest eyes I'd ever seen, bright green like emeralds, plus a heart as big as the planet itself. Always helping others, constantly bringing in animals and keeping them as pets. I'll never know what it was she saw in me."

The large beast has returned, the one with the red eyes and enormous horns. Drool mixed with blood falls from razor-sharp teeth so large they can't be contained within its mouth. The man in silver and blue is standing directly in front of it. He tries to lift the beast with his powers, and he gets it a few feet off the ground but then struggles and lifts no farther. The beast roars, shakes, and falls back to the ground. It forces ahead against the man's powers, but it can't break them. The man lifts it again. Sweat and blood glisten in the moonlight on his face. Then he doubles his hands over and the beast crashes to its side. The ground shakes. Thunder and lightning fill the sky but there's no rain to go with them.

"She was a late sleeper, and I always woke before she did. I would sit in the den and read the paper, make breakfast, go for a walk. Some mornings I would come back and she would still be sleeping. I was impatient, couldn't wait to start the day together. She made me feel good just to be around her. I would go in and try to rouse her. She would pull the covers over her head and growl at me. Almost every morning, always the same thing."

The beast flails but the man is still in control. Other Garde have joined in, every one of them using a power on the mammoth beast, fire and lightning raining down upon it, streaks of lasers coming from all directions. Some Garde are doing damage unseen, standing away from it and holding their hands out in concentration. And then high up a collective storm brews, one major cloud growing and glowing in an otherwise cloudless sky, some sort of energy collecting within it. All Garde are in on it, all of them helping to create this cataclysmic haze. And then a final, massive bolt of lightning drops down and hits the beast where it lies. And there it dies.

"What could I do? What could anyone do? In total there were nineteen of us on that ship. You nine children and us nine Cêpan, chosen by no means other than where we happened to be that night, and the pilot who brought us here. We Cêpan couldn't fight, and what difference would it have made if we could? The Cêpan are bureaucrats, meant to keep the planet running, meant to teach, meant to train new Garde how to understand and manipulate their powers. We were never meant to be fighters. We would have been ineffective. We would have died like the rest. All we could do was leave. Leave with you to live and to one day restore to glory the most beautiful planet in all of the universe."

I close my eyes and when I reopen them the fight has ended. Smoke rises from the ground among the dead and the dying. Trees broken, the forests burned, nothing standing save the few Mogadorians that have lived to tell the tale. The sun rising to the south and a pale glow growing on the barren land bathed in red. Mounds of bodies, not all of them intact, not all of them whole. On top of one mound is the man in silver and blue, dead like the rest. There are no discernible marks on his body, but he is dead all the same.

My eyes snap open. I can't breathe, and my mouth is dry, parched.

"Here," Henri says. He helps me off the coffee table, guides me into the kitchen and pulls out a chair for me. Tears are coming to my eyes though I try to blink them back. Henri brings me a glass of water and I drink every bit of it without stopping. I give him the glass and he refills it. I drop my head, still struggling to breathe. I drink the second glass, then look at Henri.

"Why didn't you ever tell me about a second ship?" I ask.

"What are you talking about?"

"There was a second ship," I say.

"Where was there a ship?"

"On Lorien, the day we left. A second ship that took off after ours."

"Impossible," he says.

"Why is it impossible?"

"Because the other ships were destroyed. I saw it with my own eyes. When the Mogadorians landed they took out our ports first. We traveled in the only ship that survived their offensive. It was a miracle that we made it off."

"I saw a second ship. I'm telling you. It wasn't like the others, though. It ran on fuel, a ball of fire following behind it."

Henri watches me closely. He is thinking hard, his brows crinkled.

"Are you sure, John?"

"Yes."

He leans back in his chair, looks out the window. Bernie Kosar is on the ground, staring up at us both.

"It made it off Lorien," I say. "I watched it the whole way until it disappeared."

"That makes no sense," Henri says. "I don't see how it could be possible. There was nothing left."

"There was a second ship."

We sit through a long silence.

"Henri?"

"Yes?"

"What was on that ship?"

He fixes me with a stare.

"I don't know," he says. "I truly don't know."

We sit in the living room, a fire in the hearth, Bernie Kosar in my lap. An occasional pop from the logs breaks the silence.

"On!" I say, and snap my fingers. My right hand illuminates, not as brightly as I've seen it before, but close. In the short amount of time since Henri started coaching me I've learned to control the glow. I can concentrate it, making it wide, like the light in a house, or narrow and focused, like a flashlight. My ability to manipulate it is coming more quickly than I expected. The left hand is still dimmer than the right, but it's catching up. I snap my fingers and say "on" just to show off, but I don't need to do either to control the light, or to have it come on. It just happens from within, as effortlessly as twitching a finger or blinking an eye.

"When do you think the other Legacies will develop?" I ask.

Henri looks up from the paper. "Soon," he says. "The next one should start within the month, whatever it is. You just have to keep a close watch. Not all the powers will be obvious like your hands."

"How long will it take for them all to come?"

He shrugs. "Sometimes all is complete within two months, sometimes it takes up to a year. It varies from Garde to Garde. But however long it takes, your major Legacy will be the last to develop."

I close my eyes and lean back against the couch. I think about my major Legacy, the one that will allow me to fight. I'm not sure what I want it to be. Lasers? Mind control? The ability to manipulate the weather as I had seen the man in silver and blue do? Or do I want something darker, more sinister, like the ability to kill without touching?

I run my hand down Bernie Kosar's back. I look over at Henri. He's wearing a nightcap and a pair of spectacles on the tip of his nose like a storybook rat.

"Why were we at the airfield that day?" I ask.

"We were there for an air show. After it was over we took a tour of some of the ships."

"Was that really the only reason?"

He turns back to me and nods. He swallows hard, and it makes me think that he's keeping something from me.

"Well, how was it decided that we would leave?" I ask. "I mean, surely a plan like that would've needed more time than a few minutes' notice, right?"

"We didn't take off until three hours after the invasion started. Do you not remember any of it?"

"Very little."

"We met your grandfather at the statue of Pittacus. He gave you to me and told me to get you to the airfield, that that was our only chance. There was an underground compound beneath the airfield. He said there had always been a contingency plan in case something of the sort occurred, but it was never taken seriously because the threat of an attack seemed ludicrous. Just like it would be here, on Earth. If you were to tell any human now that there is a threat of an attack by aliens, well, they would laugh at you. It was no different on Lorien. I asked him how he knew about the plan and he didn't answer, just smiled, and said good-bye. It makes sense that no one would really know about the plan, or only a few would."

I nod. "So just like that, you guys came up with a plan to come to Earth?"

"Of course not. One of the planet's Elders met us at the airfield. He's the one who cast the Loric charm that branded your ankles and tied you all together, and gave you each an amulet. He said you were special children, blessed children, by which I assume he meant you were getting a chance to escape. We originally planned to take the ship up and wait out the invasion, wait for our people to fight back and win. But that never happened . . . ," he says, trailing off. Then he sighs. "We stayed in orbit for a week. That was how long it took for the Mogadorians to strip Lorien of everything. After it became clear that there would be no going back, we set our course for Earth."

"Why didn't he cast a charm so that none of us could be killed, regardless of numbers?"

"There's only so much that can be done, John. What you are talking about is invincibility. It's not possible."

I nod. The charm only does so much. If one of the Mogadorians tries killing us out of order, whatever damage it attempts is reversed and done to it instead. If one had tried shooting me in the head the bullet would have gone through its own head. But not anymore. Now if they catch me, I die.

I sit in silence for a moment thinking about it all. The airfield. Lorien's lone remaining Elder who cast the charm on us, Loridas, now dead. The Elders were the first inhabitants of Lorien, those beings who made it what it was. There were ten of them in the beginning, and they contained all Legacies within them. So old, so long ago that they seem more of a myth than anything based in reality. Aside from Loridas, no one knew what had happened to the rest of them, if they were dead.

I try to remember what it was like orbiting the planet waiting to see if we could go back, but I don't remember any of it. I can recall bits and pieces of the journey. The interior of the ship we traveled in was round and open aside from the two bathrooms that had doors. There were cots pushed to one side; the other side was devoted to exercise and games to keep us from getting too antsy. I can't remember what the others look like. I can't remember the games we played. I remember being bored, an entire year being spent inside an airship with seventeen others. There was a stuffed animal I slept with at night, and though I'm sure the memory is wrong, I seem to recall the animal playing back.

"Henri?"

"Yes?"

"I keep having images of a man in a silver and blue suit. I saw him at our house, and on the battlefield. He could control the weather. And then I saw him dead."

Henri nods. "Every time you travel back it'll only be to those scenes holding relevance to you."

"He was my father, wasn't he?"

"Yes," he says. "He wasn't supposed to come around much, but he did anyway. He was around a lot."

I sigh. My father had fought valiantly, killing the beast and many of the soldiers. But in the end it still wasn't enough.

"Do we really have a chance to win?"

"What do you mean?"

"We were defeated so easily. What hope is there for a different outcome if we're found? Even when we have all developed our powers, and when we finally come together and are ready to fight, what hope do we have against things like those?"

"Hope?" he says. "There is always hope, John. New developments have yet to present themselves. Not all the information is in. No. Don't give up hope just yet. It's the last thing to go. When you have lost hope, you have lost everything. And when you think all is lost, when all is dire and bleak, there is always hope."

CHAPTER TWELVE

HENRI AND I GO INTO TOWN ON Saturday for the Halloween parade, almost two weeks after arriving in Paradise. I think the solitude is getting to us both. Not that we aren't used to solitude. We are. But the solitude in Ohio is different from that of most other places. There is a certain silence to it, a certain loneliness.

It's a cold day, the sun peeking intermittently through thick white clouds gliding by overhead. The town is bustling. All the kids are in costume. We have bought a leash for Bernie Kosar, who is wearing a Superman cape draped over his back, a large "S" on his chest. He seems unimpressed with it. He's not the only dog dressed as a superhero.

Henri and I stand on the sidewalk in front of the Hungry Bear, the diner just off the circle in the center of town, to watch the parade. In its front window hangs a clipping of the *Gazette* article on Mark James. He's pictured standing on the fifty-yard line of the football field, wearing his letterman jacket, his arms crossed, his right foot resting atop a football, a wry, confident grin on his face. Even I have to admit he looks impressive.

Henri sees me staring at the paper.

"It's your friend, right?" he asks with a smile. Henri now knows the story, from the near fight to the cow manure to the crush I have on his ex-girlfriend. Since finding out all this information he has only referred to Mark as my "friend."

"My *best* friend," I correct him.

Just then the band starts. It's at the head of the parade, followed by various Halloween-themed floats, one of which is carrying Mark and a few of the football players. Some I recognize from class, some I don't. They throw handfuls of candy to the kids. Then Mark catches sight of me and he nudges the guy beside him—Kevin, the kid I knee in the groin in the cafeteria. Mark points at me and says something. They both laugh.

"That's him?" Henri asks.

"That's him."

"Looks like a dick."

"I told you."

Then come the cheerleaders, walking, all in

uniform, hair pulled back, smiling and waving to the crowd. Sarah is walking alongside them, taking pictures. She gets them in action, while they're jumping, doing their cheers. Despite the fact that she's wearing jeans and no makeup, she's far more beautiful than any of them. We've been talking more and more at school, and I can't stop thinking about her. Henri sees me staring at her.

Then he turns back to the parade. "That's her, huh?"

"That's her."

She sees me and waves, then points to the camera, meaning she'd come over but wants to take pictures. I smile and nod.

"Well," Henri says. "I can certainly see the appeal."

We watch the parade. The mayor of Paradise passes by, sitting on the back of a red convertible. He throws more candy to the children. There will be a lot of hyper kids today, I think.

I feel a tap on my shoulder and turn around.

"Sam Goode. What's the word?"

He shrugs. "Nothin'. What's up with you?"

"Watching the parade. This is my dad, Henri."

They shake hands. Henri says, "John has told me a lot about you."

"Really?" Sam asks with a crooked grin.

"Really," Henri responds. Then he pauses a

minute and a smile takes shape. "You know, I've been reading. Maybe you've heard it already, but did you know that aliens are the reason we have thunderstorms? They create them in order to enter our planet unnoticed. The storm creates a diversion, and the lightning you see is really coming from the spaceships entering Earth's atmosphere."

Sam smiles and scratches his head. "Get out of here," he says.

Henri shrugs. "That's what I've heard."

"All right," Sam says, more than willing to oblige Henri. "Well, did you know that the dinosaurs really didn't go extinct? Aliens were so fascinated by them that they decided to gather them all up and take them to their own planet."

Henri shakes his head. "I didn't know that," he says. "Did you know that the Loch Ness monster was really an animal from the planet Trafalgra? They brought him here as an experiment, to see if he could survive, and he did. But when he was discovered the aliens had to take him back, which is why he was never spotted again."

I laugh, not at the theory, but at the name Trafalgra. There is no planet named Trafalgra and I wonder if Henri has made it up on the fly.

"Did you know the Egyptian pyramids were built by aliens?"

"I've heard that," Henri says, smiling. This is funny to him because though the pyramids weren't actually built by aliens, they were built using Lorien knowledge and with Lorien help. "Did you know the world is supposed to end on December 21, 2012?"

Sam nods and grins. "Yeah, I've heard that. Earth's supposed expiration date, the end of the Mayan calendar."

"Expiration date?" I chime in. "Like, a 'best if used before' date that's printed on milk cartons? Is Earth going to curdle?"

I laugh at my own joke, but Sam and Henri pay me no attention.

Then Sam says, "Did you know crop circles were originally used as a navigational tool for the Agharian alien race? But that was thousands of years ago. Today they are only created by bored farmers."

I laugh again. I have the urge to ask what sorts of people create alien conspiracies if it is bored farmers who create crop circles, but I don't.

"How about the Centuri?" asks Henri. "Do you know of them?"

Sam shakes his head.

"They're a race of aliens living at Earth's core. They are a contentious race, in constant discord with one another, and when they have civil wars Earth's surface is thrown off-kilter. That's when things such as earthquakes and volcanic eruptions occur. The tsunami of 2004? All because the Centuri king's daughter went missing."

"Did they find her?" I ask.

Henri shakes his head, looks at me, then back at Sam, who is still smiling at the game. "They never did. Theorists believe she is able to shift her shape, and that she is living somewhere in South America."

Henri's theory is so good, I think there's no way he made it up that quickly. I stand there and actually ponder it, even though I've never heard of aliens called the Centuri, even when I know for a fact that nothing lives at Earth's core.

"Did you know . . ." Sam pauses. I think Henri has stumped him, and as soon as that thought pops into my mind Sam says something so frightening that a wave of terror shoots through me.

"Did you know that the Mogadorians are on a quest for universal domination, and that they have already wiped out one planet and are planning to wipe Earth out next? They're here seeking human weakness so that they can exploit us when the war begins."

My mouth drops open and Henri stares at Sam, dumbfounded. He's holding his breath. His hand tightens around his coffee cup until I'm afraid that if it tightens any further the cup will crumple. Sam glances at Henri, then at me.

"You guys look like you've seen a ghost. Does this mean I win?"

"Where did you hear that?" I ask. Henri looks at me so fiercely that I wish I had remained silent.

"From *They Walk Among Us.*"

Henri still can't think of how to respond. He opens his mouth to speak but nothing comes. Then a petite woman standing behind Sam interrupts.

"Sam," she says. He turns and looks at her. "Where have you been?"

Sam shrugs. "I was standing right here."

She sighs, then says to Henri, "Hi, I'm Sam's mother."

"Henri," he says, and shakes her hand. "Pleased to meet you."

She opens her eyes in surprise. Something in Henri's accent has excited her.

"*Ah bon! Vous parlez français? C'est super! J'ai personne avec qui je peux parler français depuis longtemps.*"

Henri smiles. "I'm sorry. I don't actually speak French. I know my accent sounds like it, though."

"No?" She is disappointed. "Well hell, here I thought some dignity had finally come to town."

Sam looks at me and rolls his eyes.

"All right, Sam, let's get going," she says.

He shrugs. "You guys gonna go to the park and the hayride?"

I look at Henri, then at Sam. "Yeah, sure," I say. "Are you?"

He shrugs.

"Well, try to come meet us if you can," I say.

He smiles and nods. "Okay, cool."

"Time to go, Sam. And you might not be able to go on the hayride. I need your help at home," his mother says. He starts to say something but she walks away. Sam follows her.

"Very nice woman," Henri says sarcastically.

"How did you make all that up?" I ask.

The crowd begins migrating up Main Street, away from the circle. Henri and I follow it up to the park, where cider and food are being served.

"You lie long enough and you start to get used to it."

I nod. "So what do you think?"

He takes a deep breath and exhales. The temperature is cold enough so that I can see his breath. "I have no idea. I don't know what to think at this point. He caught me off guard."

"He caught us both off guard."

"We're going to have to look into the publication he's getting his information from, find out who is writing it and where it's being written."

He looks over at me expectantly.

"What?"

"You're going to have to get a copy," he says.

"I will," I say. "But still, it makes no sense. How could somebody know that?"

"It's being supplied from somewhere."

"Do you think it's one of us?"

"No."

"Do you think it's them?"

"It could be. I've never thought to check the conspiracy-theory rags. Perhaps they think we read them and can root us out by leaking information like that. I mean . . ." He pauses, thinks about it for a minute. "Hell, John, I don't know. We'll have to look into it, though. It's not a coincidence, that's for sure."

We walk in silence, still a little stunned, turning possible explanations over in our minds. Bernie Kosar trots along between us, tongue dangling, his cape falling to one side and dragging on the sidewalk. He's a big hit with the kids and many of them stop us to pet him.

The park is situated on the southern edge of town. At the far border are two adjacent lakes separated by a narrow strip of land leading into the forest beyond them. The park itself is made up of three baseball fields, a playground, and a large pavilion where volunteers serve cider and slices of pumpkin pie. Three hay wagons are off to the side of the gravel drive, with a large sign reading:

BE SCARED OUT OF YOUR WITS!
HALLOWEEN HAUNTED HAYRIDES
START @ SUNDOWN
$5 PER PERSON

The drive segues from gravel to dirt before it reaches the woods, the entrance to which is decorated with cutouts of ghost and goblin caricatures. It appears that the haunted hayride travels through the woods. I look around for Sarah but don't see her anywhere. I wonder if she'll be going on it.

Henri and I enter the pavilion. The cheerleaders are off to the side, some of them doing Halloween-themed face paintings for the kids, the others selling raffle tickets for the drawing to be held at six p.m.

"Hi, John," I hear behind me. I turn around and there's Sarah, holding her camera. "How did you like the parade?"

I smile at her and slide my hands into my pockets. There's a small white ghost painted on her cheek.

"Hey, you," I say. "I liked it. I think I'm getting used to this small-town Ohio charm."

"Charm? You mean boringness, right?"

I shrug. "I don't know, it isn't bad."

"Hey, it's the little guy from school. I remember you," she says, bending down to pet Bernie Kosar. He wags his tail wildly, jumps up and tries to lick her face. Sarah laughs. I look over my shoulder. Henri is twenty feet away, talking to Sarah's mom at one of the picnic tables. I'm curious to know what they're talking about.

"I think he likes you. His name is Bernie Kosar."

"Bernie Kosar? That's no name for an adorable dog. Look at this cape. It's, like, cute overload."

"You know if you keep that up I'm going to be jealous of my own dog," I say.

She smiles and stands.

"So are you going to buy a raffle ticket from me or what? It's to rebuild a not-for-profit animal shelter destroyed in a fire last month in Colorado."

"Really? How does a girl from Paradise, Ohio, learn of an animal shelter in Colorado?"

"It's my aunt's. I've convinced all the girls on the cheerleading squad to participate. We're going to take a trip and assist in the construction. We'll be helping the animals and getting out of school and Ohio for a week. It's a win-win situation."

I picture Sarah dressed in a hard hat, wielding a hammer. The thought brings a grin to my face. "So you're saying I'm going to have to cover the kitchen alone for a whole week?" I fake an exasperated sigh and shake my head. "I don't know if I can support such a trip now, even if it is for the animals."

She laughs and punches me in the arm. I take out my wallet and give her five dollars for six tickets.

"These six are good luck," she says.

"They are?"

"Of course. You bought them from me, silly."

Just then, over Sarah's shoulder, I see Mark and the rest of the guys from the float walk into the pavilion.

"Are you going on the haunted hayride tonight?" Sarah asks.

"Yeah, I was thinking about it."

"You should, it's fun. Everybody does it. And it actually gets pretty scary."

Mark sees Sarah and me talking and scrunches his face into a scowl. He comes walking our way. Same outfit as always—letterman jacket, blue jeans, hair full of gel.

"So you're going?" I ask Sarah.

Before she can respond Mark interrupts. "How'd you like the parade, Johnny?" he asks. Sarah quickly turns around and glares at him.

"I liked it a lot," I reply.

"You going on the haunted hayride tonight, or are you going to be too scared?"

I smile at him. "As a matter of fact, I am going."

"You going to have a freak-out like in school and run out of the woods crying like a baby?"

"Don't be an ass, Mark," Sarah says.

He looks at me, seething. With the crowd around there is nothing he can do without causing a scene—and I don't think he would do anything anyway.

"All in due time," Mark says.

"You think?"

"Yours is coming," he says.

"That might be true," I say. "But it won't be coming from you."

"Stop it!" Sarah yells. She works her way in between us, pushing us away from each other. People are watching. She glances around as though embarrassed by the attention, then scowls at Mark first, then at me.

"Fine, then. You guys fight if that's what you want to do. Good luck with it," Sarah says, and turns and walks away. I watch her go. Mark doesn't.

"Sarah," I call, but she keeps walking and disappears past the pavilion.

"Soon," Mark says.

I look back to him. "I doubt it."

He retreats to his group of friends. Henri walks up to me.

"I don't suppose he was inquiring about yesterday's math homework?"

"Not quite," I say.

"I wouldn't worry about him," Henri says. "He looks to be all talk."

"I'm not," I say, and then glance at the spot where Sarah disappeared. "Should I go after her?" I ask, and look at him, pleading to the part of him that was once married and in love, that part that still misses his wife every day, and not the part of him that wants to keep me safe and hidden.

He nods his head. "Yeah," he says with a sigh. "As much as I hate to admit it, you should probably go after her."

CHAPTER
THIRTEEN

KIDS RUNNING, SCREAMING, ON SLIDES and jungle gyms. Every kid with a bag of candy in his or her hand, with a mouth stuffed full of sweets. Kids dressed as cartoon characters, monsters, ghouls and ghosts. Every resident of Paradise must be at the park right now. And in the midst of all the madness I see Sarah, sitting alone, gently pushing herself on the swing.

I weave my way through the screams and shrieks. When Sarah sees me she smiles, those big blue eyes of hers like a beacon.

"Need a push?" I ask.

She nods to the swing that has just opened beside her and I sit.

"Doing okay?" I ask.

"Yeah, I'm fine. He just wears me down. He always has to act so tough and he's downright mean when he's around friends."

She twists herself on the swing until the rope becomes taut, then she lifts her feet and it spins her around, slowly at first, then gaining speed. She laughs the whole time, her blond hair a trail behind her. I do the same thing. When the swing finally stops the world keeps spinning.

"Where is Bernie Kosar?"

"I left him with Henri," I say.

"Your dad?"

"Yes, my dad." I am constantly doing that, calling Henri by his name when I should be saying "Dad."

The temperature is quickly dropping, and my hands are white knuckled on the rope chain, becoming cold. We watch the kids run amok around us. Sarah looks at me and her eyes seem bluer than ever in the coming dusk. Our gaze stays locked, each of us just staring at the other, no words being said but much passing between us. The children seem to fade into the background. Then she smiles shyly and looks away.

"So what are you going to do?" I ask.

"About what?"

"Mark."

She shrugs. "What can I do? I've already broken up with him. I keep telling him I have no interest in getting back together."

I nod. I'm not sure how to respond to that.

"But anyway, I should probably try to sell the

rest of these tickets. Only an hour before the raffle."

"Do you want any help?"

"No, that's okay. You should go have fun. Bernie Kosar is probably missing you right now. But you should definitely stick around for the hayride. Maybe we can go on it together?"

"I will," I say. A happiness blooms inside of me, but I try to keep it hidden.

"I'll see you in a little while, then."

"Good luck with the tickets."

She reaches over and grabs my hand and holds it for a good three seconds. Then she lets go, jumps off the swing, and hurries away. I sit there, gently swinging, enjoying the brisk wind that I haven't felt in a very long time because we spent the last winter in Florida, and the one before that in south Texas. When I head back to the pavilion Henri is sitting at a picnic table eating a slice of pie with Bernie Kosar lying at his feet.

"How'd it go?"

"Good," I say with a smile.

From somewhere an orange and blue firework shoots up and explodes in the sky. It makes me think of Lorien and of the fireworks I saw on the day of the invasion.

"Have you thought any more about the second ship I saw?"

Henri looks around to make sure there's nobody within earshot. We have the picnic table to ourselves, positioned in the far corner away from the crowd.

"A little. I still have no idea what it means, though."

"Do you think it could have traveled here?"

"No. It wouldn't be possible. If it ran on fuel, like you say, it wouldn't have been able to travel far without refueling."

I sit for a moment.

"I wish it could have."

"Could have what?"

"Traveled here, with us."

"It's a nice thought," says Henri.

An hour or so passes and I see all the football players, Mark in front, walk across the grass. They are dressed up as mummies, zombies, ghosts, twenty-five of them in total. They sit in the bleachers of the nearest baseball field and the cheerleaders who were drawing on the children begin applying makeup to complete the costumes of Mark and his friends. It's only then that I realize the football players will be the ones doing the scaring on the haunted hayride, the ones waiting for us in the woods.

"See that?" I ask Henri.

Henri looks at them all and nods, then picks

up his coffee and takes a long drink.

"Think you should still go on the ride?" he asks.

"No," I say. "But I'm going to anyway."

"I figured you would."

Mark is dressed as a zombie of sorts, wearing dark tattered clothes, with black and gray makeup on his face, splotches of red in random places to simulate blood. When his costume is complete Sarah walks up to him and says something. His voice becomes raised but I can't hear what he's saying. His movements are animated and he talks so fast that I can tell he's stumbling over his words. Sarah crosses her arms and shakes her head at him. His body tenses. I move to stand, but Henri grabs my arm.

"Don't," he says. "He's only pushing her further away."

I look at them and wish with everything that I could hear what is being said, but there are too many screaming kids around to focus in. When the yelling stops they both stand looking at each other, a hurtful scowl on Mark's face, an incredulous grin on Sarah's. Then she shakes her head and walks away.

I look at Henri. "What should I do now?"

"Not a thing," he says. "Not a thing."

Mark walks back to his friends, head hung, scowling. A few of them look in my direction.

Smirks appear. Then they start walking towards the forest. A slow methodical march, twenty-five guys in costume receding in the distance.

To kill time I walk back to the center of town with Henri and we eat dinner at the Hungry Bear. When we walk back the sun has set and the first trailer piled with hay and pulled by a green tractor takes off for the woods. The crowd has thinned considerably and those left are mostly high schoolers and free-spirited adults who total a hundred or so people. I look for Sarah among them but I don't see her. The next trailer leaves in ten minutes. According to the pamphlet the whole ride is half an hour long, the tractor going through the woods slowly, the anticipation building, and then it stops and the riders are to get off and follow a different trail on foot, at which point the scares begin.

Henri and I stand beneath the pavilion and I again scan the long line of people waiting their turn. I still don't see her. Just then my phone vibrates in my pocket. I can't remember the last time my phone rang when it wasn't Henri calling. The caller ID reads SARAH HART. Excitement rushes through me. She must have entered my number into her phone the same day she entered hers into mine.

"Hello?" I say.

"John?"

"Yeah."

"Hey, it's Sarah. Are you still at the park?" she says. She sounds as though her calling me is normal, that I shouldn't think twice about her already having my number despite my never having given it to her.

"Yes."

"Great! I'm going to be back there in about five minutes. Have the rides started?"

"Yeah, a couple minutes ago."

"You haven't gone yet, have you?"

"No."

"Oh, good! Wait so we can ride together."

"Yeah, definitely," I say. "The second one is about to leave now."

"Perfect. I'll be there in time for the third."

"See you then."

I hang up, a huge smile on my face.

"Be careful out there," Henri says.

"I will." Then I pause and try to bring lightness to my voice. "You don't have to stick around. I'm sure I can get a ride home."

"I'm willing to stay and live in this town, John. Even when it's probably smarter for us to leave given the events that have already happened. But you're going to have to meet me halfway on things. And this is one of them. I don't like the looks those guys gave you earlier one bit."

I nod. "I'll be fine," I say.

"I'm sure you will. But just in case I'm going to be right here waiting."

I sigh. "Fine."

Sarah pulls up five minutes later with a pretty friend who I've seen before but have never been introduced to. She has changed into jeans, a wool sweater, and a black jacket. She has wiped away the painted ghost that was on her right cheek and her hair is down, falling past her shoulders.

"Hey, you," she says.

"Hi."

She wraps her arms around me in a tentative hug. I can smell the perfume wafting up from her neck. Then she pulls away.

"Hi, John's dad," she says to Henri. "This is my friend Emily."

"Pleased to meet you both," Henri says. "So you guys are off into the unknown terror?"

"You bet," Sarah says. "Will this one be okay out there? I don't want him getting too scared on me," Sarah says to Henri, motioning to me with a smile.

Henri grins and I can tell he already likes Sarah. "You better stay close just in case."

She looks over her shoulder. The third trailer is a quarter full. "I'll keep him safe," she says. "We better get going."

"Have a great time," Henri says.

Sarah surprises me by taking my hand and the

three of us rush off towards the hay wagon a hundred yards away from the pavilion. There is a line about thirty people long. We get to the back of it and start talking, though I'm feeling a little shy and mostly just listen to the two girls talk. As we're waiting I see Sam hovering off to the side as though contemplating whether or not to approach us.

"Sam!" I yell with more enthusiasm than I intended. He stumbles over. "You coming on the ride with us?"

He shrugs. "Do you mind?"

"Come on," Sarah says, and motions him in. He stands next to Emily, who smiles at him. He immediately starts blushing and I'm ecstatic he's along for the ride. Suddenly a kid holding a walkie-talkie comes over. I recognize him from the football team.

"Hi, Tommy," Sarah says to him.

"Hey," he says. "There are four spots left on this wagon. You guys want them?"

"Really?"

"Yeah."

We skip the line and jump up onto the trailer, where the four of us sit on a bale of hay together. I find it odd that Tommy doesn't ask us for tickets. I'm curious as to why he let us skip the line altogether. Some of the people waiting look at us with disgust. I can't say that I blame them.

"Enjoy the ride," Tommy says with a grin, the kind I've seen people wear when told something bad has happened to someone they despise.

"That was weird," I say.

Sarah shrugs. "He probably has a crush on Emily."

"Oh God, I hope not," Emily says, and then fake-gags.

I watch Tommy from the bale of hay. The trailer is only half full, which is another thing that strikes me as strange since there are so many people waiting.

The tractor pulls away, bumps along the pathway, and drives through the entrance of the forest, where ghastly sounds come through hidden speakers. The forest is thick and no light penetrates other than what shines from the front of the tractor. *Once that is off,* I think, *there will be nothing but darkness.* Sarah takes hold of my hand again. She's cold to the touch, but a sense of warmth floods through me. She leans over to me and whispers, "I'm a little scared."

Figures of ghosts hang just over us from the low branches, and off the drive grimacing zombies lean against various trees. The tractor stops and kills its headlight. Then come intermittent strobes that flash for ten seconds. There is nothing scary about them and only when they stop do I understand their effect: our eyes take a few seconds to adjust and we can't see a thing. Then a scream shoots through the night and Sarah tenses against me as figures sweep around us. I squint to focus and I see that Emily has moved next to Sam, and that he is smiling widely. I'm actually a little scared myself. I put my arm carefully around Sarah. A hand grazes our backs and Sarah grips tightly to my leg. Some of the others scream. With a jolt the tractor turns back on and continues forward, nothing but the outlines of the trees in its light.

We drive for another three or four minutes. The anticipation builds, the foreboding fear of having to walk the distance we just drove. Then the tractor pulls into a circular clearing and stops.

"Everybody off," the driver yells.

When the last person is off, the tractor pulls away. Its light recedes in the distance, then disappears, leaving nothing but the night and not a single sound other than what we make.

"Shit," somebody says, and all of us laugh.

In total there are eleven of us. A path of lights turns on, showing us the way, then turns off. I close my eyes to focus on the feel of Sarah's fingers interlocked with mine.

"I have no idea why I do this every year," Emily says nervously, her arms wrapped around herself.

The other people have started down the trail

and we follow. The pathway of lights occasionally flickers on to keep us on our way. The others are far enough ahead that we can't see them. I can barely see the ground at my feet. Three or four screams suddenly ring out in front of us.

"Oh no," Sarah says, and squeezes my hand. "Sounds like trouble ahead."

Just then something heavy falls on us. Both girls scream and so does Sam. I trip and hit the ground, scraping my knee, tangled in whatever the hell the thing is. Then I realize it's a net!

"What the hell?" Sam asks.

I tear straight through the twisted rope but the second I'm free I get shoved hard from behind. Someone grabs me and drags me away from the girls and Sam. I break free and stand, but am immediately hit from behind again. This isn't part of the ride.

"Let go of me!" one of the girls yells. A guy laughs in response. I can't see a thing. The girls' voices are moving away from me.

"John?" Sarah calls.

"Where are you, John?" shouts Sam.

I stand to go after them but am hit again. No, that's not right. I am tackled. The wind is knocked out of me when I'm plowed to the ground. I rush up and try to catch my breath, my hand against a tree for support. I pick dirt and leaves from my mouth.

I stand there a few seconds and don't hear a single sound other than my own labored breathing. Just when I think I've been left alone, somebody shoulders into me and sends me flying into a nearby tree. My head slams against the trunk and I briefly see stars. I'm surprised by the person's strength. I reach up and touch my forehead and feel blood on my fingertips. I look around again but can't see anything other than the silhouetted trees.

I hear a scream from one of the girls, followed by the sounds of struggle. I grit my teeth. I am shaking. Are there people mixed in with the wall of trees around me? I can't tell. But I feel a set of eyes on me, somewhere.

"Get off of me!" Sarah yells. She is being pulled away, I can tell that much.

"Okay," I say to the darkness, to the trees. Anger surges through me. "You want to play games?" I say, loudly this time. Somebody laughs nearby.

I take a step towards the sound. I get shoved from behind but I catch my balance before I fall. I throw a blind punch and the back of my hand scrapes against the bark of a tree. There is nothing left to do. What point is there in having Legacies if they are never used when needed? Even if it means Henri and I load the truck tonight and drive off to yet another town, at least

I will have done what I needed to do.

"You want to play games?" I yell again. "I can play games too!"

A trickle of blood runs down the side of my face. Okay, I think, let's do this. They can do all they want to me, but they will not harm a single hair on Sarah's head. Or Sam's, or Emily's.

I take a deep breath and adrenaline races through me. A malicious smile takes shape and my body feels as though it has grown bigger, stronger. My hands come on and glow brilliantly with bright light that sweeps through the night, the world suddenly ablaze.

I look up. I flash my hands across the trees and sprint off into the night.

CHAPTER FOURTEEN

KEVIN STEPS FROM THE TREES, dressed as a mummy. He's the one who tackled me. The lights stun him and he seems dumbfounded, trying to figure out where they're coming from. He's wearing night-vision goggles. *So that is how they are able to see us*, I think. Where did they get them?

He charges me and at the last second I step out of the way and trip him.

"Let go of me!" I hear from down the trail. I look up and sweep my lights across the trees but nothing moves. I can't tell if the voice is Emily's or Sarah's. A guy's laughter follows.

Kevin tries to stand but I kick him in the side before he gets to his feet. He falls back to the ground with an *"Ummpf!"* I rip the goggles from his face and throw them as far as I can and know they will land at least a mile away, maybe two or three because I'm so angry that my strength is out of control. Then I race off through the woods before Kevin can even sit up.

The trail winds left, then right. My hands glow only when I need to see. I sense that I'm close. Then I see Sam up ahead, standing with a zombie's arms around him. Three others are close by.

The zombie lets go of him. "Chill out, we're just kidding around. If you don't resist, you won't get hurt," he says to Sam. "Sit down or something."

I snap my hands on and flash the lights in their eyes to blind them. The closest person steps towards me and I swing and hit him in the side of the face and he falls motionless to the ground. His goggles sail into the overgrown brambles and disappear. The second person tries to bear-hug me, but I break his grip and lift him off the ground.

"What the hell?" he says, confused.

I throw him and he hits the side of a tree twenty feet away. The third guy sees this and runs away. That just leaves the fourth, the one who was holding Sam. He lifts his hands in front of him as though I'm aiming a gun at his chest.

"It wasn't my idea," he says.

"What does he have planned?"

"Nothing, man. We just wanted to play a joke on you guys, scare you a little."

"Where are they?"

"They let Emily go. Sarah is up ahead."

"Give me your goggles," I say.

"No way, man. We're borrowing them from the police. I'll get in trouble."

I step towards him.

"Fine," he says. He takes them off and hands them to me. I throw them even harder than I did the previous pair. I hope they land in the next town. Let them explain that one to the police.

I grab Sam's shirt with my right hand. I can't see a thing without turning on my light. Only then do I realize I should have kept the two pairs of goggles for us to wear. But I didn't, so I take a deep breath and let my left hand glow and begin guiding us up the path. If Sam finds it suspicious, he doesn't let on.

I stop to listen. Nothing. We continue on, weaving through the trees. I turn the light off.

"Sarah!" I yell.

I stop to listen and hear nothing but the wind blowing through the branches and Sam's heavy breathing.

"How many people are with Mark?" I ask.

"Five or so."

"Do you know which way they went?"

"I didn't see."

We push on and I have no idea in which direction we are headed. From far off I hear the groan of the tractor motor. The fourth ride is starting. I feel frantic inside and want to sprint, but I know that Sam can't keep up. He's breathing heavily already and even I'm sweating despite the temperature being only forty-five degrees. Or maybe I'm mistaking blood for sweat. I can't tell.

As we pass a thick tree with a knotted trunk I get tackled from behind. Sam yells as a fist hits me in the back of the head and I'm momentarily stunned, but then I pivot and grab the guy by the throat and shine the light in his face. He tries to peel my fingers away but it's useless.

"What is Mark planning?"

"Nothing," he says.

"Wrong answer."

I thrust him into the nearest tree five feet away, then I pick him up and lift him a foot off the ground with my hand again around his throat. His legs kick wildly, hitting me, but I tighten my muscles so that the kicks do no damage.

"What is he planning to do?"

I lower him until his feet touch solid ground, loosening my grip to allow him to speak. I sense Sam watching, drinking all of this in, but there is nothing I can do about it.

"We just wanted to scare you guys," he gasps.

"I swear I will break you in half if you don't tell me the truth."

"He thinks that the others are dragging you two to Shepherd Falls. That's where he took Sarah. He wanted her to see him beat the crap out of you, and then he was going to let you go."

"Lead me," I say.

He shuffles forward and I turn my light off. Sam takes hold of my shirt and follows behind us. When we walk through a small clearing lit by the moonlight overhead I can see that he's looking at my hands.

"They're gloves," I say. "Kevin Miller was wearing them. Some sort of Halloween prop."

He nods but I can tell he's freaked out. We walk for nearly a minute until we hear the sound of running water just ahead of us.

"Give me your goggles," I say to the guy leading us.

He hesitates and I twist his arm. He writhes in pain and quickly rips them from his face.

"Take them, take them," he yells.

When I put them on the world turns to a shade of green. I push him hard and he falls to the ground.

"Come on," I say to Sam, and we walk ahead, leaving the guy behind.

Up ahead I see the group. I count eight guys, plus Sarah.

"I can see them now. Do you want to wait here or come with me? It might get ugly."

"I want to come," Sam says. I can tell he's scared, though I'm not sure if it's because of what he's seen me do or the football players ahead of us.

I walk the rest of the way as silently as I can, Sam tiptoeing behind me. When we are just a few feet away a twig snaps beneath Sam's foot.

"John?" Sarah asks. She's sitting on a large rock with her knees to her chest and her arms wrapped around them. She isn't wearing goggles and squints in our direction.

"Yes," I say. "And Sam."

She smiles. "Told you," she says, and I assume she's talking to Mark.

The water I heard is nothing more than a small babbling brook. Mark steps forward.

"Well, well, well," he says.

"Shut up, Mark," I say. "Manure in my locker was one thing, but you've gone way too far with this one."

"You think? It's eight on two."

"Sam has nothing to do with this. You scared to face me alone?" I ask. "What are you expecting to happen? You've tried kidnapping two people. Do you really think they'll keep silent?"

"Yeah, I do. When they see me whip your ass."

"You're delusional," I say, then turn to the others. "For those of you who don't want to go into the water, I suggest you leave now. Mark is going in no matter what. He's lost his chance to barter."

All of them snicker. One of them asks what "barter" means.

"Now's your last chance," I say.

Every one of them stands firm.

"So be it," I say.

A nervous excitement plants itself in the center of my chest. As I take one step forward Mark steps back and trips over his own feet, falling to the ground. Two of the guys come at me, both bigger than me. One swings but I duck his punch and send one of my own into his gut. He doubles over with his hands holding his stomach. I shove the second guy and his feet leave the ground. He lands with a thud five feet away and the momentum pushes him into the water. He comes up splashing. The others stand rooted, shocked. I sense Sam moving over toward Sarah. I grab hold of the first guy and drag him across the ground. His errant kicks slice through the air but hit nothing. When we are at the bank of the brook I lift him by the waistband of his jeans and throw him into the water. Another guy lunges at me. I merely sidestep him and he lands face-first in the brook. Three down, four to go. I wonder how much of this Sarah and Sam can see without goggles on.

"You guys are making it too easy for me," I say. "Who's next?"

The biggest of the group throws a punch that

comes nowhere near hitting me, though I counter so swiftly that his elbow catches me in the face and the goggle strap snaps. The goggles fall to the ground. I can only see slight shadows now. I throw a punch and hit the guy in the jaw and he falls to the ground like a sack of potatoes. He looks lifeless, and I fear that I've hit him too hard. I rip his goggles from his face and put them on.

"Any volunteers?"

Two of them hold their hands up in front of them in surrender; the third stands with his mouth gaping open like an idiot.

"That leaves you, Mark."

Mark turns as though he intends to run, but I lunge forward and grab him before he can, pulling his arms up into a full nelson. He writhes in pain.

"This ends right now, do you understand me?"

I squeeze tighter and he grunts in pain. "Whatever you have against me, you drop it now. That includes Sam and Sarah. You understand?"

My grip tightens. I fear that if I squeeze any tighter his shoulder will pop from its socket.

"I said, do you understand me?"

"Yes!"

I drag him over to Sarah. Sam is sitting on the rock beside her now.

"Apologize."

"Come on, man. You've proven your point."

I squeeze.

"I'm sorry!" he yells.

"Say it like you mean it."

He takes a deep breath. "I'm sorry," he says.

"You're an asshole, Mark!" Sarah says, and slaps him hard across the face. He tenses, but I'm holding him firmly and there isn't a thing he can do about it.

I drag him to the water. The rest of the guys stand watching in shock. The guy I had knocked out is sitting up scratching his head as though trying to figure out what has happened. I breathe a sigh of relief that he isn't badly hurt.

"You're not going to say a word to anybody about this, you understand me?" I say, my voice so low that only Mark can hear me. "Everything that has happened tonight, it dies here. I swear, if I hear one word about it in school next week this is nothing compared to what will happen to you. Do you understand me? Not a single word."

"Do you really think I would say anything?" he asks.

"You make sure you tell your friends the same. If they tell a single soul it will be *you* that I come for."

"We won't say anything," he says.

I let go, put my foot on his butt, and push him face-first into the water. Sarah is standing at the rock with Sam beside her. She hugs me tightly when I get to her.

"Do you know kung fu or something?" she asks.

I laugh nervously. "Could you see much?"

"Not a lot, but I could tell what was happening. I mean, have you been training in the mountains your whole life or what? I don't understand how you did that."

"I was just scared something would happen to you, I guess. And yeah, there was the past twelve years of martial arts training high in the Himalayas."

"You're amazing." Sarah laughs. "Let's get out of here."

None of the guys say a word to us. After ten feet I realize I have no idea where I'm going so I give the goggles to Sarah to lead the way.

"I can't friggin' believe that," Sarah says. "I mean, what an asshole. Wait till they try to explain it to the police. I'm not letting him get away with it."

"Are you really going to the police? Mark's dad is the sheriff, after all," I say.

"Why wouldn't I after that? It was bullshit. Mark's dad's job is to enforce law, even when his son breaks it."

I shrug in the darkness. "I think they received their punishment."

I bite my lip, terrified of the police getting involved. If they do I'll have to leave, no way around it. We'll be packed up and headed out of town within the hour of Henri knowing. I sigh.

"Don't you think?" I ask. "I mean, they've already lost several of the night-vision goggles. They'll have to explain that. And that's not to mention the icy cold water."

Sarah doesn't say anything. We walk in silence and I pray that she is debating the merits of letting it go.

Eventually the end of the woods comes into view. Light reaches in from the park. When I stop, Sarah and Sam both look at me. Sam has been silent the entire time and I'm hoping that it's because he couldn't really see what was happening, the dark for once serving as an unexpected ally, that maybe he's a little shaken up by everything.

"It's up to you guys," I say, "but I'm all for just letting the matter die. I really don't want to have to talk to police about what happened."

The light falls on Sarah's skeptical face. She shakes her head.

"I think he's right," Sam says. "I don't want to have to sit and write a stupid statement for the next half hour. I'll be in deep crap; my mom thinks I went to bed an hour ago."

"You live nearby?" I ask.

He nods. "Yeah, and I gotta go before she checks my room. I'll see you guys around."

Without another word, Sam hurries away. He's clearly rattled. He's probably never been in a fight and certainly never one where he was kidnapped and attacked in the woods. I'll try talking to him tomorrow. If he did see something he shouldn't have, I'll convince him his eyes were playing tricks on him.

Sarah turns my face to hers and traces the line of my cut with her thumb, moving it very gently across my forehead. Then she traces both my brows, staring into my eyes.

"Thank you for tonight. I knew you were going to come."

I shrug. "I wasn't going to let him scare you."

She smiles and I can see her eyes glistening in the moonlight. She moves towards me and as I realize what's about to happen my breath catches in my throat. She presses her lips to mine and everything inside of me turns to rubber. It's a soft kiss, lingering. My first. Then she pulls away and her eyes take me in. I don't know what to say. A million different thoughts run through my head. My legs feel wobbly and I'm barely able to stay upright.

"I knew you were special the first time I saw you," she says.

"I felt the same with you."

She reaches up and kisses me again, her hand lightly pressed to my cheek. For the first few seconds I'm lost in the feel of her lips on mine and in the idea that I'm with this beautiful girl.

She pulls away and both of us smile at each other, saying nothing, staring into each other's eyes.

"Well, I think we better go see if Emily is still here," Sarah says after about ten seconds. "Or else I'll be stranded."

"I'm sure she is," I say.

We hold hands on the walk to the pavilion. I can't stop thinking about our kisses. The fifth tractor chugs along the trail. The trailer is full and there's still a line ten or so people long waiting their turn. And after everything that happened in the woods, with Sarah's warm hand in mine, the smile doesn't leave my face.

CHAPTER FIFTEEN

THE FIRST SNOWFALL COMES TWO weeks later. A slight dusting, just enough to cover the truck with a fine powder. Since just after Halloween, once the Loric crystal spread the Lumen throughout my body, Henri has begun my real training. We've worked every day, without fail, through the cold weather and the rain and now the snow. Though he doesn't say it I believe he's impatient for me to be ready. It started with disconcerted looks, his brows crinkled while he chewed on his bottom lip, followed by deep sighs and eventually sleepless nights, the floorboards creaking under his feet while I lay awake in my room, to where we are now, an inherent desperation in Henri's strained voice.

We stand in the backyard, ten feet apart, facing each other.

"I'm not really in the mood today," I say.

"I know you're not, but we have to anyway."

I sigh and look at my watch. It's four o'clock.

"Sarah will be here at six," I say.

"I know," Henri says. "That's why we must hurry."

He holds a tennis ball in each hand.

"Are you ready?" he asks.

"As ready as I'll ever be."

He throws the first ball high in the air, and as it reaches its apex, I try to conjure a power deep within me to keep it from falling. I don't know how I'm supposed to do it, only that I should be *able* to do it, with time and practice, says Henri. Each Garde develops the ability to move objects with their mind. Telekinesis. And instead of letting me discover it on my own—as I did my hands—Henri seems hell-bent on waking the power from whatever cave it's hibernating in.

The ball drops just as the thousand or so balls before it did, without a single interruption, bouncing twice, then lying motionless in the snow-covered grass.

I let out a deep sigh. "I'm not feeling it today."

"Again," Henri says.

He throws the second ball. I try to move it, to stop it, everything inside of me straining to just make the damn thing move a single inch to the right or left, but no luck. It hits the ground as well. Bernie Kosar, who has been watching us, walks out to it, picks it up, and walks away.

"It'll come in its own time," I say.

Henri shakes his head. The muscles in his jaw are flexed. His moods and impatience are getting to me. He watches Bernie Kosar trot off with the ball, then he sighs.

"What?" I ask.

He shakes his head again. "Let's keep trying."

He walks over and picks up the other ball. Then he flings it high in the air. I try to stop it but of course it just falls.

"Maybe tomorrow," I say.

Henri nods and looks at the ground. "Maybe tomorrow."

I am covered in sweat and mud and melted snow after our workout. Henri pushed me harder than normal today and came at me with an aggression that could only be steeped in panic. Beyond the telekinesis practice, most of our session was spent drilling technique in fighting—hand-to-hand combat, wrestling, mixed martial arts—followed by elements of composure—grace under pressure, mind control, how to spot fear in the eyes of an opponent and then know how best to expose it. It wasn't Henri's hard training that got to me, but rather the look in his eyes. A distressed look, tinged with fear, despair, disappointment. I don't know if he's just concerned about progress, or if it's something deeper, but these sessions are becoming very exhausting—emotionally and physically.

Sarah arrives right on time. I walk outside and kiss her as she's coming up to the front porch. I take her coat from her and hang it when we're inside. Our home-ec midterm is a week away, and it was her idea to cook the meal before we'll have to prepare it in class. As soon as we begin cooking Henri grabs his jacket and goes for a walk. He takes Bernie Kosar with him and I'm thankful for the privacy. We make baked chicken breasts and potatoes and steamed vegetables, and the meal comes out far better than I had hoped. When all is ready the three of us sit and eat together. Henri is silent through most of it. Sarah and I break the awkward silence with small talk, about school, about our going to the movies the following Saturday. Henri rarely looks up from his plate other than to offer how wonderful the meal is.

When dinner is over Sarah and I wash the dishes and retreat to the couch. Sarah brought a movie over and we watch it on our small TV, but Henri mostly stares out the window. Halfway through he gets up with a sigh and walks outside. Sarah and I watch him go. We hold hands and she leans against me with her head on my shoulder. Bernie Kosar sits beside her with his head in her lap, a blanket draped over both of them. It may be cold and blustery outside, but it's warm and cozy in our living room.

"Is your dad okay?" Sarah asks.

"I don't know. He's been acting weird."

"He was really quiet during dinner."

"Yeah, I'm going to go check on him. I'll be right back," I say, and follow Henri outside. He's standing on the porch—looking out into the darkness.

"So what's going on?" I ask.

He looks up at the stars in contemplation.

"Something doesn't feel right," he says.

"What do you mean?"

"You're not going to like it."

"Okay. Let's have it."

"I don't know how much longer we should stay here. It doesn't feel safe to me."

My heart sinks and I stay silent.

"They're frantic, and I think they're getting close. I can feel it. I don't think we're safe here."

"I don't want to leave."

"I knew you wouldn't."

"We've kept hidden."

Henri looks at me with a raised brow. "No offense, John, but I hardly think you've stayed in the shadows."

"I have where it counts."

He nods. "I guess we'll see."

He walks to the edge of the porch and places his hands on the rail. I stand beside him. New snowflakes start falling, sifting down, specks of white shimmering on an otherwise dark night.

"That's not all," Henri says.

"I didn't think it was."

He sighs. "You should have already developed telekinesis. It almost always comes with your first Legacy. Very rarely does it come after, and when it does, it's never longer than a week later."

I look over at him. His eyes are full of concern, and creases of worry traverse the length of his forehead.

"Your Legacies come from Lorien. They always have."

"So what are you telling me?"

"I don't know how much we can expect from here on out," he says, and pauses. "Since we're no longer on the planet, I don't know if the rest of your Legacies will come at all. And if that is true, we have no hope of fighting the Mogadorians, much less defeating them. And if we can't defeat them, we'll never be able to go back."

I watch the snowfall, unable to decide whether I should be worried or relieved, relieved since perhaps that would bring an end to our moving and we could finally settle. Henri points at the stars.

"Right there," he says. "Right there is where Lorien is."

Of course I know full well where Lorien is without having to be told. There is a certain pull, a certain way that my eyes always gravitate towards the spot where, billions of miles away, Lorien sits. I try to catch a snowflake on the tip of my tongue, then close my eyes and breathe in the cold air. When I open them I turn around and look at Sarah through the window. She's sitting with her legs beneath her, Bernie Kosar's head still in her lap.

"Have you ever thought of just settling here, of saying to hell with Lorien and making a life here on Earth?" I ask Henri.

"We left when you were pretty young. I don't imagine you remember much of it, do you?"

"Not really," I say. "Bits and pieces come to me from time to time. Though I can't necessarily say whether they are things I remember or things I've seen during our training."

"I don't think you would feel that way if you could remember."

"But I don't remember. Isn't that the point?"

"Maybe," he says. "But whether or not you want to go back doesn't mean the Mogadorians are going to stop searching for you. And if we get careless and settle, you can be assured they'll find us. And as soon as they do, they'll kill us both. There's no way to change that. No way."

I know he's right. Somehow, like Henri, I can sense that much, can feel it in the dead of night when the hairs on my arms stand at attention, when a slight shiver crawls up my spine even though I'm not cold.

"Do you ever regret sticking with me for this long?"

"Regret it? Why do you think I would regret it?"

"Because there's nothing for us to go back to. Your family is dead. So is mine. On Lorien there is only a life of rebuilding. If it wasn't for me you could easily create an identity here and spend the rest of your days becoming a part of someplace. You could have friends, maybe even fall in love again."

Henri laughs. "I'm already in love. And I'll continue to be until the day that I die. I don't expect you to understand that. Lorien is different from Earth."

I sigh with exasperation. "But still, you could be a part of somewhere."

"I am a part of somewhere. I'm a part of Paradise, Ohio, right now, with you."

I shake my head. "You know what I mean, Henri."

"What is it that you think I'm missing?"

"A life."

"You are my life, kiddo. You and my memories are my only ties to the past. Without you I have nothing. That's the truth."

Just then the door opens behind us. Bernie Kosar comes trotting out ahead of Sarah, who is standing in the doorway half in and half out.

"Are you two really going to make me watch this movie all by my lonesome?" she asks.

Henri smiles at her. "Wouldn't dream of it," he says.

After the movie Henri and I drive Sarah home. When we get there I walk her to her front door and we stand on the stoop smiling at each other. I kiss her good night, a lingering kiss while holding both her hands gently in mine.

"See you tomorrow," she says, giving my hands a squeeze.

"Sweet dreams."

I walk back to the truck. Henri pulls out of Sarah's driveway and steers towards home. I can't help feeling a sense of fear while remembering Henri's words the day he picked me up from my first full day of school: "Just keep in mind we might have to leave at a moment's notice." He's right, and I know it, but I've never felt this way about anyone before. Like I'm floating on air when we're together, and I dread the times when we're apart, like now, despite having just spent the last couple of hours with her. Sarah gives some purpose to our running, and hiding, a reason that transcends mere survival. A reason to win. And to know that I may be putting her life in danger by being with her—well, it terrifies me.

When we get back, Henri walks into his bedroom and comes out carrying the Chest. He drops it on the kitchen table.

"Really?" I ask.

He nods. "There's something in here I've wanted to show you for years."

I can't wait to see what else is in the chest. We pop the lock together and he lifts the lid in such a way that I can't peer in. Henri removes a velvet bag, closes the Chest, and relocks it.

"These aren't part of your Legacy, but the last time we opened the Chest I slipped them in because of the bad feeling I've been having. If the Mogadorians catch us, they'll never be able to open this," he says, and motions to the Chest.

"So what's in the bag?"

"The solar system," he says.

"If they aren't part of my Legacy then why have you never shown me?"

"Because you needed to develop a Legacy in order to activate them."

He clears the kitchen table and then sits across

from me with the bag in his lap. He smiles at me, sensing my enthusiasm. Then he reaches down and removes seven glass orbs of varying sizes from the bag. He holds them up to his face in his cupped hands and blows on the glass orbs. Tiny flickers of light come from within them, then he tosses them up in the air and all at once they come to life, suspended above the kitchen table. The glass balls are a replica of our solar system. The largest of them is the size of an orange—Lorien's sun—and it hangs in the middle emitting the same amount of light as a lightbulb while looking like a self-contained sphere of lava. The other balls orbit around it. Those closest to the sun move at a faster rate, while those farthest away seem to only creep by. All of them spinning, days beginning and ending at hyperspeed. The fourth globe from the sun is Lorien. We watch it move, watch the surface of it begin to form. It is about the size of a racquetball. The replica must not be to scale because in reality Lorien is far smaller than our sun.

"So what's happening?" I ask.

"The ball is taking on the exact form of what Lorien looks like at this moment."

"How is this even possible?"

"It's a special place, John. An old magic exists at its very core. That's where your Legacies come from. It's what gives life and reality to the objects contained within your Inheritance."

"But you just said that this isn't part of my Legacy."

"No, but they come from the same place."

Indentations form, mountains grow, deep creases cut across the surface where I know rivers once ran. And then it stops. I look for any sort of color, any movement, any wind that might blow across the land. But there is nothing. The entire landscape is a monochromatic patch of gray and black. I don't know what I had hoped to see, what I had expected. Movement of some kind, a hint of fertileness. My spirits fall. Then the surface dims away so that we can see through it and at the very core of the globe a slight glow begins to form. It glows, then dims, then glows again as though replicating the heartbeat of a sleeping animal.

"What is that?" I ask.

"The planet still lives and breathes. It has withdrawn deep into itself, biding its time. Hibernating, if you will. But it will wake one of these days."

"What makes you so sure?"

"That little glow right there," he says. "That is hope, John."

I watch it. I find an odd pleasure in seeing it glow. They tried to wipe away our civilization, the planet itself, and yet it still breathes. *Yes*, I think, *there is always hope, just as Henri has said all along.*

"That isn't all."

Henri stands and snaps his fingers and the planets stop moving. He moves his face to within inches of Lorien, then cups his hands around his mouth and again breathes onto it. Hints of green and blue sweep across the ball and begin to fade almost immediately as the mist from Henri's breath evaporates.

"What did you do?"

"Flash your hands on it," he says.

I make them glow and when I hold them over the ball the green and blue come back, only this time they stay as my hands shine upon it.

"It's how Lorien looked the day before the invasion. Would you look how beautiful it all is? Sometimes even I forget."

It *is* beautiful. Everything green and blue, plush and verdant. The vegetation seems to waver beneath gusts of wind that I can somehow feel. Slight ripples appear on the water. The planet is truly *alive*, flourishing. But then I turn my glow back off and it all fades away, back to shades of gray.

Henri points at a spot on the globe's surface.

"Right here," he says, "is where we took off from on the day of the invasion." Then he moves his finger half an inch from the spot. "And right here is where the Loric Museum of Exploration used to be."

I nod and look at the spot he is pointing to. More gray.

"What do museums have to do with anything?" I ask. I sit back in the chair. It's hard to look at this without feeling sad.

He looks back at me. "I've been thinking a lot about what you saw."

"Uh-huh," I say, urging him on.

"It was a huge museum, devoted entirely to the evolution of space travel. One of the wings of the building held early rockets that were thousands of years old. Rockets that used to run on a kind of fuel known only to Lorien," he says, and stops, looking back to the small glass orb hanging two feet above our kitchen table. "Now, if what you saw did in fact happen, if a second ship managed to take off and escape from Lorien during the height of the war, then it would have to have been housed at the space museum. There's no other explanation for it. I'm still having a tough time believing that it would have worked, and even if it did, that it would have gotten very far."

"So if it wouldn't have gotten very far, then why are you still thinking about it?"

Henri shakes his head. "You know, I'm not really sure. Maybe because I've been wrong before. Maybe because I'm hoping I am wrong now. And, well, if it *had* made it anywhere, then it would have made it here, the closest life-sustaining planet aside from Mogadore. And that's to assume that there was life on it in the first place, that it wasn't just full of artifacts, or that it wasn't just empty, meant to confuse the Mogadorians. But I think there had to have been at least one Loric manning the ship because, well, as I'm sure you know, ships of that nature couldn't steer themselves."

Another night of insomnia. I stand shirtless in front of the mirror, staring into it with both lights in my hands turned on. "I don't know how much we can expect from here on out," Henri said today. The light at Lorien's core still burns, and the objects we brought from there still work, so why would that magic have ended there? And what about the others: are they now running into the same problems? Are they without their Legacies?

I flex in front of the mirror, then punch the air, hoping that the mirror will break, or a thud will be heard on the door. But there is nothing. Just me looking like an idiot standing shirtless, shadowboxing with myself while Bernie Kosar watches from the bed. It's nearly midnight and I'm not tired in the least. Bernie Kosar jumps off the bed, sits beside me, and watches my reflection. I smile at him and he wags his tail.

"How about you?" I ask Bernie Kosar. "Do you have any special powers? Are you a superdog? Should I put your cape back on so you can go flying through the air?"

His tail keeps wagging and he paws the ground while looking at me through the tops of his eyes. I lift him up and over my head and fly him around the room.

"Look! It's Bernie Kosar, the magnificent superdog!"

He squirms under my grip, so I set him down. He plops on his side with his tail thumping against the mattress.

"Well, buddy, one of us should have superpowers. And it doesn't look like it's going to be me. Unless we go back to the Dark Ages and I can supply the world with light. Otherwise, I'm afraid I'm useless."

Bernie Kosar rolls onto his back and stares at me with big eyes, wanting me to rub his belly.

CHAPTER
SIXTEEN

SAM IS AVOIDING ME. AT SCHOOL HE
seems to disappear when he sees me, or always
makes sure we're in a group. At the urging of
Henri—who's desperate to get his hands on Sam's
magazine after combing through everything that
came up on the internet and finding nothing like
Sam's magazine—I decide to just go over to his
place unannounced. Henri drops me off after
we've trained for the day. Sam lives on the out-
skirts of Paradise in a small, modest house. There's
no answer when I knock so I try the door. It's
unlocked and I open it and walk through.

Brown shag carpet covers the floors, and family
photographs from when Sam was very young hang
on wood-paneled walls. Him, his mother, and a
man who I assume is his father, who is wearing
glasses every bit as thick as Sam's. Then I look
closer. They look like the exact same pair of glasses.

I creep down the hallway until I find the door that must be to Sam's bedroom; a sign reading ENTER AT YOUR OWN RISK hangs from a tack. The door is open a crack and I peer inside. The room is very clean, everything consciously put in a place. His twin bed is made, has a black comforter with the planet Saturn repeated across it. Matching pillowcases. The walls are covered with posters. There are two NASA ones, the movie poster from *Alien*, a movie poster from *Star Wars*, and one that is a blacklight poster of a green alien head surrounded by dark felt. In the center of the room, hanging from clear thread, is the solar system, all nine planets and the sun. It makes me think of what Henri showed me earlier in the week. I think that Sam would lose his mind if he were to see the same thing. And then I see Sam, hunched over a small oak desk, with headphones on. I push the door open and he looks over his shoulder. He isn't wearing his glasses, and without them his eyes look very small and beady, almost cartoonlike.

"What's up?" I ask casually, as if I'm at his house every day.

He looks shocked and scared and he frantically pulls the headphones off to reach in one of the drawers. I look at his desk and see that he's reading a copy of *They Walk Among Us*. When I look back up he is pointing a gun at me.

"Whoa," I say, instinctively lifting my hands in front of me. "What's going on?"

He stands up. His hands are shaking. The gun is pointed at my chest. I think that he's lost his mind.

"Tell me what you are," he says.

"What are you talking about?"

"I saw what you did in those woods. You're not human." I was afraid of this, that he saw more than I had hoped.

"This is crazy, Sam! I got into a fight. I've been doing martial arts for years."

"Your hands lit up like flashlights. You could throw people around like they were nothing. That's not normal."

"Don't be stupid," I say, my hands still in front of me. "Look at them. Do you see any lights? I told you, they were gloves that Kevin was wearing."

"I asked Kevin! He said he wasn't wearing gloves!"

"Do you really think he would tell you the truth after what happened? Put the gun down."

"Tell me! What are you?"

I roll my eyes. "Yes, I'm an alien, Sam. I'm from a planet hundreds of millions of miles away. I have superpowers. Is that what you want to hear?"

He stares at me, his hands still shaking.

"Do you realize how stupid that sounds? Quit being crazy and put the gun down."

"Is what you just said true?"

"That you're being stupid? Yes, it's true. You're too obsessed with this stuff. You see aliens and alien conspiracies in every part of your life, including in your only friend. Now quit pointing that damn gun at me."

He stares at me, and I can tell he's thinking about what I said. I drop my hands. Then he sighs and lowers the gun. "I'm sorry," he says.

I take a deep, nervous breath. "You should be. What the hell were you thinking?"

"It wasn't actually loaded."

"You should have told me that earlier," I say. "Why do you want so badly to believe in this stuff?"

He shakes his head and puts the gun back in the drawer. I take a minute to calm myself down and try to act casual, like what just happened is no big deal.

"What are you reading?" I ask.

He shrugs. "Just more alien stuff. Maybe I should cool it a bit."

"Or just read it as fiction instead of fact," I say. "The stuff must be pretty convincing, though. Can I see it?"

He hands me the latest copy of *They Walk Among Us* and I sit tentatively on the edge of his bed. I think he's calmed down enough to not spring a gun on me again at least. Again, it is a bad photocopy, the print slightly unaligned with the paper. It isn't very thick—eight pages, twelve at the most, printed on legal-sized sheets. The date at the top reads DECEMBER. It must be the newest issue.

"This is weird stuff, Sam Goode," I say.

He smiles. "Weird people like weird stuff."

"Where do you get this?" I ask.

"I subscribe to it."

"I know, but how?"

Sam shrugs. "I don't know. It just started arriving one day."

"Are you subscribed to some other magazine? Perhaps they pulled your contact info from there."

"I went to a convention once. I think I signed up for some contest or something while I was there. I can't remember. I've always assumed that's where they got my address."

I scan the cover. There's no website listed anywhere on it, and I didn't expect there to be, considering that Henri has already searched the internet high and low. I read the headline of the top story:

IS YOUR NEIGHBOR AN ALIEN?
TEN FAILSAFE WAYS TO TELL!

In the middle of the article there's a picture of a man holding a bag of trash in one hand and the lid to the trash can in the other. He is standing at the end of the driveway and we're to assume he's in the process of dropping the bag into the can. Though the whole publication is in black-and-white, there is a certain glow to the man's eyes. It's a horrible image—as though somebody took a picture of an unsuspecting neighbor and then drew around his eyes with a crayon. It makes me laugh.

"What?" Sam asks.

"This is a terrible picture. It looks like something from *Godzilla*."

Sam looks at it. Then he shrugs. "I dunno," he says. "It could be real. Like you said, I see aliens everywhere, and in everything."

"But I thought aliens looked like that," I say, and nod to the blacklight poster on his wall.

"I don't think all of them do," he says. "Like you said, you're an alien with superpowers and you don't look like that."

We both laugh, and I wonder how I'm going to get myself out of that one. Hopefully Sam never finds out I was telling him the truth. Part of me wants to tell him, though—about me, about Henri, about Lorien—and I wonder what his reaction would be. Would he believe me?

I flip the paper open to look for the publishing page that all newspapers and magazines have. There isn't one here, only more stories and theories.

"There isn't a publisher info page."

"What do you mean?"

"You know how magazines and newspapers always have that page listing staff, editors, writers, where it's being printed, and all that? You know, 'For questions, contact so and so.' All publications have them, but this doesn't."

"They have to protect their anonymity," Sam says.

"From what?"

"Aliens," he says, and smiles, as though acknowledging the absurdity of it.

"Do you have last month's issue?"

He grabs it from his closet. I quickly flip through it, hoping that the Mogadorian article is in this one and not an earlier month. And then I find it on page 4.

THE MOGADORIAN RACE SEEK TO TAKE OVER EARTH

The Mogadorian alien race, from the planet Mogadore of the 9th Galaxy, have been on Earth for over ten years now. They are a vicious race on a quest for universal domination. They are rumored to have wiped out another planet not unlike Earth, and are planning to expose Earth's weaknesses in a quest to inhabit our planet next.

(more to follow next issue)

I read the article three times. I was hoping there might be more to it than what Sam already said, but no such luck. And there is no Ninth Galaxy. I wonder where they got that from. I flip through the new issue twice. There is no mention of the Mogadorians. My first thought is that there was nothing left to report, that more news failed to present itself. But I don't believe that's the case. My second thought is that the Mogadorians read the issue and then fixed the problem, whatever the problem was.

"Do you mind if I borrow this?" I ask, holding up last month's issue.

He nods. "But be careful with it."

Three hours later, at eight o'clock, Sam's mother still isn't home. I ask Sam where she is and he shrugs as though he doesn't know and her absence is nothing new. Mostly we just play video games and watch TV and for dinner we eat microwavable meals. The whole time I'm there he doesn't once wear his glasses, which is odd since I've never seen him without them before. Even when we ran the mile in gym class, he kept them on. I grab them from the top of his dresser and put them on. The world becomes an instant blur and they give me a headache almost immediately.

I look at Sam. He's sitting cross-legged on the

floor, his back against his bed, with a book of aliens in his lap.

"Jesus, is your vision really this bad?" I ask.

He looks up at me. "They were my dad's."

I take them off.

"Do you even need glasses, Sam?"

He shrugs. "Not really."

"So why do you wear them?"

"They were my dad's."

I put them back on. "Wow, I don't see how you can even walk straight with these on."

"My eyes are used to them."

"You know these will screw up your vision if you continue wearing them, right?"

"Then I'll be able to see what my dad saw."

I take them off and put them back where I found them. I don't really understand why Sam wears them. For sentimental reasons? Does he really think it's worth it?

"Where is your dad, Sam?"

He looks up at me.

"I don't know," he says.

"What do you mean?"

"He disappeared when I was seven."

"You don't know where he went?"

He sighs, drops his head, and resumes reading. Obviously he doesn't want to talk about it.

"Do you believe in any of this stuff?" he asks after a few minutes of silence.

"Aliens?"

"Yeah."

"Yes, I believe in aliens."

"Do you think they really abduct people?"

"I have no idea. I guess we can't rule it out. Do you believe they do?"

He nods. "Most days. But sometimes the idea just seems stupid."

"I can understand that."

He looks up at me. "I think my dad was abducted," he says.

He tenses the second the words leave his mouth and a look of vulnerability crosses his face. It makes me believe that he has shared his theory before, with someone whose response was less than kind.

"Why do you think that?"

"Because he just disappeared. He went to the store to buy milk and bread, and he never came back. His truck was parked right outside the store but nobody there had seen him. He just vanished, and his glasses were on the sidewalk beside his truck." He pauses for a second. "I was worried you were here to abduct me."

It's a hard theory to believe. How could nobody have seen his father abducted if the incident occurred in the middle of town? Perhaps his dad had reason to leave and he plotted his own disappearance. It's not hard to make yourself disappear; Henri and I have been doing it for ten years now. But all of a sudden Sam's interest in aliens makes perfect sense. Perhaps Sam just wants to see the world as his dad did, but maybe part of him truly believes that his dad's final sight is captured in the glasses, somehow etched into the lenses. Maybe he thinks that with persistence one day he'll eventually come to see it as well, and that his dad's last vision will confirm what is already in his head. Or maybe he believes that if he searches long enough he'll finally come across an article that proves his father was abducted, and not only that, but that he can be saved.

And who am I to say that he won't one day find that proof?

"I believe you," I say. "I think alien abductions are very possible."

CHAPTER SEVENTEEN

THE NEXT DAY I WAKE EARLIER THAN normal, crawl out of bed, and walk out of my room to find Henri sitting at the table scanning the papers with his laptop open. The sun is still hidden, and the house is dark, the only light coming from his computer screen.

"Anything?"

"Nah, nothing really."

I turn on the kitchen light. Bernie Kosar paws at the front door. I open it and he shoots out into the yard and patrols as he does every morning, head up, trotting around the perimeter looking for anything suspicious. He sniffs at random places. Once satisfied that everything is as it should be, he bolts into the woods and disappears.

Two issues of *They Walk Among Us* are lying atop the kitchen table, the original and a photocopy that Henri has made to keep for himself. A magnifying glass lies between them.

"Anything unique on the original?"

"No."

"So, now what?" I ask.

"Well, I have had some luck. I cross-referenced some of the other articles in the issue and got a few hits, one of which led me to a man's personal website. I sent him an email."

I stare at Henri.

"Don't worry," he says. "They can't track emails. At least not the way I send them."

"How do you send them?"

"I reroute them through various servers in cities across the world, so that the original location is lost along the way."

"Impressive."

Bernie Kosar scratches at the door and I let him in. The clock on the microwave reads 5:59. I have two hours before I have to be at school.

"Do you really think we want to go digging around in all this?" I ask. "I mean, what if it's all a trap? What if they are simply trying to root us out of hiding?"

Henri nods. "You know, if the article had mentioned anything about us, that might have given me pause. But it didn't. It was about their invading Earth, much the same way they did Lorien. There is so much about it that we don't understand. You were right a few weeks ago when you said we were defeated so easily. We were. It doesn't make sense. The entire situation with the disappearance of the Elders also doesn't make sense. Even getting you and the other children off of Lorien, which I have never questioned, seems odd. And while you've seen what happened—and I've had the same visions, too—something is still missing from the equation. If we one day make it back, I think it's imperative to understand what happened in order to prevent it from happening again. You know the saying: he who doesn't understand history is doomed to repeat it. And when it's repeated, the stakes are doubled."

"Okay," I say. "But according to what you said Saturday night, the chance of us going back seems slimmer every day. So, with that, do you think it's worth it?"

Henri shrugs. "There are still five others out there. Perhaps they've received their Legacies. Perhaps yours are merely delayed. I think it's best to plan for all possibilities."

"Well, what are you planning to do?"

"Just make a phone call. I'm curious to hear what this person knows. I wonder what caused him to not follow up. One of two possibilities: either he found no other information and lost interest in the story, or somebody got to him after the publication."

I sigh. "Well, be careful," I say.

I pull on a pair of sweatpants and a sweatshirt over two T-shirts, tie my tennis shoes and stand and stretch. I toss into my backpack the clothes I plan to wear to school, along with a towel, a bar of soap and a small bottle of shampoo so I can shower when I get there. I'll now be running to school each morning. Henri ostensibly believes the additional exercise will help in my training, but the real reason is that he hopes it will help my body's transition and pull my Legacies from their slumber, if that is indeed what they are doing.

I look down at Bernie Kosar. "Ready for a run, boy? Huh? Want to go for a run?"

His tail wags and he turns in circles.

"See you after school."

"Have a good run," says Henri. "Be careful on the road."

We walk out the door and cold, brisk air meets us. Bernie Kosar barks excitedly a few times. I start at a slight jog, down the drive, out onto the gravel road, the dog trotting beside me as I thought he would. It takes a quarter mile to warm up.

"Ready to step it up a notch, boy?"

He pays me no attention, just keeps trotting along with his tongue dangling, looking happy as can be.

"All right then, here we go."

I kick it into high gear, moving into a run, and then into a dead sprint shortly after, going as fast as I can. I leave Bernie Kosar in the dust. I look behind me and he is running as fast as he can, yet I am pulling ahead of him. The wind through my hair, the trees passing in a blur. It all feels great. Then Bernie Kosar bolts into the woods and disappears from sight. I'm not sure if I should stop and wait for him. Then I turn around and Bernie Kosar jumps out of the woods ten feet in front of me.

I look down at him and he looks up at me, tongue to the side, a sense of glee in his eyes.

"You're an odd dog, you know that?"

After five minutes the school comes into view. I sprint the remaining half mile, exerting myself, running as hard as I can because it is so early that there is no one out and about to see me. Then I stand with my fingers interlocked behind my head, catching my breath. Bernie Kosar arrives thirty seconds later and sits watching me. I kneel down and pet him.

"Good job, buddy. I think we have a new morning ritual."

I pull my bag from over my shoulders, unzip it, and remove a package with a few strips of bacon and I give them to him. He scarfs them down.

"Okay, boy, I'm heading in. Go on home. Henri's waiting."

He watches me for a second, and then goes off trotting towards home. His comprehension completely amazes me. Then I turn and walk into the building and head for the shower.

I am the second person to enter astronomy. Sam is the first, already sitting in his normal seat at the back of the class.

"Whoa," I say. "No glasses. What gives?"

He shrugs. "I thought about what you said. It's probably stupid for me to wear them."

I sit beside him and smile. It's hard to imagine I'll ever get used to his eyes looking so beady. I give him back the issue of *They Walk Among Us*. He tucks it into his bag. I hold up my fingers like a gun and nudge him.

"Bang!" I say.

He starts laughing. Then I do, too. Neither of us can stop. Every time one of us is close the other starts laughing and it begins all over again. People stare at us when they enter. Then comes Sarah. She walks in by herself, saunters up to us with a look of confusion and sits in the seat beside me.

"What are you guys laughing at?"

"I'm not really sure," I say, and then laugh a little more.

Mark is the last person to walk in. He sits in his usual seat, but instead of Sarah sitting beside him today there's another girl. I think she's a senior. Sarah reaches beneath the table and grabs hold of my hand.

"There is something I need to talk to you about," she says.

"What?"

"I know it's last-minute, but my parents want to have you and your dad over for Thanksgiving dinner tomorrow."

"Wow. That would be awesome. I have to ask, but I know we don't have plans, so I assume the answer is yes."

She smiles. "Great."

"Since it's just the two of us, we don't usually even do Thanksgiving."

"Well, we really go all out. And my brothers will both be home from college. They want to meet you."

"How do they know about me?"

"How do you think?"

The teacher walks in and Sarah winks, then we both start taking notes.

Henri is waiting for me as usual, Bernie Kosar propped up on the passenger seat with his tail wagging, thumping the side of the door the second he sees me. I slide in.

"Athens," says Henri.

"Athens?"

"Athens, Ohio."

"Why?"

"That's where the issues of *They Walk Among Us* are being written, and printed. It's where they are being mailed."

"How did you find that out?"

"I have my ways."

I look at him.

"Okay, okay. It took three emails and five phone calls, but now I have the number." He looks over at me. "That is to say, it wasn't all that hard to find with a little effort."

I nod. I know what he is telling me. The Mogadorians would have found it just as easily as he did. Which means, of course, that the scale now tips in favor of Henri's second possibility— that somebody got to the publisher before the story further developed.

"How far away is Athens?"

"Two hours by car."

"Are you going?"

"I hope not. I'm going to call first."

When we get home Henri immediately picks up the phone and sits at the kitchen table. I sit down across from him and listen.

"Yes, I'm calling to inquire about an article in last month's issue of *They Walk Among Us*."

A deep voice responds on the other end. I can't hear what is said.

Henri smiles. "Yes," he says, then pauses.

"No, I'm not a subscriber. But a friend of mine is."

Another pause. "No, thank you."

He nods his head.

"Well, I'm curious about the article written on the Mogadorians. There was never a follow-up in this month's issue as expected."

I lean in and strain to hear, my body tense and rigid. When the reply comes the voice sounds shaken, disturbed. Then the phone goes dead.

"Hello?"

Henri pulls the phone away from his ear, looks at it, then brings it back in.

"Hello?" he says again.

Then he closes the phone and sets it on the table. He looks at me.

"He said, 'Don't call here again.' Then he hung up on me."

CHAPTER

EIGHTEEN

AFTER DEBATING IT FOR SEVERAL hours, Henri wakes up the next morning and prints door-to-door directions from here to Athens, Ohio. He tells me he'll be home early enough so we can go to Thanksgiving dinner at Sarah's house, and he hands me a slip of paper with the address and the phone number of where he's going.

"Are you sure this is worth it?" I ask.

"We have to figure out what's going on."

I sigh. "I think we both know what is going on."

"Maybe," he says, but with full authority and none of the uncertainty usually accompanying the word.

"You do realize what you would tell me if the roles were reversed, right?"

Henri smiles. "Yes, John. I know what I

would say. But I think this will help us. I want to find out what they have done to scare this man so badly. I want to know if they have mentioned us, if they are searching for us by means that we haven't yet thought of. It will help us to stay hidden, stay ahead of them. And if this man has seen them, we'll learn what they look like."

"We already know what they look like."

"We knew what they looked like when they attacked, over ten years ago, but they might have changed. They've been on Earth a long time now. I want to know how they're blending in."

"Even if we know what they look like, by the time we see them on the street, it's probably going to be too late."

"Maybe, maybe not. I see one, I'm going to try and kill it. There's no guarantee it's going to be able to kill me," he says, this time with the uncertainty and none of the authority.

I give up. I don't like a single thing about him driving to Athens while I sit around at home. But I know my objections will continue to fall on deaf ears.

"You sure you'll be back on time?" I ask.

"I'm leaving now, which puts me there about nine. I doubt I'll stay more than an hour, two at the most. I should be back by one."

"So why do I have this?" I ask, and hold up the

slip of paper with the address and phone number.

He shrugs. "Well, you never know."

"Which is precisely why I don't think you should go."

"Touché," he says, bringing an end to the discussion. He gathers his papers, stands from the table, and pushes in the chair.

"I'll see you this afternoon."

"Okay," I say.

He walks out to the truck and gets inside. Bernie Kosar and I walk out to the front porch and watch him drive away. I don't know why, but I have a bad feeling. I hope he makes it back.

It's a long day. One of those days where time slows down and every minute seems like ten, every hour seems like twenty. I play video games and surf the internet. I look for news that might be related to one of the other children. I don't find anything, which makes me happy. That means we're staying under the radar. Avoiding our enemies.

I periodically check my phone. I send a text message to Henri at noon. He doesn't reply. I eat lunch and feed Bernie, and then I send another. No reply. A nervous, unsettled feeling creeps in. Henri has never failed to text back immediately. Maybe his phone is off. Maybe his battery has died. I try to convince myself of these possibilities, but I know that neither of them is true.

At two o'clock I start to get worried. Really worried. We're supposed to be at the Harts' in an hour. Henri knows the dinner is important to me. And he would never blow it off. I get in the shower with the hope that by the time I get out, Henri will be sitting at our kitchen table drinking a cup of coffee. I turn the hot water all the way up and don't bother with the cold at all. I don't feel a thing. My entire body is now impervious to heat. It feels like lukewarm water is streaming over my skin, and I actually miss the feeling of heat. I used to love taking hot showers. Standing under the water for as long as it lasted. Closing my eyes and enjoying the water hitting my head and running down. It took me away from my life. It let me forget about who and what I am for a little while.

When I get out of the shower, I open my closet and look for the nicest clothes I have, which are nothing special: khakis, a button-down shirt, a sweater. Because we live our life on the run, all I have are running shoes, which is so ridiculous it makes me laugh—the first time I've laughed all day. I go to Henri's room and look in his closet. He has a pair of loafers that fit me. Seeing all his clothes makes me more worried, more upset. I want to believe he's just taking longer than he should, but he would have contacted me. Something has to be wrong.

I walk to the front door, where Bernie is sitting, staring out the window. He looks up at me and whines. I pat him on the head and go back to my room. I look at the clock. It's just after three. I check my phone. No messages, no texts. I decide to go to Sarah's and if I don't hear from Henri by five, I'll figure out a plan then. Maybe I'll tell them Henri is sick and that I'm not feeling well either. Maybe I'll tell them Henri's truck broke down and I need to go help him. Hopefully he shows up and we can just have a nice Thanksgiving dinner. It will actually be the first one we've ever had. If not, I'll tell them something. I'll have to.

Without the truck I decide I'll run. I probably won't even break a sweat, and I will be able to get there faster than I would in the truck. And because of the holiday, the roads should be empty. I say good-bye to Bernie, tell him I'll be home later, and take off. I run on the edges of the fields, through woods. It feels good to burn some energy. It takes the edge off my anxiety. A couple times I get up near full speed, which is probably somewhere around sixty or seventy miles per hour. The cold air feels amazing whipping across my face. The sound of it is great, the same sound I hear when I stick my head out the window of the truck as we're driving down a highway. I wonder how fast I'll be able to run when I'm twenty, or twenty-five.

I stop running about a hundred yards from Sarah's house. I'm not short of breath at all. As I walk up the driveway I see Sarah peek out the window. She smiles and waves, opening the front door just as I step onto her porch.

"Hey, handsome," she says.

I turn and look over my shoulder to pretend she's talking to somebody else. Then I turn back around and ask her if she's talking to me. She laughs.

"You're silly," she says, and punches me in the arm before pulling me close to give me a lingering kiss. I take a deep breath and can smell the food: turkey and stuffing, sweet potatoes, brussels sprouts, pumpkin pie.

"Smells great," I say.

"My mom has been cooking all day."

"Can't wait to eat."

"Where is your dad?"

"He got held up. He should be here in a little while."

"Is he okay?"

"Yeah, it's not a big deal."

We go inside and she takes me on a tour. It's a great house. A classic family home with bedrooms on the second floor, an attic where one of her brothers has his room, and all of the living spaces—the living room, dining room, kitchen and family room—on the first floor. When we get to her room, she closes the door and kisses me. I'm surprised, but thrilled.

"I've been looking forward to doing that all day," she says softly when she pulls away. As she walks towards the door, I pull her back to me and kiss her again.

"And I'm looking forward to kissing you again later," I whisper. She smiles and punches me on the arm again.

We head back downstairs and she takes me to the family room, where her two older brothers, home from college for the weekend, are watching football with her father. I sit with them, while Sarah goes to the kitchen to help her mother and her younger sister with dinner. I've never been that into football. I guess, because of the way Henri and I have lived, I've never really gotten into anything outside of our life. My concerns were always with trying to fit into wherever we were, and then getting ready to go somewhere else. Her brothers, and her father, all played football in high school. They love it. And in today's game, one of her brothers and her father like one of the teams, while her other brother likes the other team. They argue with each other, taunt each other, cheer and groan depending on what's happening in the game. They've clearly been doing this for years, probably for their entire lives, and they're clearly having a great time. It makes me wish Henri and I had something, besides my training and our endless running and hiding, that we were both into and that we could enjoy with each other. It makes me wish I had a real father and brothers to hang out with.

At halftime Sarah's mother calls us in for dinner. I check my phone and still nothing. Before we sit down I go to the bathroom and try to call Henri and it goes straight to voice mail. It's almost five o'clock, and I'm starting to panic. I come back to the table, where everyone is sitting. The table looks amazing. There are flowers in the center, with place mats and table settings meticulously placed in front of each of the chairs. Serving dishes of food are spread around the inside of the table, with the turkey sitting in front of Mr. Hart's place. Just after I sit down, Mrs. Hart comes into the room. She has taken off her apron and is wearing a beautiful skirt and sweater.

"Have you heard from your dad?" she says.

"I just tried calling him. He, uh, is running late and asked us not to wait. He's very sorry for the inconvenience," I say.

Mr. Hart starts carving the turkey. Sarah smiles at me from across the table, which makes me feel better for about half a second. The food starts being passed, and I take small portions of everything. I don't think I'm going to be able to eat very much. I keep my phone out and on my lap, and have it set to vibrate if a call or text comes through. With each passing second, however, I don't believe anything is going to come through, or that I will ever see Henri again. The idea of living by myself—with my Legacies developing, and without anyone to explain them to me or train me, of running on my own, of hiding on my own, of finding my own way, of fighting the Mogadorians, fighting them until they are defeated or I am dead—terrifies me.

Dinner takes forever. Time is moving slowly again. Sarah's whole family peppers me with questions. I've never been in a situation where I've been asked so many things by so many people in such a short period of time. They ask about my past, the places I've lived, about Henri, about my mother—who, I say as I always do, died when I was very young. It's the only answer I give that has even the smallest sliver of truth. I have no idea if my answers even make sense. The phone on my leg feels like it weighs a thousand pounds. It doesn't vibrate. It just sits there.

After dinner, and before dessert, Sarah asks everyone to go out to the backyard so she can take some pictures. As we go outside, Sarah asks if something is wrong. I tell her I'm worried about Henri. She tries to calm me down and tell me everything is fine, but it doesn't work. If anything, it makes me feel worse. I try to imagine where he is and what he's doing, and the only image I can bring is him standing before a Mogadorian, looking terrified, and knowing he's about to die.

As we gather for the pictures, I start to panic. How could I get to Athens? I could run, but it might be hard to find my way, especially because I would have to avoid traffic and stay off the major highways. I could take a bus, but it would take too long. I could ask Sarah, but that would involve a huge amount of explaining, including telling her I was an alien and that I believed Henri had been either captured or killed by hostile aliens who were searching for me so that they could kill me. Not the best idea.

As we pose I get a desperate urge to leave, but I need to do it in a way that doesn't make Sarah or her family mad at me. I focus on the camera, staring directly into it while trying to think of an excuse that will get the least amount of questions. I'm wracked with full-on panic now. My hands begin to shake. They feel hot. I look down at them to make sure they aren't glowing. They're not, but when I look back up I see that the whole camera is shaking in Sarah's hands. I know that somehow I'm doing it, but I have no idea how or what I can do to make it stop. A chill shoots up my back. My breath catches in my throat and at the same time the glass lens of the camera cracks and shatters. Sarah screams, then pulls the camera down and stares at it in confusion. Her mouth drops open and tears well up in her eyes.

Her parents rush over to her to see if she's okay. I just stand there in shock. I'm not sure what to do. I'm bummed about her camera, and that she's upset about it, but I'm also thrilled because my telekinesis has clearly arrived. Will I be able to control it? Henri will be beside himself when he finds out. Henri. The panic returns. I clench my hands into fists. I need to get out of here. I need to find him. If the Mogadorians have him, which I hope they don't, I'll kill every damn one of them to get him back.

Thinking quickly, I walk over to Sarah and pull her away from her parents, who are examining the camera to figure out what has just happened.

"I just got a message from Henri. I'm really sorry, but I need to go."

She's clearly distracted, glancing from me to her parents.

"Is he all right?"

"Yes, but I have to go—he needs me." She nods and we kiss gently. I hope it's not for the last time.

I thank her parents and her brothers and sister and I leave before they can ask me too many questions. I walk through the house and as soon as I'm out the front door, I start running. I take the same route home that I took to get to Sarah's house earlier. I stay off the main roads, run through the trees. I'm back in a few minutes. I hear Bernie Kosar scratching at the door as I sprint up the drive. He's clearly anxious, as though he also senses something amiss.

I go straight to my room. I retrieve from my bag the piece of paper containing the phone number and address Henri gave me before leaving. I dial the number. A recording comes on. "I'm sorry, the number you are trying to reach has been disconnected or is no longer in service." I look down at the piece of paper and try the number again. The same recording.

"Shit!" I yell. I kick a chair and it sails across the kitchen and into the living room.

I walk into my room. I walk out. I walk back in again. I stare in the mirror. My eyes are red; tears have surfaced but none are falling. Hands shaking. Anger and rage and a terrible fear that Henri is dead consume me. I squeeze my eyes shut and squeeze all the rage into the pit of my stomach. In a sudden burst I scream and open my eyes and thrust my hands towards the mirror and the glass shatters though I am ten feet away. I stand looking at it. Most of the mirror is still attached to the wall. What happened at Sarah's was no fluke.

I look at the shards on the floor. I reach a hand out in front of me and while concentrating on one particular shard, I try to move it. My breathing is controlled, but all the fear and anger remain within me. Fear is too simple a word. Terror. That is what I feel.

The shard doesn't move at first, but then after fifteen seconds it begins to shake. Slowly at first, then rapidly. And then I remember. Henri said that it's usually emotions that trigger Legacies. Surely that is what is happening now. I strain to lift the shard. Beads of sweat stand out on my forehead. I concentrate with everything that I have and everything that I am despite all that is going on. It's a struggle to breathe. Ever so slowly the shard begins to rise. One inch. Two inches. It is a foot above the floor, continuing up, my right arm extended and moving with it until the shard of glass is at eye level. I hold it there. *If only Henri could see this,* I think. And in a flash, through the excitement of my newly discovered happiness, panic and fear return. I look at the shard, at the way it reflects the wood-paneled wall looking old and brittle in the glass. Wood. Old and brittle. And then my eyes snap open wider than they ever have before in all of my life.

The Chest!

Henri had said it: "Only the two of us can open it together. Unless I die; then you can open it yourself."

I drop the shard and sprint from my bedroom into Henri's. The Chest is on the floor beside his bed. I snatch it, run into the kitchen, and throw it on the table. The lock in the shape of the Loric emblem is looking me in the face.

I sit at the table and stare at the lock. My lip is quivering. I try to slow my breathing but it is useless; my chest is heaving as though I just finished a ten-mile sprint. I'm scared of feeling a click beneath my grip. I take a deep breath and close my eyes.

"Please don't open," I say.

I grab hold of the lock. I squeeze as tightly as I can, my breath held, vision blurry, the muscles in my forearm flexed and straining. Waiting for the click. Holding the lock and waiting for the click.

Only there is no click.

I let go and slouch in the chair and hold my head in my hands. A small glimmer of hope. I run my hands through my hair and stand. On the counter five feet away is a dirty spoon. I focus on it and sweep my hand across my body and the spoon goes flying. Henri would be so happy. *Henri,* I think, *where are you? Somewhere, and still alive, too. And I'm going to come get you.*

I dial Sam's number, the only friend besides Sarah I've made in Paradise, the only friend I've ever had, if I'm to be honest. He answers on the second ring.

"Hello?"

I close my eyes and pinch the bridge of my nose. I take a deep breath. The shaking has returned, if it ever left in the first place.

"Hello?" he says again.

"Sam."

"Hey," he says, then, "You sound like hell. Are you okay?"

"No. I need your help."

"Huh? What's happened?"

"Is there any way your mom can bring you over?"

"She's not here. She's working a shift at the hospital because she gets paid double time on holidays. What's going on?"

"Things are bad, Sam. And I need help."

Another silence, then, "I'll get there as quickly as I can."

"You sure?"

"I'll see you soon."

I close my phone and drop my head to the table. Athens, Ohio. That is where Henri is. Somehow, some way, that is where I have to go.

And I need to get there fast.

CHAPTER NINETEEN

WHILE I WAIT FOR SAM I WALK through the house lifting inanimate objects up in the air without touching them: an apple from the kitchen counter, a fork in the sink, a small potted plant sitting beside the front window. I can only lift the small things, and they rise in the air somewhat timidly. When I try for something heavier—a chair, a table—nothing happens.

The three tennis balls Henri and I use for training sit in a basket on the other side of the living room. I bring one of them to me, and as it crosses his line of sight Bernie Kosar stands at attention. Then I throw it without touching it and he sprints after it; but before he can get to it, I pull it back, or when he does manage to get it, I pull it from his mouth, all while sitting in the chair in the living room. It keeps my mind from Henri, from the harm that may have found him, and from the guilt of the lies I'll have to tell Sam.

It takes him twenty-five minutes to ride his bike the four miles to my house. I hear him ride up the drive. He jumps off of it and it crashes to the ground while he runs through the front door without knocking, out of breath. His face is streaked with sweat. He looks around and surveys the scene.

"So what's up?" he asks.

"This is going to sound absurd to you," I say. "But you have to promise to take me seriously."

"What are you talking about?"

What am I talking about? I'm talking about Henri. He has disappeared because of carelessness, the same carelessness he has always preached against. I'm talking about the fact that when you had that gun on me, I told you the truth. I am an alien. Henri and I came to Earth ten years ago, and we are being hunted by a malicious race of aliens. I'm talking about Henri thinking that he could somehow evade them by understanding them a little more. And now he is gone. That is what I'm talking about, Sam. Do you understand? But no, I can't tell him any of these things.

"My dad's been captured, Sam. I'm not entirely sure by who, or what is being done to him. But something has happened, and I think he's being held prisoner. Or worse."

A grin spreads on his face. "Get out of here," he says.

I shake my head and close my eyes. The gravity of the situation again makes it difficult to breathe. I turn and stare pleadingly at Sam. Tears well up in my eyes.

"I'm not kidding."

Sam's face becomes stricken. "What do you mean? Who has captured him? Where is he?"

"He tracked the writer of one of the articles in your magazine back to Athens, Ohio, and he went there today. He went there and he hasn't come back. His phone is off. Something has happened to him. Something bad."

Sam becomes more confused. "What? Why would he care? I'm missing something. It's just some stupid paper."

"I don't know, Sam. He's like you—he loves aliens and conspiracy theories and all that stuff," I say, thinking quickly. "It's always been a stupid hobby of his. One of the articles piqued his interest and I guess he wanted to know more, so he drove down."

"Was it the article on the Mogadorians?"

I nod. "How did you know?"

"Because he looked like he had seen a ghost when I mentioned it on Halloween," he says, and he shakes his head. "But why would somebody care if he asked questions about a stupid article?"

"I don't know. I mean, I would imagine these people aren't the sanest in the world. They're probably paranoid and delusional. Maybe they thought he was an alien, the same reason you aimed a gun at me. He was supposed to be home by one and his phone is off. That's all I can say."

I stand and walk to the kitchen table. I grab the slip of paper with the address and phone number of where Henri has gone.

"This is where he went today," I say. "Do you have any idea where it is?"

He looks at the slip, then at me.

"You want to go there?"

"I don't know what else to do."

"Why can't you just call the cops and tell them what happened?"

I sit down on the couch, thinking of the best way to respond. I wish I could tell him the truth, that the best-case scenario with the cops getting involved would be Henri and I leaving. The worst case would be Henri being questioned, maybe fingerprinted, thrust into the sluggish-paced bureaucracy, which would give the Mogadorians the chance to move. And once they find us, death is imminent.

"Call which cops? The ones in Paradise? What do you think they would do if I told them the truth? It would take days for them to take me seriously, and I don't have days."

Sam shrugs. "They might take you seriously. Besides, what if he just got held up, or his phone broke? He might be on his way home now."

"Maybe, but I don't think so. Something feels off, and I have to get there as soon as possible. He was supposed to be home hours ago."

"Maybe he got into an accident."

I shake my head. "Maybe you're right, but I don't think you are. And if he's being harmed, then we're wasting time."

Sam looks at the sheet of paper. He bites his lip and remains silent for fifteen seconds.

"Well, I know vaguely how to get to Athens. No idea how to get to this address once we're there, though."

"I can print directions from the internet. I'm not worried about that. The thing I am worried about is transportation. I have a hundred and twenty dollars in my room. I can pay someone to drive us, but I have no idea who I would ask. There aren't exactly a whole lot of taxis in Paradise, Ohio."

"We can take our truck."

"What truck?"

"I mean my dad's truck. We still have it. It's sitting in the garage. It hasn't been touched since he disappeared."

I look at him. "Are you serious?"

He nods.

"How long has it been? Does it even still run?"

"Eight years. Why wouldn't it still run? It was nearly new when he bought it."

"Wait, let me get this right. You're suggesting we drive there ourselves, me and you, two hours to Athens?"

Sam's face twists into a devious smile. "That's exactly what I'm suggesting."

I lean forward on the sofa. I can't help but smile as well.

"You know we'll be in deep shit if we get caught, right? Neither of us has our license."

Sam nods. "My mom will kill me, and she'll maybe kill you, too. And then there is the law. But yeah, if you really think your dad is in trouble, what other choice do we have? If the roles were reversed, and it was my dad who was in trouble, I would go in a second."

I look at Sam. There isn't an ounce of hesitation on his face in his suggesting that we drive illegally to a town two hours away, and that's not to mention that neither of us knows how to drive and that we have no idea what to expect once getting there. And yet Sam is on board. It was his idea even.

"All right then, let's drive to Athens," I say.

I throw my phone in my bag, make sure everything is zipped and in order. Then I walk through the house, taking everything in as though it will be the last time I see any of it. It's foolish thinking, and I know I'm merely being sentimental, but I'm nervous and there is a sort of calming sensation to it. I pick things up, then I set them down. After five minutes I am ready.

"Let's go," I say to Sam.

"You want to ride on the back of my bike?"

"You ride; I'll jog alongside."

"What about your asthma?"

"I think I'll be okay."

We leave. He gets on his bike. He tries to ride as fast as he can, but he is not in great shape. I jog a few feet behind and pretend that I'm winded. Bernie follows us as well. By the time we get to his house, Sam is dripping with sweat. Sam runs into his room and comes out with a backpack. He sets it on the kitchen counter and goes to change his clothes. I peer inside of it. There is a crucifix, a few cloves of garlic, a wooden stake, a hammer, a blob of Silly Putty, and a pocketknife.

"You do realize these people aren't vampires, right?" I say when Sam walks back in.

"Yeah, but you never know. They're probably crazy, like you said."

"And even if we were hunting vampires, what the hell is the Silly Putty for?"

He shrugs. "Just want to be prepared."

I pour a bowl of water for Bernie Kosar and he

laps it all up immediately. I change clothes in the bathroom and remove the door-to-door directions from my bag. Then I walk out and through the house and into the garage, which is dark and smells of gasoline and old grass clippings. Sam flips on the light. Various tools have rusted with disuse and hang on the Peg-Board walls. The truck sits in the center of the garage, covered with a large blue tarp that's coated with a thick layer of dust.

"How long has it been since this tarp was removed?"

"Not since Dad went missing."

I grab one corner, Sam takes the other, and together we peel it away and I set it in the corner. Sam stares at the truck, his eyes big, a smile on his face.

The truck is small, dark blue, room inside for only two people, or maybe a third if they don't mind an uncomfortable ride sitting in the center. It will be perfect for Bernie Kosar. None of the dust from the past eight years has made it onto the truck, so it sparkles as though it was recently waxed. I throw my bag into the bed.

"My dad's truck," Sam says proudly. "All these years. It looks exactly the same."

"Our golden chariot," I say. "Do you have the keys?"

He walks to the side of the garage and lifts a set of keys from a hook on the wall. I unlock the garage door and open it.

"Do you want to paper-rock-scissors to see who drives?" I ask.

"Nope," Sam says, and then he unlocks the driver's side door and gets in behind the wheel. The engine cranks over and finally starts. He rolls down the window.

"I think my dad would be proud to see me driving it," he says.

I smile. "I think so, too. Pull it out and I'll close the door."

He takes a deep breath, and then puts the truck in drive and slowly, timidly, inches it out of the garage. He hits the brakes too hard too soon and the truck slams to a stop.

"You aren't all the way out yet," I say.

He eases his foot off the brake and then inches the rest of the way out. I close the garage door behind him. Bernie Kosar jumps up and in of his own volition and I slide in beside him. Sam's hands are white knuckled at the ten and two positions of the wheel.

"Nervous?" I ask.

"Terrified."

"You'll be fine," I say. "We've both seen it done a thousand times before."

He nods. "Okay. Which way do I turn out of the driveway?"

"We really going to do this?"

"Yes," he says.

"We turn right, then," I say, "and head in the direction away from town."

We both buckle our seat beats. I crack the window enough so that Bernie Kosar can fit his head out, which he does immediately, standing with his hind legs in my lap.

"I'm scared shitless," Sam says.

"Me too."

He takes a deep breath, holds the air in his lungs, and then slowly exhales.

"And . . . away . . . we . . . go," he says, taking his foot off the brake when he says the last word. The truck goes bouncing down the driveway. He hits the brakes once and we skid to a stop. Then he starts again and inches down the drive more slowly this time until he stops at the end of it, looks both ways, and then turns out onto the road. Again, slow at first, then gaining speed. He is tense, leaning forward, and then after a mile a grin begins to form on his face and he leans back.

"This isn't so hard."

"You're a natural."

He keeps the truck close to the painted line on the right side of the road. He tenses every time a car passes in the opposite direction, but after a while he relaxes and pays the other cars little attention. He makes one turn, then another, and

in twenty-five minutes we pull onto the interstate.

"I can't believe we're doing this," Sam finally
says. "This is the craziest shit I've ever done."

"Me too."

"Do you have any plan when we get there?"

"None whatsoever. I'm hoping we'll be able to
scope the place out and go from there. I have no
idea if it's a house or an office building or what.
I don't even know if he is there."

He nods. "Do you think he's okay?"

"I have no idea," I say.

I take a deep breath. We have an hour and a
half to go. Then we'll reach Athens.

Then we'll find Henri.

CHAPTER TWENTY

WE DRIVE SOUTH UNTIL, NESTLED IN the foothills of the Appalachian Mountains, Athens comes into view: a small city sprouting through the trees. In the waning light I can see a river curling gently around that seems to cup the city, serving as the border to the east, south and west, and to the north lie hills and trees. The temperature is relatively warm for November. We pass the college football stadium. A white-domed arena stands a little beyond it.

"Take this exit," I say.

Sam guides the truck off the interstate and turns right onto Richland Avenue. Both of us are elated we made it in one piece, and without being caught.

"So this is what a college town looks like, huh?"

"I guess so," Sam says.

Buildings and dorms are on each side of us. The grass is green, meticulously trimmed even though it is November. We drive up a steep hill.

"At the top of this is Court Street. We want to turn left."

"How far are we?" Sam asks.

"Less than a mile."

"Do you want to drive by it first?"

"No. I think we should park the first opportunity we get and walk."

We drive down Court Street, which is the main artery in the center of town. Everything is closed for the holiday—bookstores, coffeehouses, bars. Then I see it, standing out like a jewel.

"Stop!" I say.

Sam slams on the brakes.

"What?!"

A car honks behind us.

"Nothing, nothing. Keep driving. Let's park."

We drive another block until we find a lot to park in. By my guess we are a five-minute walk at most from the address.

"What was that? You scared the crap out of me."

"Henri's truck is back there," I say.

Sam nods. "Why do you sometimes call him Henri?"

"I don't know, I just do. Sort of a joke between

us," I say, and look at Bernie Kosar. "Do you think we should take him?"

Sam shrugs. "He might get in the way."

I give Bernie Kosar a few treats and leave him in the truck with the window cracked. He is not happy about it and begins whining and scratching at the window, but I don't think we'll be long. Sam and I walk back up Court Street, the straps of my bag pulled over my shoulders, Sam holding his in his hand. He has removed the Silly Putty and is squeezing it like people do with those foam balls when they're stressed. We reach Henri's truck. The doors are locked. There is nothing of importance on the seats or dash.

"Well, this means two things," I say. "Henri is still here, and whoever has him hasn't discovered his truck yet, which means he hasn't talked. Not that he ever would."

"What would he say if he talked?"

For a brief moment I had forgotten that Sam knows nothing of Henri's true reasons for being here. I've already slipped and called him Henri. I need to be careful not to reveal anything else.

"I don't know," I say. "I mean, who knows what sorts of questions these weirdos are asking."

"Okay, now what?"

I pull out the map to the address Henri had given me that morning. "We walk," I say.

We walk back the way we came. The buildings

end and houses begin. Unkempt and dirty looking. In no time at all we reach the address and
stop.

I look at the slip of paper, then at the house. I
take a deep breath.

"This is us," I say.

We stand looking up at the two-story house
with gray vinyl siding. The front walk leads to an
unpainted front porch with a broken swing
hanging unevenly to the side. The grass is long
and untended. It looks uninhabited, but there is
a car in the driveway at the rear. I don't know
what to do. I remove my phone. It is 11:12. I call
Henri even though I know he won't answer. It's
an attempt to establish my wits, to come up with
a plan. I hadn't thought this far ahead, and now
that the reality is here my mind is blank. My call
goes straight to voice mail.

"Let me go knock on the door," Sam says.

"And say what?"

"I don't know, whatever comes to my mind."

But he doesn't get a chance to because just
then a man walks out of the front door. He is
huge, at least six feet six, two hundred fifty
pounds. He has a goatee and his head is shaved.
He's wearing work boots, blue jeans, and a black
sweatshirt pulled up to his elbows. There is a tattoo on his right forearm, but I am too far away to
see what it is. He spits into the yard, then turns

around and locks the front door, walking off the porch and heading our way. I stiffen as he approaches. The tattoo is of an alien holding a bouquet of tulips in one hand as though offering them to some unseen entity. Then the man walks right past us without saying a word. Sam and I turn and watch him go.

"Did you see his tattoo?" I ask.

"Yeah. And so much for the stereotype of scrawny nerds being the only ones fascinated by aliens. That man is huge, and mean looking."

"Take my phone, Sam."

"What? Why?" he asks.

"You have to follow him. Take my phone. I'll go into the house. It's obvious there is nobody there or he wouldn't have locked the door. Henri might be in there. I'll call you as soon as I can."

"How are you going to call me?"

"I don't know. I'll find a way. Here." He reluctantly takes it.

"What if Henri isn't in there?"

"That's why I want you to follow that guy. He might be going to Henri now."

"What if he comes back?"

"We'll figure it out. But you have to go now. I promise, I'll call you the first chance I get."

Sam turns and looks at the man. He is fifty yards away from us now. Then he looks back at me.

"Okay, I'll do it. But be careful in there."

"You be careful, too. Don't let him out of your sight. And don't let him see you."

"Not a chance."

He turns and hurries after the man. I watch them go and, once they vanish from sight, I walk up to the house. The windows are dark, each one covered with a white shade. I can't see in. I walk around to the back. There is a small concrete patio leading to a back door, which is locked. I walk the rest of the way around the house. Overgrown weeds and bushes left over from summer. I try a window. Locked. All of them are locked. Should I break one? I look for rocks among the brambles, and the second I see one and lift it from the ground with my mind an idea occurs to me, an idea so crazy that it just might work.

I drop the rock and walk to the back door. It has a simple lock, no deadbolt. I take a deep breath, close my eyes in concentration, and grab hold of the doorknob. I give it a shake. My thoughts move from head to heart to stomach; everything is centered there. My grip tightens, my breath is held in anticipation as I try to envision the inner workings. Then I feel and hear a click in the hand holding the knob. A smile forms on my face. I turn the knob and the door swings open. I can't believe I can unlock doors by imagining what is inside of them.

The kitchen is surprisingly clean, the surfaces wiped down, the sink free of dirty dishes. A new loaf of bread sits on the counter. I walk through a narrow corridor into a living room with sports posters and banners on the walls, a big-screen TV sitting in a corner. The door to a bedroom is off to the left side. I poke my head in. It's in a state of disarray, covers thrown aside on the bed, clutter atop the dresser. The foul stench of dirty laundry covered in sweat that has never dried.

At the front of the house, beside the door, a flight of stairs ascends to the second level. I begin walking up them. The third step groans under my foot.

"Hello?" a voice yells from the top of the stairs.

I freeze, holding my breath.

"Frank, is that you?"

I stay silent. I hear somebody stand from a chair, the creak of footsteps on a hardwood floor approaching. A man appears at the top of the stairs. Dark shaggy hair, sideburns, an unshaven face. Not as big as the man who left earlier, but not exactly small either.

"Who the hell are you?" he asks.

"I'm looking for a friend of mine," I say.

He screws his face up into a scowl, vanishes

and reappears five seconds later holding a wooden baseball bat in his hand.

"How did you get in here?" he asks.

"I would put the bat down if I were you."

"How did you get in here?"

"I am faster than you are and I am far stronger."

"Like hell you are."

"I'm looking for a friend of mine. He came here this morning. I want to know where he is."

"You're one of them, aren't you?"

"I don't know who you are talking about."

"You're one of them!" he screams. He holds the bat as a baseball player would, both white-knuckled hands at the thin base poised to swing. There is genuine fear in his eyes. His jaw is tightly clenched. "You're one of them! Why don't you just leave us alone already!?"

"I am not one of them. I've come for my friend. Tell me where he is."

"Your friend is one of them!"

"No he isn't."

"So you know who I'm talking about?"

"Yes."

He takes a step down.

"I'm warning you," I say. "Drop the bat and tell me where he is."

My hands are shaking from the uncertainty of the situation, from the fact that he has a bat in his hands while I have nothing but my own abilities. I'm unnerved by the fear in his eyes. He takes another step down. There are only six stairs between us.

"I'm going to take your head off. That'll send your friends a message."

"They aren't my friends. And I assure you, you'd be doing them a favor if you hurt me."

"Let's see then," he says.

He comes racing down the stairs. There is nothing I can do but react. He swings the bat. I duck and it hits the wall with a thud, leaving a large splintered hole in the wood panel. I come up after him and lift him in the air, one hand gripping his throat, the other in his armpit, carrying him back up the stairs. He flails, landing kicks to my legs and groin. The bat drops from his hands. It bounces hollowly down the stairs and I hear one of the windows break behind me.

The second floor is a wide-open loft. It is dark. The walls are covered with issues of *They Walk Among Us*, and where the issues end, alien paraphernalia takes up the rest—but unlike Sam's, the posters are actual photographs taken over the years, blown up and grainy so that it is hard to make them out, mostly white blips on black backdrops. A rubber alien dummy with a noose around its neck sits in the corner. Somebody has added a Mexican sombrero to its head. Glow-in-the-dark stars are stuck to the ceiling. They seem out of place, more like something belonging in a ten-year-old girl's room.

I throw the man to the ground. He scoots away from me and stands up. When he does I put all my power into the pit of my stomach and direct it towards him with a hard forward-thrusting motion, and he goes flying backwards and crashes into the wall.

"Where is he?" I ask.

"I'll never tell you. He's one of you."

"I'm not who you think I am."

"You guys will never succeed! Just leave Earth alone!"

I lift my hand and choke him. I can feel the flexed tendons beneath my hand even though I am not touching him. He can't breathe and his face turns red. I let go.

"I'll ask again."

"No."

I choke him once more, but this time when his face turns red I squeeze tighter. When I let go he begins to cry and I feel bad for him, for what I've done to him. But he knows where Henri is, has done something to him, and my sympathy ends almost as soon as it began.

After he catches his breath, and between sobs, he says, "He's downstairs."

"Where? I didn't see him."

"In the basement. The door is behind the Steelers banner in the living room."

I dial my phone number from the telephone atop the middle desk. Sam doesn't answer. Then I pull the phone from the wall and break it in half.

"Give me your cell phone," I say.

"I don't have one."

I walk to the dummy and remove the noose from around its neck.

"Come on, man," he pleads.

"Shut up. You've kidnapped my friend. You're holding him against his will. You're lucky all I'm doing is tying you up."

I pull his arms behind him and tie the rope tightly around them, then tie him to one of the chairs. I don't think that it will hold him for very long. Then I duct-tape his mouth shut so that he can't yell and I sweep down the stairs and rip the Steelers banner from the wall, revealing a black door that is locked. I unlock it as I did the other. A set of wooden stairs leads down to total darkness.

The smell of mildew reaches my nose. I flip the light switch on and begin walking down, slowly, terrified at what I might find. The rafters are littered with cobwebs. I reach the bottom and immediately feel the presence of somebody else, somebody there with me. I stiffen, take a deep breath, and then turn.

There, in the corner of the basement, sits Henri.

"Henri!"

He is squinting from the light, his eyes adjusting. A length of duct tape is across his mouth. His hands are bound behind him, his ankles tied to the legs of the chair in which he is sitting. His hair is tousled, and down the right side of his face is a line of dried blood that looks almost black. The sight of it fills me with rage.

I rush over to him and rip the piece of tape from his mouth. He takes a deep breath.

"Thank God," he says. His voice is weak. "You were right, John. It was foolish to come here. I'm sorry. I should have listened."

"Shh," I say.

I bend down and begin untying his ankles. He smells like urine.

"I was ambushed."

"How many are there?" I ask.

"Three."

"I've tied one of them up upstairs," I say.

I free his ankles. He stretches his legs out and sighs with relief.

"I've been in this damn chair all day."

I begin working his hands free.

"How in the hell did you get here?" he asks.

"Sam and I came together. We drove down."

"You're kidding me?"

"I had no other way."

"What did you drive?"

"His father's old truck."

Henri is silent a minute while he ponders what that means.

"He doesn't know anything," I say. "I told him aliens are a hobby of yours, nothing more."

He nods. "Well, I'm happy you made it. Where is he now?"

"Trailing one of them. I don't know where they went."

The creak of a floorboard comes from above us. I stand, Henri's hands only halfway untied.

"Did you hear that?" I whisper.

We both watch the door with our breaths held. A foot steps onto the top stair, and then a second, and all at once the large man I passed earlier, the one Sam was trailing, comes into view.

"The party's over, fellas," he says. He is holding a gun aimed at my face. "Now, step away."

I hold my hands up in front of me and take a step back. I think of using my powers to pull the gun away, but what if I somehow cause it to fire by accident? I'm not confident in my abilities just yet. It's too risky.

"They told us you might be coming. That you

would look like humans. That you were the real enemy," the man says.

"What are you talking about?" I ask.

"They're delusional," Henri says. "They think we're the enemy."

"Shut up!" the man screams.

He takes three steps towards me. Then he moves the gun from me and fixes it straight on Henri.

"One false move by you and he gets it. You understand?"

"Yes," I say.

"Now, catch this," he says. He pulls down a roll of duct tape from the shelf beside him and throws it towards me. As it moves through the air, I stop it, suspended about eight feet off the ground, halfway between us. I start spinning it very quickly. The man stares at it, confused.

"What the . . ."

While he's distracted, I move my arm towards him with a throwing motion. The roll of tape flies back and slams him in the nose. Blood starts gushing, and as he reaches for it he drops the gun, which hits the ground and goes off. I point my hand towards the bullet and I make it stop, and behind me I hear Henri laugh. I move the bullet so that it hangs in front of the man's face.

"Hey, fat boy," I say.

He opens his eyes and sees the bullet in the air

in front of his face.

"You're gonna need to bring more."

I let the bullet fall to the ground at his feet. He turns to run, but I bring him back across the room and slam him against a large support pole. It knocks him out and he slumps to the floor. I grab the tape and tie him to the pole. After I'm sure he's secured, I turn to Henri and finish freeing him.

"John, I think that's the best surprise I've ever seen in my entire life," he says in a whisper, such relief in his voice that I think tears might come next.

I smile proudly. "Thanks. It showed at dinner."

"Sorry I missed it."

"I told them you were tied up."

He smiles.

"Thank God the Legacy came," he says, and I realize that the stress of my Legacies forming—or the fear of them not forming—took a far greater toll on Henri than I imagined.

"So what happened to you?" I ask.

"I knocked on the door. All three of them were home. When I walked in one of them clubbed me in the back of the head. Then I woke up in this chair." He shakes his head and says a long string of words in Loric that I know are curses. I finish untying him and he stands and stretches his legs.

"We need to get out of here," he says.
"We have to find Sam."
And then we hear him.
"John. You down there?"

CHAPTER TWENTY-ONE

EVERYTHING SLOWS. I SEE A SECOND person at the top of the stairs. Sam yelps in surprise and I turn to him, silence filling my ears with the discordant hum that comes with slow motion. The man behind him gives him a hard shove that causes his feet to leave the ground, and, when he hits, it will be at the bottom of the stairs, where the concrete floor awaits. I watch him sail through the air, flailing his arms with a look of terror on his anguished face. Without giving it a single thought, my instinct takes over and I lift my hands at the very last second and catch him, his head a mere two inches above the basement floor. I set him down gently.

"Shit," Henri says.

Sam sits up and crawls backwards like a crab until he reaches the cinder-block wall. His eyes are wide-open, staring at the steps, his mouth moving but no words coming out. The figure who pushed him stands at the top of the stairs trying to figure out, like Sam, what just happened. It must be the third one.

"Sam, I tried to—" I say.

The man at the top of the stairs turns and tries to sprint away but I force him down two of the stairs. Sam looks at the man being held by an unseen force, then looks at my one arm extended towards him. He is shocked and speechless.

I grab the duct tape and lift the man in the air and carry him up to the second floor, keeping him suspended the entire way. He yells obscenities while I tape him into a chair, but I hear none of them because my mind is racing to figure out what we will say to Sam about what just happened.

"Shut up," I say.

He unloads another string of cuss words. I decide I've had enough so I tape his mouth shut and walk back to the basement. Henri is standing near Sam, who is still sitting there, with the same blank stare on his face.

"I don't get it," he says. "What just happened?"

Henri and I look at each other. I shrug.

"Tell me what's happening," Sam says, his voice pleading with us, tinged with desperation to know the truth, to know that he's not crazy and that he didn't imagine what he just saw.

Henri sighs and shakes his head. Then he says, "What the hell's the point?"

"The point in what?" I ask.

He ignores me, and instead turns to Sam. He purses his lips together, looks at the man slumped in the chair to make sure he is still out and then at Sam. "We aren't who you think we are," he says, and pauses. Sam stays silent, staring at Henri. I can't read his face, and I have no idea what Henri is about to tell him—if he will again make up some elaborate story or, for once, tell him the truth—and it's this latter that I'm truly hoping for. He looks at me and I nod my head in agreement.

"We came to Earth ten years ago from a planet named Lorien. We came because it was destroyed by the inhabitants of another planet named Mogadore. They destroyed Lorien for its resources because they had turned their own planet into a cesspool of decay. We came here to hide until we could return to Lorien, which we will one day do. But we were followed by the Mogadorians. They are here hunting us. And I believe they are here to take over Earth, and that is why I came here today, to find out a little more."

Sam says nothing. Had it been me who told him as much, I'm sure that he wouldn't believe me, that he might become angry, but it is Henri who has told him, and there is a certain integrity within Henri that I have always felt, and I have no doubt that Sam feels it also. He looks over at me.

"I was right: you're an alien. You weren't joking when you admitted it," Sam says to me.

"Yes, you were right."

He looks back at Henri. "And those stories you told me on Halloween?"

"No. Those were just that," Henri says. "Ridiculous stories that made me smile when I stumbled across them on the internet, nothing more. But what I told you now is the honest truth."

"Well . . . ," Sam says, and trails off, grasping for words. "What happened just now?"

Henri nods to me. "John is in the process of developing certain powers. Telekinesis is one of them. When you were pushed, John saved you."

Sam still smiles beside me, watching me. When I look at him he nods his head.

"I knew you were different," he says.

"Needless to say," Henri says to Sam, "you're going to have to be quiet about this." Then he looks over at me. "We need information and we need to get out of here. They're probably nearby."

"The guys upstairs might still be conscious."

"Let's go talk to them."

Henri walks over and picks the gun up from the floor and pulls the clip. It's full. He removes all the bullets and sets them on a nearby shelf, then snaps the clip back in and tucks the gun in the waistband of his jeans. I help Sam to his feet and we all go upstairs to the second floor. The man I brought up with my telekinesis is still struggling. The other one is sitting still. Henri walks over to him.

"You were warned," Henri says.

The man nods.

"Now you're going to talk," Henri says, and he pulls the tape from the man's mouth. "And if you don't . . ." He pulls the slide back on the gun and aims it at the man's chest. "Who visited you?"

"There were three of them," he says.

"Well, there are three of us. Who cares? Keep talking."

"They told me if you showed up and I said anything, they'd kill me," the man says. "I won't tell you anything more."

Henri presses the barrel of the gun against the man's forehead. For some reason it makes me uncomfortable. I reach out and move the gun down so it points only at the floor. Henri looks at me curiously.

"There are other ways," I say.

Henri shrugs and sets the gun down. "The floor is yours," he says.

I stand five feet in front of the man. He looks at me with fear. He is heavy, but after catching Sam as he sailed through the air, I know that I can lift him. I hold my arms out, my body straining in concentration. Nothing at first, and then very slowly he begins to rise off the floor. The man struggles but he is taped to the chair and there is nothing he can do. I concentrate with everything I have, and yet in my peripheral vision I can see that Henri is smiling proudly, and that Sam is, too. Yesterday I couldn't lift a tennis ball; now I'm lifting a chair with a two-hundred-pound man sitting in it. How quickly the Legacy has developed.

When I have raised him to face level, I flip the chair over and he hangs upside down.

"Come on!" he yells.

"Start talking."

"No!" he yells. "They said they'd kill me."

I let go of the chair and it falls. The man screams but I catch him before he hits the ground. I raise him back up.

"There were three of them!" he yells, talking fast. "They showed up the same day we sent out the magazines. They showed up that night."

"What did they look like?" Henri asks.

"Like ghosts. They were pale, almost like albinos. They wore sunglasses, but when we wouldn't talk one of them took the sunglasses off. They had black eyes and pointy teeth, but they didn't look natural like an animal's would. Theirs looked as though they had been broken and chiseled. They all wore long coats and hats like some shit out of an old spy movie. What the hell more do you want?"

"Why did they come?"

"They wanted to know our source for the story. We told them. A man had called, said he had an exclusive for us, started raging about a group of aliens that wanted to destroy our civilization. But he called on the day we were printing, so instead of writing the full story, we put in a small quip and said more to follow next month. He talked so fast that we hardly grasped what he was saying. We were planning on calling him the next night, only that didn't happen, because the Mogadorians showed up instead."

"How did you know they were Mogadorians?"

"What the hell else could they have been? We wrote a story about the Mogadorian race of aliens and lo and behold a group of aliens shows up on our doorstep the same day wanting to know where we got the story. It wasn't hard to figure out."

The man is heavy and I'm having trouble holding him. My forehead is beaded with sweat and it's a struggle to breathe. I flip him back over, begin to lower him. When he is within a foot of the floor I drop him the rest of the way and he lands with an *Oomphf.* I bend over with my hands on my knees to catch my breath.

"What the hell, man? I'm answering your questions," he says.

"I'm sorry," I say. "You're too heavy."

"And that's the only time they came?" says Henri.

The man shakes his head. "They came back."

"Why?"

"To make sure we didn't print anything else. I don't think they trusted us, but the man who called us never answered his phone again, so we had nothing else to print."

"What happened to him?"

"What do you think happened?" the man asks.

Henri nods. "So they knew where he lived?"

"They had the phone number we were supposed to call him back on. I'm sure they could have figured it out."

"Did they threaten you?"

"Hell, yes. They trashed our office. They screwed with my mind. I haven't been the same since."

"What'd they do to your mind?"

He closes his eyes and takes another deep breath.

"They didn't even look real," he says. "I mean,

here are these three men standing in front of us talking in deep, raspy voices, all in trench coats and hats and sunglasses even though it was night-time. It looked like they were dressed up for a Halloween party or something. They looked funny and out of place, so at first I laughed at them . . . ," he says, his voice trailing off.

"But the second I laughed I knew I had made a mistake. The other two Mogadorians started towards me with their sunglasses off. I tried to look away, but I couldn't. Those eyes. I had to look, as though something was pulling me there. It was like seeing death. My own death, and the deaths of all the people I know and love. Things weren't so funny anymore. Not only did I have to witness the deaths, but I could feel them, too. The uncertainty. The pain. The complete and utter terror. I wasn't in that room anymore. And then came things I've always feared as a kid. Images of stuffed animals that came to life, with sharp teeth as mouths, razor blades for claws. The usual stuff all kids are afraid of. Werewolves. Demonic clowns. Giant spiders. I viewed them all through the eyes of a child, and they absolutely terrified me. And every time one of those things bit into me, I could feel its teeth rip the flesh from my body, I could feel the blood pour from the wounds. I couldn't stop screaming."

"Did you try to fight back at all?"

"They had two of these little weasel-looking

things, fat, with short legs. No bigger than a dog. They were frothing at the mouth. One of the men was holding them on a leash, but you could tell they were hungry for us. They said they would turn them loose if we resisted. I'm telling you, man, these things weren't from Earth. If they were dogs, big deal, we would have fought back. But I think those things would have eaten us whole despite our size. And they were pulling against the leash, growling, trying to get to us."

"So you talked?"

"Yes."

"When did they come back?"

"The night before the next magazine went out, a little over a week ago."

Henri gives me a concerned look. Only one week ago the Mogadorians were within a hundred miles of where we live. They could still be here somewhere, maybe monitoring the paper. Perhaps that is why Henri has felt their presence of late. Sam stands beside me, taking everything in.

"Why didn't they just kill you like they did your source?"

"How the hell do I know? Maybe because we publish a respectable paper."

"How did the man who called know about the Mogadorians?"

"He said he had captured one of them and tortured it."

"Where?"

"I don't know. His phone number was from the area code near Columbus. So north of here. Maybe sixty or eighty miles north."

"You spoke to him?"

"Yeah. And I wasn't sure if he was crazy or not, but we had heard rumors about something like this before. He started talking about them wanting to wipe out civilization as we know it, and sometimes he talked so fast that it was hard to make sense of anything he said. One thing he kept repeating was that they were here hunting something, or somebody. Then he started spouting numbers."

My eyes open wide. "What numbers? What did they mean?"

"I have no idea. Like I said, he was talking so fast that it was all we could do to write it all down."

"You wrote while he talked?" Henri says.

"Of course we did. We're journalists," he says incredulously. "Do you think we make up the stories we write?"

"Yeah, I do," says Henri.

"Do you still have the notes that you wrote?" I say.

He looks at me and nods. "I'm telling you, they're worthless. Most of what I wrote are scribbles on their plan to destroy the human race."

"I need to see them," I nearly bellow. "Where, where are they?"

He motions towards a desk against one of the walls.

"On the desk. On sticky notes."

I walk over to the desk, which is covered with papers, and start looking through the sticky notes. I find some very vague notes on the Mogadorians' hope to conquer Earth. Nothing concrete, no plans or details, just a few indistinct words:

"Overpopulation"

"Earth's resources"

"Biological warfare?"

"The Planet Mogadore."

I come to the note I'm looking for. I read it carefully three or four times.

PLANET LORIEN? THE LORIC?
1–3 DEAD
4 ?
7 TRAILED IN SPAIN.
9 ON THE RUN IN SA

(WHAT IS HE TALKING ABOUT?
WHAT DO THESE NUMBERS HAVE
TO DO WITH INVADING EARTH?)

"Why is there a question mark after the number 4?" I ask.

"Because he said something about it but he talked too fast and I didn't get it."

"You've got to be kidding me?"

He shakes his head. I sigh. *Just my luck,* I think. *The one thing said about me is the one thing that wasn't written.*

"What does 'SA' mean?" I ask.

"South America."

"Did he say where in South America?"

"No."

I nod, stare at the slip of paper. I wish I could have heard the conversation, that I could have asked questions of my own. Do the Mogadorians really know where Seven is? Are they really following him or her? If so, the Loric charm still holds. I fold the sticky notes and slip them into my back pocket.

"Do you know what the numbers mean?" he asks.

I shake my head. "I have no idea."

"I don't believe you," he says.

"Shut up," Sam says, and pokes him in the gut with the heavy end of the bat.

"Is there anything else you can tell me?" I ask.

He thinks about it for a moment, then says, "I think bright light bothers them. It seemed to cause them pain when they took their sunglasses off."

We hear a noise downstairs. Like someone trying to slowly open the door. We look at each other. I look to the man in the chair.

"Who is that?" I quietly say.

"Them."

"What?"

"They said they'd be watching. That they knew someone might be coming."

We hear quiet footsteps on the first floor.

Henri and Sam look at each other, both terrified.

"Why didn't you tell us?"

"They said they'd kill me. And my family."

I run to the window, look out the back. We're on the second floor. It's a twenty-foot drop to the ground. There's a fence around the yard. Eight feet of wood slats. I move quickly back to the stairs, and peer down. I see three huge figures, in long black trench coats, black hats, and sunglasses. They're carrying long gleaming swords. There's no way we're going to make it down the stairs. My Legacies are growing stronger, but they aren't strong enough to take on three Mogadorians. The only way out is through one of the windows or over a small porch at the front of the room. The windows are smaller but the backyard will allow us to escape unseen. If we go out the front, we will most likely be visible. I hear noise coming from the basement and the Mogadorians talking to each other in an ugly, guttural language. Two of them move towards the basement while the third starts walking towards the stairs that lead to us.

I have a second or two to act. The windows will break if we go through them. Our only chance is the doors leading to the second-floor porch. I open them using telekinesis. It's black outside. I hear footsteps coming up the stairs. I pull Sam and Henri over to me and I throw each of them over my shoulders like sacks of potatoes.

"What are you doing?" whispers Henri.

"I have no idea," I say. "But I hope it works."

Just as I see the top of the first Mogadorian's hat, I sprint towards the doors and right before the ledge of the porch, I jump. We go flying into the night sky. For two or three seconds we're floating. I see cars moving down the street beneath us. I see people on the sidewalk. I don't know where we're going to land, or if my body will support all the weight I'm carrying when we do. When we hit the roof of a house across the street I collapse, with Sam and Henri on top of me. I get my breath knocked out of me, and it feels like my legs are broken. Sam starts to stand, but Henri keeps him down. He drags me to the far end of the roof and asks if I can use my telekinesis to get him and Sam onto the ground. I can and I do. He tells me I need to jump. I stand on legs that are wobbly and still hurt, and just before I jump, I turn and see the three Mogadorians are standing on the porch across the street, looking confused. Their swords are gleaming. Without a second to spare, we got away without them seeing us.

We get to Sam's truck. Henri and Sam have to help me walk. Bernie is there waiting for us. We decide to leave Henri's truck because they most likely know what it looks like and would track it. We pull out of Athens and Henri starts driving back to Paradise, which it really might be after the night we just had.

Henri starts from the beginning, telling Sam everything. He doesn't stop until we are pulling into our driveway. It's still dark. Sam looks over at me.

"Unbelievable," he says, and smiles. "It's the coolest thing I've ever heard of." I look at him and I see the validation he has always looked for in his life, an affirmation that the time he's spent with his nose in the conspiracy rags, looking for clues to his father's disappearance, wasn't in vain.

"Are you really resistant to fire?" he asks.

"Yes," I say.

"God, that's awesome."

"Thanks, Sam."

"Can you fly?" he asks. At first I think he is joking, but then I see that he isn't.

"I can't fly. I'm resistant to fire and can turn my hands into lights. I have telekinesis, which I only learned to use yesterday. More Legacies are supposed to come soon. We think so, anyhow. But I have no idea what they will be until they actually develop."

"I hope you learn to make yourself invisible," Sam says.

"My grandfather could. And anything he touched also became invisible."

"Seriously?"

"Yes."

He starts laughing.

"I still can't believe you two drove all the way to Athens by yourselves," Henri says. "You guys are really something. When we stopped for gas I saw that the plates have been expired for four years. I really don't see how you made it without getting stopped."

"Well, you can count on me from now on," says Sam. "I'll do whatever it takes to help stop them. Especially because I bet they're the ones who took my dad."

"Thanks, Sam," says Henri. "The most important thing you could do is stay quiet with our secret. If anyone else finds out about this it could lead to our deaths."

"Don't worry. I'll never tell anyone. I don't want John using his powers on me."

We laugh and thank Sam again and he pulls away. Henri and I go inside. Even though I slept on the drive back, I'm still exhausted. I lie down on the couch. Henri sits in a chair across from me.

"Sam won't say anything," I say.

He doesn't respond, just stares at the floor.

"They don't know we're here," I say.

He looks up at me.

"They don't," I say. "If they knew they'd be following us now."

He stays silent. I can't take it.

"I'm not leaving Ohio on nothing more than speculation."

Henri stands.

"I'm happy that you've made a friend. And I think Sarah is great. But we can't stay. I'm going to start packing," he says.

"No."

"When we're packed I'll go into town and buy a new truck. We need to get out of here. They might not have followed us, but they know how close they were at catching us, and that we might still be nearby. I believe the man who called the magazine did in fact capture one of them. That was his story, that he captured one and tortured it until it talked and then he killed it. We don't know what kind of tracking technology they have, but I don't think it will take them long to find us. And when they do, we'll die. Your Legacies are emerging, and your strength is growing, but you're nowhere near ready to fight them."

He walks out of the room. I sit up. I don't want to leave. I have a real friend for the first time in my life. A friend who knows what I am and isn't scared, doesn't think I'm a freak. A friend who is willing to fight with me, and go into danger with me. And I have a girlfriend. Someone who wants to be with me, even without knowing who I am. Someone who makes me happy, someone I would fight for, or go into danger in order to protect. My Legacies haven't all emerged yet, but enough of them have. I took down three grown men. They didn't stand a chance. It was like fighting with little kids. I could do anything I wanted to them. We also now know that humans can also fight, and capture, and hurt, and kill Mogadorians. If they can, then I definitely can. I don't want to leave. I have a friend, and I have a girlfriend. I am not going to leave.

Henri walks back out of his room. He is carrying the Loric Chest that is our most prized possession.

"Henri," I say.

"Yes?"

"We're not leaving."

"Yes we are."

"You can if you want, but I'll go live with Sam. I'm not leaving."

"This is not your decision to make."

"It's not? I thought I was the one being hunted. I thought I was the one in danger. You could walk away right now and the Mogadorians would never look for you. You could live a nice, long, normal life. You could do whatever you want. I can't. They will always be after me. They will always be trying to find me and kill me. I'm fifteen years old. I'm not a kid anymore. It is my decision to make."

He stares at me for a minute. "That was a good speech, but it doesn't change anything. Pack your stuff. We're leaving."

I raise my hand and point it at him and lift him off the ground. He's so shocked that he doesn't say anything. I stand and move him into the corner of the room, up near the ceiling.

"We're staying," I say.

"Put me down, John."

"I'll put you down when you agree to stay."

"It's too dangerous."

"We don't know that. They're not in Paradise. They might not have any idea where we are."

"Put me down."

"Not until you agree to stay."

"PUT ME DOWN."

I don't say anything back. I just hold him

there. He struggles, tries to push off the wall and the ceiling, but he can't move. My power holds him in place. And I feel strong doing it. Stronger than I've ever felt in my life. I am not leaving. I am not running. I love my life in Paradise. I love having a real friend, and I love my girlfriend. I'm ready to fight for what I love, be it with the Mogadorians, or be it with Henri.

"You know you're not coming down until I bring you down."

"You're acting like a child."

"No, I'm acting like someone who is starting to realize who he is and what he can do."

"And you're really going to keep me up here?"

"Until I fall asleep or get tired, but I'll just do it again once I get some rest."

"Fine. We can stay. With certain conditions."

"What?"

"Put me down and we'll talk about it."

I lower him, set him on the floor. He hugs me. I'm surprised; I expected him to be pissed. He lets go of me and we sit down on the couch.

"I'm proud of how far you've come. I've spent many years waiting and preparing for these things to happen, for your Legacies to arrive. You know my entire life is devoted to keeping you safe, and making you strong. I would never forgive myself if something happened to you. If you died on my watch, I'm not sure how I would go on. In time the Mogadorians will catch up with us. I want to be ready for them when they come. I don't think you are yet, even though you do. You have a long way to go. We can stay here, for now, if you agree that training comes first. Before Sarah, before Sam, before everything. And at the first sign that they're nearby, or are on our trail, we leave, no questions asked, no fighting about it, no levitating me up to the ceiling and holding me there."

"Deal," I say, and smile.

CHAPTER TWENTY-TWO

WINTER COMES EARLY AND WITH full force to Paradise, Ohio. First the wind, then the cold, then the snow. Light dustings to start, then a storm blows through and buries the land so that the scraping sound of snowplows is as consistently heard as the wind itself, leaving a coat of salt over everything. School is canceled for two days. The snow near the roads segues from white to dingy black and eventually melts to standing puddles of slush that refuse to drain. Henri and I spend my time off training, indoors, outdoors. I can now juggle three balls without touching them, which also means I can lift more than one thing at a time. The heavier and larger objects have come, the kitchen table, the snow-blower Henri bought the week before, our new truck, which looks almost exactly like the old one and like millions of other pickup trucks in

America. If I can lift it physically, with my body, then I can lift it with my mind. Henri believes that the strength of my mind will eventually transcend that of my body.

In the backyard the trees stand sentinel around us, frozen branches like figurines of hollow glass, an inch of a fine white powder piled atop each one. The snow is up to our knees aside from the small patch Henri has cleared away. Bernie Kosar sits watching from the back porch. Even he wants nothing to do with the snow.

"Are you sure about this?" I ask.

"You need to learn to embrace it," Henri says. Over his shoulder, watching with morbid curiosity, stands Sam. It is his first time watching me train.

"How long will this burn?" I ask.

"I don't know."

I am wearing a highly combustible suit made mostly of natural fibers soaked in oils, some of which are slow burning, some of which are not. I want to set it on fire just to be rid of the smells that are making my eyes water. I take a deep breath.

"Are you ready?" he asks.

"As ready as I'll ever be."

"Don't breathe. You're not immune to the smoke or fumes and your internal organs will burn."

"This seems foolish to me," I say.

"It's part of your training. Grace under pressure. You need to learn to multitask while consumed in flames."

"But why?"

"Because when the battle comes, we're going to be greatly outnumbered. Fire will be one of your great allies in war. You need to learn to fight while burning."

"Ugh."

"If you get in trouble, jump into the snow and start rolling."

I look at Sam, who has a big grin spread across his face. He is holding a red fire extinguisher in his hand just in case it's needed.

"I know," I say.

Everyone is silent while Henri messes with the matches.

"You look like Sasquatch wearing that suit," Sam says.

"Eat it, Sam," I say.

"Here we go," says Henri.

I take a deep breath just before he touches a match to the suit. Fire sweeps across my body. It feels unnatural for me to keep my eyes open, but I do. I look up. The fire rises eight feet above me. The whole world is shrouded in shades of orange, red, yellow that dance in my line of sight. I can feel the heat, but only slightly as one feels the sun's rays on a summer day. Nothing more than that.

"Go!" Henri yells.

I hold my arms out to my sides, eyes wide-open, breath held. I feel as though I'm hovering. I enter the deep snow and it begins to sizzle and melt underfoot, a slight steam rising while I walk. I reach my right hand forward and lift a cinder block, which feels heavier than normal. Is it because I'm not breathing? Is it the stress of the fire?

"Don't waste time!" Henri yells.

I hurl the block as hard as I can against a dead tree fifty feet away. The force causes it to smash into a million little pieces, leaving an indentation in the wood. Then I raise three tennis balls soaked in gasoline. I juggle them in midair, one over the other. I bring them in towards my body. They catch fire, and still I juggle them—and while doing so I lift a long, thin broomstick. I close my eyes. My body is warm. I wonder if I'm sweating. If I am, the sweat must be evaporating the second it reaches the skin's surface.

I grit my teeth, open my eyes, thrust my body forward and direct all of my powers into the stick's very core. It explodes, splintering into small bits. I don't let any of them fall to the ground; instead I keep them suspended, collectively looking like a cloud of dust hovering in midair. I pull them to me and let them burn. The wood pops through the flicker and hum of the flames. I force them back together into a tightly compacted spear of fire that looks as though it has sprung straight from the depths of hell.

"Perfect!" Henri yells.

One minute has passed. My lungs begin to burn from the fire, from my breath still held. I put everything that I am into the spear and I hurl it so hard that it speeds through the air like a bullet and hits the tree, and hundreds of tiny fires spread throughout the vicinity and extinguish almost immediately. I had hoped the dead wood would catch fire but it does not. I have also dropped the tennis balls. They sizzle in the snow five feet away from me.

"Forget the balls," Henri yells. "The tree. Get the tree."

The dead wood looks ghastly with its arthritic limbs silhouetted against the world of white beyond it. I close my eyes. I can't hold my breath much longer. Frustration and anger begin to form, fueled by the fire and the discomfort of the suit and the tasks that are left undone. I focus on the large branch coming off the tree's trunk and I try to break that branch away but it won't come. I grit my teeth and furrow my brows and finally a loud snap rings through the air like a shotgun blast and the branch comes sailing towards me. I catch it in my hands and hold it straight above me. *Let it burn,* I think. It must be twenty feet long. It finally catches fire and I lift it into the air forty or fifty feet above me and, without touching it, I drive it straight into the ground as though I'm staking my claim like some old-world swordsman standing atop the hill after winning the war. The stick totters back and forth smoking, flames dancing along the upper half of it. I open my mouth and instinctively take a breath, and the flames come rushing in; an instant burning spreads throughout my body. I'm so shocked and it hurts so much that I don't know what to do.

"The snow! The snow!" Henri yells.

I dive in headfirst and begin rolling. The fire goes out almost immediately but I keep rolling and the sizzle of snow touching the tattered suit is all I hear while wisps of steam and smoke rise off of me. And then Sam finally pulls the clip from the extinguisher and unloads with a thick powder that makes it even harder to breathe.

"No," I yell.

He stops. I lie there trying to catch my breath, but each inhalation brings about a pain in my lungs that reverberates throughout my body.

"Damn, John. You weren't supposed to

breathe," Henri says, standing over me.

"I couldn't help it."

"Are you okay?" Sam asks.

"My lungs are burning."

Everything is blurry but slowly the world comes into focus. I lie there looking up into the low gray sky at the flakes of snow sifting sullenly down upon us.

"How'd I do?"

"Not bad for your first try."

"We're going to do it again, aren't we?"

"In time, yes."

"That was wicked cool," Sam says.

I sigh, then take a deep, labored breath. "That sucked."

"You did well for your first time," Henri says. "You can't expect everything to come easily."

I nod from the ground. I lie there a good minute or two, and then Henri extends a hand and helps me up, bringing about the end of training for the day.

I wake in the middle of the night two days later, 2:57 on the clock. I can hear Henri working at the kitchen table. I crawl out of bed and walk out of the room. He is hunched over a document, wearing bifocals and holding some sort of stamp with a pair of tweezers. He looks up at me.

"What are you doing?" I ask.

"Creating forms for you."

"For what?"

"I got to thinking about you and Sam driving down to get me. I think it's foolish of us to keep using your real age when we can just as easily change it according to our needs."

I pick up a birth certificate that he has already finished. The name written is James Hughes. The date of birth would make me a year older. I'd be sixteen and able to drive. Then I bend over and look at the one he is in the process of creating. The name listed is Jobie Frey, age eighteen, a legal adult.

"Why didn't we ever think to do this before?" I ask.

"We never had reason to."

Papers of different shapes and sizes and densities are scattered across the table, a large printer off to the side. Bottles of ink, rubber stamps, notary stamps, metal plate-looking things, various tools that look as though they belong in a dentist's office. The process of document creation has always remained foreign to me.

"Are we going to change my age now?"

Henri shakes his head. "It's too late to change your age in Paradise. These are mostly for the future. Who knows what will happen that will give you reason to use them."

The thought of moving in the future makes

me nauseous. I would rather stay fifteen and unable to drive forever than move someplace new.

Sarah returns from Colorado a week before Christmas. I haven't seen her in eight days. It feels as though it's been a month. The van drops all the girls off at the school and one of her friends drives her straight to my house without first taking her home. When I hear the tires come up the drive I meet her with a hug and a kiss and I lift her off the ground and twirl her in the air. She has just been in a plane and a car for ten hours and she is wearing sweatpants and no makeup with her hair pulled into a ponytail and yet she is the most beautiful girl I have ever seen and I don't want to let go of her. We stare into each other's eyes beneath the moonlight and all either of us can do is smile.

"Did you miss me?" she asks.

"Every second of every day."

She kisses the tip of my nose.

"I missed you, too."

"So do the animals have a shelter again?" I ask.

"Oh, John, it was amazing! I wish you could have been there. There were probably thirty people helping out at all times, around the clock. The building went up so fast and it's so much nicer than it was before. We built this cat tree in one of the corners, and I swear the whole time we were there, there were cats playing on it."

I smile. "It sounds great. I wish I could have been there, too."

I take her bag and we walk into the house together.

"Where's Henri?" she asks.

"Grocery shopping. He left about ten minutes ago."

She walks through the living room and drops her coat onto the back of a chair on her way into my bedroom. She sits on the edge of my bed and kicks her shoes off.

"What should we do?" she asks.

I stand there watching her. She is wearing a red hooded sweatshirt with a zipper down the front. It is only halfway zipped. She smiles and looks at me through the tops of her eyes.

"Come here," she says, and holds her hand out to me.

I walk to her and she takes my hand in hers. She looks up at me and squints her eyes from the light shining overhead. I snap my fingers with my free hand and the light turns off.

"How'd you do that?"

"Magic," I say.

I sit beside her. She tucks a few loose strands of hair behind her ear, then leans over and kisses me on the cheek. Then she cups my chin and pulls my head to hers and kisses me again, softly, delicately. My whole body tingles in response. She pulls away, her hand still on my cheek. She traces my brow with her thumb.

"I really did miss you," she says.

"Me, too."

A silence passes between us. Sarah bites her lower lip.

"I couldn't wait to get here," she says. "The whole time I was in Colorado, you were all I could think of. Even when playing with the animals, I was wishing you were there with me playing with them, too. And then when we finally left this morning, the entire trip was hell even though every mile we traveled was another mile I was closer to you."

She smiles, mostly with her eyes, her lips a thin upturned crescent that keeps her teeth hidden. She kisses me again, a kiss that starts as slow and lingering and goes from there. Both of us are sitting on the edge of the bed, her hand on the side of my face, mine on the small of her back. I can feel the tight contours beneath the tips of my fingers, can taste the berry gloss on her lips. I pull her to me. I feel as though I can't get close enough to her despite our bodies being pressed tightly together. My hand running up her back, the smooth porcelain feel of her skin. Her hands through my hair, both of us breathing heavily. We fall back on the bed, on our sides. Our eyes are closed. I keep opening mine to see her. The room is dark aside from the moonlight entering through the windows. She catches me watching her and we stop kissing. She puts her forehead to mine and stares at me.

She places her hand on the back of my neck and pulls me to her and all at once we're kissing again. Entangled. Meshed. Our arms tightly around the other. My mind clear of every plague that normally visits and every thought of other planets, my mind free of the hunt and pursuit by the Mogadorians. Sarah and I on the bed kissing each other, falling into each other. Nothing else in the world matters.

And then the door opens in the living room. We both jump up.

"Henri's home," I say.

We stand and quickly brush the wrinkles from our clothes, smiling, a secret shared between us that makes us giggle as we walk out of the bedroom holding hands. Henri is setting a bag of groceries on the kitchen table.

"Hi, Henri," Sarah says.

He smiles at her. She lets go of my hand and walks over and hugs him and they start talking about her trip to Colorado. I walk outside to get the rest of the groceries. I breathe in the cold air, try to shake my limbs free of the tension of what just happened, and the disappointment of Henri coming home when he did. I'm still breathing heavily as I grab the rest of the groceries and carry them into the house. Sarah is telling Henri about some of the cats that were at the shelter.

"And you didn't bring one of them back for us?"

"Now Henri, you know I would have happily brought you one if you had told me," Sarah says, her arms folded across her chest with her hip cocked to the side.

He smiles at her. "I know you would've."

Henri puts the groceries away and Sarah and I head out into the frigid air to go for a walk before her mom arrives to take her home. Bernie Kosar comes with us. He takes the lead and runs ahead. Sarah and I hold hands, walking through the yard, the temperature slightly above freezing. The snow melting, the ground wet and muddy. Bernie Kosar disappears for a time into the woods and then comes running back out. His bottom half is filthy.

"What time is your mom coming?" I ask.

She looks at her watch. "Twenty minutes."

I nod. "I'm so happy you're back."

"Me too."

We go to the edge of the woods but it is too dark for us to enter. We instead walk along the perimeter of the yard, hand in hand, occasionally stopping to kiss with the moon and stars as witnesses. Neither of us talks about what just happened, but it's obvious that it is on both of our minds. When we make the first lap Sarah's mother pulls into the drive. She's ten minutes early. Sarah runs up and hugs her. I walk inside and grab Sarah's bag. After we say good-bye, I walk to the road and watch their taillights recede in the distance. I stand outside for a while and then Bernie Kosar and I go back into the house. Henri is halfway through making dinner. I give the dog a bath. When I'm finished dinner is ready.

We sit at the table and eat, not a word passing between us. I can't stop thinking of her. I stare blankly into my plate. I'm not hungry but I try to force the food down anyhow. I manage a few bites, and then I push the plate out in front of me and I sit there in silence.

"So are you going to tell me?" Henri asks.

"Tell you what?"

"What's on your mind."

I shrug. "I don't know."

He nods, goes back to eating. I close my eyes. I can still smell Sarah on the collar of my shirt, can still feel her hand on my cheek. Her lips to mine, the texture of her hair when I ran my hand through it. All I can think about is what she must be doing, and how I wish she were still here.

"Do you think it's possible for us to be loved?" I ask.

"What are you talking about?"

"By humans. Do you think we can be loved, like, truly be loved by them?"

"I think they can love us the way they love each other, especially if they don't know what we are, but I don't think it's possible to love a human the way you would love a Loric," he says.

"Why?"

"Because deep down we're different from them. And we love differently. One of the gifts our planet gave us is to love completely. Without jealousy or insecurity or fear. Without pettiness. Without anger. You may have strong feelings for Sarah, but they aren't what you would feel for a Loric girl."

"There aren't many Loric girls available for me."

"Even more reason to be careful with Sarah. At some point, if we last long enough, we will need to regenerate our race and repopulate our planet. Obviously you're a long way from having to worry about that, but I wouldn't count on Sarah being your partner."

"What happens if we try to have children with humans?"

"It's happened many times before. Usually it results in an exceptional and gifted human.

Some of the greatest figures in Earth's history were actually the product of humans and the Loric, including Buddha, Aristotle, Julius Caesar, Alexander the Great, Genghis Khan, Leonardo da Vinci, Isaac Newton, Thomas Jefferson, and Albert Einstein. Many of the ancient Greek gods, who most people believe were mythological, were actually the children of the humans and Loric, mainly because it was much more common then for us to be on this planet and we were helping them develop civilizations. Aphrodite, Apollo, Hermes, and Zeus were all real, and had one Loric parent."

"So it is possible."

"It was possible. In our current situation it's reckless and impractical. In fact, though I don't know her number, or have any idea where she is, one of the children who came to Earth with us was the daughter of your parents' best friends. They used to joke that it was fate that the two of you would end up together. They may well have been right."

"So what do I do?"

"Enjoy your time with Sarah, but don't get too attached to her, and don't let her get too attached to you."

"Really?"

"Trust me, John. If you never believe another word I say, then believe that."

"I believe all the words you say even if I don't want to."

Henri winks at me. "Good," he says.

Afterwards I go into my room and call Sarah. I think about what Henri said to me before I do it, but I can't help myself. I am attached to her. I think I'm in love with her. We talk for two hours. It is midnight when the call ends. Then I lie in bed smiling through the darkness.

CHAPTER TWENTY-THREE

THE DAY HAS GROWN DARK. THE warm night carries a soft wind and the sky is scattered with intermittent flashes of light, clouds turning to brilliant colors of blue and red and green. Fireworks at first. Fireworks that segue to something else, louder, more menacing, the *ooh*s and *aah*s turning to shrieks and screams. A chaos erupts. People running, children crying. Me, standing in the middle of it all, watching without the benefit of being able to do anything to help. The soldiers and the beasts pour onto the scene from all directions as I have seen before, the continuous fall of bombs so loud that it hurts the ears, the reverberations felt in the pit of my stomach. So deafening it makes my teeth ache. Then the Loric charge back with such intensity, with such courage, that it makes me proud to be among them, to be one of them.

Then I am gone, sweeping through the air at a rate that causes the world beneath to pass in a blur so that I can't focus on any one thing. When I stop I am standing on the tarmac of an airfield. A silver airship is fifteen feet away and forty or so people stand at the ramp leading up to its entrance. Two people have already entered, standing in the doorway with their eyes on the sky, a very young girl and a woman Henri's age. And then I see myself, four years old, crying, shoulders slumped. A much younger version of Henri just behind me. He, too, is watching the sky. On bended knee in front of me is my grandmother, gripping me by the shoulders. My grandfather stands behind her, his face set hard, distracted, the lenses of his glasses gathering the light from the sky.

"Come back to us, you hear? Come back to us," my grandmother says, finishing speaking. I wish I could have heard the words that came before them. Up until now I have never remembered anything that was spoken to me that night. But now I have something. My four-year-old self doesn't respond. My four-year-old self is too scared. He doesn't understand what is happening, why there is urgency and fear in the eyes of everyone around him. My grandmother pulls me to her and then she lets go. She stands and turns her back to keep me from seeing her cry. My four-year-old self knows that she is crying, but he doesn't know why.

Next is my grandfather, who is covered in sweat, grime, and blood. He has clearly been fighting, and his face is twisted as though he is straining, ready to fight more, ready to go and do all he can in the struggle to survive. His, and the planet's. He drops to a knee as my grandmother did before him. For the first time I look around. Twisted heaps of metal, chunks of concrete, large holes in the ground where the bombs have fallen. Scattered fires, shattered glass, dirt, splintered trees. And in the middle of it all a single airship, unharmed, the one that we are boarding.

"We gotta go!" somebody yells out. A man, dark hair and eyes. I don't know who he is. Henri looks at him and nods. The children walk up the ramp. My grandfather fixes me with a hard stare. He opens his mouth to speak. But before the words come.I am again swept away, hurled up through the air, the world below again passing in a blur. I try to make it out, but I am moving too fast. The only discernible sights are the bombs, continually falling, large displays of fire of all colors that sweep through the night sky and the perpetual explosions that follow.

Then I stop again.

I am inside of a large, open building that I have never seen before. It is silent. The ceiling is domed. The floor is one great slab of concrete the size of a football field. There are no windows, but the sounds of the bombs still penetrate, echoing off the walls around me. Standing in the very middle of the building, tall and proud, alone, is a white rocket that extends all the way to the apex of the ceiling.

Then a door slams open in the far corner. My head snaps around to it. Two men enter, frantic, talking quickly and loudly. All at once a herd of animals rush in behind the men. Fifteen, give or take, continually changing shape. Some flying, some running, on two legs, then on four. Bringing up the rear, a third man follows and the door is shut. The first man reaches the spacecraft, opens a sort of hatch on the ship's bottom, and begins ushering the animals in.

"Go! Go! Up and in, up and in," he yells.

The animals go, all of them changing their shapes in order to do so. Then the last animal enters and one of the men pulls himself in. The other two begin throwing bags and boxes up to him. It takes them a good ten minutes to get everything on board. Then all three scatter around the rocket, preparing it. The men are sweating, moving frantically until everything is ready. Just before the three of them climb inside the rocket, someone runs up with a bundle that looks like a swaddled child, though I can't see well enough to tell. They take whatever it is and go inside. Then the door snaps shut behind them and is sealed. Minutes pass. The bombs must be just outside the walls now. And then from nowhere an explosion occurs inside the building and I see the beginnings of fire shoot from the bottom of the rocket, a fire that quickly grows, a fire that consumes everything inside the building. A fire that consumes even me.

My eyes snap open. I am back home, in Ohio, lying in bed. The room is dark, but I can sense that I am not alone. A figure moves, a shadow thrown across the bed. I tense myself to it, ready to snap my lights on, ready to hurl it against the wall.

"You were talking," Henri says. "In your sleep just now, you were talking."

I turn on my lights. He is standing beside the bed, wearing pajamas pants and a white T-shirt. His hair is tousled; his eyes are red with sleep.

"What was I saying?"

"You said 'Up and in, up and in.' What was happening?"

"I was just on Lorien."

"In a dream?"

"I don't think so. I was there, just like before."

"What did you see?"

I scoot up the bed so my back rests against the wall.

"The animals," I say.

"What animals?"

"In the spaceship I saw take off. The old one, at the museum. In the rocket that left after ours. I watched animals being loaded into it. Not many. Fifteen, maybe. With three other Loric. I don't think they were Garde. And something else. A bundle. It looked like a baby, but I couldn't tell."

"Why don't you think they were Garde?"

"They loaded the rocket with supplies, fifty or so boxes and duffel bags. They didn't use telekinesis."

"Into the rocket inside the museum?"

"I think it was the museum. I was inside a large, domed building with nothing inside of it but a rocket. I can only assume it was the museum."

Henri nods. "If they worked at the museum then they would have been Cêpan."

"Loading animals," I say. "Animals that could change their shape."

"Chimæra," Henri says.

"What?"

"Chimæra. Animals on Lorien that could change their shape. They were called Chimæra."

"Is that what Hadley was?" I ask, remembering back to the vision I had a few weeks ago, the vision of playing in the yard of my elders' home when I was lifted in the air by the man wearing a silver and blue suit.

Henri smiles. "You remember Hadley?"

I nod. "I've seen him the way that I've seen everything else."

"You're having the visions even when we're not training?"

"Sometimes."

"How often?"

"Henri, who cares about the visions? Why were they loading animals into a rocket? What was a baby doing with them, or was it even a baby? Where did they go? What purpose could they possibly have had?"

Henri thinks about it a moment. He shifts the weight of his body to his right leg. "Probably the same purpose we had. Think about it, John. How else could animals repopulate Lorien? They too would have to go to some sort of sanctuary. Everything was wiped out. Not just the people, but also the animals, and all plant life. Maybe the bundle was just another animal. A fragile one, or maybe a young one."

"Well, where would they go? What other sanctuary exists besides Earth?"

"I think they went to one of the space stations. A rocket with Loric fuel would have been able to make it that far. Maybe they thought the invasion would be short-lived, and they thought they could wait it out. I mean, they would have been able to live on the space station for as long as their supplies lasted."

"There are space stations close to Lorien?"

"Yes, two of them. Well, there *were* two of them. I know for sure the larger of the two was destroyed at the same time as the invasion. We lost contact with it less than two minutes after the first bomb fell."

"Why didn't you mention that before, when I first told you about the rocket?"

"I had assumed that it was empty, that it went up in the air as a decoy. And I think that if one space station was destroyed, then the other was as well. Their trip, unfortunately, was probably done in vain, whatever their goal was."

"But what if they came back when their supplies ran out? Do you think they could survive on Lorien?" I ask in desperation. I already know the answer, already know what Henri will say, but I ask anyway in order to hold on to some sort of hope that we aren't alone in all this. That maybe, somewhere far away, there are others like us, waiting, monitoring the planet so that they, too, might one day return and we won't be alone when we go back.

"No. There is no water there now. You saw that for yourself. Nothing but a barren waste-land. And nothing can survive without water."

I sigh and scoot back down into the bed. I drop my head onto the pillow. What's the point in arguing? Henri is right and I know it. I saw it for myself. If the globes that he pulled from the Chest are to be trusted, then Lorien is nothing more than wasteland, a dump. The planet still lives but on the surface there is nothing. No water. No plants. No life. Nothing but dirt and rocks and the rubble of the civilization that once existed.

"Did you see anything else?" Henri asks.

"I saw us on the day we left. All of us at the airship right before we took off."

"It was a sad day."

I nod. Henri crosses his arms and gazes out the window, lost in thought. I take a deep breath. "Where was your family during it all?" I ask.

My lights have been off for a good two or three minutes, but I can see the whites of Henri's eyes staring back at me.

"Not with me, not on that day," he says.

We are both silent for a time and then Henri shifts his weight.

"Well, I better get back to bed," he says, bringing an end to the conversation. "Get some sleep."

After he leaves I lie there thinking of the animals, of the rocket, of Henri's family and how I'm sure he never got the chance to say good-bye to them. I know I won't be able to go back to sleep. I never can when the images visit me, when I feel Henri's sadness. It must be a thought constantly on his mind, as it would be for anyone who left under the same circumstances, leaving the only home you've ever known, all the while knowing you will never see the people you love again.

I grab my cell phone and text Sarah. I always text her when I can't sleep, or she texts me if it's the other way around. Then we'll talk for as long as it takes to become tired. She calls me twenty seconds after I hit the send button.

"Hey, you," I answer.

"You can't sleep?"

"No."

"What's the matter?" she asks. She yawns on the other end of the line.

"Was just missing you is all. Been lying in bed staring at the ceiling for like an hour now."

"You're silly. You saw me like six hours ago."

"I wish you were still here," I say. She moans. I can hear her smile through the darkness. I roll to my side and hold the phone between my ear and the pillow.

"Well, I wish I was still there, too."

We talk for twenty minutes. The last half of the call is both of us just lying there listening to the other breathe. I feel better after having talked to Sarah, but I find it even harder to fall back asleep.

CHAPTER TWENTY-FOUR

FOR ONCE, SINCE WE ARRIVED IN Ohio, things seem to slow for a time. School ends quietly and for winter break we have eleven days off. Sam and his mother spend most of it visiting his aunt in Illinois. Sarah stays home. We spend Christmas together. We kiss when the ball drops at midnight on New Year's Eve. Despite the snow and the cold, or maybe even in retaliation against it, we go for long walks through the woods behind my house, holding hands, kissing, breathing in the chilly air beneath the low gray skies of winter. We spend more and more time together. Not a day passes during that whole break that we don't see each other at least once.

We walk hand in hand beneath an umbrella of white from the snow piled atop the tree branches overhead. She has her camera with her and occasionally stops to take pictures. Most of the snow on the ground lies undisturbed aside from the tracks we have made on the walk out. We follow them back now, Bernie Kosar in the lead, darting in and out of the brambles, chasing rabbits into small groves and thickets of thorny bush, chasing squirrels up trees. Sarah wears a pair of black earmuffs. Her cheeks and the tip of her nose are red with the cold, making her eyes look bluer. I stare at her.

"What?" she asks, smiling.

"Just admiring the view."

She rolls her eyes at me. For the most part the woods are dense aside from sporadic clearings we continually stumble upon. I'm not sure how far in any one direction the woods extend, but in all of our walks we have yet to reach their end.

"I bet it's beautiful here in the summer," Sarah says. "We can probably picnic in the clearings."

An ache forms in my chest. Summer is still five months away and if Henri and I are here in May, we will have made it seven months in Ohio. That is very nearly the longest we have ever stayed in one place.

"Yeah," I agree.

Sarah looks at me. "What?"

I look at her questioningly. "What do you mean, 'what?'"

"That wasn't very convincing," she says. A mess of crows fly by overhead, squawking noisily.

"I just wish it was summer now."

"Me too. I can't believe we have to go back to school tomorrow."

"Ugh, don't remind me."

We enter another clearing, larger than the others, an almost perfect circle a hundred feet in diameter. Sarah lets go of my hand, runs into the middle of it, and drops into the snow, laughing. She rolls to her back and begins making a snow angel. I drop beside her and do the same. The tips of our fingers just barely touch while we make the wings. We get up.

"It's like we're holding wings," she says.

"Is that possible?" I ask. "I mean, how would we fly if we're holding wings?"

"Of course it's possible. Angels can do anything."

Then she turns and nuzzles into me. Her cold face against my neck makes me squirm away from her.

"Ahh! Your face is like ice."

She laughs. "Come warm me up."

I take her in my arms and kiss her beneath the open sky, the trees surrounding us. There are no sounds save the birds and the occasional pack of snow falling from the nearby branches. Two cold faces pressed tightly together. Bernie Kosar comes trotting up, out of breath, tongue dangling, tail wagging. He barks and sits in the snow staring at us, his head cocked to the side.

"Bernie Kosar! Were you off chasing rabbits?" Sarah asks.

He barks twice and runs over and jumps up on her. He barks again and pushes off and then looks up expectantly. She grabs a stick from the ground, shakes the snow off it, and then hurls it into the trees. He races after it and disappears from sight. He emerges from the trees ten seconds later, but instead of returning to the clearing where he had exited it, he comes from the opposite side. Sarah and I both spin around to watch him.

"How'd he do that?" she asks.

"Don't know," I say. "He's a peculiar dog."

"Did you hear that, Bernie Kosar? He just called you peculiar!"

He drops the stick at her feet. We walk towards home, holding hands, the day nearing dusk. Bernie Kosar trots beside us the whole way out, his head on a swivel as though ushering us along, keeping us safe from what may or may not lurk in the outer dark beyond our line of sight.

Five newspapers are stacked on the kitchen table, Henri at his computer, the overhead light on.

"Anything?" I ask out of habit, nothing more. There hasn't been a promising story in months, which is a good thing, but I can't help but always hope for something every time I ask.

"Actually, yes, I think so."

I perk up, then walk around the table and look over Henri's shoulder at the computer screen. "What?"

"There was an earthquake in Argentina yesterday evening. A sixteen-year-old girl pulled an elderly man free from a pile of rubble in a tiny town near the coast."

"Number Nine?"

"Well, I certainly think she's one of us. Whether she's Number Nine or not remains to be seen."

"Why? There's nothing really extraordinary about pulling a man from rubble."

"Look," Henri says, and then scrolls to the top of the article. There is a picture of a large slab of concrete at least a foot thick, eight feet long and wide. "This is what she lifted to save him. It must weigh five tons. And look at this," he says, and scrolls back to the bottom of the page. He highlights the very last sentence. It reads: "Sofia García could not be found for comment."

I read the sentence three times. "She couldn't be found," I say.

"Exactly. She didn't *decline* to comment; she simply couldn't be found."

"How did they know her name?"

"It's a small town, less than a third the size of

Paradise. Most everyone would know her name there."

"She left, didn't she?"

Henri nods. "I think so. Probably before the paper was even published. That's the downfall of small towns; it's impossible to remain unnoticed."

I sigh. "Hard for the Mogadorians to go unnoticed too."

"Precisely."

"Sucks for her," I say, and stand up. "Who knows what she must have left behind."

Henri gives me a skeptical look, opens his mouth to say something, but then thinks better of it and goes back to the computer. I return to my bedroom. I pack my bag with a fresh change of clothes and the books I'll need for the day. Back to school. I'm not looking forward to it, though it'll be nice to see Sam again, whom I haven't seen in nearly two weeks.

"Okay," I say. "I'm off."

"Have a good day. Be safe out there."

"See you this afternoon."

Bernie Kosar rushes out of the house ahead of me. He's a ball of energy this morning. I think he's come to look forward to our morning runs, and the fact that we haven't done one in a week and a half has him chomping at the bit to get back to it. He keeps up with me for most of the run. Once we make it I give him a good pet and scratch behind his ears.

"All right, boy, go home," I say. He turns and starts trotting back to the house.

I take my time in the shower. By the time I finish, other students are beginning to arrive. I walk the hall, stop by my locker, then go to Sam's. I slap him on the back. It startles him, then he flashes a big toothy grin when he sees that it's me.

"I thought I was going to have to whip somebody's ass there for a minute," he says.

"Just me, my friend. How was Illinois?"

"Ugh," he says, and rolls his eyes. "My aunt made me drink tea and watch reruns of *Little House on the Prairie* nearly every day."

I laugh. "That sounds awful."

"It was, trust me," he says, and reaches into his bag. "This was waiting in the mail when we got back."

He hands me the latest issue of *They Walk Among Us*. I begin flipping through it.

"There is nothing on us or the Mogadorians," he says.

"Good," I say. "They must fear us after you visited them."

"Yeah, right."

Over Sam's shoulder I see that Sarah is coming our way. Mark James stops her in the middle of the hallway and hands her a few sheets of orange paper. Then she continues on her way.

"Hi, gorgeous," I say when she reaches us. She stands on her toes to kiss me. Her lips taste like strawberry lip balm.

"Hi, Sam. How are you?"

"Good. How're you?" he asks. He seems at ease with her now. Before the incident with Henri, which was a month and a half ago, being in Sarah's presence would have made him uncomfortable, and he wouldn't have been able to meet her eye or know what to do with his hands. But now he looks at her and smiles, speaking with confidence.

"Good," she says. "I'm supposed to give you both one of these."

She hands us each one of the orange sheets Mark just gave her. It's a party invitation for this upcoming Saturday night at his house.

"I'm invited?" Sam asks.

Sarah nods. "All three of us are."

"Do you want to go?" I ask.

"Maybe we could give it a shot."

I nod. "You interested, Sam?"

He looks past Sarah and me. I turn to see what he is looking at, or rather who. At a locker across the hall is Emily, the girl who was on the hayride with us, and who Sam has been pining for ever since. When she walks past she sees that

Sam is watching her and she smiles politely.

"Emily?" I say to Sam.

"Emily what?" Sam asks, looking back at me.

I look at Sarah. "I think Sam likes Emily Knapp."

"I do not," he says.

"I could ask her to come to the party with us," Sarah says.

"Do you think she would go?" Sam asks.

Sarah looks at me. "Well, maybe I shouldn't invite her since Sam doesn't like her."

Sam smiles. "Okay, fine. I just, I don't know."

"She kept asking why you never called after the hayride. She kind of likes you."

"That is true," I say. "I've heard her say it."

"Why didn't you tell me?" says Sam.

"You never asked."

Sam looks down at the flyer. "So it's this Saturday?"

"Yes."

He looks up at me. "I say we go."

I shrug. "I'm in."

Henri is waiting for me when the final bell rings. As always, Bernie Kosar is in the passenger seat, and when he sees me, his tail begins wagging a hundred miles an hour. I jump into the truck. Henri puts it into gear and drives away.

"There was a follow-up article on the girl in Argentina," Henri says.

"And?"

"Just a short article saying that she has disappeared. The mayor of the town is offering a modest reward for information on her whereabouts. It sounds like they believe she's been kidnapped."

"Are you worried about the Mogadorians having gotten to her first?"

"If she's Nine, like the note we found indicated, and the Mogadorians were tracking her, it's a good thing that she vanished. And if she's been captured, the Mogadorians can't kill her—they can't even hurt her. That gives us hope. The good thing, aside from the news itself, is that I imagine every Mogadorian on Earth has poured into Argentina."

"Speaking of which, Sam had the latest issue of *They Walk Among Us* today."

"Was there anything in it?"

"Nope."

"I didn't think there would be. Your levitation trick seemed to affect them rather profoundly."

When we arrive home I change clothes and meet Henri in the backyard for our day of training. Working while consumed with fire has gotten easier. I don't get as flustered as I did on that first day. I can hold my breath longer, close to four minutes. I have more control over the objects I lift, and I can lift more of them at the same time. Little by little, the look of worry I saw on Henri's face during the first days has melted away. He nods more. He smiles more. On the days it goes really well he gets a crazed look in his eyes and he raises his arms in the air and yells "Yes!" as loudly as he can. In that way I am gaining confidence in my Legacies. The rest have yet to come, but I don't think they're far off. And the major one, whatever it will be. The anticipation of it keeps me up most nights. I want to fight. I hunger for a Mogadorian to saunter into the backyard so that I may finally seek revenge.

It's an easy day. No fire. Mostly just me lifting things and manipulating them while they are suspended in the air. The last twenty minutes pass with Henri throwing objects at me—sometimes just allowing them to fall to the ground, other times deflecting them in a way that emulates a boomerang so that they twist in the air and go blazing back towards Henri. At one point a meat tenderizer flies back so fast that Henri dives face-first into the snow to keep from being hit by it. I laugh. Henri does not. Bernie Kosar lies on the ground the whole time watching us, seeming to offer his own encouragement. After we are done I shower, do my homework, and sit at the kitchen table for dinner.

"So there is a party this Saturday that I'm going to go to."

He looks up at me, stops chewing. "Whose party?"

"Mark James's."

Henri looks surprised.

"All that's over," I say before he can object.

"Well, you know best, I suppose. Just remember what's at stake."

CHAPTER TWENTY-FIVE

AND THEN THE WEATHER WARMS. Brisk winds, bitter cold, and continuous snow showers are followed by blue skies and fifty-degree temperatures. The snow melts. At first there are standing puddles in the driveway and the yard, the road wet with the sounds of splashing tires, but after a day all the water drains and evaporates and the cars pass as they do on any other day. A lull in the action, a brief reprieve before old man winter takes up the reins again.

I sit on the porch waiting for Sarah, staring up at the night sky full of twinkling stars and a full moon. A thin, knifelike cloud cuts the moon in two and then quickly disappears. I hear the crunch of gravel under tires; then headlights come into view and the car pulls into the driveway. Sarah gets out of the driver's side. She's dressed in dark gray pants flared at the ankles, a navy blue cardigan sweater beneath a beige jacket. Her eyes are accentuated by the blue shirt peeking out where the jacket's zipper ends. Her blond hair falling past her shoulders. She smiles coyly and looks at me, fluttering her eyelashes as she approaches. There are butterflies in my stomach. Almost three months together and yet I still grow nervous when I see her. A nervousness that's hard to imagine time will ever assuage.

"You look gorgeous," I say.

"Well, thank you," she says, and bobs a curtsy. "You don't look so bad yourself."

I kiss Sarah on the cheek. Then Henri walks out of the house and waves to Sarah's mom, who is sitting in the passenger seat of the car.

"So you'll call when you're ready to be picked up, right?" Henri asks me.

"Yes," I say.

We walk to the car and Sarah gets behind the wheel. I sit in the back. She's had her learner's permit for a few months now, which means she can drive so long as a licensed driver sits in the passenger seat beside her. Her actual driver's test is on Monday, two days away. She's been anxious about it ever since making the appointment over winter break. She backs out of the driveway and pulls away, eventually flipping the visor down and smiling at me through the mirror. I smile back.

"So how was your day, John?" her mother turns and asks me. We make small talk. She tells me of the trip to the mall that the two of them made earlier in the day, and how Sarah drove. I tell her about playing with Bernie Kosar in the yard, and about the run we went on after. I *don't* tell her about the training session that lasted for three hours in the backyard after the run. I don't tell her how I split the dead tree's trunk straight down the middle through telekinesis, or how Henri threw knives at me that I deflected into a sandbag fifty feet away. I don't tell her about being lit on fire or the objects that I lifted and crushed and splintered. Another kept secret. Another half-truth that feels like a lie. I would like to tell Sarah. I somehow feel that I'm betraying her by keeping myself hidden, and over the last few weeks the burden has really begun to weigh on me. But I also know I have no other choice. Not at this point, anyhow.

"So it's this one?" Sarah asks.

"Yes," I say.

She pulls into Sam's driveway. He paces at the end of it, dressed in jeans and a wool sweater. He looks up at us with a deer-caught-in-the-headlights blank stare. There is gel in his hair. I've never seen gel in his hair before. He walks to the side of the car, opens the door, and slides in beside me.

"Hi, Sam," Sarah says, then introduces him to her mom.

Sarah reverses the car out of the driveway and pulls onto the road. Both of Sam's hands are planted firmly on the seat in nervousness. Sarah turns down a road I've never seen before and makes a right turn into a winding driveway. Thirty or so cars are parked along the side of it. At the end of the driveway, surrounded by trees, is a large, two-story house. We can hear the music well before we reach the house.

"Jeez, nice house," Sam says.

"You guys be good in there," Sarah's mom says. "And be safe. Call if you need anything, or if you can't get ahold of your father," she says, looking at me.

"Will do, Mrs. Hart," I say.

We get out of the car and begin walking to the front door. Two dogs run up to us from the side of the house, a golden retriever and a bull-dog. Their tails are wagging and they're sniffing spastically at my pants, smelling the scent of Bernie Kosar. The bulldog is carrying a stick in his mouth. I wrestle it away from him and throw it across the yard and both dogs sprint after it.

"Dozer and Abby," Sarah says.

"I take it Dozer is the bulldog?" I ask.

She nods and smiles at me as though in

apology. I'm reminded how well she must know this house. I wonder if it's odd for her to be back now, with me.

"This is a horrible idea," Sam says. He looks at me. "I'm only now realizing that."

"Why do you think so?"

"Because only three months ago the guy who lives here filled both our lockers with cow manure and hit me in the back of the head with a meatball during lunch. And now we're here."

"I bet Emily is already here," I say, and nudge him with my elbow.

The door opens into the foyer. The dogs come rushing in past us and disappear into the kitchen, which lies straight ahead. I can see that Abby is now holding the stick. We're met with loud music that we have to yell over to be heard. People are dancing in the living room. There are cans of beer in most of their hands, a few people drinking bottled water or soda. Apparently Mark's parents are out of town. The whole football team is in the kitchen, half of them wearing their letterman jackets. Mark comes up and hugs Sarah. Then he shakes my hand. He holds my gaze for a second and then looks away. He doesn't shake Sam's hand. He doesn't even look at him. Perhaps Sam is right. This may have been a mistake.

"Happy you guys could make it. Come on in. Beer's in the kitchen."

Emily stands in the far corner talking to other people. Sam looks her way, then asks Mark where the bathroom is. He points the way.

"Be right back," Sam says to me.

Most of the guys are standing around the island in the middle of the kitchen. They look at me when Sarah and I enter. I look at each of them in turn, and then grab a bottle of water from the ice bucket. Mark hands Sarah a beer and opens it for her. The way he looks at her makes me realize yet again just how little I trust him. And I realize now just how bizarre this whole situation is. Me, being in his house now, with Sarah, his ex-girl-friend. I'm happy that Sam is with me.

I reach down and play with the dogs until Sam comes out of the bathroom. By then Sarah has made her way to the corner of the living room and is talking to Emily. Sam tenses beside me when he realizes that there is nothing else for us to do but walk up to them and say hello. He takes a deep breath. In the kitchen two of the guys have lit a corner of the newspaper on fire for no other reason than to watch it burn.

"Make sure you compliment Emily," I say to Sam as we approach. He nods.

"There you guys are," Sarah says. "I thought you had left me all by my lonesome."

"Wouldn't dream of it," I say. "Hi, Emily. How are you?"

"I'm good," she says, then to Sam, "I like your hair."

Sam just looks at her. I nudge him. He smiles.

"Thank you," he says. "You look very nice."

Sarah gives me a knowing look. I shrug and kiss her on the cheek. The music has grown even louder. Sam talks to Emily, somewhat nervously, but she laughs and after a while he eases a little.

"So are you okay?" Sarah asks me.

"Of course. I'm with the prettiest girl at the party. How could things be better?"

"Oh shush," she says, and pokes me in the stomach.

The four of us dance for an hour or so. The football players keep drinking. Somebody shows up with a bottle of vodka and not long after that one of them—I don't know which—throws up in the bathroom so that the smell of vomit wafts throughout the whole downstairs. Another one passes out on the living-room sofa and some of the others draw with marker on his face. People keep filtering in and out of the doorway leading to the basement. I have no idea what is going on down there. I haven't seen Sarah for the past ten minutes. I leave Sam and walk through the living room and the kitchen, then walk up the stairs. White, thick carpet, walls lined with art and family portraits. Some of the bedroom doors are open. Some are closed. I don't see Sarah. I walk back downstairs. Sam is standing sullenly by himself in the corner. I walk over to him.

"Why the long face?" I ask.

He shakes his head.

"Don't make me lift you in the air and turn you upside down like the guy in Athens."

I smile, Sam doesn't.

"I just got cornered by Alex Davis," he says.

Alex Davis is another of Mark James's brood, a wide receiver for the team. He's a junior, tall and thin. I've never talked to him before, and likewise know little else about him.

"What do you mean by 'cornered'?"

"We just talked. He saw that I've been talking to Emily. I guess they dated over the summer."

"So what. Why does that bother you?"

He shrugs. "It just sucks, and it bothers me, okay?"

"Sam, do you know how long Sarah and Mark dated?"

"For a long time."

"Two years," I say.

"Does it bother you?" he asks.

"Not in the least. Who cares about her past? Besides, look at Alex," I say, and nod to him standing in the kitchen. He is slumped against the kitchen counter, his eyes aflutter, a thin layer of sweat glistening on his forehead. "Do you really think she misses being with that?"

Sam looks at him, shrugs.

"You're a good dude, Sam Goode. Don't get down on yourself."

"I'm not down on myself."

"Well then, don't worry about Emily's past. We don't have to be defined by the things we did or didn't do in our past. Some people allow themselves to be controlled by regret. Maybe it's a regret, maybe it's not. It's merely something that happened. Get over it."

Sam sighs. He's still wrestling with it.

"Go on. She likes you. There's nothing to be scared of," I say.

"I am, though."

"Best way to deal with fear is to confront it. Just walk up to her and kiss her. I bet you she kisses you back."

Sam looks at me and nods, then goes to the basement, where Emily is hanging out. The two dogs come wrestling into the living room. Tongues dangling. Tails wagging. Dozer drops his chest to the ground and waits for Abby to come near enough and then he jumps at her and she jumps away. I watch them until they disappear up the stairs, playing tug-of-war with a rubber toy. It's a quarter till midnight. A couple is making out on the couch across the room. The football players are still drinking in the kitchen. I'm starting to get sleepy. I still can't find Sarah.

Just then one of the football players comes rushing up the basement stairs, a crazed, frantic look in his eyes. He rushes to the kitchen sink, turns on the water as high as it will go, and begins throwing open the kitchen-cupboard doors.

"There's a fire downstairs!" he says to the guys nearby.

They begin filling pots and pans with water, and one by one they rush down the stairs.

Emily and Sam come up the stairs. Sam looks shaken.

"What's wrong?" I say.

"The house is on fire!"

"How bad?"

"Is any fire good? And I think we started it. We, uh, knocked a candle into a curtain."

Sam and Emily both look disheveled and have clearly been making out. I make a mental note to congratulate Sam later.

"Have you seen Sarah?" I ask Emily.

She shakes her head.

More guys rush up the stairs, Mark James with them. There is fear in his eyes. For the first time I smell smoke. I look at Sam.

"Go outside," I say.

He nods and takes Emily's hand and they leave together. Some of the others follow, but some stay where they are, watching with drunken curiosity.

A few people stand around stupidly patting the football players on the back as they rush up and down the basement stairs, cheering them on as though it's all a joke.

I go to the kitchen and grab the largest thing left, a medium-sized metal pot. I fill it with water and then go downstairs. Everybody has evacuated aside from us battling the blaze, which is far bigger than I expected. Half the basement is consumed in flames. Dousing it with the little water I have left is completely futile. I don't try, and instead drop the pot and dash back up. Mark comes flying down. I stop him in the middle of the stairway. His eyes are swimming in booze but through it I can see that he is terrified, that he is desperate.

"Forget about it," I say. "It's too big. We have to get everyone out."

He looks down the stairs at the fire. He knows that what I've said is true. The tough-guy front is gone. There is no more pretending.

"Mark!" I yell.

He nods and drops the pot and we go back up together.

"Everybody out! Now!" I yell when I get to the top of the stairs.

Some of the drunker ones don't move. Some of them laugh. One person says, "Where's the marshmallows?" Mark slaps him across the face.

"Get out!" he screams.

I rip the cordless phone from the wall and shove it into Mark's hand.

"Dial 911," I yell over the loud voices and the music that still blares from somewhere like a sound track to the erupting pandemonium. The floor is getting warm. Smoke begins to billow up from beneath us. Only then do people take it seriously. I start pushing them towards the door.

I dart past Mark as he begins dialing and rush through the house. I take the stairs three at a time and kick through the open doors. One couple is making out on a bed. I yell at them both to get out. Sarah's nowhere to be found. I sprint back down the stairs and through the door into the dark, cold night. People are standing around, watching. Some of them I can tell are excited by the prospect of the house burning down. Some laugh. I can feel myself begin to panic. Where is Sarah? Sam stands at the back of the crowd, which must total a hundred people. I run to him.

"Have you seen Sarah?" I ask.

"No," he says.

I look back at the house. People are still coming out. The basement windows glow red, flames licking against the panes of glass. One of them is open. Black smoke pours out of it and floats high in the air. I weave through the crowd. Just then an explosion rattles the house. All the basement windows shatter. Some of the people cheer. The flames have reached the first floor, and they're moving fast. Mark James stands at the front of the crowd, unable to divert his gaze away from it. His face is illuminated by the orange glow. There are tears in his eyes, a look of despair, the same look that I saw in the eyes of the Loric on the day of the invasion. What an odd thing it must be to watch everything you've ever known be destroyed. The fire spreads with hostility, with disregard. All Mark can do is watch. Flames are beginning to rise up past the first-floor windows. We can feel the heat on our faces from where we stand.

"Where's Sarah?" I ask him.

He doesn't hear me. I shake him by the shoulder. He turns and looks at me with a blankness that suggests he still doesn't believe what his own eyes are telling him.

"Where's Sarah?" I ask again.

"I don't know," he says.

I start to weave through the crowd looking for her, getting more and more frantic. Everyone is watching the blaze. The vinyl siding has begun to bubble and melt. The curtains in the windows have all burned away. The front door stands open, smoke pouring out of the top of it like an upside-down waterfall. We can see all the way into the kitchen, which is an inferno. On the left side of the house the fire has reached the second floor. And that's when we all hear it.

A long terrible scream. And dogs barking. My heart drops. Every person there strains to listen while hoping like hell we didn't hear what we all know we did. And then it comes again. Unmistakable. It comes in a torrent and this time it doesn't let up. Gasps filter throughout the crowd.

"Oh no," Emily says. "Oh God no, please no."

CHAPTER TWENTY-SIX

NOBODY SPEAKS. ALL EYES ARE wide-open, staring up in shock. Sarah and the dogs must be somewhere in the back. I close my eyes and lower my head. All I can smell is the smoke. "Just remember what's at stake," Henri had warned. I know damn well what's at stake, but still his voice echoes. My life, and now Sarah's life. There is another scream. Terrified. Severe.

I feel Sam's eyes on me. He has seen first-hand my resistance to fire. But he also knows how I am hunted. I glance around. Mark is on his knees, rocking himself back and forth. He wants it over with. He wants the dogs to stop barking. But they don't stop, and he takes each bark as though being stabbed in the gut with a knife.

"Sam," I say so that only he can hear, "I'm

going in." He closes his eyes, takes a deep breath, fixes me with a stare.

"Go get her," he says.

I hand him my phone and tell him to call Henri if for some reason I don't make it out. He nods. I begin moving to the back of the crowd, weaving in and out of the mass of bodies. Nobody pays me any attention. When I finally reach the back I make a mad dash for the yard's perimeter and then sprint to the rear of the house so that I can enter without being seen. The kitchen is completely submerged in flame. I watch it for a brief moment. I can hear Sarah and the dogs. They sound closer now. I take a deep breath and with that breath other things come. Anger. Determination. Hope and fear. I let them in, I feel them all. And then I lunge forward and sweep across the yard and burst into the house. I am swallowed by the inferno immediately, hearing nothing but the crackle and hum of the flames. My clothes catch fire. There is no end to the blaze. I move to the front of the house and half of the stairs have burned away. What is left is on fire, looking brittle, but there isn't time to test them. I rush up but they collapse under my weight when I reach the half-way point. I tumble down with them, the fire rising as though someone has stoked the flames. Something pierces my back. I grit my teeth, still holding my breath. I stand from the rubble and listen to Sarah screaming. She's screaming and she's scared and she's going to die, die a hideous miserable death if I don't get to her. Time is short. I'll have to jump to the second floor.

I jump and grab hold of the edge of the floor and pull myself up. The fire has spread to the other side of the house. She and the dogs are somewhere to my right. I leap down the hallway, checking rooms. The pictures on the walls have burned in their frames, nothing more than blackened silhouettes melted to the wall. Then my foot falls through the floor and my breath catches in surprise and I breathe in. Nothing but smoke and flame enter. I begin coughing. I cover my mouth with my arm but it does little to help. Smoke and fire are burning my lungs. I drop to a knee, coughing, gasping. Then a fury surges through me and I stand back up and I move on, hunched over, gritting my teeth, determined.

And then I find them in the last room on the left. Sarah is screaming, "HELP!" The dogs are whining and crying. The door is closed and I kick it open, send it flying off its hinges. All three of them are huddled as tightly against one another as far into the corner as they can get. Sarah sees me and yells my name and starts to stand. I motion to her to stay where she is, and as I step into the room, a huge flaming support beam falls between us. I raise my hand and send it upwards, crashing through what remains of the roof. Sarah seems confused by what she's just seen. I leap towards her, covering twenty feet in a single bound, moving straight through the flames without them affecting me at all. The dogs are at her feet. I push the bulldog into her arms and pick up the retriever. With my other arm I help her stand.

"You came," she says.

"No one, and nothing, will ever hurt you as long as I'm alive," I say back to her.

Another huge beam falls and takes out part of the floor, landing in the kitchen below us. We need to get out the back of the house so no one sees me, or sees what I think I'm going to need to do. I hold Sarah tight against my side and the dog against my chest. We take two steps, then leap over the flaming chasm created by the fallen beam. As we start to move down the hall, a huge explosion below takes out most of it. The hallway is gone; where it used to be are a wall and a window, quickly being consumed by flames. Our only chance is through the window. Sarah is screaming again, clutching my arm, and I can feel the dog's claws digging into my chest. I lift my hand towards the window, stare at it, and focus—and it blows out of its frame, leaving us the opening we need. I look at Sarah, pulling her securely against my side.

"Hold on tight," I say.

I take three steps and dive forward. The flames swallow us whole but we fly through the air like a bullet, heading straight towards the opening. I'm worried we're not going to make it. We barely clear it, and I feel the edge of the shattered frame scrape against my arms and the tops of my legs. I hold Sarah and the dog as best as I can, and twist my body so that I'll land on my back and everyone else will be on top of me. We hit the ground with a thud. Dozer goes rolling. Abby yelps. I hear the breath go out of Sarah. We're about thirty feet behind the house. I feel a cut on the top of my head from the broken glass of the window. Dozer is the first one up. He seems fine. Abby is a little slower. She limps on her front paw, but I don't think it is anything serious. I lie on my back and hold Sarah. She is starting to cry. I can smell her singed hair. Blood drips down the side of my face and gathers in my ear.

I sit in the grass to catch my breath. Sarah is in my arms. The bottoms of my shoes have melted. My shirt has completely burned away, and so have most of my jeans. Small cuts traverse the length of both arms. But I am not burned at all. Dozer walks over and licks my hand. I pet him.

"You're a good boy," I say between Sarah's sobs. "Go on. Get your sister and go back up front."

There are sirens in the distance that should be here within the next minute or two. The woods are about a hundred yards from the back of the house. Both dogs sit watching me. I nod to the front of the house and they get up as if they understand and both begin walking that way. Sarah is still in my arms. I turn her so she is cradled in them and I stand and head to the woods, carrying her as she cries on my shoulder. Just as I enter them I hear the whole crowd erupt in cheers. Dozer and Abby must have been seen.

The woods are dense. The full moon still shines but there is little light coming from it. I turn my hands on so we can see. I start to shiver. Panic sweeps through me. How will I explain this to Henri? I'm wearing what now look like singed cutoffs. My head is bleeding. So is my back, along with various cuts on my arms and legs. My lungs feel as though they are on fire with every breath I take. And Sarah is in my arms. She now must know what I can do, what I am capable of, or at least some of it. I'm going to have to explain everything to her. I'll have to tell Henri she knows. I already have too many strikes against me. He'll say someone will slip at some point. He'll insist we leave. There's no way around it.

I set Sarah down. She's stopped crying. She looks at me, confused, scared, bewildered. I know I need to get some clothes and get back to the party so that people aren't suspicious. I need to get Sarah back so people don't think she's dead.

"You're okay to walk?" I say.

"I think so."

"Follow me."

"Where are we going?"

"I need to get some clothes. Hopefully, one of the football players has a change of clothes for after practice."

We start walking through the woods. I'm going to circle around and look inside people's cars for something to wear.

"What just happened, John? What is happening?"

"You were in a fire, and I got you out of it."

"What you did isn't possible."

"It is for me."

"What's that supposed to mean?"

I look at her. I had hoped never to have to tell her what I'm about to tell her. Even though I knew it probably wasn't realistic, I had hoped to stay hidden in Paradise. Henri has always said never to get too close to anyone. Because if you do, at some point they're going to notice that you're different, and that will require an explanation. And that means we have to leave. My heart is pounding, my hands are shaking, but not because I'm cold. If I have any hope of staying, or of getting away with what I did tonight, I have to tell her.

"I am not who you think I am," I say.

"Who are you?"

"I am Number Four."

"What's that supposed to mean?"

"Sarah, it's going to sound stupid and crazy, but what I'm about to say is the truth. You have to believe me."

She touches her hand to the side of my face. "If you say it's the truth, then I'll believe you."

"It is."

"Then tell me."

"I'm an alien. I am the fourth of nine kids sent to Earth after our planet was destroyed. I have powers, powers unlike any human, powers that allow me to do things like I did in the house. And there are other aliens here on Earth who are hunting me, the ones who attacked my planet, and if they find me they will kill me."

I expect her to slap me, or laugh at me, or scream, or turn and run away from me. She stops and looks at me. Looks right into my eyes.

"You're telling me the truth," she says.

"Yes, I am." I look into her eyes, willing her to believe me. She stares searchingly at me for a long moment, and then nods.

"Thank you for saving my life. I don't care what you are or where you're from. To me you're John, the boy I love."

"What?"

"I love you, John, and you saved my life, and that's all that's important."

"I love you too. And I always will."

I wrap my arms around her and kiss her. After a minute or so, she pulls away.

"Let's go find you some clothes and get back so people know we're okay."

⌗

Sarah finds a change of clothes in the fourth car we check. They're close enough to what I was wearing—jeans and a button-down shirt—that no one will notice the difference. When we reach the house we stand as far away as possible while still being able to see. The house has collapsed in on itself and is now nothing more than a twisted heap of blackened coals soggy with water. Wisps of smoke sporadically rise, looking ghastly in the night sky. There are three fire trucks. I count six cop cars. Nine sets of flashing lights but no sound to go with them. Few people, if any, have left. They've been pushed back, the house cordoned off with yellow tape. The police officers are questioning some of them. Five firemen stand in the middle of it all, sifting through the rubble.

Then I hear "There they are!" yelled from behind me. Every set of eyes in the crowd turns my way. It takes me a full five seconds to realize that it is me the person is referring to.

Four police officers walk towards us. Behind them is a man holding a notepad and tape recorder. While we were looking for the clothes, Sarah and I agreed on a story. I came around the back of the house where she was watching the fire. She had jumped out of the second-floor window with the dogs, who had run away. We had watched away from the crowd, but eventually drifted over and joined it. I explained to her that we couldn't tell anyone about what happened, not even Sam or Henri, that if anyone found out the truth, I would have to leave immediately. We agreed that I would answer the questions and she would agree with whatever I said.

"Are you John Smith?" one of the cops asks me. The officer is of medium height, and stands with his shoulders hunched. He isn't overweight but is far from being in shape, with a slight paunch and an overall look of softness.

"Yes, why?"

"Two people said they saw you run into that house and then come flying out the back of it like Superman, with the dogs and the girl in your arms."

"Seriously?" I ask in disbelief. Sarah stays beside me.

"That's what they said."

I fake a laugh. "The house was on fire. Do I look like I was inside a burning house?"

He scrunches his eyebrows together and rests his hands on his hips. "So you're telling me you didn't go in there?"

"I came around the back to try and find Sarah," I say. "She had gotten out with the dogs. We stayed back there and watched the fire and then came over here."

The officer looks at Sarah. "Is that true?"

"Yes."

"Well, who ran into that house, then?" the reporter beside him chimes in. It's his first time speaking. He watches me with shrewd, judging eyes. I can already tell that he doesn't believe my story.

"How do I know?" I say.

He nods his head and writes something in his notebook. I can't read what it says.

"So you're telling me these two witnesses are liars?" the reporter asks.

"Baines," the officer says, shaking his head at him.

I nod. "I didn't go into the house and save her or the dogs. They were outside."

"Who said anything about saving her or the

dogs?" Baines asks.

I shrug. "I thought that's what you were implying."

"I didn't imply anything."

Sam walks up with my phone. I try to fix him with a stare to tell him the timing is bad, but he doesn't understand and he hands me my phone anyway.

"Thanks," I say.

"I'm happy you're okay," he says. The officers glare at him and he slinks away.

Baines watches with his eyes squinted. He's chewing gum, trying to piece the information together. He nods to himself.

"So you handed your phone to your friend before you went for a walk?" he asks.

"I handed him my phone during the party. It was uncomfortable in my pocket."

"I bet it was," Baines says. "So where did you go?"

"All right, Baines, that's enough questions," the officer says.

"Can I leave?" I ask him. He nods his head. I walk away with my phone in my hand, dialing Henri's number with Sarah at my side.

"Hello," answers Henri.

"I'm ready to be picked up," I say. "There's been a terrible fire here."

"What?"

"Can you just pick us up?"

"Yes. I'll be right there."

"So how do you explain the cut on the top of your head?" Baines asks from behind me. He had been following me, listening to my call to Henri.

"I cut it on a branch in the woods."

"How convenient," he says, and again writes something in his notebook. "You know I can tell when I'm being lied to, right?"

I ignore him, keep walking away with Sarah's hand in mine. We head over to Sam.

"I'll find the truth, Mr. Smith. I always do," Baines yells behind me.

"Henri is on the way," I say to Sam and Sarah.

"What the hell was that all about?" Sam asks.

"Who knows? Somebody thinks they saw me run in, probably somebody who drank too much," I say more at Baines than Sam.

We stand at the end of the driveway until Henri arrives. When he pulls up he steps out of the truck and looks at the smoldering house far off in the distance.

"Ah, hell. Promise me you weren't a part of this," he says.

"I wasn't," I say.

We get into the truck. He pulls away while looking at the smoking rubble.

"You guys smell like smoke," Henri says.

None of us reply, making the drive in silence.

Sarah sits on my lap. We drop Sam off first, then Henri pulls out of the driveway and points the truck towards Sarah's home.

"I don't want to leave you tonight," Sarah says to me.

"I don't want to leave you either."

When we arrive at her house I get out with her and walk her to the door. She won't let go of me when I hug her good night.

"Will you call me when you get home?"

"Of course."

"I love you."

I smile. "I love you too."

She goes inside. I walk back to the truck, where Henri is waiting. I have to figure out a way to keep him from finding out the truth about tonight, from making us leave Paradise. Henri pulls out and drives home.

"So what happened to your jacket?" he asks.

"It was in Mark's closet."

"What happened to your head?"

"I hit it trying to get out when the fire first started."

He looks over at me doubtfully. "You're the one who smells like smoke."

I shrug. "There was a lot of it."

"So what started it?"

"Drunkenness is my guess."

Henri nods and turns down our road.

"Well," he says. "It will be interesting to see what's in the papers on Monday." He turns and looks at me, studying my reaction.

I keep silent.

Yes, I think, *it most certainly will be.*

CHAPTER TWENTY-SEVEN

I CAN'T SLEEP. I LIE IN BED STARING through the darkness at the ceiling. I call Sarah and we talk until three; I hang up and lie there with my eyes wide-open. At four I crawl out of bed and walk out of the room. Henri sits at the kitchen table, drinking coffee. He looks up at me, bags beneath his eyes, hair tousled.

"What are you doing?" I ask.

"I couldn't sleep either," he says. "Scouring the news."

"Find anything?"

"Yes, but I'm not sure what it means to us yet. The men who wrote and published *They Walk Among Us*, the men we met, were tortured and killed."

I sit across from him. "What?"

"Police found them when the neighbors called after hearing screams coming from the house."

"They didn't know where we lived."

"No, they didn't. Thankfully. But it means the Mogadorians are getting bolder. And they're close. If we see or hear anything else out of the ordinary, we're going to need to leave immediately, no questions asked, no discussion."

"Okay."

"How's your head?"

"Sore," I say. It took seven stitches to close the cut. Henri did it himself. I'm wearing a baggy sweatshirt. I'm certain one of the cuts on my back needs stitches as well, but that would require me to take my shirt off, and how would I explain the other cuts and scrapes to Henri? He'll know for sure what has happened. My lungs still burn. If anything, the pain has grown worse.

"So, the fire started in the basement?"

"Yes."

"And you were in the living room?"

"Yes."

"How did you know it started in the basement?"

"Because all the guys came running up."

"And you knew everyone was out of the house by the time you went outside?"

"Yes."

"How?"

I can tell he's trying to get me to contradict myself, that he's skeptical of my story. I'm certain he doesn't believe that I merely stood out front watching like everyone else.

"I didn't go in," I say. It pains me to do so, but I look him in the eye and I lie.

"I believe you," he says.

I wake close to noon. Birds are chirping beyond the window, and sunlight is pouring in. I breathe a sigh of relief. The fact that I was allowed to sleep this late means that there was no news to incriminate me. If there had been, I would have been pulled from bed and told to pack.

I roll off my back and that's when the pain hits. My chest feels as though somebody is pushing down on it, squeezing me. I can't take full breaths. When I try there is a sharp pain. It scares me.

Bernie Kosar is snoring in a ball at my side. I wake him by wrestling with him. He groans at first, then wrestles back. That is the beginning to our day. Me rousing the snoring dog beside me. His wagging tail, his dangling tongue immediately make me feel better. Never mind the pain in my chest. Never mind what the day might bring.

Henri's truck is gone. On the table is a note that reads: "Ran to the store. Be back at one." I walk outside. I have a headache and my arms are red and splotchy, the cuts slightly raised as though I've been scratched by a cat. I don't care about the cuts, or my headache, or the burning in my chest. What I care about is that I'm still here, in Ohio, that tomorrow I'll be going back to the same school I've gone to for three months now, and that I will see Sarah tonight.

Henri gets home at one. There is a haggard look in his eyes that tells me he still hasn't slept. After he unloads the groceries he goes into his bedroom and closes the door. Bernie Kosar and I go for a walk in the woods. I try to run, and I'm able to for a little while, but after a half mile or so the pain is too great and I have to stop. We walk on for what must be five miles. The woods end at another country road that looks similar to ours. I turn around and walk back. Henri is still in his room with the door closed when I return. I sit on the porch. I tense every time a car passes. I keep thinking one of them will stop, but none of them do.

The confidence I felt when I woke up is slowly chipped away as the day wanes. The *Paradise Gazette* isn't printed on Sunday. Will there be a story tomorrow? I suppose I expected a call to arrive, or the same reporter to show up at our doorstep, or one of the officers to ask more questions. I don't know why I'm so worried about a small-time reporter, but he'd been persistent— too persistent. And I know he didn't believe my story.

But nobody comes to our house. No one calls. I expected something, and when that something doesn't come, a dread creeps in that I'm about to be exposed. "I'll find the truth, Mr. Smith. I always do," Baines said. I consider running into town, trying to find him to dissuade him from any such truth, but I know that would only encourage suspicion. All I can do is hold my breath and hope for the best.

I wasn't in that house.

I have nothing to hide.

Sarah comes over that night. We go to my room and I hold her in my arms, lying on my back on the bed. Her head is against my chest and her leg is draped over me. She asks me questions about who I am, my past, about Lorien, about the Mogadorians. I'm still amazed at how quickly, and easily, Sarah believed everything, and how she's accepted it. I answer everything truthfully, which feels good after all the lies I've told over the last few days. But when we talk about the Mogadorians, I start to get scared. I'm worried that they'll find us. That what I did will expose us. I would do it again, for if I didn't Sarah would be dead, but I'm scared. I'm also scared of what Henri is going to do if he finds out. Though he is not biologically, for all intents and purposes he is my father. I love him and he loves me and I don't want to disappoint him. And as we lie there, my fear begins to reach new levels. I can't take not knowing what the next day will bring—the uncertainty is sawing me in two. The room is dark. A flickering candle burns on the window ledge a few feet away. I take a deep breath, which is to say, as deep a breath as I *can* take.

"Are you okay?" Sarah asks.

I wrap my arms around her. "I miss you," I say.

"You miss me? But I'm right here."

"That's the worst way to miss somebody. When they're right beside you and you miss them anyway."

"You're talking crazy." She reaches up and pulls my face to hers and kisses me, her soft lips on mine. I don't want her to stop. I don't ever want her to stop kissing me. As long as she is, then everything is fine. Everything is right. I would stay in this room forever if I could. The world can pass by without me, without us. Just as long as we can stay here, together, in each other's arms.

"Tomorrow," I say.

She looks up at me. "Tomorrow, what?"

I shake my head. "I don't really know," I say. "I guess I'm just scared."

She flashes a confused look at me. "Scared of what?"

"I don't know," I say. "Just scared."

When Henri and I get home after dropping her off I go back into my bedroom and lie in the same spot where she was. I can still smell her on my bed. I won't sleep tonight. I won't even try. I pace the room. When Henri goes to bed I walk out and sit at the kitchen table and write under candlelight. I write about Lorien, about Florida, about the things that I've seen when our training first began—the war, the animals, childhood images. I hope for some sort of cathartic release, but there isn't one. It only makes me sadder.

When my hand cramps I walk out of the house and stand on the porch. The cold air helps ease the pain of breathing. The moon is nearly full, a side of it ever so subtly shaved away. Sunrise is two hours away, and with that sunrise comes a new day, and the news of the weekend. The paper falls on our doorstep at six, sometimes six thirty. I'll already be at the school by the time it arrives and, if I'm in the news, I refuse to leave without seeing Sarah again, without saying good-bye to Sam.

I walk into the house, change clothes, and pack my bag. I tiptoe back through and quietly close the door behind me. I take three steps on the porch when I hear a scratching at the door. I turn around and open it and Bernie Kosar comes trotting out. *Okay,* I think, *let us go together.*

We walk, stopping often, standing and listening to the silence. The night is dark but after a while a pale glow grows in the eastern sky just as we enter the school grounds. There are no cars in the lot and all the lights are off inside. At the very front of the school, in front of the pirate mural, sits a large rock that has been painted by previous graduating classes. I sit on it. Bernie Kosar lies in the grass a few feet away from me. I'm there for half an hour before the first vehicle arrives, a van, and I assume it's Hobbs, the janitor, arriving early to get the school in order, but I'm wrong. The van pulls up to the front doors and the driver gets out and leaves it idling. He's carrying a stack of newspapers bound by wire. We nod at each other and he drops the stack by the door and then drives off. I stay on the rock. I glance contemptuously at the papers. In my mind I'm hurling curses at them, threatening them to deliver the bad news I'm terrified of.

"I wasn't in that house on Saturday," I say out loud, and as soon as I do I feel stupid. Then I look away, sigh, and jump off the rock.

"Well," I say to Bernie Kosar. "This is it, for good or bad."

He opens his eyes briefly, then closes them and resumes his nap on the cold ground.

I tear the binding away and lift the top paper. The story has made the front page. At the very top is a picture of the burned rubble taken the next morning at dawn. There is a gothic, foreboding feel to it. Blackened ash is forefront to naked trees and frost-covered grass. I read the headline:

JAMES HOUSE GOES *UP IN SMOKE*

I hold my breath, a miserable feeling centered in my gut as though horrible news is about to find me. I race through the article. I don't read it, only look for my name. I reach the end. I blink my eyes and shake my head to rid myself of the cobwebs. A cautious smile forms. Then I scan through it again.

"No way," I say. "Bernie Kosar, my name isn't here!"

He pays me no attention. I run across the grass and jump back on the rock.

"My name isn't here!" I yell again, this time as loudly as I can.

I sit back down and read the story. The headline is a play on Cheech and Chong's *Up in Smoke*, which is apparently a movie about drugs. What the police believe started the blaze was a marijuana joint being smoked in the basement. How that information was discovered, I have no idea, especially because it is so wrong. The article itself is callous and mean, almost an attack on the James family. I didn't like the reporter. It's apparent that he doesn't like the Jameses. Who knows why?

I sit on the rock and read the article three times before the first person arrives to unlock the doors. I can't stop smiling. I'm staying in Ohio, in Paradise. The town name doesn't seem so foolish to me anymore. Through my excitement I feel as though I'm overlooking something, that I've forgotten a key component. But I'm so happy that I don't care. What harm can come now? My name isn't in the article. I didn't run into that house. The proof is right here, in my hands. Nobody can say otherwise.

"What are you so happy about?" Sam asks in astronomy class. I haven't stopped smiling.

"Didn't you read the paper this morning?"

He nods.

"Sam, I wasn't in it! I don't have to leave."

"Why would they put you in the paper?" he asks.

I'm dumbfounded. I open my mouth to argue with him but just then Sarah walks into the room. She comes sauntering up the aisle.

"Hey, gorgeous," I say.

She bends down and kisses me on the cheek, something I'll never take for granted.

"Somebody's in a happy mood today," she says.

"Happy to see you," I say. "Nervous about your driver's test?"

"Maybe a little. Just can't wait until it's over."

She sits down beside me. *This is my day,* I think. *This is where I want to be and this is where I am. Sarah on one side, Sam on the other.*

I go to class as I've done all the other days. I sit with Sam at lunch. We don't talk about the fire. We must be the only two in the whole school not talking about it. The same story, over and over. I never hear my name spoken once. As I expected, Mark isn't in school. A rumor spreads that he and several of the others will be suspended for the theory the paper has spouted. I don't know if it's true or not. I don't know if I care.

By the time Sarah and I enter the kitchen for eighth-period home ec, my certainty that I'm safe has taken a firm hold. Such a strong certainty that I'm confident I must be wrong, that something has been overlooked. The doubt has been creeping up throughout the day but I've been quick to push it back down.

We make tapioca pudding. An easy day. In the middle of class, the kitchen door opens. It's the hall monitor. I look at him and I know immediately what it means. The harbinger of bad news. The messenger of death. He walks straight up to me and hands me a slip of paper.

"Mr. Harris wants to see you," he says.

"Now?"

He nods.

I look at Sarah and shrug. I don't want her to see my fear. I smile at her and walk to the door. Before I leave I turn around and look at her again. She's bent over the table mixing our ingredients, wearing the same green apron that I tied on her my first day, the day we made pancakes and ate them off the same plate. Her hair is in a ponytail and loose strands dangle in front of her face. She tucks them behind her ear and as she does she sees me standing in the doorway watching her. I keep staring, trying to remember every minute detail of this moment, the way she grips the wooden spoon in her hand, the ivory look to her skin with the light coming in the windows behind her, the tenderness in her eyes. Her shirt has a loose button at the collar. I wonder if she knows about it. Then the hall monitor says something behind me. I wave at Sarah, shut the door, and walk down the hall. I take my time, trying to convince myself that it's just a formality, some document we forgot to sign, some question about transcripts. But I know it's not just a formality.

Mr. Harris sits at his desk when I enter the office. He is smiling in a way that terrifies me, the same prideful smile that he had on the day he pulled Mark from class to do the interview.

"Sit down," he says. I sit. "So, is it true?" he asks. He glances at his computer screen, then he looks back at me.

"Is what true?"

On his desk there is an envelope with my name handwritten in black ink. He sees me looking at it.

"Oh yes, this was faxed to you about half an hour ago."

He picks the envelope up and tosses it to me. I catch it.

"What is it?" I ask.

"No idea. My secretary sealed it in the envelope as soon as it arrived."

Several things happen at once. I open the envelope and remove its contents. Two sheets of paper. The top is a cover page with my name on it and "CONFIDENTIAL" written in large black letters. I shuffle it behind the second sheet. A single sentence written in all capitals. No name. Just four black words on a white canvas.

"So, Mr. Smith, is it true? Did you run into that burning house to save Sarah Hart and those dogs?" Mr. Harris asks. Blood rushes to my face. I look up. He turns his computer monitor towards me so that I can read the screen. It's the blog affiliated with the *Paradise Gazette*. I don't need to look at the name of the author to know who has written it. The title is more than enough.

THE JAMES HOUSE FIRE: THE UNTOLD STORY

My breath catches in my throat. My heart races. The world stops, or at least it seems to. I feel dead inside. I look back down at the sheet of paper I'm holding. White paper, smooth in my fingertips. It reads:

ARE YOU NUMBER 4?

Both sheets fall from my hands, drift away, and float to the floor, where they lie motionless. *I don't understand,* I think. *How can this be?*

"So is it?" Mr. Harris asks.

My mouth drops open. Mr. Harris is smiling, proud, happy. But it's not him that I see. It's what's behind him, seen through the windows of his office. A blur of red coming around the corner, moving faster than what is normal, than what is safe. The squeal of tires as it zips into the lot. The pickup truck throwing gravel as it makes a second turn. Henri leaning over the wheel like some crazed maniac. He hits the brakes so forcefully that his whole body jerks and the truck comes screeching to a stop.

I close my eyes.

I place my head in my hands.

Through the window I hear the truck door open. I hear it close.

Henri will be in this office within the minute.

CHAPTER TWENTY-EIGHT

"ARE YOU OKAY, MR. SMITH?" THE principal asks. I look up at him. He attempts his best look of concern, a look that lasts only a second before the toothy grin returns to his face.

"No, Mr. Harris," I say. "I'm not okay."

I pick the sheet up off the floor. I read it again. Where did it come from? Are they merely screwing with us now? There is no phone number or address, no name. Nothing but four words and a question mark. I look up and out the window. Henri's truck is parked, fumes rising from the exhaust. In and out as quickly as he can. I look back at the computer screen. The article was posted at 11:59 a.m., almost two hours ago. I'm amazed it took Henri this long to arrive. A sense of vertigo seeps in. I feel myself sway.

"Do you need the nurse?" Mr. Harris asks.

The nurse, I think. *No, I don't need the nurse.*

The nurse's station is the room beside the home economics kitchen. *What I need, Mr. Harris, is to go back there, fifteen minutes ago, before the hall monitor arrived.* Sarah must have the pudding on the stove by now. I wonder if it's boiling yet. Is she looking towards the door, waiting for me to return?

The faint echo of the school doors slamming shut reaches the principal's office. Fifteen seconds until Henri is here. Then to his truck. Then home. Then where? To Maine? Missouri? Canada? A different school, a new beginning, another new name.

I haven't slept in almost thirty hours and only now do I feel the exhaustion. But then something else enters with it, and in that split second between instinct and action, the reality that I'm going away forever without the chance to say good-bye is suddenly too much to bear. My eyes narrow, my face twists in agony, and—without thinking, without truly knowing what it is that I'm doing—I lunge over Mr. Harris's desk and crash through the plate-glass window, which shatters into a million little pieces behind me. A scream of shock follows.

My feet land in the outside grass. I turn right and run across the schoolyard, the classrooms passing in a blur to my right, across the lot and into the woods that lie beyond the baseball field.

There are cuts on my forehead and left elbow from the glass. My lungs are burning. The hell with the pain. I keep going, the sheet of paper still in my right hand. I shove it into my pocket. Why would the Mogadorians send a fax? Wouldn't they just show up? That is their main advantage, to arrive unexpectedly, without warning. The benefit of surprise.

I take a hard left in the middle of the woods, weaving in and out of the forest's density until it ends and a field begins. Cows chewing cud watch with blank eyes as I streak past. I beat Henri to the house. Bernie Kosar is nowhere to be seen. I burst through the door and stop dead in my tracks. My breath catches in my throat. At the kitchen table, in front of Henri's open laptop, sits a person I immediately think is one of them. They've beat me here, have worked it out so that I am alone, without Henri. The person turns around and I clench my hands into fists and am ready to fight.

But it's Mark James.

"What are you doing here?" I ask.

"I'm trying to figure out what's going on," he says, a look of fright evident in his eyes. "Who the hell *are* you?"

"What are you talking about?"

"Look," he says, pointing to the computer screen.

I walk to him, but I don't look at the screen, my eyes instead focusing on the white sheet of paper sitting beside the computer. It's an exact replica of the sheet in my pocket except for the paper that it's printed on, which is thicker than the fax. And then I notice something else. At the bottom of Henri's, in very small handwriting, is a phone number. Surely they can't expect us to call? "Yes, it's me, Number Four. I am here waiting for you. We've been running for ten years, but please, come kill us now; we won't put up a fight." It makes no sense at all.

"Is this yours?" I ask.

"No," he says. "But it was delivered by UPS at the same time that I got here. Your dad read it as I showed him the video, and then he sprinted out of the house."

"What video?" I ask.

"Watch," he says.

I look at the computer and see that he's pulled up YouTube. He presses the play button. It's a grainy video, of poor quality as though it has been shot on somebody's cell phone. I recognize his house immediately, the front of which is in flames. The camera is shaky, but through it can be heard the dogs barking and the filtered gasps throughout the crowd. Then the person begins walking away from the crowd, to the side of the house, and eventually to the back. The camera zooms in to the rear window where the bark is coming from. The bark stops and I close my eyes because I know what is coming. About twenty seconds pass, and in the moment that I fly through the window with Sarah in one arm and the dog in the other, Mark hits the pause button on the video. The camera is zoomed in, and our faces are unmistakable.

"Who are you?" Mark asks.

I ignore his question, instead ask one of my own: "Who took this?"

"I have no idea," he answers.

The gravel pops beneath the truck tires in the front of the house as Henri pulls in. I stand straight and my first instinct is to run, get out of the house and get back to the school, where I know Sarah will be staying late to develop photos—until her driver's test at four thirty. Her face is just as obvious as mine is in that video, which puts her in as much danger as me. But something keeps me from fleeing, and I instead move around to the other side of the table and wait. The truck door slams shut. Henri walks into the house five seconds later, Bernie Kosar dashing in ahead of him.

"You lied to me," he says in the doorway, his face set hard, the muscles in his jaw flexed.

"I lie to everybody," I say. "I learned that from you."

"We don't lie to each other!" he screams.

Our eyes stay locked.

"What's going on?" Mark asks.

"I'm not leaving without finding Sarah," I say. "She's in danger, Henri!"

He shakes his head at me. "Now isn't the time for sentimentality, John. Do you not see this?" he says, and walks across the room and lifts the sheet of paper and begins waving it at me. "Where the hell do you think this came from?"

"What in the hell is going on?" Mark nearly bellows.

I ignore the sheet and Mark, and keep my eyes on Henri's. "Yes, I've seen it, and that's why I need to get back to the school. They'll see her and go after her."

Henri starts towards me. After his second step I lift my hand and stop him where he stands, ten or so feet away. He tries to keep walking but I hold him in place.

"We need to get out of here, John," he says, a hurt, almost pleading tone in his voice.

While holding him at a distance, I begin walking backwards towards my bedroom. He stops trying to walk. He says nothing, standing there watching me with pain in his eyes, a look that makes me feel worse than I've ever felt before. I have to look away. When I get to my doorway our eyes meet again. His shoulders are slumped, arms at his sides as though he doesn't know what to do with himself. He just stares at me, looking as though he may cry.

"I'm sorry," I say, giving myself enough of a head start to get away, and turn and sprint across my bedroom, grab from my drawer a knife I used to scale fish when we still lived in Florida, and jump out the window and race into the woods. Bernie Kosar's bark follows, nothing else. I run for a mile and stop in the big clearing where Sarah and I made snow angels. Our clearing, she had called it. The clearing in which we would have our summer picnics. A pain in my chest at the thought that I won't be here for summer, a pain so great that I bend over and grit my teeth. If only I could call her and warn her to get out of the school. My phone, along with everything else I took to school, is in my locker. I'll get her out of harm's way and then I'll get back to Henri and we'll leave.

I turn and run towards school, run as hard as my lungs will permit me. I reach the school just as the buses have begun pulling out of the lot. I watch them from the border of the woods. At the front of the school Hobbs is standing outside the front window measuring a large sheet of plywood to cover the window I broke. I slow my breathing, try my best to clear my mind. I watch the cars trickle out until there are only a few left. Hobbs covers the hole, disappears into the school. I wonder if he has been warned about me, if he has been instructed to call the police if he sees me. I look at my watch. Though it is only 3:30, the darkness seems to have come on faster than normal, a darkness steeped in density, a darkness that is heavy, consuming. The lights in the lot have come on, but even they seem dulled and stunted.

I leave the woods and walk across the baseball field and into the lot. Ten or so cars stand alone. The door to the school is already locked. I grab hold of it and close my eyes and focus and the lock clicks. I walk inside, and I don't see anyone. Only half of the hallway lights are on. The air is still and quiet. Somewhere I hear the floor polisher running. I turn into the lobby and the door to the photography darkroom comes into view. Sarah. She was going to develop some pictures today before her test. I pass by my locker and open it. My phone isn't there; the locker is completely empty. Somebody, hopefully Henri, has it. By the time I reach the darkroom I haven't seen a single person. Where are the athletes, the members of the band, the teachers who often stay late to grade papers or do whatever it is they do? A bad feeling creeps into my bones, and I'm terrified that something awful has already happened to Sarah. I press my ear against the darkroom door to listen, but hear nothing aside from the drone of the floor polisher coming from far down the hallway. I take a deep breath and try the door. It's locked. I press my ear to it again and gently knock. There's no answer, but I hear a slight rustling on the other side. I take a deep breath, tense myself to what I might find inside, and unlock the door.

The room is pitch-black. I turn on my lights and sweep my hands one way, then the other. I see nothing and think the room is empty, but in the corner, I see a very slight movement. I crouch down to look, and beneath the counter, trying to remain unseen, is Sarah. I dim my lights so that she can see it's me. From the shadows, she looks up and smiles, and breathes a sigh of relief.

"They're here, aren't they?"

"If they aren't yet, they will be soon."

I help her up from off the floor and she wraps her arms around me and squeezes me so tightly that I don't think she intends to ever let go.

"I came in here right after eighth period, and as soon as school ended, all these weird noises started coming from the halls. And it got really dark, so I locked myself in here and stayed beneath the counter, too scared to move. I just knew something was wrong, especially after I heard about you jumping through the window and you weren't answering your phone."

"That was smart, but now we have to get out of here, and fast."

We leave the room, holding hands. The hall-way lights flicker off, the whole school engulfed in darkness, even though dusk is still an hour or so away. After about ten seconds, they come back on.

"What's happening?" Sarah whispers.

"I don't know."

We move down the hallway as quietly as we can, and any noise we do make seems deadened, muffled. The quickest way out is the back door that opens onto the teachers' lot, and as we head that way, the sound of the floor polisher grows. I assume that we'll run into Hobbs. I assume he knows that I'm the one who broke the window. Will he fend me off with a broomstick and call the police? I guess at this point it doesn't matter.

When we reach the back hallway the lights turn off again. We stop and wait for them to come back on, but they don't. The floor polisher continues, a steady hum. I can't see it, but it is only twenty or so feet away in the impenetrable darkness. I find it odd that the machine keeps running, that Hobbs keeps polishing in the dark. I turn on my lights, and Sarah lets go of my hand and stands behind me with her hands on my hips. I find the plug in the wall first, then the cord, then the machine itself. It stands in one place, bumping against the wall, unmanned, running itself. Panic sweeps through me, with fear close behind. Sarah and I have to get out of the school.

I rip the cord from the outlet and the polisher stops, replaced by the soft hum of silence. I turn my lights off. Somewhere far down the hall a door slowly creaks open. I crouch down, my back against the wall, Sarah holding tightly to my arm. Both of us are too scared to say a word. Instinct caused me to pull the cord to stop the polisher, and I have the urge to plug it back in, but I know it'll give us away if they're here. I close my eyes and strain to listen. The creaking door stops. A soft wind seems to materialize from nowhere. Surely there isn't a window open. I think that maybe the wind is entering from the window I broke. Then the door slams shut and glass breaks and shatters on the floor.

Sarah screams. Something sweeps by us but I don't see what it is and I don't care to find out. I pull Sarah by the hand and sprint down the hall. I shoulder the door and rush out into the parking lot. Sarah gasps and both of us stop dead in our tracks. My breath catches in my throat and chills shoot up my spine. The lights are still on but dimmed and looking ghastly in the heavy dark. Beneath the nearest light we both see it, trench coat swaying in the breeze, hat pulled low so that I can't see its eyes. It lifts his head and grins at me.

Sarah's grip tightens on my hand. We both take one step backwards and trip in our rush to get away. We move the rest of the way back in a crab walk until we hit the door.

"Come on," I yell as I rush to my feet. Sarah stands. I try the latch but the door automatically locked behind us.

"Shit!" I yell.

I see another in the corner of my eye, standing still at first. I watch as it takes its first step towards me. There is another one behind it. The Mogadorians. All these years and they are finally here. I try to focus but my hands are shaking too badly to open the door. I feel them bearing down, closing in. Sarah presses close to me and I can feel her trembling.

I can't focus to get the door unlocked. What happened to grace under pressure, to all those days of training in the backyard? *I don't want to die,* I think. *I don't want to die.*

"John," Sarah says, and in her voice there is such fear that it causes my eyes to open wide, and twist in determination.

The lock clicks. The door opens. Sarah and I push through and I slam it shut. There is a thud on the other side as though one of them has kicked it. We run down the hall. Noises follow. I don't know if any of the Mogadorians are in the school. Another window breaks off to the side and Sarah screams in surprise.

"We have to be quiet," I say.

We try opening classroom doors but all of them are locked. I don't think there is enough time for me to open one of them. Somewhere a door is slammed shut and I can't tell if it was ahead of us or behind us. Noises follow close behind, closing in, filling our ears. Sarah takes my hand and we run faster, my mind rushing ahead to remember the layout of the building so I can keep my lights off, keep from being seen. Finally a door opens and we fall headlong into it. It's the history classroom, at the left of the school overlooking a slight hill, and because of the twenty-foot drop, there are bars over the windows. Darkness is pressing firmly against the glass and no light enters. I silently shut the door and hope they didn't see us. I sweep my lights across the room and quickly turn them off. We're alone and we hide beneath the teacher's desk. I try to catch my breath. Sweat runs down the sides of my face and stings my eyes. How many of them are here? I saw at least three. Surely those aren't the only ones out there. Did they bring the beasts with them, the small weasels that the writers in Athens were so scared of? I wish that Henri were here, or even Bernie Kosar.

The door slowly opens. I hold my breath, listening. Sarah leans into me and we put our arms around each other. The door closes very quietly and clicks into place. No footsteps follow. Did they merely open the door and stick their heads in to see if we were inside? Did they move on without entering? They found me after all this time; surely they aren't that lazy.

"What are we going to do?" Sarah whispers after thirty seconds.

"I don't know," I whisper back.

The room is wrapped in silence. Whatever opened the door must have left, or is out in the hall waiting. I know, though, the longer we sit, the more of them will arrive. We need to get out of here. We'll have to risk it. I take a deep breath.

"We have to leave," I whisper. "We're not safe here."

"But they're out there."

"I know, and they aren't going to leave. Henri is at home, and is in just as much danger as we are."

"But how are we going to get out?"

I have no idea, don't know what to say. Only one way out and that's the way we came in. Sarah's arms stay around me.

"We're sitting ducks, Sarah. They'll find us, and when they do, it will be with all of them. At least we'll have the element of surprise this way. If we can get out of the school, I think I can start a car. If I can't, we'll have to fight our way back."

She nods in agreement.

I take a deep breath and move out from underneath the desk. I reach for Sarah's hand and she stands with me. Together we take one step, quietly as possible. Then another. It takes a full minute to cross the room and nothing meets us in the darkness. A very slight glow comes from my hands, emitting almost no light, only enough to keep from running into a desk. I stare at the door. I'll open it and have Sarah jump on my back and I'll run as hard and as fast as I can, lights on, down the hall, out of the school and into the lot or, failing that, into the woods. I know the woods and the way home. There are more of them, but Sarah and I will have the home-field advantage.

As we near the door, I can feel my heart pounding so hard that I fear the Mogadorians can hear it. I close my eyes and slowly reach for the knob. Sarah tenses, gripping my hand as tightly as she can. When my hand is an inch away, so close to the knob that I can feel the cold coming off of it, we are both grabbed from behind and pulled to the ground.

I try to scream but a hand covers my mouth. Fear rushes through me. I can feel Sarah struggling beneath the grip and I do the same thing but the grip is too strong. I never anticipated this, the Mogadorians being stronger than I am. I've greatly underestimated them. There is no hope now. I've failed. I have failed Sarah and Henri and I'm sorry. *Henri, I hope you put up a better fight than I did.*

Sarah is breathing heavily and with all my might I try to free myself but I can't.

"Shhh, stop struggling," the voice whispers in my ear. A girl's voice. "They're out there waiting. Both of you have to be quiet."

It's a girl, every bit as strong as I am, maybe even stronger. I don't understand. Her grip loosens and I turn and face her. We take each other in. Above the glow of my hands I see a face slightly older than mine. Hazel eyes, high cheekbones, long dark hair pulled into a ponytail, a wide mouth and strong nose, olive-toned skin.

"Who are you?" I ask.

She looks to the door, still silent. *An ally,* I think. Somebody besides the Mogadorians knows we exist. Somebody is here, to help.

"I am Number Six," she says. "I tried to get here before they did."

CHAPTER
TWENTY-NINE

"HOW DID YOU KNOW IT WAS ME?" I ask.

She looks to the door. "I've been trying to find you ever since Three was killed. But I'll explain it all later. First, we have to get out of here."

"How did you get in without them seeing you?"

"I can make myself invisible."

I smile. The same Legacy my grandfather had. Invisibility. The ability to make those things he touches invisible as well, like the house on Henri's second day of work.

"How far do you live from here?" she asks.

"Three miles."

I feel her nod through the darkness.

"Do you have a Cêpan?" she asks.

"Yes, of course. Don't you?"

Her weight shifts and she pauses before

speaking, as though drawing strength from some unseen entity. "I did," she says. "She died three years ago. I've been on my own since then."

"I'm sorry," I say.

"It's a war, people are going to die. Right now we have to get out of here or we'll die as well. If they're in the area, then they already know where you live, which means they're already there, so it's pointless to try to be secretive once we're out of here. These are only scouts. The soldiers are on the way. They have the swords. The beasts won't be far behind. Time is short. At best we have a day. At worst they're already here."

My first thought: *They already know where I live.* I panic. Henri is at home, with Bernie Kosar, and the soldiers and beasts may already be there. My second thought: her Cêpan, dead three years now. Six has been alone that long, alone on a foreign planet since what, the age of thirteen? Fourteen?

"He's at home," I say.

"Who?"

"Henri, my Cêpan."

"I'm sure he's fine. They won't touch him as long as you're free. It's you they want, and they'll use him to try to lure you," Six says, then lifts her head towards the barred window. We turn and look with her. Speeding around the bend coming towards the school, very faintly so that nothing else can be seen, is a pair of headlights that slow, pass the exit, then turn into the entrance and quickly disappear. Six turns back to us. "All the doors are blocked. How else can we get out?"

I think about it, figuring that one of the unbarred windows in a different classroom is our best bet.

"We can get out through the gymnasium," Sarah says. "There's a passageway beneath the stage that opens like a cellar door in the back of the school."

"Really?" I ask.

She nods, and I feel a sense of pride.

"Each of you take a hand," Six says. I take her right, Sarah her left. "Be as quiet as possible. As long as you hold my hands, you'll both be invisible. They won't be able to see us, but they'll hear us. Once we're outside we'll run like hell. We'll never be able to escape them, not since they've found us. The only way to escape is to kill them, every last one of them, before the others arrive."

"Okay," I say.

"Do you know what that means?" Six says.

I shake my head. I'm not sure what she is asking me.

"There's no escaping them now," she says. "It means you're going to have to fight."

I mean to respond, but the shuffling I had heard earlier stops outside the door. Silence.

Then the doorknob is jiggled. Number Six takes a deep breath and lets go of my hand.

"Never mind sneaking out," she says. "The war starts now."

She rushes up and thrusts her hands forward and the door breaks away from the jamb and crashes across the hallway. Splintered wood. Shattered glass.

"Turn your lights on!" she yells.

I snap them on. A Mogadorian stands amid the rubble of the broken door. It smiles, blood seeping from the corner of its mouth, where the door has hit it. Black eyes, pale skin as though the sun has never touched it. A cave-dwelling creature risen from the dead. It throws something that I don't see and I hear Six grunt beside me. I look into its eyes and a pain tears through me so that I'm stuck where I am, unable to move. Darkness falls. Sadness. My body stiffens. A haze of pictures of the day of the invasion flicker through my mind: the death of women and children, my grandparents; tears, screams, blood, heaps of burning bodies. Six breaks the spell by lifting the Mogadorian in the air and hurling it against the wall. It tries standing and Six lifts it again, this time throwing it as hard as she can against one wall and then the other. The scout falls to the ground twisted and broken, its chest rising once and then becoming still. One or two seconds pass. Its entire body collapses into a pile of ash, accompanied by a sound similar to a bag of sand being dropped to the ground.

"What the hell?" I ask, wondering how it's possible for the body to completely disintegrate like it just did.

"Don't look into their eyes!" she yells, ignoring my confusion.

I think of the writer of *They Walk Among Us*. I now understand what he went through when looking into their eyes. I wonder if he welcomed death when the time finally came, welcomed it just to be rid of the images that perpetually played in his mind. I can only imagine how intense they would have become had Six not broken the spell.

Two other scouts sweep towards us from the end of the hall. A shroud of darkness surrounds them, as though they consume everything around them and turn it into black. Six stands tall in front of me, firm, chin held high. She is two inches shorter than I am, but her presence makes her seem two inches taller. Sarah stands behind me. Both Mogadorians stop where the hallway intersects with another, their teeth bared in a sneer. My body is tense, muscles burning with exhaustion. They take deep, rasping breaths, which is what we heard outside the door, their breathing, not their walking. Watching us. And then a different noise fills the hallway, and the Mogadorians both turn their attention to it. A door being shaken as though somebody is trying to force it open. From out of nowhere there comes the sound of a gun blast, followed by the school door being kicked open. They both look surprised, and as they turn to flee, two more blasts boom through the hallway and both scouts are blown backwards. We hear the approaching sound of two sets of shoes and the click of a dog's toenails. Six tenses beside me, ready for whatever is coming our way. Henri! It was his truck's lights we saw enter the school grounds. He has a double-barreled shotgun I have never seen before. Bernie Kosar is at his side, and he comes sprinting towards me. I crouch down and lift him off the floor. He licks wildly at my face, and I'm so excited to see him that I almost forget to tell Six who the man with the shotgun is.

"It's Henri," I say. "My Cêpan."

Henri comes walking down, vigilant, looking at the classroom doors as he passes them, and behind him, carrying the Loric Chest in his arms, is Mark. I have no idea why Henri has brought him along. There is a crazed look in Henri's eyes, one of exhaustion, full of fear and worry. I expect the worst after the way I left the house, some sort of scolding, perhaps a slap across the face, but he instead switches the shotgun to his left hand and hugs me as tightly as he can. I hug him back.

"I'm sorry, Henri. I didn't know this would happen."

"I know you didn't. I'm just happy you're okay." He says, "Come on, we have to get out of here. The whole damn school is surrounded."

Sarah leads us to the safest room she can think of, which is the home economics kitchen down the hall. We lock the door behind us. Six moves three refrigerators in front of it to keep anything from entering while Henri rushes to the windows and pulls the blinds down. Sarah walks straight into the kitchen we normally use, opens the drawer, and removes the biggest butcher's knife she can find. Mark watches her, and when he sees what she has done, he drops the Chest to the floor and grabs a knife of his own. He rifles through other drawers and removes a meat-tenderizer hammer and tucks it into the waistband of his pants.

"You guys okay?" Henri asks.

"Yes," I say.

"Aside from the dagger in my arm, yes, I'm fine," Six says.

I turn my lights on dimly and look at her arm. She wasn't kidding. Where the biceps meets the shoulder a small dagger is sticking out. That was why I heard her gasp before she killed the scout. It had thrown a knife at her. Henri reaches up and pulls it free. She grunts.

"Thankfully it's just a dagger," she says, looking at me. "The soldiers will have swords that glow with different sorts of powers."

I mean to ask what kind of powers, but Henri interrupts.

"Take this," he says, and holds the shotgun out for Mark to take. He accepts it in his free hand without protest, staring in awe at everything he is witnessing around him. I wonder how much Henri has told him. I wonder why Henri brought him along in the first place. I look back at Six. Henri presses a rag to her arm and she holds it in place. He steps over and lifts the Chest and sets it on the nearest table.

"Here, John," he says.

Without explanation I help him unlock it. He throws the top open, reaches in, removes a flat rock every bit as dark as the aura surrounding the Mogadorians. Six seems to know what the rock is for. She takes her shirt off. Beneath it she is wearing a black and gray rubber suit very similar to the silver and blue suit I saw my father wear in my flashbacks. She takes a deep breath, offers Henri her arm. Henri thrusts the rock against the gash, and Six, with her teeth clenched tightly, grunts and writhes in pain. Sweat beads across her forehead, her face bright red under the strain, tendons standing out on her neck. Henri holds it there for nearly a full minute. He pulls the stone away and Six bends over at the waist, taking deep breaths to compose herself. I look at her arm. Aside from a bit of blood still glistening, the cut is completely healed, no scars, nothing aside from the small tear in the suit.

"What is that?" I ask, nodding to the rock.

"It's a healing stone," says Henri.

"Stuff like that really exists?"

"On Lorien it does, but the pain of healing is double that of the original pain caused by whatever has happened, and the stone only works when the injury was done with the intent to harm or kill. And the healing stone has to be used right away."

"Intent?" I ask. "So, the stone wouldn't work if I tripped and cut my head by accident?"

"No," Henri says. "That's the whole point of Legacies. Defense and purity."

"Would it work on Mark or Sarah?"

"I have no idea," Henri says. "And I hope we don't have to find out."

Six catches her breath. She stands straight, feeling her arm. The red in her face begins to fade. Behind her, Bernie Kosar is running back and forth from the blocked door to the windows, which are placed too high off the ground for him to see out of, but he stands on his hind legs and tries anyway, growling at what he feels is out there. *Maybe nothing*, I think. Occasionally he bites at the air.

"Did you get my phone today when you were at the school?" I ask Henri.

"No," he says. "I didn't grab anything."

"It wasn't there when I went back."

"Well, it wouldn't work here anyway. They've done something to our house and the school. The power is off, and no signals penetrate whatever sort of shield they've set up. All the clocks have stopped. Even the air seems dead."

"We don't have much time," Six interrupts.

Henri nods. A slight grin appears while he looks at her, a look of pride, maybe even relief.

"I remember you," he says.

"I remember you, too."

Henri reaches out his hand and Six shakes it. "It's shit good to see you again."

"*Damn* good," I correct him, but he ignores me.

"I've been looking for you guys for a while," Six says.

"Where is Katarina?" Henri asks.

Six shakes her head. A mournful look crosses her face.

"She didn't make it. She died three years ago. I've been looking for the others since, you guys included."

"I'm sorry," Henri says.

Six nods. She looks across the room at Bernie Kosar, who has just begun to growl ferociously. He seems to have grown tall enough so that his head is able to peek out the bottom of the window. Henri picks the shotgun up off the floor and walks to within five feet of the window.

"John, turn your lights off," he says. I comply. "Now, on my word, pull the blinds."

I walk to the side of the window and wrap the cord twice around my hand. I nod to Henri, and over his shoulder I see that Sarah has placed her palms against her ears in anticipation of the blast. He cocks the shotgun and aims it.

"It's payback time," he says, then, "now!"

I pull the cord and the blind flies up. Henri fires the shotgun. The sound is deafening, echoing in my ears for seconds after. He cocks the gun again, keeps it aimed. I twist my body to look out. Two fallen scouts are lying in the grass, unmoving. One of them is reduced to ash with the same hollow thud as the one in the hallway. Henri shoots the other a second time and it does the same. Shadows seem to swarm around them.

"Six, bring a fridge over," Henri says to her.

Mark and Sarah watch with amazement as the fridge floats in the air towards us and is positioned in front of the window to block the

Mogadorians from entering or seeing into the room.

"Better than nothing," Henri says. He turns to Six. "How much time do we have?"

"Time is short," she says. "They have an outpost three hours from here, in a hollowed-out mountain in West Virginia."

Henri snaps the gun open, slides in two new cartridges, snaps it shut.

"How many bullets does that hold?" I ask.

"Ten," he says.

Sarah and Mark whisper to each other. I walk over to them.

"You guys okay?" I ask.

Sarah nods, Mark shrugs, neither really knowing quite what to say in the terror of the situation. I kiss Sarah on the cheek and take hold of her hand.

"Don't worry," I say. "We'll get out of this."

I turn to Six and Henri. "Why are they just out there waiting?" I ask. "Why don't they break a window and rush in? They know they have us outnumbered."

"They only want to keep us here, inside," Six says. "They have us exactly where they want us, all together, confined to one place. Now they're waiting for the others to arrive, the soldiers with the weapons, the ones who are skilled at killing. They're desperate now because they know we're developing our Legacies. They can't afford to screw it up and risk us getting stronger. They know that some of us can now fight back."

"We have to get out of here then," Sarah pleads, her voice soft and shaky.

Six nods reassuringly to her. And then I remember something I had forgotten in all the excitement.

"Wait, your being here, us being together, that breaks the charm. All the others are fair game now," I say. "They can kill us at will."

I can see by the look of horror on Henri's face that it had slipped his mind as well.

Six nods. "I had to risk it," she says. "We can't keep running, and I'm sick of waiting. We're all developing, all of us are ready to hit back. Let's not forget what they did to us that day, and I'm not going to forget what they did to Katarina. Everybody we know is dead, our families, our friends. I think they're planning to do the same thing to Earth as they did to Lorien, and they are almost ready. To sit back and do nothing is to allow that same destruction, that same death and annihilation. Why stand back and let it happen? If this planet dies, we die with it."

Bernie Kosar is still barking at the window. I almost want to let him outside, see what he can do. His mouth is frothing with his teeth bared, hair standing tall down the center of his back. *The dog is ready,* I think. *The question is, are the rest of us?*

"Well, you're here now," Henri says. "Let's hope the others are safe; let's hope they can fend for themselves. Both of you will know immediately if they can't. As for us, war has come to our doorstep. We didn't ask for it, but now that it's here we have no choice but to meet it, head on, with full force," he says. He lifts his head and looks at us, the whites of his eyes glistening through the dark of the room.

"I agree with you, Six," he says. "The time has come."

CHAPTER
THIRTY

WIND FROM THE OPEN WINDOW rushes into the home economics room, the refrigerator in front of it doing little to prevent the cold air. The school is already chilly from the electricity being off. Six is now wearing only the rubber suit, which is entirely black aside from a gray band slicing diagonally down the front of it. She is standing in the middle of our group with such poise and confidence that I wish I had a Loric suit of my own. She opens her mouth to speak but is interrupted by a loud boom from outside. All of us rush to the windows but can see nothing of what is happening. The crash is followed by several loud bangs, and the sounds of tearing, gnashing, something being destroyed.

"What's happening?" I ask.

"Your lights," Henri says over the sounds of destruction.

I turn them on and sweep them across the yard outside. They reach but ten feet before being swallowed by the darkness. Henri steps back and tilts his head, listening to the sounds in extreme concentration, and then he nods in resigned acceptance.

"They are destroying all the cars out there, my truck included," he says. "If we survive this and escape this school, it'll have to be on foot."

Terror sweeps across both Mark's and Sarah's faces.

"We can't waste any more time," Six says. "Strategy or no strategy, we have to go before the beasts and soldiers arrive. She said we can get out through the gymnasium," Six says, and nods at Sarah. "It's our only hope."

"Her name is Sarah," I say.

I sit in a nearby chair, unnerved by the urgency in Six's voice. She seems to be the steady one, the one who has remained calm under the weight of the terrors we have seen thus far. Bernie Kosar is back at the door, scratching at the fridges that are blocking it, growling and whining in impatience. Since my lights are on, Six has a good look at him for the first time. She stares at Bernie Kosar, then squints her eyes and inches her face forward. She walks over and bends down to pet him. I turn and look at her. I find it odd that she is grinning.

"What?" I ask.

She looks up at me. "You don't know?"

"Know what?"

Her grin widens. She looks back at Bernie Kosar, who races away from her and charges back to the window, scratching at it, growling, the occasional bark in frustration. The school is surrounded, death imminent, almost certain, and Six is grinning. It irritates me.

"Your dog," she says. "You really don't know?"

"No," says Henri. I look at him. He shakes his head at Six.

"What the hell?" I ask. "What?"

Six looks at me, then at Henri. She emits a half laugh and opens her mouth to speak. But just before any words escape something catches her eye and she rushes back to the window. We follow and, as before, the very subtle glow of a set of headlights sweeps around the bend in the road and into the lot of the school. Another car, maybe a coach or teacher. I close my eyes and take a deep breath.

"It could mean nothing," I say.

"Turn your lights off," Henri says to me.

I turn them off, clench my hands into fists. Something about the car outside causes anger within me. The hell with the exhaustion, with the shakes that have been present ever since I jumped through the principal's window. I can't take being confined in this room any longer, knowing that the Mogadorians are out there, waiting, and plotting our doom. That car outside may be the first of the soldiers arriving on the scene. But just when that thought pops into my mind, we see the lights quickly retreat from the lot, and speed away in a hurry, down the same road they came.

"We have to get out of this damn school," Henri says.

Henri sits in a chair ten feet away from the door with the shotgun aimed right at it. He is breathing slowly though he is tense and I can see the muscles flexed in his jaw. None of us says a word. Six made herself invisible and slipped out to do some exploring. We're just waiting, and finally it comes. Three slight taps on the door, Six's knock so that we know it's her and not a scout trying to enter. Henri lowers the gun and she walks in and I return one of the fridges to block the door behind her. She was gone for a full ten minutes.

"You were right," she says to Henri. "They've destroyed every car in the lot, and have somehow moved the wreckage to block every door from being opened. And Sarah is right; they've overlooked the stage hatch. I counted seven scouts outside and five inside walking the halls. There was one outside this door but it's been disposed of. They seem to be getting antsy. I think that means the others should have been here already, which means they can't be far."

Henri stands and grabs the Chest and nods at me. I help him open it. He reaches in and pulls out a few small round pebbles that he sticks in his pocket. I have no idea what they are. Then he closes and locks the Chest and slides it into one of the ovens and closes the door. I move a refrigerator up against the oven to keep it from being opened. There really is no other choice. The Chest is heavy, it would be impossible to fight while carrying it, and we need every available hand to get out of this mess.

"I hate to leave it behind," Henri says, shaking his head. Six nods uneasily. Something in the thought of the Mogadorians getting ahold of the Chest terrifies them both.

"It'll be fine here," I say.

Henri lifts the shotgun and pumps it once, looks at Sarah and Mark.

"This isn't your fight," he tells them. "I don't know what to expect out there, but if this thing goes badly you guys get back in this school and stay hidden. They aren't after you, and I don't think they'll care to come looking if they already have us."

Sarah and Mark both look stricken with

fear, both holding their respective knives with white-knuckled grips in their right hands. Mark has lined his belt with everything from the kitchen drawers that might be of use—more knives, the meat tenderizer, cheese grater, a pair of scissors.

"We go left out of this room, and when we reach the end of the hall, the gymnasium is past double doors twenty or so feet to the right," I say to Henri.

"The hatch is in the very middle of the stage," Six says. "It's covered with a blue mat. There were no scouts in the gym, but that doesn't mean they won't be there this time around."

"So we're just going to go outside and try to outrun them?" Sarah asks. Her voice is full of panic. She's breathing heavily.

"It's our only choice," says Henri.

I grab her hand. She is shaking badly.

"It'll be okay," I say.

"How do you know that?" she says in a more demanding tone than a questioning one.

"I don't," I say.

Six moves the fridge from the door. Bernie Kosar immediately starts scratching at the door, trying to get out, growling.

"I can't make you all invisible," Six says. "If I disappear, I'll still be nearby."

Six grabs hold of the doorknob and Sarah takes

a deep, shaky breath beside me, squeezing my hand as tightly as she can. I can see the knife quivering in her right hand.

"Stay close to me," I say.

"I'm not leaving your side."

The door swings open and Six jumps out into the hall, Henri close behind. I follow and Bernie Kosar races ahead of us all, a ball of fury speeding away. Henri points the shotgun one way, then the other. The hallway is empty. Bernie Kosar has already reached the intersection. He disappears. Six follows suit and makes herself invisible and the rest of us run towards the gym, Henri in the lead. I make Mark and Sarah go ahead of me. None of us can really see a thing, can only hear each other's footsteps. I turn my lights on to help guide the way, and that's the first mistake I make.

A classroom door to my right swings open. Everything happens in a split second and, before I have a chance to react, I am hit in the shoulder with something heavy. My lights shut off. I crash straight through a glass display window. I'm cut on the top of my head and blood runs down the side of my face almost immediately. Sarah screams. Whatever it was that hit me clubs me again, a hollow thud in my ribs that knocks the wind from me.

"Turn your lights on!" Henri yells. I do. A

scout stands over me, holding a six-foot-long piece of wood that it must have found in the industrial arts classroom. It raises it in the air to hit me again, but Henri, standing twenty feet away, fires the shotgun first. The scout's head disappears, blown to pieces. The rest of its body turns to ash before it even hits the floor.

Henri lowers the gun. "Shit," he says, catching sight of the blood. He takes a step towards me and then from the corner of my eye I see another scout, in the same doorway, a sledgehammer raised over its head. It comes charging forward and, with telekinesis, I throw the nearest thing to me without even knowing what that thing is. A golden glinting object that speeds through the air with violence. It hits the scout so hard that its skull cracks on impact, and then it falls to the ground and lies motionless. Henri, Mark, and Sarah rush over. The scout is still alive and Henri takes Sarah's knife and thrusts it through its chest, reducing it to a pile of ash. He hands Sarah back her knife. She holds it out in front of her, between thumb and forefinger, as though she's just been handed a pair of somebody's dirty underwear. Mark bends down and lifts the object I had thrown, now in three separate pieces.

"It's my all-conference trophy," he says, and then can't help but chuckle to himself. "It was given to me last month."

I stand. It was the trophy case that I crashed through.

"You okay?" Henri asks, looking at the cut.

"Yeah, I'm fine. Let's keep going."

We rush down the hall and into the gymnasium, sprint across the floor, jump up onto the stage. I flip my lights on to see the blue mat being moved away as though of its own volition. Then the hatch is thrown up. Only then does Six make herself visible again.

"What happened back there?" she asks.

"Ran into a little bit of trouble," Henri says, climbing down the ladder first to make sure the coast is clear. Then Sarah and Mark go.

"Where is the dog?" I ask.

Six shakes her head.

"Go on," I say. She goes down first, leaving only me on the stage. I whistle as loudly as I can, knowing full well that I'm giving away my position by doing so. I wait.

"Come on, John," Henri calls up from below.

I crawl into the hatch, my feet on the ladder, but from the waist up I'm still on the stage, watching.

"Come on!" I say to myself. *"Where are you?"* And in that split second when I have no choice but to give up, but just before I drop down, Bernie Kosar materializes on the far side of the gym and comes sprinting my way, ears pinned

to the sides of his head. I smile.

"Come on!" Henri yells this time.

"Hold on!" I yell back.

Bernie Kosar jumps onto the stage and into my arms.

"Here!" I yell, and hand the dog to Six. I drop down, close and lock the hatch and turn my lights on as brightly as they'll go.

The walls and floor are made of concrete, reeking of mildew. We have to walk in a low crouch to keep from hitting our heads. Six leads the way. The tunnel is about a hundred feet long and I have no idea what purpose this could have served at one time. We reach the end; a short flight of steps leads to a pair of metal cellar doors. Six waits until everyone is together.

"Where does this open?" I ask.

"Behind the faculty lot," Sarah says. "Not far from the football field."

Six presses her ear to listen in the small crack between the closed doors. Nothing but the wind. Everyone's face is streaked with sweat, dust, and fear. Six looks at Henri and nods. I turn my lights off.

"All right," she says, and makes herself invisible.

She inches the door up just enough to stick her head out and have a look around. The rest of us watch with bated breath, waiting, listening, all of us wracked with nerves. She turns one way, then the other. Satisfied we've made it unnoticed, she pushes the door all the way open and we file out one by one.

Everything is dark and silent, no wind, the forest trees to our right standing motionless. I look around, can see the busted silhouettes of the twisted cars piled in front of the doors of the school. No stars or moon. No sky at all, almost as though we're beneath a bubble of darkness, some sort of dome where only shadows remain. Bernie Kosar begins to growl, low at first so that my initial thought is that it's done for reasons of anxiety only; but the growl grows into something more ferocious, more menacing, and I know that he senses something out there. All of our heads turn to see what he is growling at but nothing moves. I take a step forward to put Sarah behind me. I think to turn on my lights but I know that will give us away even more so than the dog's growl. Suddenly, Bernie Kosar takes off.

He charges ahead thirty yards before leaping through the air and sinking his teeth deeply into one of the unseen scouts, who materializes from out of nowhere as though some spell of invisibility has been broken. In an instant, we're able to see them all, surrounding us, no fewer than twenty of them, who begin closing in.

"It was a trap!" Henri yells, and fires twice and drops two scouts immediately.

"Get back in the tunnel!" I scream to Mark and Sarah.

One of the scouts comes charging towards me. I lift it in the air and hurl it as hard as I can against an oak tree twenty yards away. It hits the ground with a thud, quickly stands, and hurls a dagger my way. I deflect it and lift the scout again and throw it even harder. It bursts into ash at the base of the tree. Henri unloads more rounds, the shots echoing. Two hands grab me from behind. I almost deflect them until I realize that it's Sarah. Six is nowhere to be seen. Bernie Kosar has brought a Mogadorian to the ground, his teeth now sunk deeply into its throat, hell ablaze in the dog's eyes.

"Get into the school!" I yell.

She doesn't let go. A clap of thunder breaks through the silence and a storm begins to brew, dark clouds now forming overhead with flashes of lighting and thunder tearing through the night sky, loud pounding thunder that makes Sarah jump each time one booms. Six has reappeared, standing thirty feet away, her eyes to the sky and her face twisted in concentration with both arms raised. She's the one creating the storm, controlling the weather. Bolts of lightning begin raining down, striking the scouts dead where they stand, creating small explosions that form clouds of ash that drift listlessly across the yard. Henri stands off to the side, loading more shells into the shotgun. The scout that Bernie Kosar is choking finally succumbs to death and bursts into a heap of ash covering the dog's face. He sneezes once, shakes the ash from his coat and then rushes off and chases the closest scout until they both disappear into the dense woods fifty yards away. I have this unbearable fear that I've seen him for the very last time.

"You have to go into the school," I say to Sarah. "You have to go now and you have to hide. Mark!" I yell. I look up and don't see him. I snap around. I catch sight of him sprinting towards Henri, who is still loading his gun. At first I don't understand why, and then I see what is happening: a Mogadorian scout has snuck up on Henri without his knowing it.

"Henri," I scream to get his attention. I lift my hand to stop the scout with its knife raised high in the air, but Mark tackles the thing first. A wrestling match ensues. Henri snaps the shotgun closed, and Mark kicks the scout's knife away. Henri fires and the scout explodes. Henri says something to Mark. I yell for Mark again and he sprints over, breathing heavily.

"You have to take Sarah into the school."

"I can help here," he says.

"It's not your fight. You have to hide! Get in the school and hide with Sarah!"

"Okay," he says.

"You have to stay hidden, no matter what!" I yell over the storm. "They won't come for you. It's me they want. Promise me, Mark! Promise me you'll stay hidden with Sarah!"

Mark nods rapidly. "I promise!"

Sarah is crying and there's no time to comfort her. Another clap of thunder, another shotgun blast. She kisses me one time on the lips, her hands holding tightly to my face and I know she would stay like this forever. Mark pulls her off, begins leading her away.

"I love you," she says, and in her eyes she is staring at me in the same way that I had stared at her earlier, before I left home ec, as though she may be seeing me for the final time, wanting to remember it so that this last image might last a lifetime.

"I love you too," I mouth back just as the two of them reach the steps of the tunnel, and as soon as the words leave my lips, Henri cries out in pain. I turn. One of the scouts has thrust a knife into his gut. Terror sweeps through me. The scout pulls the knife from Henri's side, the blade glistening with his blood. It thrusts down to stab Henri a second time. My hand reaches out for it and I rip the knife away at the last second so that it is only a fist that hits Henri. He grunts, gathers himself, and presses the barrel of the shotgun to the chin of the scout and fires. The scout drops, headless.

The rain starts, a cold, heavy rain. In no time at all I'm soaked to the bone. Blood leaks from Henri's gut. He's aiming the shotgun into the darkness, but all of the scouts have moved into the shadows, away from us, so that Henri can't get a good enough aim. They're no longer interested in attacking, knowing that two of us have retreated and a third has been wounded. Six is still reaching for the sky. The storm has grown; the wind is beginning to howl. She seems to be having trouble controlling it. A winter storm, thunder in January. As quickly as everything started, it all seems to stop—the thunder, the lightning, the rain. The wind dies away and a low groan begins to grow from off in the distance. Six lowers her arms, all of us straining to listen. Even the Mogadorians turn. The groan grows, unmistakably coming our way, some sort of deep mechanical groan. The scouts step from the shadows and begin to laugh. Despite our killing at least ten of them, there are many more than before. From far off a cloud of smoke rises over the tops of the trees as if a steam engine is coming around the bend. The scouts nod to one another, smiling their wicked smiles, and re-form their circle around us in what is an apparent attempt to get us back into the school. And it's obvious that that is our only choice. Six walks over.

"What is it?" I ask.

Henri hobbles, the shotgun hanging limply at his side. He's breathing heavily, a gash on his cheek below his right eye, a circular puddle of blood on his gray sweater from the knife wound.

"It's the rest of them, isn't it?" Henri asks Six.

Six looks at him, stricken, her hair wet and clinging to the sides of her face.

"The beasts," she says. "And the soldiers. They're here."

Henri cocks the shotgun and takes a deep breath. "And so the real war begins," he says. "I don't know about you two, but if this is it, then this is it. I, for one . . . ," he says, and trails off. "Well, I'll be damned if I'll go down without a fight."

Six nods. "Our people fought back till the end. And so shall I," she says.

A mile off the smoke still rises. *Live cargo*, I think. *That is how they transport them, by over-sized semitrucks.* Six and I follow Henri back down the steps. I yell for Bernie Kosar but he's nowhere to be seen.

"We can't wait for him again," Henri says. "There isn't time."

I look around one final time, and slam the cellar doors shut. We rush back through the tunnel, up onto the stage, across the gymnasium. We don't see a single scout, nor do we see Mark and Sarah, and I'm relieved by that. I hope they are well hidden, and I hope Mark keeps his promise and that they stay that way. When we make it back to the home-ec room I slide the fridge out of the way and grab the Chest. Henri and I open it. Six takes the healing stone out and thrusts it against Henri's gut. He is silent, his eyes closed, holding his breath. His face is red under the strain but not a single sound escapes. A minute of this and Six pulls the stone away. The cut has healed. Henri exhales, his forehead covered in sweat. Then it's my turn. She presses it to the gash on my head and a pain far greater than anything I've ever felt before rips through me. I grunt and groan, every muscle in my body flexing. I can't breathe until it's over, and when it finally is, I bend over and catch my breath for a full minute.

Outside the mechanical groan has stopped. The semi is hidden from view. While Henri closes up the Chest and places it back in the same oven as before, I look out the window hoping to catch sight of Bernie Kosar. I don't see him.

Another set of headlights passes by the school. As before, I can't tell if it's a car or truck, and it slows as it drives by the entrance, then quickly speeds away without turning in. Henri pushes his shirt down, picks up the shotgun. As we move towards the door, a sound stops the three of us dead in our tracks.

A roar comes from outside, loud, animal-like, a sinister roar unlike anything I have ever heard before, followed by the sound of the metallic clicks of a gate being unlocked, low-ered, and opened. A loud bang snaps us all back to attention. I take another deep breath. Henri shakes his head and sighs in what is an almost hopeless gesture, a gesture made when the fight is lost.

"There's always hope, Henri," I say. He turns and looks at me. "New developments have yet to present themselves. Not all the information is in. Don't give up hope just yet."

He nods and the tiniest trace of a smile forms. He looks at Six, a new development that I don't think either of us could have imagined. Who's to say that there aren't more waiting? And then he picks up where I left off, quoting the exact words he spoke to me when I was the one who was discouraged, the day I asked how we could possibly expect to win this fight, alone and outnumbered, far from home—against the

Mogadorians, who seem to take great joy in war and death. "It's the last thing to go," Henri says. "When you have lost hope, you have lost everything. And when you think all is lost, when all is dire and bleak, there is always hope."

"Exactly," I say.

CHAPTER THIRTY-ONE

ANOTHER ROAR CUTS THROUGH THE night air, through the walls of the school, a roar that makes my blood turn cold. The ground begins to rumble under the footsteps of the beast that must now be on the loose. I shake my head. I saw firsthand how big they were during the flashbacks of the war on Lorien.

"For your friends' sake and ours," Six says, "we better get the hell out of this school while there's still time. They'll destroy the entire building trying to get to us."

We nod to one another.

"Our only hope is to get to the woods," Henri says. "Whatever that thing is, we might be able to escape it if we can stay invisible."

Six nods. "Just keep ahold of my hands."

Needing no other motivation than that, Henri and I each take a hand.

"As quietly as we can," Henri says.

The hallway is dark and silent. We walk with a quiet urgency, moving as swiftly as we can while making little noise. Another roar, and in the middle of it, another roar begins. We stop. Not one beast, but *two*. We continue on and enter the gymnasium. No sign of the scouts. When we reach the very center of the court, Henri stops. I look over but can't see him.

"Why are we stopped?" I whisper.

"Shh," he says. "Listen."

I strain to listen, but hear nothing aside from the steady hum of blood filling my ears.

"The beasts have stopped moving," Henri says.

"So what?"

"Shh," he says. "There's something else out there."

And then I hear it too, slight high-pitched yipping sounds as though coming from small animals. The sounds are muffled, though obviously growing louder.

"What the hell?" I ask.

Something begins banging at the stage hatch, the hatch we are hoping to escape through.

"Turn your lights on," he says.

I let go of Six's hand, snap them on, and aim them towards the stage. Henri looks down the end of the shotgun barrel. The hatch bounces up as though something is trying to force itself through but lacks the strength to do so. *The weasels,* I think, *the stout-bodied little creatures that the guys in Athens were terrified of.* One of them hits the hatch so hard that it breaks away from the stage and rattles across the floor. So much for thinking they lacked strength. Two of them come bursting forth, and upon catching sight of us, come racing our way so swiftly that I can hardly make them out. Henri stands watching with the gun aimed, an amused grin on his face. Their paths diverge and both leap from about twenty feet away, one jumping at Henri, the other coming at me. Henri fires once and the weasel explodes and covers him with its blood and guts; and just as I'm about to rip apart the second with telekinesis, it is snatched out of midair by Six's unseen hand and spiked to the ground like a football, killing it instantly.

Henri cocks the shotgun. "Well, that wasn't so bad," he says, and before I can respond, the entire wall along the stage is smashed in by the fist of a beast. It draws back and punches again, smashing the stage to smithereens and exposing the night sky. The impact pushes both Henri and me backwards.

"Run!" Henri yells, and he immediately unloads every shell in the shotgun into the beast. They have no effect upon it. The beast leans forward and roars so loudly that I feel my clothes flutter. A hand reaches out and grabs hold of me, turning me invisible. The beast charges ahead, moving straight for Henri, and I'm gripped with terror at what it might do.

"No!" I scream. "To Henri, get to Henri!" I twist under Six's grip, finally grabbing hold of her and pushing her away. I become visible; she stays hidden. The beast surges towards Henri, who stands firm and watches it come. Out of bullets. Out of options. "Get to him!" I scream again. "Get to him, Six!"

"Go to the woods!" she yells back.

All I can do is watch. The beast must stand thirty feet tall, maybe forty, towering over Henri. It roars, pure wrath in its eyes. Its muscled and bulging fist rushes high in the air, so high that it breaks straight through the rafters and the roof of the school gymnasium. And then it falls, speeding down with such swiftness that it becomes a blur, like the blades of a spinning fan. I cry out in horror, knowing that Henri is about to be crushed. I can't look away, Henri seeming tiny standing there with the shotgun limply at his side. When the fist of the beast is a split second from him, Henri disappears. The fist crashes through the gymnasium floor, the wood splintering, the impact sending me crashing into the stands twenty feet away. The beast turns to me, blocking from view the place where Henri had just stood.

"Henri!" I yell. The beast roars so that any response that might have come is drowned out. It takes one step towards me. To the woods, Six had said. Go to the woods. I stand and run as fast as I can to the back of the gym, where the beast had just broken through. I turn to see if the beast is following. It is not. Perhaps Six has done something to divert its attention. All I know is that I'm on my own now, alone.

I leap over the pile of rubble and sprint away from the school, running as hard as I can for the woods. The shadows swarm around me, following like villainous wraiths. I know that I can outrun them. The beast roars and I hear another wall crumble. I reach the trees and the swarming shadows seem to have disappeared. I stop and listen. The trees sway under a light breeze. There is a wind here! I've escaped whatever dome the Mogadorians have created. Something warm collects at the waistband of my pants. The cut I suffered at Mark James's has reopened on my back.

The school's silhouette is faint from where I stand. The entire gymnasium is gone, a pile of brick. The beast's shadow stands tall in the rubble of the cafeteria. Why hasn't it run after me? And where is the second beast we all heard? The

beast's fist falls again, another room demolished.
Mark and Sarah are there somewhere. I told them
to go back and I realize how foolish it was. I
didn't anticipate the beast destroying the school if
it knew I wasn't there. I have to do something to
get the beast away. I take a deep breath to gather
my strength, and as soon as I take that first step,
something hard hits me in the back of the head.
I fall face-first into the mud. I touch where I've
been hit and my hand is covered in blood, drips
of it falling from my fingertips. I turn around
and see nothing at first, and then it steps out of
the shadows and grins.

A soldier. This is what they look like. Taller
than the scouts—seven, maybe eight feet tall—
its muscles bulging beneath a black ragged cloak.
Large, raised veins traverse the length of each
arm. Black boots. Nothing covering its head, and
its hair falling to its shoulders. The same pale,
waxy skin as the scouts. A grin of self-assurance,
of finality. In one of its hands is a sword. Long
and shimmering, made of some kind of metal I've
never seen here on Earth or in my visions of
Lorien, and it appears to be pulsing, as if it is
somehow alive.

I begin to crawl away, the blood dripping
down my neck. The beast at the school lets out
another roar, and I reach for the low branches of
a nearby tree and pull myself up. The soldier is

ten feet away. I grip both hands into fists. It motions the sword nonchalantly towards me, and something comes out of its tip, something that looks like a small dagger. I watch the dagger twist in an arc, leaving a slight trail behind it like smoke from a plane. The light casts a spell that I can't look away from.

A flash of bright light devours everything, the world dimming away into a soundless void. No walls. No sound. No floor or ceiling. Very slowly the shapes of things return, the trees standing like ancient effigies whispering of the world that once was in some alternate realm where only shadows reside.

I reach out to feel the nearest tree, the only touch of gray in an otherwise white world. My hand goes through it and for a moment the tree shimmers as if it were liquid. I take a deep breath. When I exhale the pain returns to the gash on the back of my head and the tears down my arms and body from the James house fire. A sound of dripping water comes from somewhere. Slowly, the soldier takes form, twenty or thirty feet away. Giantlike. We take each other in. Its sword glowing more brightly in this new world. Its eyes narrow and my hands again clench into fists. I've lifted objects far heavier than it; I've split trees and I've caused destruction. Surely I can match its strength with my own. I push everything that

I feel into the core of my being, everything that I am and everything that I will be, until I feel as though I'm about to burst.

"Yahhhh!" I yell, and I thrust my arms forward. The brute force leaves my body, raging towards the soldier. At the same time it sweeps the sword across its body as though swatting a fly. The power deflects into the trees, which dance for a brief moment like the grain in a wheat field waving in a light wind, and then they become still. It laughs at me, a deep, guttural laugh meant to taunt. Its red eyes begin to glow, swirling as though lava filled. It lifts its free hand and I tense myself against the unknown. And without my knowing what has happened, my throat is in its grip, the gap that had separated us closed in the blink of an eye. It lifts me, one handed, breathing with its mouth open so that I can smell the sour stench of its breath, the smell of decay. I thrash, try to pry its fingers from around my throat, but they are like iron.

And then it throws me.

I land on my back forty feet away. I stand and it charges, swinging the sword at my head, which I duck and counter by pushing it as hard as I can. It stumbles back but stays standing. I try to lift it with telekinesis but nothing happens. In this alternate world my powers are dimmed, almost ineffectual. The Mogadorian has the advantage here.

It smiles at my futility and raises the sword with both hands. The sword comes alive, turning from shimmering silver into ice blue. Blue flames lick across the blade. A sword that glows with power, just as Six had talked about. It swings the sword in my direction and another dagger comes flying off the tip, straight at me. *This I can do,* I think. All the hours in the backyard with Henri preparing for this very thing. Always the knives, more or less the same as a dagger. Did Henri know they would use them? Certainly, though in my flashbacks of the invasion I had never seen them. But I had never seen these creatures, either. They were different on Lorien, not quite as sinister looking. On the day of the invasion they looked sickly and starved. Is it Earth's fault for this convalescence, have the resources here caused them to grow stronger and healthier?

The dagger literally screams as it rages towards me. It grows and becomes consumed in flames. Just when I am about to deflect it, it explodes into a ball of fire, and the flames jump to me. I'm trapped within it, consumed in a perfect sphere of fire. Anyone else would burn, but not me, and somehow it causes my strength to return. I'm able to breathe. Without the soldier knowing it, it has made me stronger. Now it's my turn to smile at its own futility.

"Is this all you've got?" I yell.

Its face turns into rage. It defiantly reaches one hand over its shoulder and returns with a cannonlike gun that begins conforming to its body, the gun wrapping around its forearm. Its arm and the gun becoming one and the same. I pull the knife from my back pocket, the knife that I grabbed from home before returning to school. Small, ineffectual, but better than nothing. I open the blade and charge. The ball of fire charges with me. The soldier squares its body and brings down its sword with force. I deflect it with the pocketknife but the weight of the sword snaps the blade in two. I drop the remaining pieces and swing as hard as I can. My fist slams into the soldier's gut. It doubles over but comes right back up and swings the sword again. I duck beneath the blade at the last second. It singes the hair on top of my head. Right behind the sword comes the cannon. No time to react. It hits me in my shoulder and I grunt and fall backwards. The soldier regroups and points the cannon in the air. I'm confounded at first. The gray from the trees is being pulled away and sucked into the gun. Then I understand. The gun. It needs to be charged before it can be fired, needs to steal Earth's essence in order to be used. The gray in the trees isn't shadows; the gray is the life of the trees at its most elemental level. And now those lives are being stolen, consumed by the Mogadorians. A race of aliens that depleted their planet's resources in the quest for advancement, now doing the same thing here. That is the reason they attacked Lorien. The same reason they will attack Earth. One by one the trees fall and crumble into heaps of ash. The gun glows brighter and brighter, so bright that it hurts the eyes to look at. No time to spare.

I charge. It keeps the gun pointed at the sky and swings the sword. I duck and plow straight into it. Its body tenses and it writhes in agony. The fire surrounding me burns it where it stands. But I've left myself open. It swings the blade feebly, not enough to cut me, but there is nothing I can do to prevent its fall. It hits me and my body is hurled backwards fifty feet as though I've been struck by a bolt of lightning. I lie there, my body shaking with postelectrocution tremors. I lift my head. Thirty piles of ash from the fallen trees surround us. How many times will that allow him to fire? A slight wind kicks up and the ash begins filtering across the empty space between us. The moon returns. This world to which it has brought me is beginning to fail. It knows it. The gun is ready. I wrestle myself up from the ground. Sitting a couple feet away, still glowing, is one of the daggers it fired at me. I pick it up.

It lowers the cannon and aims. The white

surrounding us is beginning to dim, color returning. And then the cannon fires, a bright flash of
light containing the ghoulish forms of everyone I
have ever known—Henri, Sam, Bernie Kosar,
Sarah—all of them dead in this alternate realm and
the light so bright that they are all I can see, trying
to take me with them, raging forward in a ball of
energy growing as it nears. I try to deflect the blast
but it's too strong. The white makes it as far as the
fiery enclosure, and when the two touch an explosion erupts and the power sends me backwards. I
land with a thud. I take inventory. I am unharmed.
The ball of fire has extinguished. Somehow it has
absorbed the blast, has saved me from what I am
certain would have been death. Surely that is how
the cannon works, the death of one thing for the
death of another. The power of mind control,
manipulation that plays on fear, possible through
the destruction of the elements of the world. The
scouts have learned to do this weakly with their
minds. The soldiers rely on weapons that produce
a much greater effect.

I stand, the glowing knife still in my hand.
The soldier pulls some sort of lever on the side of
the cannon as though to reload it. I sprint
towards it. When I'm close enough, I aim for its
heart and hurl the knife as hard as I can. It fires
a second shot. A torpedo of orange raging its way,
the certainty of a white death coming mine. They

cross in midair without touching. Just when I expect that second shot to hit, to bring upon that death, something else happens instead.

My knife strikes first.

The world vanishes. The shadows fade and the cold and the dark return as though they had never left. A vertiginous transition. I take a step backwards and fall. My eyes adjust to the dearth of light. I fix them on the dark figure of the soldier hovering over me. The cannon blast didn't travel with us. The glowing knife did, the blade sunk deeply into its heart, the handle pulsating orange beneath the moonlight overhead. The soldier staggers, and then the knife is sucked in deeper and disappears. It grunts. Spurts of black blood pump from the open wound. Its eyes go blank, then roll back into its head. It falls to the ground, lies motionless, and then explodes into a cloud of ash that covers my shoes. A soldier. I've killed my first. May it not be the last.

Something about being in the alternate realm has weakened me. I place my hand on a nearby tree to steady myself and catch my breath, only the tree is no longer there. I look around. All the trees surrounding us have collapsed into heaps of ash just as they did in the other realm, just as the Mogadorians do when they die.

I hear the roar of the beast and I look up to see

how much of the school is left standing. But instead of the school there is something else, fifteen feet away, standing tall with a sword in one hand and a similar-looking cannon in the other. The cannon is aimed right at my heart, a cannon that has already been charged, glowing with power. Another soldier. I don't think I have the strength to fight this one as I did the last.

There is nothing I can throw, and the gap between us is too great to charge before it fires. And then its arm twitches and the sound of a gunshot rings through the air. My body instinctively jerks, expecting the cannon to rip me in half. But I am fine, unharmed. I look up confused, and there, in the soldier's forehead, is a hole the size of a quarter spurting its hideous blood. Then it drops and disintegrates.

"That's for my dad," I hear behind me. I turn. Sam, holding a silver pistol in his right hand. I smile at him. He lowers the gun. "They passed right through the center of town," he says. "I knew it was them as soon as I saw the trailer."

I try to catch my breath, staring in awe at Sam's figure. Just moments before, in the first soldier's blast, he was a decaying corpse sprung from hell to take me away. And now he just saved me.

"You okay?" he asks.

I nod. "Where did you just come from?"

"I followed them in my dad's truck after they passed my house. I pulled in fifteen minutes ago and got swarmed by the ones that were already here. So I left and parked in a field a mile away and walked through the woods."

The second set of lights we had seen from the window of the school came from Sam's truck. I open my mouth to respond but a clap of thunder shakes the sky. Another storm begins to brew, and relief courses through me that Six is still alive. A bolt of lightning cuts the sky and clouds begin rushing in from all directions, being pulled together into one giant mass. An even greater darkness falls, followed by a rain so heavy that I have to squint to see Sam five feet away from me. The school is blotted out. But then a great bolt of lightning strikes and everything brightens for a split second, and I see that the beast has been hit. An agonizing roar follows.

"I have to get to the school!" I yell. "Mark and Sarah are somewhere inside."

"If you're going, then I'm going," he yells back over the rumble of the storm.

We take no more than five steps before the wind comes howling, pushing us back, torrential rain stinging our faces. We're soaked, shivering and cold. But if I'm shivering then I know I'm alive. Sam drops to a knee, then lies on his stomach to keep from being blown backwards. I do the same. Through squinted eyes I look into the clouds—heavy, dark, ominous—swirling in small concentric circles and, in the center, the center I'm trying mightily to reach, a face begins to form.

It's an old, weathered face, bearded, tranquil looking as though it sleeps. A face that looks older than Earth itself. The clouds begin to lower, slowly nearing the surface and consuming everything, everything darkening, a dark so deep and impenetrable that it's hard to imagine that somewhere, anywhere, a sun still exists. Another roar, a roar of anger and doom. I try to stand but am quickly knocked back down, the wind too great. The face. It's coming alive. An awakening. The eyes opening, the face upturned into a grimace. Is this Six's creation? The face becomes the look of rage itself, a look of revenge. Coming down fast. Everything seems to hang in the balance. And then the mouth opens, hungry, its lips curling to show teeth and its eyes squinted in what can only be described as pure malice. A complete and utter wrath.

And then the face touches down and a sonic blast shakes the ground, an explosion reaching out over the school, everything illuminated in red, orange, and yellow. I'm thrust backwards. Trees break in half. The ground rumbles. I land with a thud, branches and mud falling atop me.

My ears ring as they've never rung before. A boom so loud that it must have been heard fifty miles away. And then the rain stops, and everything falls silent.

I lie in the mud, listening to the beat of my heart. The clouds clear away, revealing a hanging moon. Not a single gust of wind. I look around but don't see Sam. I yell for him but get no response. I yearn to hear something, anything, another roar, Henri's shotgun, but there is nothing.

I pull myself up off the forest floor, wipe away the mud and the twigs as best as I can. I exit the woods for the second time. The stars have reappeared, a million of them twinkling high in the night sky. Is it over? Have we won? Or is it just a lull in the action? The school, I think. I have to get to the school. I take one step forward, and that's when I hear it.

Another roar, coming from within the woods behind me.

Sound returns. Three successive gunshots ring through the night, echoing so that I have no idea from which direction they have come. I hope with everything inside of me that they are from Henri's shotgun, that he is still alive, still fighting.

The ground begins to shake. The beast is on the run, coming for me, no mistaking it now, trees broken and uprooted behind me. They don't seem to slow it down at all. Is this one even bigger than the other? I don't care to find out. I take off running for the school, but then realize that's the absolute worst place I can go. Sarah and Mark are still there, still hiding. Or at least I hope they are.

Everything returns to the way it was before the storm, the shadows following, looming. Scouts. Soldiers. I veer to the right and sprint along the tree-lined path that leads to the football field, the beast hot on my trail. Can I really expect to outrun it? If I can make it to the woods beyond the field, maybe I can. I know those woods, the woods that lead to our house. Within them I'll have the home-field advantage. I look around and see the figures of the Mogadorians in the schoolyard. There are too many of them. We're greatly outnumbered. Did we ever really believe we could win?

A dagger flies by me, a flash of red missing my face by mere inches. It sticks into the trunk of a tree beside me and the tree ignites in flame. Another roar. The beast is keeping pace. Which of us has the greater endurance? I enter the stadium, sprint straight across the fifty-yard line and pass through the visiting team's side. Another knife whizzes by, a blue one this time. The woods are near, and when I finally sprint into them a smile forms on my face. I've led it away from the others. If everyone else is safe then I've done my job. Just when a sense of triumph blooms within me, the third dagger strikes.

I cry out, fall face-first into the mud. I can feel the dagger between my shoulder blades. A pain so sharp that it paralyzes me. I try to reach to pull it free but it is up too high. It feels as though it's moving, digging itself deeper, the pain spreading as if I've been poisoned. On my stomach, in agony. I can't pull it free with telekinesis, my powers somehow failing me. I begin dragging myself forward. One of the soldiers—or maybe it's a scout; I can't tell which—places a foot on my back, reaches down, and pulls the knife free. I grunt. The knife is gone but the pain stays. It takes its foot off of me but I can still feel its presence, and I wrestle myself onto my back to face it.

Another soldier, standing tall and smiling with hatred. The same look as the one before, the same type of sword. The dagger that was in my back twists in its grip. That is what I felt, the blade turning while imbedded in my flesh. I lift a hand towards the soldier to move it but I know it's in vain. I can't focus, everything blurry. The soldier raises its sword in the air. The blade tastes death, starts glowing in the night sky behind it. *I'm gone,* I think. *Nothing I can do.* I look into its eyes. Ten years on the run and this is how easily it ends, how quietly. But behind it lurks something else. Something far more menacing than a million soldiers with a million swords. Teeth every bit as long as the soldier is tall, teeth glowing white in a mouth too small to hold them. The beast with its evil eyes hovering over us.

A sharp intake of breath catches in my throat, and my eyes open wide in terror. It'll take us both out, I think. The soldier is oblivious. It tenses and grimaces at me and starts to bring the sword down to split me in two. But it is too slow and the beast strikes first, its jaws clamping down like a bear trap. The bite doesn't stop until the beast's teeth come together, the soldier's body cut cleanly in half just below the hips, leaving nothing behind but two stumps still standing. The beast chews twice and swallows. The soldier's legs fall hollowly to the ground, one dropping to the right, the other to the left, and quickly disintegrate.

It takes every ounce of strength I have to reach out and grab the dagger that has fallen at my feet. I tuck it into the waistband of my jeans, and begin crawling away. I feel the beast hovering over me, feel its breath upon the nape of my neck. The smell of death and rotting meat. I enter a small clearing. I expect the beast's wrath to fall any second, expect its teeth and claws to rip me to shreds. I pull myself forward until I can go no more, my back against an oak tree.

The beast stands in the very center of the clearing, thirty feet away from me. I look at it fully for the first time. A looming figure, hazy in the dark and the cold of the night. Taller and bigger than the beast at the school, forty feet, standing upright on two hind legs. Thick, gray skin stretched tightly over slabs of bulging muscle. No neck, its head sloped so that its lower jaw protrudes farther out than its upper. A set of fangs points towards the sky, another set points to the ground, dripping blood and drool. Long, thick arms hang a foot or two above the ground even while the beast stands straight, giving it the appearance of slightly leaning forward. Yellow eyes. Round disks at the sides of its head that pulsate with the beating of its heart, the only sign that it has any sort of heart at all.

It leans forward and brings its left hand to the ground. A hand, complete with stubby short fingers with claws like a raptor, claws meant to rip apart anything they touch. It sniffs at me, and roars. An ear-splitting roar that would have pushed me backwards if I weren't already against a tree. Its mouth opens, showing what must be fifty other teeth, each one every bit as sharp as the next. Its free hand thrusts away from its side and splits in half every tree that it strikes, ten, fifteen of them.

No more running. No more fighting. Blood from the knife wound runs down my back; my hands and legs are both shaking. The dagger is still tucked into the waistband of my jeans, but what's the point in grabbing it? What faith is there in a four-inch blade against a forty-foot beast? It would be the equivalent of a splinter. It'll only make it angrier. My only hope is to bleed to death before I am killed and eaten.

I close my eyes and accept death. My lights are off. I don't want to see what is about to happen. I hear movement behind me. I open my eyes. One of the Mogadorians must be moving in for a closer look; I think at first, but I know immediately that I am wrong. There is something familiar about the loping gait, something I recognize in the sound of his breathing. And then he enters the clearing.

Bernie Kosar.

I smile, but the smile quickly fades. If I am doomed, there is no point in him dying too. *No, Bernie Kosar. You can't be here. You need to leave and you need to run like the wind, get as far away as you can. Pretend you've just finished our early-morning jog to school and that it's time to return home.*

He looks at me as he walks up. *I am here,* he seems to say. *I am here and I will stand with you.*

"No," I say aloud.

He stops long enough to give my hand a reassuring lick. He looks up at me with his big, brown eyes. *Get away, John,* I hear in my mind. *Crawl if you have to crawl, but get away now.* The blood loss has made me delusional. Bernie seems to be communicating with me. Is Bernie Kosar even here, or am I imagining that as well?

He stands in front of me as though in protection. He begins to growl, low at first, but it grows to a growl every bit as ferocious as the beast's own roar. The beast fixates on Bernie Kosar. A staredown. Bernie Kosar's hair is raised down the center of his back, his tan ears pinned to his head. His loyalty, his bravery very nearly make me weep. He's a hundred times smaller than the beast yet he stands tall, vowing to fight. One quick strike from the beast and all is done.

I reach my hand out to Bernie Kosar. I wish I could stand and grab him and get away. His growls are so fierce that his whole body shakes, tremors coursing through him.

And then something begins to happen.

Bernie Kosar begins to grow.

CHAPTER THIRTY-TWO

AFTER ALL THIS TIME, ONLY NOW do I understand. The morning runs when I would run too fast for him to keep pace. He would disappear into the woods, reappear seconds later in front of me. Six tried to tell me. Six took one look at him and she knew immediately. On those runs Bernie Kosar went into the woods to change himself, to turn himself into a bird. The way he would rush outside each morning, nose to the ground, patrolling the yard. Protecting me, and Henri. Looking for signs of the Mogadorians. The gecko in Florida. The gecko that used to watch from the wall while I ate breakfast. How long has he been with us? The Chimæra, the ones I watched being loaded into the rocket—did they make it to Earth after all?

Bernie Kosar continues to grow. He tells me to run. I can communicate with him. No, that's not all. I can communicate with all animals. Another Legacy. It started with the deer in Florida on the day that we left. The shudder that ran up my spine as it passed something along to me, some feeling. I attributed it to the sadness of our leaving, but I was wrong. Mark James's dogs. The cows I passed on my morning runs. The same thing. I feel like such a fool to discover it only now. So blatantly obvious, right in front of my face. Another of Henri's adages: Those things that are most obvious are the very things we're most likely to overlook. But Henri knew. That is why he said no to Six when she tried to tell me.

Bernie Kosar is done growing; his hair has fallen away, replaced by oblong scales. He looks like a dragon, but without the wings. His body is thick with muscle. Jagged teeth and claws, horns that curl like a ram's. Thicker than the beast, but far shorter. Looking every bit as menacing. Two giants on opposite sides of the clearing, roaring at one another.

Run, he tells me. I try to tell him that I can't. I don't know if he can understand me. *You can,* he says. *You must.*

The beast swings. A hammer swing that starts in the clouds and pours down with brutality. Bernie Kosar blocks it with his horns and then charges before the beast can swing again. A colossal collision in the very center of the clearing. Bernie Kosar thrusts up, sinks his teeth into the beast's side. The beast knocks him back. Both of them so quick that it defies all logic. Bleeding gashes already down the sides of each. I watch with my back against the tree. I try to help. But my telekinesis is still failing me. Blood still pours down my back. My limbs feel heavy, as though my blood has turned to lead. I can feel myself fading.

The beast is still upright on two legs while Bernie Kosar must fight on four. The beast makes a charge. Bernie Kosar lowers his head and they smash into one another, crashing through the trees off to my right side. Somehow the beast ends up on top. It sinks its teeth deep in Bernie Kosar's throat. It thrashes, trying to tear his throat out. Bernie Kosar twists under the beast's bite but he can't shake free. He tears at the beast's hide with his paws but the beast doesn't let go.

Then a hand reaches out behind me, grabs my arm. I try to push it away but I'm incapable of doing even that. Bernie Kosar's eyes are closed tightly. He is straining under the beast's jaws, his throat constricted, unable to breathe.

"No!" I yell.

"Come on!" the voice yells behind me. "We need to get out of here."

"The dog," I say, not comprehending whose voice it is. "The dog!"

Bernie Kosar is being bitten and choked, about to die, and there isn't a damn thing I can do about it. I won't be far behind. I would sacrifice my own life for his. I scream out. Bernie Kosar twists his head around and looks at me, his face scrunched tightly in pain and agony and the oncoming death he must feel.

"We have to go!" the voice behind me yells, the hand pulling me up from off the forest floor.

Bernie Kosar's eyes stay fixed on mine. *Go*, he says to me. *Get out of here, now, while you can. There isn't much time.*

I somehow reach my feet. Dizzy, the world cast in a haze around me. Only Bernie Kosar's eyes remain clear. Eyes that scream "Help!" even while his thoughts say otherwise.

"We have to go!" the voice yells again. I don't turn to face it, but I know whose it is. Mark James, no longer hiding in the school, trying to save me from this clash. His being here must mean that Sarah is okay, and for a brief moment I allow myself to be relieved, but then that relief vanishes as quickly as it came. In this exact moment only one thing matters. Bernie Kosar, on his side, looking at me with glassy eyes. He saved me. It's my turn to save him.

Mark reaches his hand across my chest, begins pulling me backwards, out of the clearing, away from the fight. I twist myself free. Bernie Kosar's eyes slowly begin to close. He's fading, I think. *I won't watch you die*, I tell him. *I'm willing to watch many things in this world but I'll be damned if I'll watch you die.* There's no response. The beast's bite hardens. It can sense that death is near.

I take one wobbly step and pull the dagger from the waistband of my jeans. I close my fingers tightly around it and it comes alive and starts glowing. I'll never be able to hit the beast by throwing the dagger, and my Legacies have all but vanished. An easy decision. No choice but to charge.

One deep, shaky breath. I rock my body backwards, everything tensing through the ache of exhaustion, not an inch anywhere on me that doesn't feel some sort of pain.

"No!" Mark yells behind me.

I lunge forward and sprint for the beast. The beast's eyes are closed, jaws clamped tightly around Bernie Kosar's throat so that the moonlight glows in the pools of blood around it. Thirty feet away. Then twenty. The beast's eyes snap open at the exact moment I jump. Yellow eyes that twist in rage the second they focus upon me, sailing through the air towards them, dagger in both hands held high over my head as though in some heroic dream I never want to wake from. The beast lets go of Bernie Kosar's throat and moves to bite, but surely it knows that it has sensed me too late. The blade of the dagger glows in anticipation, and I jam it deeply into the eye of the beast. A liquid ooze immediately bursts out. The beast lets out a blood-curdling scream so loud that it's hard to imagine the dead being able to sleep through it.

I fall flat on my back. I lift my head and watch the beast totter over me. It tries in vain to pull the dagger from its eye, but its hands are too big and the dagger is too small. The Mogadorian weapons function in some way that I don't think I'll ever understand, because of the mystical gateways between the realms. The dagger is no different, the black of the night rushing into the eye of the beast in a vortexlike funnel cloud, a tornado of death.

The beast falls silent as the last of the great black cloud enters its skull, and the dagger is sucked in with it. The beast's arms fall limply to its sides. Its hands begin to shake. A violent shake that reverberates throughout the entirety of its massive body. When the convulsions end the beast hunches over and then falls to the ground with its back against the trees. Sitting, but yet still towering some twenty-five feet over me. Everything silent, hanging in anticipation of what is to come. A gun fires once, very close so that my ears ring for seconds afterward. The beast takes a great breath and holds it in as though in meditation, and suddenly its head explodes, raining down pieces of brain and flesh and skull over everything, all of which quickly turn to ash and dust.

The woods fall silent. I turn my head and look at Bernie Kosar, who still lies motionless on his side, his eyes closed. I can't tell if he's alive or not. As I look at him, he begins to change again, shrinking down to his normal size, while remaining lifeless. I hear the sound of crunching leaves and snapping twigs nearby.

It takes all the strength I have just to lift my head an inch off the ground. I open my eyes and peer up into the haze of night, expecting to see Mark James. But it's not him standing over me. My breath catches in my throat. A looming figure, indistinct with the moon's light hovering just over it. Then he takes one step forward, blotting out the moon, and my eyes widen in anticipation and dread.

CHAPTER THIRTY-THREE

THE HAZY IMAGE SHARPENS. THROUGH the exhaustion and pain and fear, a smile comes to my face, coupled with a sense of relief. Henri. He throws the shotgun into the bushes and drops to one knee beside me. He face is bloodied, his shirt and jeans in tatters, cuts down the length of both arms and on his neck, and beyond that I see that his eyes are fear-stricken from what he sees in mine.

"Is it over?" I ask.

"Shhh," he says. "Tell me, have you been stabbed by one of their daggers?"

"My back," I say.

He closes his eyes and shakes his head. He reaches into his pocket and removes one of the small round stones I watched him grab from the Loric Chest before we left the home-ec room. His hands are shaking.

"Open your mouth," he says. He inserts one of the stones. "Keep it under your tongue. Don't swallow it." He hefts me up with his hands beneath my armpits. I get to my feet and he keeps an arm on me while I regain balance. He turns me around to look at the gash on my back. My face feels warm. A sort of rejuvenation blooms through me from the stone. My limbs still ache with exhaustion, but enough strength has returned so that I'm able to function.

"What is this?"

"Loric salt. It'll slow and numb the dagger's effects," he says. "You'll feel a burst of energy, but it won't last long and we have to get back to the school as quickly as we can."

The pebble is cold in my mouth, tastes nothing like salt—tastes like nothing at all, actually. I look down and take inventory, and then brush off with my hands the ashen residue left from the fallen beast.

"Is everyone okay?" I ask.

"Six has been badly hurt," he says. "Sam is carrying her back to the truck as we speak; then he is going to drive to the school to pick us up. That's why we have to get back there."

"Have you seen Sarah?"

"No."

"Mark James was just here," I say, and look at him. "I thought you were him."

"I didn't see him."

I look past Henri at the dog. "Bernie Kosar," I say. He is still shrinking, the scales fading away—tan, black, and brown hair taking their place—returning to the form in which I have known him most recently: floppy ears, short legs, long body. A beagle with a cold wet nose always ready to run. "He just saved my life. You knew, didn't you?"

"Of course I knew."

"Why didn't you tell me?"

"Because he watched over you when I couldn't."

"But how is he here?"

"He was on the ship with us."

And then I remember what I thought was a stuffed animal that used to play with me. It was really Bernie Kosar I was playing with, though back then his name was Hadley.

We walk to the dog together. I crouch down and run my hand along Bernie Kosar's side.

"We have to hurry," Henri says again.

Bernie Kosar isn't moving. The woods are alive, swarming with shadows that can only mean one thing, but I don't care. I move my head to the dog's rib cage. Ever so faintly I hear the *th-tump* of his beating heart. Some glimmer of life is still left. He is covered in deep cuts and gashes, and blood seems to seep from everywhere. His front leg is twisted at an unnatural angle, broken. But he is still alive. I lift him as gently as I can, cradling him like a child in my arms. Henri helps me up, then reaches into his pocket, grabs another salt pebble, and plops it into his own mouth. It makes me wonder if he was talking about himself when he said there was little time. Both of us are unsteady. And then something catches my eye in Henri's thigh. A wound glowing navy blue through the gathering blood around it. He's also been stabbed by a soldier's knife. I wonder if the salt pebble is the only reason he's now standing, as it is for me.

"What about the shotgun?" I ask.

"I'm out of ammo."

We walk out of the clearing, taking our time. Bernie Kosar doesn't move in my arms but I can feel that life hasn't left him. Not yet. We exit the woods, leaving behind us the overhanging branches and bushes and the smell of wet and rotting leaves.

"Do you think you can run?" Henri asks.

"No," I say. "But I'll run anyway."

Up ahead of us we hear a great commotion, several grunts followed by clanking of chains.

And then we hear a roar, not quite as sinister as the others, but loud enough so that we know it can only mean one thing: another beast.

"You're kidding me," Henri says.

Twigs snap behind us, coming from the

woods. Henri and I both twist around, but the woods are too dense to see. I snap the light on in my left hand and sweep it through the trees to see. There must be seven or eight soldiers standing at the entrance of the woods, and when my light hits them they all draw their swords, which come alive, glowing their various colors the second they do.

"No!" Henri yells. "Don't use your Legacies; it'll weaken you."

But it's too late. I snap the light off. Vertigo and weakness return, then the pain. I hold my breath and wait for the soldiers to come charging at us. But they don't. There follows no sound aside from the obvious struggle happening straight ahead of us. Then an uproar of yells behind us. I turn to look. The glowing swords begin swaggering forward from forty feet away. A confident laugh comes from one of the soldiers. Nine of them armed and full of strength versus three of us broken and battered and armed with nothing more than our valor. The beast one way, the soldiers the other. That is the choice that we now face.

Henri seems unfazed. He removes two more pebbles from his pocket and hands one to me.

"The last two," he says, his voice shaky as though it requires a great effort just to speak.

I plop the new pebble into my mouth and bury it beneath my tongue despite a small bit of the first still remaining. Renewed strength rushes through me.

"What do you think?" he asks me.

We are surrounded. Henri and Bernie Kosar and I are the only three left. Six badly hurt and carried away by Sam. Mark just here but now nowhere to be found. And that leaves Sarah, who I pray is tucked away safely in the school that lies a tenth of a mile ahead of us. I take a deep breath and I accept the inevitable.

"I don't think it matters, Henri," I say, and look at him. "But the school is ahead of us, and that is where Sam will be shortly."

What he does next catches me off guard: he smiles. He reaches his hand out and gives my shoulder a squeeze. His eyes are tired and red but in them I see relief, a sense of serenity as though he knows it's all about to end.

"We've done all we could. And what's done is done. But I'm damn proud of you," he says. "You did amazing today. I always knew you would. There was never a doubt in my mind."

I drop my head. I don't want him to see me cry. I squeeze the dog. For the first time since I grabbed him he shows a slight sign of life, lifting his head just enough so that he can lick the side of my face. He passes one word to me and one word only, as if that is all his strength will allow. *Courage*, he says.

I lift my head. Henri steps forward and hugs me. I close my eyes and bury my face in his neck. He is still shaking, his body frail and weak beneath my grip. I'm sure mine is no stronger. *So this is it,* I think. With our heads held high we will walk across the field to whatever awaits there. At least there is dignity in that.

"You did damn good," he says.

I open my eyes. From over his shoulder I see the soldiers are near, twenty feet away now. They have stopped walking. One of them is holding a dagger that pulsates silver and gray. The soldier tosses it in the air, catches it, and hurls it at Henri's back. I lift my hand and deflect it away and it misses by a foot. My strength leaves me almost immediately even though the pebble is only half dissolved.

Henri takes my free arm and drapes it over his shoulders and places his right arm around my waist. We stagger forward. The beast comes into view, looming just ahead in the center of the football field. The Mogadorians follow behind us. Perhaps they are curious to see the beast in action, to see the beast kill. Each step I take becomes more of an effort than the one that preceded it. My heart thuds in my chest. Death is forthcoming and of that I am terrified. But Henri is here. And so is Bernie Kosar. I'm happy not to have to face it alone. Several soldiers stand on the other side of the beast. Even if we could get past the beast, we would then have to walk straight into the soldiers, who stand with drawn swords.

We have no choice. We reach the field and I expect the beast to pounce at any moment. But nothing happens. When we are within fifteen feet of it we stop. We stand leaning against each other for support.

The beast is half the size of the other but still big enough to kill us all with no great effort of its own. Pale, almost translucent skin stretched over protruding ribs and knobby joints. Various pinkish scars down its arms and sides. White, sightless eyes. It shifts its weight and lowers itself, then swings its head low over the grass to smell what its eyes fail to see. It can sense us in front of it. It lets out a low groan. I feel none of the rage and malice that the other beasts radiated, no desire for blood and death. There is a sense of fear, a sense of sadness. I open myself to it. I see images of torture and starvation. I see the beast locked up for all its life here on Earth, a damp cave where little light reaches. Shivering through the night to stay warm, always cold and wet. I see the way the Mogadorians pit the beasts against one another, force them to fight in order to train, to toughen them and make them mean.

Henri lets go of me. I can't hold Bernie Kosar any longer. I gently place him in the grass at my feet.

I haven't felt him move in minutes and I can't tell if he's still alive. I take one step forward and drop to my knees. The soldiers yell around us. I don't understand their language but I can tell by their tones that they are impatient. One swings his sword and a dagger just misses me, a flash of white that flutters and tears the front of my shirt. I stay on my knees and I look up at the beast hovering over me. Some weapon is fired but it sails over our heads. A warning shot, meant to move the beast to action. The beast quivers. A second dagger darts through the air and hits the beast below the elbow of its left arm. It lifts its head and roars in pain.

I am sorry, I try to tell it. *I am sorry for the life you've been forced to live. You've been wronged. No living creature deserves such treatment. You've been forced to endure hell, plucked from your own planet to fight a war that isn't yours. Beaten and tortured and starved. The blame for all the pain and agony you've experienced lies with them. You and I share a common bond. Both wronged by these monsters.*

I try with everything to pass along my own images, the things that I've seen and felt. The beast doesn't look away. My thoughts, on some level, are reaching it. I show it Lorien, the vast ocean and thick forests and verdant hills teeming with life and vitality. Animals drinking from the cold blue waters. A proud people content to pass the days in harmony. I show it the hell that followed, the slaying of men, women, and children. The Mogadorians. Cold-blooded murderers. Draconian killers destroying all that lies within their path due to their own recklessness and pathetic beliefs. Destroying even their own planet. Where does it end? I show it Sarah, show it every emotion that I've ever felt with her. Happiness and bliss, this is how I feel with her. And this is the pain I feel in having to leave her, all because of them. *Help me,* I say. *Help me end this death and slaughter. Let us fight together. I have so little left but if you stand with me, I'll stand with you.*

The beast lifts its head to the sky and it roars. A roar both long and deep. The Mogadorians can sense what is happening and have seen enough. Their weapons begin firing. I look over and one of the cannons is aimed right at me. It fires and the white death surges forth, but the beast drops its head in time and absorbs the shot instead. Its face twists in pain, its eyes squeeze tightly shut, but almost immediately they snap back open. This time I see the rage.

I fall face-first in the grass. I'm grazed by something but I don't see what it is. Henri cries out in pain behind me and he is flung thirty feet away, his body lying in the mud, face up, smoking. I have no idea what has hit him. Something big and deadly. Panic and fear hit me. *Not Henri,* I think. *Please not Henri.*

The beast throws a hard sweeping blow that takes out several of the soldiers and quiets many of their guns. Another roar. I look up and see the beast's eyes have turned red, ablaze with fury. Retribution. Mutiny. It looks my way once and swiftly rushes off to follow its captors. Guns blaze but many of them are quick to be silenced. *Kill them all,* I think. *Fight nobly and honorably and may you kill them all.*

I lift my head. Bernie Kosar is motionless in the grass. Henri, thirty feet away, is motionless as well. I place a hand in the grass and pull myself forward, across the field, inch by inch, dragging myself to Henri. When I get there his eyes are open slightly; each breath is a fight. Trails of blood run from his mouth and nose. I take him into my arms and I pull him into my lap. His body is frail and weak and I can feel him dying. His eyes flutter open. He looks at me and lifts his hand and presses it to the side of my face. The second he does I begin to cry.

"I'm here," I say.

He tries to smile.

"I'm so sorry, Henri." I say. "I'm so sorry. We should have left when you wanted to."

"Shh," he says. "It's not your fault."

"I'm so sorry," I say between sobs.

"You did great," he says in a whisper. "You did so great. I always knew you would."

"We have to get you to the school," I say. "Sam could be there."

"Listen to me, John. Everything," he says. "Everything you need to know, it's all in the Chest. The letter."

"It's not over. We can still make it."

I can feel him begin to go. I shake him. His eyes reluctantly reopen. A trail of blood runs from his mouth.

"Coming here, to Paradise, it wasn't by chance." I don't know what he means. "Read the letter."

"Henri," I say, and reach down and wipe the blood off his chin.

He looks me in the eye.

"You are Lorien's Legacy, John. You and the others. The only hope the planet has left. The secrets," he says, and is gripped by a fit of coughs. More blood. His eyes close again. "The Chest, John."

I pull him more tightly to me, squeezing him. His body is going slack. Breaths so shallow that they are hardly breaths at all.

"We'll make it back together, Henri. Me and you, I promise," I say, and close my eyes.

"Be strong," he says, and is overtaken by slight coughs, though he tries to speak through them. "This war . . . Can win . . . Find the others. . . . Six. . . . The power of . . . ," he says, and trails off.

I try to stand with him in my arms but I have nothing left, hardly enough strength to even breathe. Off in the distance I hear the beast roar. Cannons are still being fired, the sounds and lights of which reach out over the stadium bleachers, but as each minute passes less and less of them are being fired until there is only one. I lower Henri in my arms. I place my hand to the side of his face and he opens his eyes and looks at me for what I know will be the final time. He takes a weak breath and exhales and then slowly closes his eyes.

"I wouldn't have missed a second of it, kiddo. Not for all of Lorien. Not for the whole damn world," he says, and when that last word leaves his mouth I know that he is gone. I squeeze him in my arms, shaking, crying, despair and hopelessness taking hold. His hand drops lifelessly to the grass. I cup his head in my hand and hold it close to my chest, and I rock him back and forth and I cry like I've never cried before. The pendant around my neck glows blue, grows heavy for just a split second, and then dims to normal.

I sit in the grass and I hold Henri while the last cannon falls silent. The pain leaves my own body and with the cold of the night I feel my own self begin to fade. The moon and the stars shine overhead. I hear a cackle of laughter carried on the wind. My ears attune to it. I turn my head.

Through the dizziness and blurry vision I see a scout fifteen feet away from me. Long trench coat, hat pulled to its eyes. It drops the coat and takes off the hat to reveal a pale and hairless head. It reaches to the back of its belt and removes a bowie knife, the blade of which is no less than twelve inches long. I close my eyes. I don't care anymore. The scout's raspy breathing comes my way, ten feet, then five. And then the footsteps end. The scout grunts in pain, and begins gurgling.

I open my eyes, the scout so close that I can smell it. The bowie knife falls from its hand, and there in its chest, where I assume its heart must be, is the end of a butcher's knife. The knife is pulled free. The scout drops to its knees, falls to its side, and explodes into a puff of ash. Behind it, holding the knife in her shaky right hand, with tears in her eyes, stands Sarah. She drops the knife and rushes over to me, wrapping her arms around me with my arms around Henri. I hold Henri as my own head falls and the world dims away into nothingness. The aftermath of war, the school destroyed, the trees fallen and heaps of ash piled in the grass of the football field and I still hold Henri. And Sarah holds me.

CHAPTER THIRTY-FOUR

IMAGES FLICKER, EACH ONE BRINGING its own sorrow or its own smile. Sometimes both. At the very worst an impenetrable and sightless black and at best a happiness so bright that it hurts the eyes to see, coming and going on some unseen projector perpetually turned by an invisible hand. One, then another. The hollow click of the shutter. Now stop. Freeze this frame. Pluck it down and hold it close and be damned by what you see. Henri always said: the price of a memory is the memory of the sorrow it brings.

A warm summer day in the cool grass with the sun high in the cloudless sky. The air coming off the water, carrying the freshness of the sea. A man walks up to the house, briefcase in hand. A younger man, brown hair cut short, freshly shaven, dressed casually. A sense of nervousness by the way he switches his briefcase from one hand to the other and the thin layer of sweat glistening on his forehead. He knocks at the door. My grandfather answers, opens the door for the man to enter, then closes it behind him. I resume my romping in the yard. Hadley changing forms, flying, then dodging, then charging. Wrestling with one another and laughing until it hurts. The day passing as time only can under the reckless abandon of childhood's invincibility, of its innocence.

Fifteen minutes pass. Maybe less. At that age a day can last forever. The door opens and closes. I look up. My grandfather is standing with the man I had seen approach, both of them looking down at me.

"There is somebody I would like you to meet," he says.

I stand from the grass and clap my hands together to knock away the dirt.

"This is Brandon," my grandfather says. "He is your Cêpan. Do you know what that means?"

I shake my head. Brandon. That was his name. All these years and only now does it come back to me.

"It means he's going to be spending a lot of time with you from here on out. The two of you, it means you are connected. You are bound to one another. Do you understand?"

I nod and walk to the man and I offer him my

hand as I have seen done many times by grown men before. The man smiles and drops to one knee. He takes my small hand in his right and he closes his fingers around it.

"Pleased to meet you, sir," I say.

Bright, kind eyes full of life look into mine as though offering a promise, a bond, yet I'm too young to know what that promise or bond really means.

He nods and brings his left hand on top of his right, my tiny hand lost somewhere in the middle. He nods at me, still smiling.

"My dear child," he says. "The pleasure is all mine."

I am jolted awake. I lie on my back, my heart racing, breathing heavily as though I had been running. My eyes stay closed but I can tell the sun has just risen by the long shadows and the crispness of air in the room. Pain returns, my limbs still heavy. With the pain comes another pain, a pain far greater than any physical ailment I could ever be afflicted with: the memory of the hours before.

I take a deep breath and exhale. A single tear rolls down the side of my face. I keep my eyes closed. An irrational hope that if I don't find the day then the day won't find me, that the things in the night will be nullified. My body shudders, a silent cry turning into a hard one. I shake my head and let it in. I know that Henri is dead and that all the hope in the world won't change it.

I feel movement beside me. I tense myself, try to remain motionless so as not to be detected. A hand reaches up and touches the side of my face. A delicate touch done with love. My eyes come open, adjusting to the postdawn light until the ceiling of a foreign room comes into focus. I have no idea where I am, nor how I could have gotten here. Sarah is sitting next to me. She brings her hand to the side of my face and traces my brow with her thumb. She leans down and kisses me, a soft lingering kiss that I wish I could bottle and save for all time. She pulls away and I take a deep breath and close my eyes and kiss her on the forehead.

"Where are we?" I ask.

"A hotel thirty miles from Paradise."

"How did I get here?"

"Sam drove us," she says.

"I mean from the school. What happened? I remember that you were with me last night, but I don't remember a thing after," I say. "It almost seems like a dream."

"I waited on the field with you until Mark arrived and he carried you to Sam's truck. I couldn't stay hidden any longer. Being in the school without knowing what was happening out there was killing me. And I felt like I could help somehow."

"You certainly helped," I say. "You saved my life."

"I killed an alien," she says, as though the fact still hasn't settled in.

She wraps her arms around me, her hand resting on the back of my head. I try to sit up. I make it halfway on my own and then Sarah helps me the rest of the way, pushing on my back but being careful not to touch the wound left by the knife. I swing my feet over the edge of the bed and reach down and feel the scars around my ankle, counting them with the tips of my fingers. Still only three, and in this way I know that Six has survived. I had already accepted the fate of the rest of my days being spent alone, an itinerant wanderer with no place to go. But I won't be alone. Six is still here, still with me, my tie to a past world.

"Is Six okay?"

"Yes," she says. "She's been stabbed and shot but she seems to be doing okay now. I don't think she would have survived had Sam not carried her to the truck."

"Where is she?"

"In the room next door, with Sam and Mark."

I stand. My muscles and joints ache in protest, everything stiff and sore. I am wearing a clean T-shirt, a pair of mesh shorts. My skin is fresh with the smell of soap. The cuts have been cleaned and bandaged, a few of them stitched.

"Did you do all of this?" I ask.

"Most of it. The stitches were hard. We only had the ones Henri put in your head to go on as an example. Sam helped with them."

I look at Sarah sitting on the bed, her legs pulled underneath her. Something else catches my eye, a small mass that has shifted beneath the blanket at the foot of the bed. I tense, and immediately my mind returns to the weasels that sped across the gym. Sarah sees what I am looking at and smiles. She crawls to the bottom of the bed on her hands and knees.

"There's somebody here who wants to say hello," she says, then takes the corner of the blanket and gently peels it back to reveal Bernie Kosar, sleeping away. A metal splint goes the length of his front leg, and his body is covered with cuts and gashes that, like mine, have been cleaned and are already beginning to heal. His eyes slowly open and adjust, eyes rimmed with red, full of exhaustion. He keeps his head on the bed but his tail gives a subtle wag, softly thumping against the mattress.

"Bernie," I say, and drop to my knees before him. I place my hand softly on his head. I can't stop smiling and tears of joy surface. His small body is curled into a ball, head resting on his front paws, his eyes taking me in, battle scarred and wounded but still here to tell the tale.

"Bernie Kosar, you made it through. I owe my life to you," I say, and kiss the top of his head.

Sarah runs her hand down the length of his back.

"I carried him to the truck while Mark carried you."

"Mark. I'm sorry I ever doubted him," I say.

She lifts one of Bernie Kosar's ears. He turns and sniffs at her hand and then licks it. "So, is it true what Mark said, that Bernie Kosar grew to thirty feet tall and killed a beast almost double his size?"

I smile. "A beast triple his size."

Bernie Kosar looks at me. *Liar,* he says. I look down and wink at him. I stand back up and look at Sarah.

"All of this," I say. "All of this has happened so fast. How are you handling it?"

She nods. "Handling what? The fact that I've fallen in love with an alien, which I only found out about three days ago, and then just happened to walk headlong into the middle of a war? Yeah, I'm handling that okay."

I smile at her. "You're an angel."

"Nah," she says. "I'm just a girl crazy in love."

She gets up from the bed and wraps her arms around me and we stand in the center of the room holding one another.

"You really have to leave, don't you?"

I nod.

She takes a deep breath and exhales shakily, willing herself not to cry. More tears in the past twenty-four hours than I have ever witnessed in all the years of my life.

"I don't know where you have to go or what you have to do, but I'll wait for you, John. Every bit of my heart belongs to you, whether you ask for it or not."

I pull her to me. "And mine belongs to you," I say.

I walk across the room. Sitting on top of the desk are the Loric Chest, three packed bags, Henri's computer, and all the money from the last withdrawal he made at the bank. Sarah must have rescued the Chest from the home-ec room. I place my hand on it. All the secrets, Henri had said. All of them contained within this. In time I'll open it and discover them, but that time is certainly not now. And what did he mean about Paradise, that our coming wasn't by chance?

"Did you pack my bags?" I ask Sarah, who is standing behind me.

"Yes, and it was probably the hardest thing I ever had to do."

I lift my bag from the table. Beneath it is a

manila envelope carrying my name across the front of it.

"What is this?" I ask.

"I don't know. I found it in Henri's bedroom. We went there after leaving the school and tried to grab everything we could; then we came here."

I open the envelope and pull out the contents. All of the documents Henri had created for me: birth certificates, social security cards, visas, and so on. I count through them. Seventeen different identities, seventeen different ages. On the very front sheet is a sticky note in Henri's writing. It reads, "Just in case." After the last sheet is another sealed envelope, across which Henri has written my name. A letter, the one he must have been talking about just before he died. I don't have the heart to read it now.

I look out the window of the hotel room. A light snow sifts down from the low, gray clouds overhead. The ground is too warm for any of it to stick. Sarah's car and Sam's father's blue truck are parked beside each other in the lot. As I stand looking down at them a knock sounds at the door. Sarah opens it and Sam and Mark walk into the room; Six limps behind them. Sam hugs me, says he's sorry.

"Thank you," I say.

"How do you feel?" Six asks. She is no longer wearing the suit but is now dressed in the pair of jeans she wore when I first saw her, and one of Henri's sweatshirts.

I shrug. "I'm okay. Sore and stiff. My body feels heavy."

"The heaviness is from the dagger. It'll eventually wear off, though."

"How badly were you stabbed?" I ask.

She lifts her shirt and shows me the gash in her side, then a different one on her back. All told, she was stabbed three times last night, and that's not to mention the various cuts along the rest of her body, or the shot that left a deep gash in her right thigh, now wrapped tightly with gauze and tape, the reason for her limp. She tells me that by the time we made it back it was too late to be healed by the stone. It amazes me that she is even alive.

Sam and Mark are wearing the same clothes as the day before, both filthy and covered in mud and dirt with smatterings of blood mixed in. Both with heavy eyes as though they've yet to sleep. Mark stands behind Sam, shifting his weight uncomfortably.

"Sam, I always knew you were a wrecking machine," I say.

He laughs uncertainly. "Are you okay?"

"Yeah, I'm fine," I say. "How about you?"

"Doing okay."

I look over his shoulder at Mark.

"Sarah told me you carried me off the field last night."

Mark shrugs. "I was happy to help."

"You saved my life, Mark."

He looks me in the eye. "I think every one of us saved somebody at some point last night. Hell, Six saved me on three separate occasions. And you saved my two dogs on Saturday. I say we're even."

I somehow manage to smile. "Fair enough," I say. "I'm just happy to find out you're not the dick I thought you were."

He half grins. "Let's just say that had I known you were an alien and could kick my ass at will, I might have been a little nicer to you that first day."

Six walks across the room and looks at my bags atop the table.

"We really should get going," she says, and then looks at me with implicit concern, her face softening. "There's really only one thing left undone. We weren't sure what you wanted us to do."

I nod. I don't need to ask to know what she is talking about. I look at Sarah. It's going to happen much sooner than I thought. My stomach turns. I feel as though I could vomit. Sarah reaches out and takes hold of my hand.

"Where is he?"

The ground is damp with the melting snow. I hold Sarah's hand in mine and we pass through the woods in silence, a mile away from the hotel. Sam and Mark walk in the lead, following the muddy footprints they created a few hours before. Up ahead I see a slight clearing, in the center of which Henri's body has been laid out on a slab of wood. He is wrapped in the gray blanket pulled from his bed. I walk to him. Sarah follows and places a hand on my shoulder. The others stand behind me. I pull the blanket down to see him. His eyes are closed, his face is ashen gray, and his lips are blue from the cold. I kiss his forehead.

"What do you want to do, John?" Six asks. "We can bury him if you want. We can also cremate him."

"How can we cremate him?"

"I can create a fire."

"I thought you could only control the weather."

"Not the weather. The elements."

I look up at her soft face, concern written upon it but also the stress of time at our having to leave before reinforcements arrive. I don't answer. I look away and squeeze Henri a final time with my face close to his and I lose myself to grief.

"I'm so sorry, Henri," I whisper in his ear. I close my eyes. "I love you. I wouldn't have missed a second of it, either. Not for anything," I whisper. "I'm going to take you back yet. Somehow I am going to get you back to Lorien. We always joked about it but you were my father, the best father I could have ever asked for. I'll never forget you, not for a minute for as long as I live. I love you, Henri. I always did."

I let go of him, pull the blanket back over his face, and lay him gently on the wooden slab. I stand and hug Sarah. She holds me until I stop crying. I wipe the tears away with the back of my hand and I nod at Six.

Sam helps me clear away the sticks and leaves and then we lay Henri's body on the ground so as not to dilute his ash with anything else. Sam lights an edge of the blanket and Six makes the fire rage from there. We watch it burn, not a dry eye among us. Even Mark cries. Nobody says a word. When the flames end I gather the ashes in a coffee can that Mark was astute enough to bring from the hotel. I'll get something better the second we stop. When we walk back I put the can on the dashboard of Sam's dad's truck. I feel comforted to know that Henri will still travel with us, that he'll look out over the roads while we leave another town as the two of us have done so many times before.

We load our belongings into the back of the truck. Along with Six's things and mine, Sam has also loaded in two bags of his own. At first I'm confused, but then I realize that between him and Six some agreement has been made that Sam will come with us. And I'm happy for that. Sarah and I walk back into the hotel room. The second the door closes she takes my hand and turns me towards her.

"My heart is breaking," she says. "I want to be strong for you right now but the thought of you leaving is killing me inside."

I kiss her on the head.

"My heart is broken already," I say. "The second I get settled I'll write. And I'll do my best to call when I know it is safe."

Six pokes her head in the doorway.

"We really have to go," she says.

I nod. She closes the door. Sarah lifts her face to mine and we kiss standing there in the hotel room. The thought of the Mogadorians returning before we've left, and thus putting her in danger yet again, is the only source of strength I can find. Else I might collapse. Else I might stay forever.

Bernie Kosar still lies waiting at the foot of the bed. He wags his tail when I carefully take him into my arms and carry him outside to the truck. Six starts the truck and lets it idle. I turn and look up at the hotel and am saddened that it's not the house, and that I know I'll never see it again. Its peeling wooden clapboards, broken windows, black shingles warped from excessive sun exposure and rain. It looks like Paradise, I once told Henri. But that will no longer hold true. Paradise lost.

I turn and nod to Six. She climbs into the truck, closes the door, and waits.

Sam and Mark shake hands but I don't hear what they say to each other. Sam climbs into the truck and waits with Six. I shake Mark's hand.

"I owe you more than I'll ever be able to repay," I say to Mark.

"You don't owe me a thing," Mark says.

"Not true," I say. "Someday."

I look away. I can feel myself wanting to collapse under the sadness of leaving. My resolve is being held by a tattered string ready to snap.

I nod. "I'll see you again someday."

"Be safe out there."

I take Sarah into my arms and squeeze her tightly, never wanting to let go.

"I'll come back to you," I say. "I promise you, if it's the last thing I do I'll come back to you."

Her face is buried in my neck. She nods.

"I'll count the minutes until you do," she says.

One last kiss. I set her on the ground and I open the door to the truck. My eyes never leave hers. She covers her mouth and her nose with her hands pressed together, neither one of us able to look away. I close the door. Six puts the truck in reverse and pulls out of the parking lot, comes to a stop, puts it in gear. Mark and Sarah walk to the end of the lot to watch us on our way, tears streaming down both sides of Sarah's face. I turn in my seat and watch from the rear window. I lift my hand to wave and Mark waves back but Sarah just watches. I watch her for as long as I can, growing smaller, one indistinct blur fading in the distance. The truck slows and turns and both of them vanish from sight. I turn back around and I watch the fields pass and I close my eyes and I picture Sarah's face and I smile. *We'll be together yet,* I tell her. *And until that day you'll be in my heart and my every thought.*

Bernie Kosar lifts his head and rests it in my lap and I place my hand upon his back. The truck bounces down the road, driving south. The four of us, together, heading for the next town. Wherever that might be.

THE POWER OF SIX

CHAPTER ONE

MY NAME IS MARINA, AS OF THE sea, but I wasn't called that until much later. In the beginning I was known merely as Seven, one of the nine surviving Garde from the planet Lorien, the fate of which was, and still is, left in our hands. Those of us who aren't lost. Those of us still alive.

I was six when we landed. When the ship jolted to a halt on Earth, even at my young age I sensed how much was at stake for us—nine Cêpan, nine Garde—and that our only chance waited for us here. We had entered the planet's atmosphere in the midst of a storm of our own creation, and as our feet found Earth for the very first time, I remember the wisps of steam that rolled off the ship and the goose bumps that covered my arms. I hadn't felt the wind in a year, and it was freezing outside. Somebody was there waiting for us. I don't know who he was, only that he handed each Cêpan two sets of clothes and a large envelope. I still don't know what was in it.

As a group we huddled together, knowing we might never see one another again. Words were said, hugs were given, and then we split up, as we knew we must, walking in pairs in nine different directions. I kept peering over my shoulder as the others receded in the distance until, very slowly, one by one, they all disappeared. And then it was just Adelina and I, trudging alone in a world we knew next to nothing about. I realize now just how scared Adelina must have been.

I remember our aimless march that went on for days, maybe weeks, then Adelina rushing us aboard a ship headed to some unknown destination. I remember two or three different trains after that. Adelina and I kept to ourselves, sticking to obscure corners, away from whoever might be around. We hiked from town to town, over mountains and across fields, knocking on doors that were quickly slammed in our faces. We were hungry, tired, and scared. I remember sitting on a sidewalk begging for change. I remember crying instead of sleeping. I'm certain that Adelina gave away some of our precious gems from Lorien for nothing more than warm meals, so great was our need. Perhaps she gave them all away. And then we found this place in Spain.

A stern-looking woman I would come to know

as Sister Lucia answered the heavy oak door. She squinted at Adelina, her gaze moving from head to toe, surely taking in her desperation, the way her shoulders drooped.

"Do you believe in the word of God?" the woman asked in Spanish, pursing her lips and narrowing her eyes in scrutiny.

"The word of God is my vow," Adelina replied with a solemn nod. I don't know how she knew this response—perhaps she learned it when we stayed in a church basement weeks before—but it was the right one. Sister Lucia opened the door.

We've been here ever since, eleven years in this stone cathedral with its musty rooms, drafty hallways, and hard floors like slabs of ice. Aside from the few visitors, the internet is my only access to the world outside our small town, and I search it constantly, looking for some indication that the others are out there, that they're searching, maybe fighting. Some sign that I'm not alone, because at this point I can't say that Adelina still believes, that she's still with me. Her attitude changed somewhere over the mountains. Maybe it was with the slam of one of the doors that shut a starving woman and her child out in the cold for another night. Whatever it was, Adelina seems to have lost her sense of the urgency of staying on the move, and her faith in the resurgence of Lorien seems to have been replaced by the faith shared by the convent's Sisters. I remember a distinct shift in Adelina's eyes, her sudden speeches on the need for guidance and structure if we were to survive.

My faith remains intact. In India, a year and a half ago, four different people witnessed a boy move objects with his mind. Not once, but twice. While the significance of the event seemed small at first, the boy's abrupt disappearance shortly thereafter created much buzz in the region, and a hunt for him began. As far as I know, he hasn't been found.

A few months ago there was news of a girl in Argentina who, in the wake of an earthquake, lifted a five-ton slab of concrete to save a man trapped beneath, and when news of this heroic act spread, she disappeared. Like the boy in India, she's still missing.

And then there's the father/son duo making all the news now in America, in Ohio, who the police are hunting after the two allegedly demolished an entire school by themselves, killing five people in the process. They left no trace behind other than mysterious heaps of ash. The authorities have no leads.

"It looks like a battle took place here. I don't know how else to explain it," the head investigator was quoted as saying. "But make no mistake, we will get to the bottom of this, and we will find Henri Smith and his son, John. You have my word on that."

Perhaps John Smith, if that's his real name, is merely a boy with a grudge who was pushed too far. But I don't think that's the case. My heart races whenever his picture appears on my screen. My breathing becomes labored, and I'm gripped with a profound desperation that I can't quite explain. I can feel in my bones that he is one of us. And I know, somehow, that I must find him.